DANCING

ON THE *Wind*

CHARLOTTE
BOYETT-COMPO

ELLORA'S CAVE
ROMANTICA PUBLISHING

An Ellora's Cave Romantica Publication

www.ellorascave.com

Dancing on the Wind

ISBN 9781419961236
ALL RIGHTS RESERVED.
Dancing on the Wind Copyright © 2008 Charlotte Boyett-Compo
Edited by Mary Moran.
Cover art by Syneca.

Electronic book publication April 2008
Trade paperback publication 2010

DANCING ON THE WIND

ജ

Trademarks Acknowledgement

ഇ

The author acknowledges the trademarked status and trademark owners of the following wordmarks mentioned in this work of fiction:

Band-Aid: Johnson & Johnson Corporation

BMW: Bayerische Motoren Werke Aktiengesellschaft

Bugs Bunny: Time Warner Entertainment Company, L.P.

"Demolition Man": Words and Music by Sting

Desert Eagle XIX: Israel Military Industries Ltd

Doctors Without Borders: Bureau International de Medecins sans Frontieres Not-For-Profit Corporation

Glock 19: Glock, Inc.

GPS: Randazzo, William Salvator

Harley-Davidsons: H-D Michigan, Inc

Ka-Bar: Alcas Corporation

Knights of Columbus: Knights of Columbus Corporation

Lear: Lear Corporation

M1: Aero Development & Engineering, Inc.

M3 Trench Knife: Camillus Cutlery, Inc.

McDonald's: McDonald's Corporation

Pepsi: Pepsico, Inc.

Porsche Boxster: Dy. Ing. h. c. F. Porsche Aktiengesellschaft

Ray-Bans: Bausch & Lomb Inc.

Ritz: Ritz-Carlton Hotel Company, L.L.C

"Soul and Inspiration": Words and Music by Barry Mann and Cynthia Weil

Star Wars: Lucasfilm Entertainment Company Ltd.

Uzi: Israel Military Industries Ltd
Wizard of Oz: Turner Entertainment Co.

Prologue
Present Day

ℰↃ

The bitter Iowa wind blowing across the grassy expanse chilled bone-deep as it skirled through the black walnut trees. Rain plinked hollowly upon a small sea of black umbrellas to stream ceaselessly to the already spongy ground. Hanging low in the sodden gray sky, the clouds looked as bruised and battered as he felt—bereft of warmth, saturated with despair. Looking up at the harsh winter heavens, blinking against the cold invasion of the falling rain striking his upturned face and splattering the dark glasses he was wearing, he thought it an appropriate day for what was happening in front of him. Lowering his head, he stared dully at the tall, cadaverously thin man dressed in white who was officiating. With detachment, he looked around him at the others who had gathered at this gloomy, freezing hour but never quite met the eyes of his fellow mourners. He was too numb, too dazed, too tired to tolerate either the pitying gazes or the pointed glares aimed his way. He had refused the place offered him beneath the protection of the canopy, preferring to stand alone in the rain—an outsider, a looker-on—alienating himself from the inner circle.

Despite his better judgment, his attention wandered to the flag-draped casket and he felt once again the force of that humbling sight to the very marrow of his bones, to the depths of his aching heart, and he jerked his gaze away again. He wanted this obligatory ceremony over and done with. He wanted to leave this wretched hilltop upon which rows of white marble markers with their small bronze emblems of faith above the name of the dead stretched out like dragon teeth tearing through the earth. He wanted to drink himself into oblivion to blot out the memories that kept assailing him at every turn.

"Eternal rest grant unto her, O Lord," the priest intoned.

"And let perpetual light shine upon her," those gathered who were of the Catholic faith responded.

"May she rest in peace," the priest said.

"Amen," replied almost every one of the assembled.

Everyone except him, he thought as his vision drifted to the mound of dirt barely covered by the tacky green carpet. His stomach roiled at the sight and bile raced up his gullet. He had to forcefully swallow to keep it down.

The priest closed the book he carried. "May her soul, and the souls of all the faithful departed, through the mercy of God rest in peace."

"Amen."

Backing away, the priest joined the two acolytes who had flanked him as the NCOIC stepped forward. "Present arms!" he called out.

The seven militiamen standing to one side snapped to attention in perfect synchronized union then shouldered their M1 carbines.

The first of the three volleys made him flinch even though he knew the sound was coming. The second doubled his fist inside the pocket of his raincoat so that he drove his nails brutally into his palms. The third started a sting behind his eyes, and as the echo died down, thirty yards away the bugler brought up his instrument and the first three notes skirled over the mourners, he began to tremble—jaw clenched tightly, teeth grinding. Throughout the hauntingly beautiful final tribute to a fallen comrade, he stood rigid at attention, his eyes never wavering from her casket. It wasn't until the casket team leader stepped forward and he and his men began the folding of the flag that he completely lost it.

Pain such as he could never have imagined ran through his entire body, nearly driving him to his knees. He spun around— staggering as the cane in his right hand dug deep into the soft earth. Leaning heavily on the silver dragon-head handle, he hobbled as fast as he could toward his parked car, the coattail of his raincoat flapping behind him. He could not stay to see that flag presented to a woman he despised and who loathed him just as deeply. He could not stay to see the casket lowered into the ground, the last memory of her presence in his world the dirt being tossed into the grave, the last sound to remember that of the dull thud as the soil hit the casket lid.

There was a bar calling to him, a bottle and glass with his name on it. Hell, why even bother with the glass? he thought as he snatched open the car door and slid behind the wheel, tossing the cane onto the floorboard of the passenger side. And why stop at one bottle when two would do the job more effectively? Vaguely he heard his name being called as he slammed the door shut, but he ignored it, jamming the key into the ignition—though it took some doing since his hand shook so badly—and gunned the powerful motor. He worked the gears of the Basalt Black Metallic Porsche Boxster S like a maniac, a low, keening sound accompanying his movements. With the 295 hp engine roaring, the sleek sports car leapt out of the line of the lesser cars of the funeral cortege and took to the gravel road like a hot knife through butter.

Jerking the wheel, he shot out of the cemetery gates and took the highway eastward—rear tires fishtailing and squealing as rubber gripped asphalt—barely missing an oncoming semi. To the shrill blast of the truck's air horn, the Boxster picked up speed, soon vanishing in the gloom, its taillights bright red glittering in the slashing rain. Darting recklessly between slower-moving cars and passing dangerously across double yellow lines, he finally found open highway ahead of him and pushed down hard on the accelerator, hitting the one hundred sixty mark without so much as a blink of his pale amber eyes.

At that moment he didn't care if he lived or died, though he would just as soon not take an innocent family with him when he checked out. He finally eased up on the gas but maintained a speed far exceeding the posted fifty-five mile per hour limit. He paid no attention at all to the scenery through which he sped, the occasional slide of the tires on the wet payment, but the sports car tracked securely to keep him on the highway. Apparently his guardian angel was working overtime.

The piercing sound of a siren caught his attention and he glanced in the rearview mirror where revolving lights had appeared suddenly as a state patrol car streaked toward him. He considered flooring it, trying to outrun the trooper, then thought better of it. Why endanger the officer's life needlessly? With a sigh, he took his foot off the gas and began braking, sliding smoothly over onto the soggy shoulder of the road. When the car rolled to a stop, he hit the button to lower the window despite the rain blowing in, switched off the engine, took off his sunglasses, tossed them to the passenger seat then sat with his hands in plain sight, gripping the wheel, eyes on the rearview mirror. Though he couldn't see through the rear windshield of the patrol car, he knew the trooper was calling in the stop. He sighed again, resisting the urge to hang his head.

He wasn't armed although there was a fully loaded Desert Eagle XIX strapped beneath the dash, a Glock 19 with a 33-round extended magazine in the glove compartment and a 50-round Uzi tucked under the seat. Even if he didn't count the two Ka-Bar knives with their seven-inch carbon steel killing blades and the double-edged M3 fighting knife in the console, he was screwed on a concealed weapons charge—especially if he counted the brace of hand grenades he kept for no other purpose than just to have them at hand. With the entire System on high alert, he'd felt he needed the protection but his overzealous approach to self-preservation might prove to be his undoing. He could feel the handcuffs clicking into place around his wrists.

"Afternoon, sir."

The voice was young, shaky and feminine—which surprised him—and he slowly turned his head toward her.

Though her eyes were hard and her mouth tight as she stood there with her hand on the butt of her service revolver, he could read her like a book. She'd already called in his license number and knew he was one of the Crew. She was afraid of him, afraid of what he might do, not sure she could handle him on her own.

"Good afternoon, Officer," he said.

"What's the hurry, Mr. Fallon?" she asked, confirming she had already run his tag.

"No reason, ma'am," he replied. "Just flat-out stupidity."

"Do you know how fast you were going?"

"Not fast enough to slide in under your radar," he said dryly, and heard her snort.

"Have you been drinking?"

"Not yet, but I was headed that way," he replied honestly.

"You could have killed somebody driving like that," she reminded him. "Or yourself."

He shrugged indifferently.

"Please take the key out of the ignition and give it to me," she ordered.

"Excuse me?" he said, surprise showing in his eyes.

"I ran your plate and was told to bring you down to the Exchange," she replied. "So please take the key out of the ignition and hand it over, sir."

For a split second he almost balked at the order, but he didn't want to cause the trooper any problems. He did as he was told although it went against the grain and made a muscle clench in his jaw.

"Now please follow me to my car," she said after he had hit the button to raise the window and she pocketed his keys. She stepped back to allow him to exit. "Be sure to lock the doors. It would be a shame for someone to come along and steal a piece of prime machinery like that."

He couldn't have cared less about the car. If it had been his bike he had taken to the funeral, that was different, but he couldn't ride the Harley VBSC with his leg torn up so he'd been forced to take the Porsche. To him it was transportation — expensive transportation but nothing more. It meant less to him than the splatters of mud on the cuff of his trousers, but he leaned over to retrieve his cane, opened the door, engaged the lock button and got out. It had stopped raining but the wind had picked up, tossing his dark hair into his eyes as he limped behind her to the cruiser. He went around to the passenger door and got in, holding the cane between his knees.

"They'll have your car brought down to the Exchange, sir," she said.

"That's damned white of them," he said.

13

"They take care of their own I hear," she commented as she started the cruiser.

"Yep," he agreed. "They even tuck us in bed at night."

She smiled. "With warm milk and a cookie if you've been good?"

"Something like that," he agreed, liking her sarcasm.

"Were you close to Miss McCullough?" she asked as she hung a U-ee and headed back the way they'd come. Asking that question, he knew she'd been told where his race had started.

"She was my partner," he said softly, and clenched his hands so hard it hurt.

"I'm sorry," she said.

"Yeah, so am I," he agreed, and turned his head to look out the window beside him, hoping she'd say nothing else, ask no more questions, make no more comments. To ensure her silence, he leaned his head against the cool glass and closed his eyes. He could feel her gaze on him but she remained quiet as she headed for the Exchange.

Ten minutes later they were passing the turnoff that led into the cemetery. He didn't look that way though he was aware of cars waiting in line to pull out on the highway. The ceremony was over. The goodbyes had been said. The mourners were going home, the wet earth being piled into Keenan McCullough's grave. Once more the debilitating pain shot through him and he wrapped his arms around himself to keep from bellowing with rage.

"I lost a partner when I was with Metro," she said in an understanding voice. "It gets better."

"Yeah," he mumbled.

The highway curved sharply to the left and suddenly in front of them was the mile upon mile of electrified fence topped with razor wire, the hooked barbs glinting in the sweep of the cruiser's headlights. They passed five miles of the ultra-maximum security barrier before the turnoff to the Exchange and the titanium-sheathed guard kiosk bracketed by twin heavy-duty gates.

"This place has security as tight as Ft. Knox," the trooper commented.

"Tighter," Fallon mumbled.

"What exactly do you guys do out here?" she asked, cutting a side glance to him. "I know its all top secret government stuff and all." When he didn't answer, she looked at him again. "Black ops, maybe?"

Fallon returned her gaze. "If I told you, I'd have to kill you."

The trooper grinned, but when he didn't echo the expression, she allowed it to fade. "You're not joking, are you?"

He looked away. "Nope."

They were nearing the security kiosk and the trooper was slowing down. Through the bullet-proof windows, he saw the four guards who controlled the entry and departure from the Exchange staring out at them. Two heavily armed men came out of the security kiosk as the trooper rolled down her window. One came to the driver side while the other skirted the front of the cruiser and headed for the passenger side. In that man's hand was a small oval-shaped device.

"I'm bringing Mr. Fallon in," she told the guard.

The guard did not reply as he leaned down to look at the trooper's passenger. "How's it going, Mr. Fallon?" he asked.

"Just peachy," came the bitter reply. He rolled down his window and turned to the second guard.

It was a retinal scanner the guard held in his hand, and the device was placed to Mikhail Fallon's right eye for a few seconds then removed when three beeps sounded.

"Welcome back, sir," the guards said, stepping back to escort a crisp salute.

"Yeah, home sweet home," Fallon drawled. "May it be ever so humble."

"Mr. Fallon will direct you to his quarters, Officer," the guard beside the trooper's window stated as he raised a hand.

The security gate in front of the cruiser engaged with a dull clank and began to slide back slowly.

"Thanks," the trooper said. She drove into the sprawling compound with a look of awe on her young face, glancing in the rearview mirror as the gate rolled shut behind them. "Man, I've never been out here before."

"You haven't missed anything," Fallon told her.

"Just the most secure installation on earth," she said.

"That and a dollar will get you a cup of coffee," he quipped, turning his head to watch the mile or so of barren land by which they passed. For as far as the eye could see there was not one tree, shrub or rock behind which a trespasser could hide. The grounds were patrolled by armed guards with vicious security dogs and by flyovers at odd times during the day and night. Over the compound was a no-fly zone that was strictly enforced.

She did exactly as he expected she would when the main building came into view—she whistled, eyes wide.

"Mother of God," she muttered.

"Special, ain't it?" he asked.

Situated in the center of a pristine white landscape of crushed marble, the black glass three-story building resembled a crouching behemoth, its front legs curved inward, paws not quite touching. On the top floor, two gleaming red lights pulsing off and on gave the impression of blinking eyes glaring back at the viewer. Twin communications obelisks in the center of the roofline looked like pointed ears and the jutting gravity-defying extension pushing out from the middle floor could have passed for a wicked snout, its twin windows the nostrils. In the gloom of the rain-washed day, the Exchange looked as menacing as it had always felt to Fallon.

"That is something else," the trooper marveled.

"It's hell on earth," Fallon said beneath his breath then lifted a hand to point to his right. "Take that street."

She took him to a building just beyond the Exchange. Curved into an arch, the four-story dormitory faced the main compound, connected to the Exchange by an elevated monorail system that ran through the back of the Exchange and then on to the maintenance complex that was a mirror construction of the arched dorm building. The twin buildings made Fallon think of

16

an enormous egg that had been cracked open to eject the monster that was the Exchange. The dark-red brick walkways that connected the buildings were like bleeding arteries stretching out upon the stark white marble stone.

Stopping the cruiser where he indicated, she turned toward him as he opened the door with a gruff thanks for the lift. He had trouble getting out since his bad leg was hurting like hell. He had to hang on to the top of the door for a moment before he could straighten.

"Mr. Fallon?" she called out to him, and he bent over to look at her through the opened door. "It does get better."

He nodded then straightened, slammed the door, pivoted around carefully then headed for the dorm. As he walked, he felt her watching him until he heard the growl of the cruiser's engine as she drove away. His shoulders relaxed. He'd never liked to be watched—especially by someone he didn't know.

"Why am I still alive?" he muttered to himself as he neared the dorm entrance.

The doorkeeper of the dormitory from long acquaintance with Fallon did not greet him. Nor did the man turn his head to watch when Fallon bypassed the elevator and shoved the stairway door open. It was a given the stairs would be taken and not the claustrophobic cage. No matter how much it hurt or how long it took, he would take the stairs.

Fallon was in agony and winded by the time he reached the fourth floor and snatched open the door. He took three steps to the right then stopped. For a long moment he just stood there bracing himself on the cane with his head down then turned around, limping along the east corridor and toward quarters that were not his own.

At this time of day, there should be no one lurking about the dorms. Those who worked at the Exchange were over there or else on assignment. The mourners would be going to the meal prepared for them at McCauley's. Maid service would have already finished for the day. He rationalized that he most likely had the entire floor to himself.

Getting into Keenan's quarters wasn't hard. He knew her personal code and punched it in without a second thought. When the door shushed open, he stood just beyond the threshold for a complete sweep of his watch's second hand before finally gathering up the courage to cross over into the great room. The door closed soundlessly behind him, shutting him into a room that still bore the weight of her aura.

He was sweating, but it wasn't from the pain or exertion that had carried him up the stairs. Lifting a hand to scrub at his face, he realized it was shaking again. Instead, he plowed it through his damp hair before lowering it to clench at his side, tightening the other hand around the cane's handle. His heart was pounding brutally, his blood racing. A sour taste had risen in his throat to choke him and once again there was a hot stinging behind his eyes. He shook his head to clear his thoughts then shrugged out of the raincoat that seemed to be weighing him down. He let it drop to the floor, jamming his hands into the pockets of his trousers as he swept his gaze around the room.

"Why?" he asked aloud. "Why am I alive?"

Everywhere he looked he saw her heart in the decoration of this space that had once been so impersonal before she put her stamp of simple elegance to it. From the soft white muslin curtains at the windows to the green-and-white-gingham upholstered sofa and identical twin loveseats grouped around a low maple coffee table, the two overstuffed dark green corduroy recliners flanking the gas fireplace, the country prints on the walls and the pieces of occasional furniture done in the same rich maple wood, the room was homey and comforting—a place to relax, unwind and recharge. The room smelled of gardenia potpourri and lemon furniture polish, and the thick floral carpet underfoot muffled his footsteps.

Going into the dining room, he wasn't surprised that everything was in precise order. That was the way she had liked it. Order reassured her. Clutter made her nervous. Chaos disturbed her, offended her soul. The table was kept to a high sheen with the floral arrangement precisely in the center and flanked by four crystal candlesticks holding tall green tapers, the burgundy cushioned chairs sitting like sentinels around it. Plain but expensive white china was housed in the chest cabinet and upon the buffet were two tall candleholders with glass chimneys to either side of another striking floral piece he knew she had created. The three pieces sat upon a long lace doily she had purchased on a long-ago trip to Ireland. In one corner of the room was a small antique cabinet with punched copper panels she used as a bar, and lining it was exquisite crystal decanters in myriad styles and shapes. A little inlaid tray with a rolled wicker edge held a Depression glass decanter filled with plum brandy and four delicate snifters.

He looked up at the chandelier that hung over the table and half smiled. He'd been with her the day she had seen it displayed in the window of an antiques shop in Missouri. She'd nearly broken his neck when she'd slammed on the brakes and whipped into a parking space in front of the store. The light with its burnished chain swags, stylish center bowl and classic amber flake glass shades was perfect in her estimation and just what she'd needed to complete her dining room. She never even blinked at the outrageous price being asked. She had to have it and it became hers, lovingly packing it herself for the trip back to the Exchange.

The kitchen was just as neat as the first two rooms but he knew from past experience anything that could spoil had already been removed from the refrigerator and pantry. Housekeeping would have seen to that as soon as they'd learned of Keenan's death. Likewise any bills she'd owed, anything left pending would be handled by Agent Affairs with alacrity and efficiency — pending final resolution of her estate.

There were three bedrooms in the suite that had been her home. On the west side of the hallway was one bedroom for guests and another used as an office set to either side of a well-appointed bathroom. On the east side of the hall was the master bedroom and bath. It was here he dreaded to go but where his footsteps carried him as though he could not stop their movement.

"By all rights, I should be dead," he said on a long sigh. "I fucking don't understand it."

A king-sized bed with intricately curled brass headboard and footboard sat along one wall, the bed was flanked by twin nightstands over which hung copper pendant lamps with beveled amber glass shades. Two enormous armoires stood beside a forty-inch-wide cabinet holding a thirty-six-inch plasma TV and a massive collection of paperback novels. Angled in the corner by the sweep of four windows covered with cheerful burgundy-and-white-calico curtains was a small desk upon which sat a laptop computer and brass pharmacy lamp with a green glass shade. In the opposite corner was a chaise lounge and floor lamp where he knew Keenan had spent many hours immersed in the trashy romance novels she'd devoured by the gross. Overhead, a copper and wicker ceiling fan circulated the air with only a small whir of sound. The fan was on a timer, and when the digital bedside clock registered noon, the speed of the rotating blades would quicken as the outside spring temperatures rose or fell. At 4 p.m. in the summer time, the blades would start spinning at top speed. In the winter the reverse blade action would go no higher than medium speed simply to circulate the warm air.

Fallon stood in the center of the room for a long time, just staring at the bed. The coverlet matched the curtains and the upholstery on the desk chair and looked as though he could sink down into its softness and all his cares would disappear, his troubles would cease to be.

He wished with all his heart that such was possible and before he knew what he was doing, he shrugged off his suit coat and draped it over the footboard, kicked off his loafers — wincing as the pain in his right leg flared brutally — then sat down on the edge of her bed. Five minutes passed as he just sat there gripping the cane then he propped it against the mattress and swung his legs up with a grunt to stretch out on her bed. He flung his arm over his head. Lying there on his back, staring up at the punched copper ceiling that he knew Keenan had paid a small fortune to obtain, he mentally traced the pattern of one beautiful square, counting the leaves on the cluster of flowers, the petals, the scrolls running along the edge.

It was her scent that pushed aside all other thoughts and he turned his head on the pillow, reaching over to pull the coverlet down so he could drag the other pillow to him. He brought it to his face and inhaled slowly, drawing in the smell of her, the essence of her presence deep into his lungs, closing his eyes as he breathed in her perfume. Above him, the fan circled lazily with that soft displacement of air.

"Keenan." He whispered her name, and it reverberated through his very soul. The sound of it made him ache. Her loss cut him to the quick.

He had lain beside Keenan many times in this bed. Never had he fallen asleep here without his body having been eased by hers. He remembered one such sweet time that brought a quiver to his lips...

That day, she had come to him fresh from a shower with her hair curling damply around her face. Beautiful beyond anything he could ever have imagined would one day be his for the simple price of a gentle smile. Her arms had opened to him. For him. And she had welcomed him inside her body with the same enthusiasm and trust they had come to need from one another.

"Love me, Fallon," she asked, and he had.

When he had begun to really love her with all his being, he had no idea. Perhaps it had been the first time they'd clashed together with an explosion of passion that had left them both stunned. Perhaps it had been the first time he'd seen her cry, or it might well have been the day she had challenged his authority and stood her ground—the only female to have ever done so and lived to remember it.

All he knew was that it had been long before that final time they'd shared her bed.

Their coming together had been slow and gentle—at first. He had taken her into his arms and tilted her chin up to kiss her, claiming her mouth softly but possessively. She fit so perfectly against him. Her scent enveloped him, drove deep into his soul. His kiss had deepened at the moment enticement wafted along his senses.

Long, silky arms had wrapped around his neck as she dropped the towel to press her body to his. She'd brought her legs up to lash them around his hips, and with his hands cupping her tight little ass, barefoot, he carried her to the bed, never breaking the dueling of their tongues as they explored each other's mouth. He had dipped a jean-clad knee to the mattress and moved them over to the center of the bed to lay her down, rubbing his crotch against the soft center of her.

She eased her mouth from his and that gentle smile no other woman had ever bestowed upon him nearly broke his heart as she gazed up at him.

"Strip for me, lineman," she demanded, sliding her arms and legs from around him.

He was on his knees between her legs, inhaling the scent of her sex calling to him.

He hadn't bothered with the buttons of his shirt. He simply tore the long-sleeved checkered shirt from his chest and threw it aside. He worked the fly of his jeans, snagged down the zipper and dropped to his side, rolled to his back to kick off the jeans. She laughed at the garment went flying from the foot of the bed.

"You are so rough on your clothes," she reprimanded on a long sigh.

He had crawled up her then, covering her with his body like a vine, wedging himself tightly between her spread thighs, nudging her knees farther apart with his own.

"I'm thinking about being rough on you, baby," he countered, a growl in his deep voice.

"Yeah?"

"Yeah."

She'd plowed her fingers through his hair when he dipped his head to her breast, drawing her nipple hard into his mouth, suckling on it with enough force to make her groan. She held him to her as a mother would her infant.

With a fierce rumble reverberating from his chest, he ground against her, letting her feel the heated erection that was hard and oozing as he dragged it along her thigh.

"This what you want?" he asked, teasing the broad tip at her velvety center.

She pretended to yawn. "I suppose if that's all you've got."

He had grinned mercilessly at her and rammed himself hard and tight inside her wet sheath, eliciting a shocked gasp from her. The look she had given him then had made him feel like a satyr, and he thrust again and again into her as she lifted her legs to lock them securely around his waist. Her breasts were pressed flat against his chest, her fingernails digging into his back as he rocked his body against hers. He ran his hands under her ass and lifted her high for deeper penetration. Beneath them, the headboard hit the wall time and again. The bed thumped along with their rhythm. Sweaty flesh slapped against sweaty flesh and he swooped down to slant his mouth brutally over hers, catching the first squeal of release as her climax pulsed like an exploding star.

After the last spasm had shook them and she lay pressed to his side—her fingers winding curls in his chest hair—he held her and knew such peace it humbled him.

"Lineman?"

"Yeah?"

She said nothing for a moment then lifted her head to look up at him. When he tilted his face toward hers, she smiled tremulously.

"I love you," she whispered. "I will always love you."

"I love you, too, *leanabh*," he replied, and kissed her forehead.

She gave him a look he would never forget as long as he lived then said, "I will go to my grave loving you."

It started as another sharp sting behind his eyes then began to build with intensity he neither could have stopped nor would have tried to. His chest felt as though a ton of weight had suddenly been laid upon it. His face grew hot. His throat closed. He made a sound that wasn't quite human then he began to shake. The tremor grew, built until he was shivering violently, the pillow clutched to him as though it were a lifeline tossed to him upon a raging sea. He heard himself moaning and his grip on the pillow tightened. He caressed it, stroked it gently—running his hand over the soft fabric—buried his face in it for a moment, but

23

the scent of her, the presence of her was so overpowering he could not take it. He pulled back with a gasp, his breath shuddering in his throat. He exhaled explosively, feeling the heavy weight in his chest, the burning behind his eyes. He groaned helplessly, mouth open, body vibrating. The burning became tears and he felt the first slide down his cheek, scalding his flesh.

"Keenan."

The name was a pitiful, tormented, tortured sound torn from the very depths of him but it broke the dam of emotions he had held so rigidly in check for the past week. The flood waters washed over him, submersing him in grief, drowning him in hopelessness, and he put his head back, howling with pain and sorrow and utter, soul-shattering despair.

"Keenan!"

This time her name was a scream of denial, of betrayal, of inhuman agony that ripped from him on a long wave of reverberation. He threw the pillow away from him with a furious snap, with such force it shook the bed beneath him. He yowled again and beat his fists savagely into the mattress, arched his back and dug in his heels. His head whipped from side to side like a man possessed, and still her name continued to pour from him in crashing waves of piteous anguish.

"Keenan!"

On the nightstand beside him, the clock's readout changed to 12 p.m. and the blades of the fan began to move faster, bringing with them a low whomping sound that was just loud enough to break through the suffering in which he was being held. The sound caught his attention and he looked up at the whirling blades, the low, swooshing sound instantly cutting off his sobbing. His lips parted, fists bunching in the coverlet.

He stared at the blades with his brows drawn together in confusion. Something was trying to come to him but it was hovering just outside his reach, beyond his ability to grasp it. Yet it remained there to taunt him. With every revolution of the blades the feeling grew that there was memory lurking there. If he tried hard enough, he would recognize it, snatch it up.

Every bone in his body began to ache. Every muscle began to burn and cramp. His head throbbed. He had trouble drawing air into his lungs. His jaws ached brutally. His back was an agony unto itself and even the tips of his fingers hurt so badly he had to release his hold on the coverlet. His vision began to blur, and with the distortion, an image rose up in his mind—the whirl of blades cutting through the air.

Whomp. Whomp. Whomp.

Suddenly he was beyond the here and now and entering a place into which no one else could follow.

He was cold. So cold his lips began to quiver. Blasts of Arctic air were blowing over him to chill to the marrow of his bones. He felt drained, depleted, destroyed. He felt encased in darkness.

Whomp. Whomp. Whomp.

He was jostled and his body screamed in protest though he knew he'd not uttered a word, wasn't capable of making a sound. He felt fresh tears gathering in his eyes, but this time from the pain and not the grief. He could barely breathe.

Whomp. Whomp. Whomp.

A blurry face came into his line of vision. He couldn't see anything except the hazy white outline, the shape, but when he heard the man's voice, he recognized it.

"They put a needle in your lung so you'll be able to breathe better now, Misha," the man said in a not-unkind voice. "You're on your way home. I couldn't let them kill you. She would have died if I had."

Whomp. Whomp. Whomp.

It was a chopper under which he was lying, a black military transport. He was strapped to a gurney that had been stopped by the hand of the faceless man. The cold air moving over him came from the spinning blades.

"I'll be coming for her," he heard the faceless man say. "Keep her safe until I do."

He felt himself being lifted into the chopper and the pain was so great he knew he lost consciousness. The last thing he remembered was the whir of the blades.

Whomp. Whomp. Whomp.

Coming back from wherever he'd been hurled, Fallon suddenly went as still as death, his eyes open wide. He stared unseeingly at the fan blades circling above him.

"Why am I still alive?" he whispered. "It doesn't make sense."

Whomp. Whomp. Whomp.

"One of these days I'll be coming for her."

"Groves," he said, and slowly sat up as memories flooded through him. Matty Groves had saved his life, had rescued him from unspeakable torment at the hands of his enemy.

Other memories assailed him like flashing neon signs on the Vegas strip. They shot past his mind's eye in rapid succession. Snatches of a long-ago conversation rumbled through his brain to shake him to the core of his being.

"When cloning becomes the norm, we'll all have expendable molds from which to take the pieces-parts we need to live fifty years longer than the norm. If I just had the money to complete my personal research, stuff I'd just as soon the Exchange not know about for now." He'd lowered his voice. *"I'm working up a facial replica right now from blood and tissue samples I received a few days ago. Sort of a living mask. Guess who the model was."*

Something snapped inside Mikhail Fallon and he sprang from the bed as though jerked by unseen hands. He didn't bother putting on his shoes, ignored the cane as it fell to the floor. Limping, hobbling, he left her room—crashing into the doorjamb but barely acknowledging the pain that shot through him. He tore down the hallway, sped through the great room and yanked open the door, not even bothering to shut it behind him. He stumbled down the corridor and shoved the stairway door open with a bang. Down the flights of stairs he flew as though demons were nipping at his heels. The pain in his injured leg didn't even register. When he slammed into the lobby of the dorm, he never heard the doorkeeper yell out to him. His objective was beyond the doorway leading outside and he plowed through it, shoving it aside as though it were nothing more than tissue paper. Distantly he heard glass shatter but he didn't give it a single thought. He stumbled on the walkway leading to the Exchange, but he managed to stay on his feet, increasing his speed as he tore across

26

the distance between the two buildings, his stocking feet tearing across the brick walkway, arms pumping.

Each of the entrances to the Exchange was governed by armed guards standing by scanners, and when he jerked open the side entrance door and came hurtling through, he saw guns come out of holsters, two men bending their knees in shooters' stances, but he shot through the scanner, ignoring them and their shouts of "Halt!" He'd gone no farther than ten feet into the building before he was tackled roughly from behind, the breath knocked from his body, sliding forward on the Terrazzo floor while his arms were jerked savagely behind him as a third guard knelt with a knee to Fallon's back, snapping handcuffs around his prisoner's wrists.

"Be careful of his leg!" someone shouted.

"What the fuck is wrong with you, Fallon?" he heard someone else growl. "Have you finally lost your mind, bro?"

"She's alive," was all he could say in between gasps for breath. *"She's alive!"*

Chapter One
Five Months Ago

စာ

"No."

"Did I ask your permission?"

Mikhail Fallon glared at the man known only as the Supervisor. "I work alone."

"You work with whomever I order you to work with," the Supervisor snapped, dark blue eyes flashing with irritation. "It has been decided that you are to have an Extension and..."

Fallon put his clenched fists on the top of the Supervisor's desk and leaned forward, chiseled features hardening with rage. "I said no."

"And an Extension has been assigned to you," the Supervisor finished as though his top agent had not interrupted him.

"You know what you can do with your Extension?" Fallon queried.

The Supervisor leaned back in his expensive formfitting chair and steepled his fingers beneath his chin. "I wish I could say it has been nice working with you, Agent Fallon, but I'm afraid I can't. I do, however, wish you luck in your next job."

Pale amber orbs narrowed dangerously. "That's the way you want to play it?"

"That's the way it will be if you refuse my orders."

Straightening, Fallon nodded slowly. "Fine. You can forward my last check to the Chelsea address." He turned toward the door.

"Have you forgotten your service with us can not be terminated under any circumstances?"

The soft words stopped Fallon in his tracks. He looked back, and the expression on the Supervisor's face made him walk back to the desk. "What does that mean?"

A nasty smile twitched the Supervisor's lips. "You know perfectly well what it means, but just in case you've had an extremely severe brain fart, let me be clear on the matter. It means, Agent Fallon, that you can never leave your employment with us. Employment with the Exchange is for life. There are no provisions within the contract you signed for you quitting or us firing you. There are no provisions for disability or retirement. Only death can sever the Connection. Now considering what I just said, let me assure you I can assign you any job within this organization I deem you capable of performing. Since you are proficient at many things, I can install you in any available position from janitor to file clerk." The smile widened. "Which position would you prefer?" One thick brow arched upward. "Or would auxiliary groundskeeper suit you better? I can't offer you the head groundskeeper position since that is already filled."

A snarl lifted Fallon's lip. "You can't keep me here if I don't..."

"How does solitary confinement for the next fifty to sixty years of your life sound?" the Supervisor inquired. "If you don't wish to work, imprisonment here at the Exchange is your only other alternative."

Fallon stared at the man everyone within the organization hated—himself more than most—and his hands curled into fists again. "You are a fucking son of a bitch," he said.

"And you are a supremely arrogant little prick but, hey, what's in a name?" the Supervisor asked with a smirk.

"I don't want a fucking Extension!" Fallon shouted so loudly the glass shade on the lamp sitting upon the Supervisor's desk rattled.

"There are perks to having a female Extension," the Supervisor said.

"Goddamn it! I..."

"We went to a great deal of trouble picking just the right woman for you, Fallon," the Supervisor cut him off. "She had to meet certain standards even to be considered."

"*I don't want a fucking Extension!*" The bellow was like that of an enraged bull. This time the force of it shook the windows.

The Supervisor smiled brutally. "Well, you don't have a say in the matter. It's settled. Live with it."

Snarling like a cornered weretiger, Fallon spun around and stalked to the door, jerking it open with a curse so vile it turned the air blue.

In the office of the Supervisor's executive assistant, Keenan McCullough looked up from the novel she was reading as two hundred and sixty pounds of irate male stormed past her. She saw him glance her way and felt the lash of his fury make landfall along her spine. He stopped in mid-stride—giving her a murderous glower that might have quelled a lesser woman—then he shocked her by hissing at her.

She blinked, taken back by the rage she saw brewing in his stormy amber eyes.

"What's your problem?" she asked.

"Before I'm through with you, you'll wish you'd never heard my name," he prophesied, his gaze raking over her insultingly.

Her eyebrows drew together. She had no idea who this towering hulk of masculinity was. Although he was movie-star handsome—devastatingly so in fact—he made her acutely uneasy. This was a man who could maim and kill without the slightest hesitation. She had the unsettling feeling he was the man they intended to hand her over to as his Extension.

"I don't want a fucking Extension!"

That said he stomped from the room, jerking open the door then letting it slam back against the wall behind his passing.

"Who the hell was that?" Keenan asked the man sitting behind the desk.

"That was Mikhail Fallon," the Supervisor's EA said dryly. "His friends—and believe it or not he actually has one or two—

call him Misha." He shuffled some papers on his desk. "He's your Alpha."

Keenan scowled. "That's *him*?" she asked. "That's the great and powerful Fallon?"

"I'm afraid that's the wizard behind the curtain," the EA replied with a sigh.

"Oh bloody swell," Keenan mumbled. "I don't need..."

A buzzer sounded and the EA stood, adjusting the fit of his suit as he did. "The Supervisor is ready for you."

By the time he reached the cafeteria, Fallon's jaws were aching from grinding his teeth. He had dug deep half-moons into his palms and his back was stiff from the rigid set of his shoulders. It had been a long time since he'd been this mad and longer still since anyone had dared to make him do something he truly didn't care to.

"Old bastard," he muttered as he strode up to the counter and ordered a cup of black coffee.

The young woman behind the counter knew better than to inform this particular man he could pour the coffee himself from the self-service end of the cafeteria. Instead, she hurried to do his bidding, making note at which table he planted his tall frame. The service workers took extra care with Fallon, spoke only when spoken directly to, and were very cautious not to garner his notice if at all possible. They were so terrified of him that when he made an appearance in the cafeteria, they mentally held their breaths until he left.

Slamming his brawny body into a chair by the far window, Fallon turned to stare out at the miles of rolling green hills that stretched as far as the eye could see beyond the Exchange. No trees dotted the landscape. No water mirrored the bright summer sky, only acre upon acre of rye grass that was mown and rolled into large round hay bales that resembled pencil erasers at harvesting time.

As his cup of coffee was placed silently before him, he acknowledged it with a quick bob of his head then took up the cup to take a long sip of the piping-hot liquid. The steam made him squint and the heat scalded his tongue but he welcomed the minor discomfort for it momentarily took his mind from the anger building within him in leaps and bounds.

"Fucking romance novel," he grumbled as he put the cup down and returned his attention to the outside scenery, reaching up to unconsciously tug at the gold hoop in his left earlobe. "The bitch was reading a fucking trashy romance novel!"

Those few people taking a late breakfast glanced toward the Exchange's main operative then quickly away. It didn't pay to gain Fallon's attention. If he wanted to talk to himself, no one would dare listen in to the one-sided conversation.

"She probably has a two-twenty-volt G-spot vibrator in her nightstand," he said, and lifted the cup to his lips.

He thought about that for a moment then a nasty smile pulled at his mouth as an idea began to take shape in his mind.

"I hope I've done nothing to cause that spiteful grin."

Fallon didn't bother to look up. At the sound of the sardonic voice, he leaned back in his chair and propped his booted feet on the one opposite. "You'd best be glad you haven't," Fallon replied.

Dr. Matt Groves set down his breakfast tray then took a seat, snapping a linen napkin into place on his lap. He reached for the salt shaker sitting in the center of the table and began sprinkling its contents onto the soft scrambled eggs on his plate. "Who's pissed you off now, you crazy Mick?" he inquired.

"The old man has gifted me with a fucking Extension."

Groves looked up, his eyebrows elevated. "The new woman who came in yesterday?" he asked in a surprised tone. "The one from Langley?"

"I don't know where the hell she came from and I don't give a rat's ass where she came from," Fallon growled. "All I know is that that rank old bastard is foisting her off on me."

Groves sat back, his meal forgotten. "Misha, what did he tell you about her?"

"Not a fucking thing," Fallon answered, and took another gulp of coffee before holding his hand to signal the counter girl he wanted a refill.

The chief physician of Operational Services stared at Fallon. "Then you don't know."

"Know what?" Fallon snapped.

"That she's an interceptor," Groves told him. "A primary channeller."

Fallon gave the man beside him a narrowed look filled with ferocity. "You've got to be shitting me. A fucking psychic?"

Shaking his head, Groves sat forward and reached for his fork. "I shit you not, my man. I'm really looking forward to meeting her because I saw her test results. They were off the chart. I studied them in detail."

"That's all the hell I need," Fallon exploded. "The Supervisor is saddling me with a tarot-reading, tea-leaf swirling, crystal ball-breaking shyster with…"

"Her talents are real, my friend, and no shit, they are fucking off the scale," Groves insisted. "She doesn't have just one or two psi abilities, Misha. She has several."

"And just what the hell am I suppose to do with this marvel of parapsychology?" Fallon demanded.

"Use her!" Groves said then shook his head as though he realized how Fallon would interpret his words. He waved a dismissive hand when Fallon would have made an obvious vulgar remark. "Use her abilities to enhance your own. That's what the Network is expecting. That's why they are pairing you two. You're a strong empath, she's a primary channeller. Together you two will rock, my man."

"I hunt bad guys, Matthew," Fallon stated. "I don't do anything but."

"She can find those bad guys for you."

Fallon snorted. "Finding them is not a problem I have ever had."

"I agree your natural abilities are a major asset, but I don't think she would have been handed over to you unless what she can do will help you on your assignments."

"How?" Fallon challenged.

"Any way the Supervisor sees fit."

"I don't want her," Fallon said, and when the man beside him made no comment to that assertion, Fallon folded his arms over his broad chest. "And I don't need her to help me do what I was born to do."

With still no response from Groves, Fallon pushed his chair back and stood. "And besides, the bitch reads romance novels."

"How positively evil of her," Groves mumbled before taking up his glass of orange juice and sipping.

"Retarded is more like it," Fallon pronounced, and sauntered off with his hand dug into the pocket of his tight jeans.

* * * * *

Keenan was mentally numb by the time she left the Supervisor's office. It was well into the afternoon before he'd allowed her to leave and she was exhausted.

"You've no reason to fear Agent Fallon, Keenan," the Supervisor had tried to assure her. *"I will keep his ass in line, believe me."*

On the way up to her floor at the dormitory she studied her reflection in the polished titanium doors of the cage. Soft, pleasant music—something Celtic she thought—was coming quietly through the overhead speaker and the interior of the elevator smelled of oranges. The scent and sound was comforting, relaxing, and when she stepped out of the cage, she felt calmer.

Until she came face-to-face with the man who would be her unwanted partner from now on.

Keenan stepped back, a deep frown between her brows. "You surprised me," she said.

"I'd have thought you would have known I'd be waiting here for you. Didn't your little inner voice tell you I would be?" he asked with a mean smirk. He was leaning with his shoulder against the wall, arms crossed over his wide chest.

34

Keenan stiffened. There was only one thing that pissed her off more than all others and that was to have her talents, her abilities, dismissed as though they were unimportant. She knew he was insulting her, and the hateful gleam in his unusual eyes made her bristle. Her chin came up.

"What exactly would you like to know, Mr. Fallon?" she queried.

Fallon's gaze narrowed dangerously. He leaned toward her—towering over her five-foot six-inch frame—and with his face set and hard replied, "Tell me what I was doing on September 5, 1977, if you know so fucking much."

He grinned nastily, knowing there was no way in hell she'd know where he'd been on that day, but she stunned him by replying, "You were in your grandfather's barn with a girl named Elana playing doctor until her older brother Feodor caught you." Her lips twisted with a smirk of her own. "Don't you think you were a little young at eight years of age to be…"

"That's enough!" he snarled, and pushed away from the wall.

"Satisfied?" she taunted, and her unease with him seemed to be melting.

He gave her a brief glower before walking past her to head in the opposite direction from her quarters. "Doesn't prove anything," she heard him growl. "That could be in a file somewhere."

"Privately you call your penis Yindy, which is short for *Yindyssagh mie*—meaning mighty good in the Manx language—so I can't help but wonder if it really is or if that's just wishful thinking on your part," she called out to him.

Fallon spun around with his eyes wide. No one—and he meant *no* one!—could have known about the nasty nickname he had for his cock. He stood there staring at her, and for the first time in his life felt the world shift beneath his feet. She said nothing, but the scorn on her face was enough to set his blood to boiling. Slowly he walked back to her, never breaking eye contact and wondering why she was standing her ground, not backing away from him since he allowed his most menacing expression to settle on his face.

"Let's you and me get something clear right up front, baby," he said as he glared down at her. Because of his six-foot six-inch height, she had to crane her neck back to look up at him. "I'll leave any guesswork about the tightness of your cunt out of our conversations if you'll leave the speculation of how good my dick is out of yours. How's that?"

Keenan ignored his crude words. "I'm good at what I do," she said, and wished she hadn't for the look he gave her had nothing to do with her abilities as a medium or his talents as an Alpha agent.

"So am I."

She watched him turn his back on her and stroll down the hall, his wide shoulders displacing more room than those of a normal man. Her gaze lowered to the tight roundness of his ass in those faded jeans, down the long legs to the well-worn sneakers then back up to the play of muscles in his back as he walked — no, *strutted* — down the hallway.

"Conceited prick," she called him before turning toward her suite. She could feel his surprised gaze on her, knew he'd intercepted her insult, but refused to look around.

As soon as she closed the door, she shrugged off her shoulder bag, hung it on the clothes tree behind the door, kicked off her shoes then bent over to neatly align them side by side at the base, then marched over to the loveseat, cracking open her book as she flopped down. She needed to dive into the story to take her mind from the unsettling thoughts that were plaguing her.

* * * * *

Fallon twisted his head around one last time before she disappeared into her new quarters. Despite his irritation at her, he liked the way she filled out her dark blue linen slacks. The curves were sweet, legs long, ass just right. There was plenty up front as well with breasts that pushed invitingly at the pale blue silk blouse — just a hint of cleavage showing in the opening. Long brown hair French braided down her back reached almost to a waist so small he knew he could encircle it with his hands. Those hazel eyes could flash verdant fire and that pleased him. Her high cheekbones gathered a blush easily, her full lips were no strangers to pouting. He had to admit she was a knock-dead gorgeous female who smelled like mangoes, their branches wrapped around on a fence ripening on a late summer afternoon.

"Wrapping around," he said as he opened the door to his quarters. For some reason those words stuck in his mind and he had a sudden vision of twisted sheets and tangled limbs, sweaty bodies cooling by a lazily moving fan overhead, a slender foot slowly traveling along his calf.

It had been a long time since he'd lain with a woman, taken comfort from a soft feminine body, was cradled by silken arms and stroked by gentle fingers. He had plunged himself into his work to push aside the need for any of that. He was a loner and preferred to keep it that way. Women needlessly complicated things. That was the main reason he'd never wanted an Extension, a fellow agent who would amplify his own powers.

But at that moment, he couldn't force his mind away from the woman at the other end of the corridor and he felt his cock swelling, aching, demanding. He put a hand to his growing erection.

"I bet if I come on hard to that prissy little bitch…"

He stopped, considered how she might react to his blatant sexual demand, and an unholy light spread over Mikhail Fallon's face.

"She'll run screaming to the Supervisor," he said aloud. "Begging him to reassign her. That's one way to get rid of her."

The more he thought about it, the more the need intensified. He reached for the door knob.

* * * * *

When the heavy, intruding knock came at her door, Keenan jumped, her head snapping up. She knew precisely who had come to call and thought of ignoring the interruption. She had been engrossed in the hot sex scene between the hero and heroine in

37

the book, had been turned on by it, and the interruption exasperated her. When the knock came again — louder this time — she hissed and swung her feet off the loveseat, snatched the bookmark from the side table to mark her place as she moved to answer the door. Even before she reached the portal, that insistent knock sounded once more.

"All right already!" she snapped. "I'm coming!"

The moment she opened the door, she knew what he wanted. She read it on his face, in the cruel set of his full lips, in the look he gave her. Hell, she could even *smell* it on him. His eyes were glowing with a preternatural light that practically singed her. That stare made her heart rate increase, her blood race, and caused a pool of heat to form between her legs. She shook her head. "No," she stated emphatically. "Don't even think you're going to…"

"You have no choice," he said, and barged right past her, "and it's what I want, and I always get what I want."

"Excuse me!" she declared, eyes snapping green fire. "I did not invite…"

Fallon whipped out an arm to encircle her waist, dragging her to him so quickly Keenan barely had time to bring her hands up to slam against his chest wall. But her strength was nothing compared to his and she could not stop him from molding his body to hers. His mouth swooped down to claim hers, slanting across her lips with hard, unrelenting pressure, his tongue slipping past the soft flesh as smoothly as a hot knife through warm butter. With careless ease he kicked the door shut and backed her against it, pressing into her without breaking the possession he had of her mouth. His hands dropped to her buttocks and he cupped her, aligning her to the hard bulge in his jeans. He ground himself against her, one hard thigh insinuating into the V of her legs. He growled low in his throat and all will to resist him flowed out of Keenan McCullough.

The romance book fell to the floor.

She ran her arms up to wrap around his neck. She lifted her legs to drape them around his lean hips, locking her ankles together. Her mouth took his with just as much heat and need, and when he turned around, started through the great room with her straddling him, her only thought was on what the weight of his body would feel like upon hers.

Fallon blinked, blinked again and lost it completely. He'd gone there to scare her—nothing more—but something else entirely was happening, something he'd damned sure never expected, and he found he had no control whatsoever over it. What was worse, he didn't want to.

Fallon carried her into the bedroom and propelled them onto the patchwork coverlet like a man possessed. The bed vibrated beneath their weight but all he could think of was writhing upon the soft body under him, entering the sweet, hot warmth between the long legs wrapped around his middle and pumping his flesh feverishly into hers. He wanted to rip the silken blouse from her and taste her nipples, remove her slacks and see if the nectar down there was as delicious as the honey from the lips his own assaulted. Jerking his hands from under her rump, he slid one onto her breast to knead her flesh—at first urgently then with thoughtful gentleness—his mouth still locked on hers.

Keenan loved his hand on her. His thumb was stroking over her engorged nipple in such a way she felt it all the way down to her bare toes. His weight was sublime and the knee he had thrust between her legs to push them apart made her want to draw her unsheathed nails down his broad back. But when he pushed up and put his hands on the front of her blouse—his intent apparent in the glittering depths of his amber eyes—she shook her head.

"Don't you dare!" she said. "This blouse cost me a small fortune."

"Then take it off!" he snarled, and rolled off her, coming to his feet beside the bed in one lithe bound. The dark burgundy pullover he was wearing was gone before she had time to take another breath, the wide expanse of his powerfully cut chest making her mouth water as he stood there running the buttons on his jeans. When he spared her a quick, impatient glance, she quickly rolled to the opposite side of the bed and began stripping off her blouse and slacks.

Fallon turned his back, sat down on the edge of her bed to take off his sneakers and socks before standing and shoving the jeans down his long legs. Facing the bed once more, the breath caught in his throat for his new partner—actually the only one he'd ever had—was standing on the other side of the mattress as naked as the day she'd been born and looking far too innocent for his state of mind. He watched her face pale and had to wonder what she'd seen in his expression that had caused that reaction.

Keenan swallowed hard for there was rampant lust flashing through those striking eyes of his and as his tongue came out to sweep across his upper lip like a man ready to feast at a banquet, she trembled.

"Don't hurt me, Fallon," she said, putting a knee to the coverlet. She had to clamp her mouth shut to stop her teeth from chattering.

Hurting her was the last thing on Fallon's mind as he got on the bed, stretching out on his side, his entire body tensed and primed. He wanted to lose himself in her silken folds, but for the first time in his life, he found himself wanting to give as much pleasure in the act as he was about to receive.

"Come here, baby," he said gruffly, lifting his left arm so she could place her body close to his. He made a mental note to go slowly with her—easy, gently—though he was on fire wanting her beneath him.

The moment they touched flesh to flesh something uncontrollable spread over the both of them. He was on his back with her atop him. He locked his arms savagely around her, her thighs outside his own. Their mouths greedily fed upon the other's lips, tongues dueling like serpents, bodies grinding together. They twisted and writhed upon the mattress, grunting and moaning until he flipped her over, sliding down her body to fasten his mouth upon one hard little nipple.

Keenan moaned and buried her hands in the thick darkness of his wavy hair. The texture of it sent shivers of delight down her arms for it was soft and clean and like dark chocolate flowing through her fingers. She closed her eyes to the sensations he was wreaking upon her body as he licked at her nipple and nibbled it, flicked his tongue across it then sucked it deep into his mouth. His right hand was beneath her left leg, his fingers stroking lightly along the ultrasensitive flesh behind her slightly upraised knee.

As he shifted his attention to her other nipple, she shivered for his hand now cupped the upper part of her calf and he was lifting her leg over his back. She slid the sole of her foot along his firm buttock and heard the growl deep in his throat.

The scent of her filled Fallon's nostrils and he released her nipple to writhe his way down her sleek, supple body until he was lapping at the sweet indention of her navel. She tasted like mangoes and where his tongue flicked, the flesh rose in gooseflesh.

He moved lower still until he was staring wide-eyed at the sensually cropped patch that grew in a heart shape upon her mons. Perfectly trimmed with no sign of stubble above the deep V of the heart or along its slightly curved sides, the hair beckoned his fingertips to touch the wiry curls, to test their springiness and softness. He threaded his fingers through the short spirals.

"How?" he asked, his breath blowing across her flesh.

She knew what he meant. "Laser."

"Ah," he sighed, and placed his lips just above the arches of the heart to place a gentle kiss there.

Keenan was stroking the lush hair back from his high forehead, grazing his widow's peak with her thumb, but when he lapped her between the legs, she sucked in a breath and her fingers tightened in his hair. She heard him chuckle a moment before both his hands were at the apex of her thighs and his thumbs were easing her folds aside. His hot breath on her most private of parts caused her to squeeze her eyes tightly closed then bury the side of her face in the pillow.

The heated scent of her sex—wet and spicy—drew him like a magnet and he flicked out his tongue to drag it up one fold, across the clit and down the opposite fold. He probed gently at her opening then licked his way up in quick little laps until he could wrap his lips around her.

"Oh my God!" she whispered as he drew on that sensitive area. He was nibbling her and sending shock waves of pure delight racing along her spine. She removed her hands from his hair—fearful she would tug too sharply—and slammed them down at her sides, gathering the coverlet in her fists and twisting the fabric as he continued to mouth her.

Fallon felt like a starving man. His nostrils were filled with the musky aroma of her juices as she wriggled her hips beneath his tender assault. He'd never taken so much time with a woman before—had never wanted to—and he was surprised at his reaction to a woman he'd developed an instant disliking to.

His hands were splayed along the creases of her taut thighs, his thumbs holding her apart for his tasting. Though he'd gone down on women in the past, he'd never taken as much pleasure from the act as it was giving him at that moment. Not a woman among them tasted as sweet and intoxicating as this one. He could hear the blood rushing through his veins in anticipation of impaling her upon his shaft, and that shaft was as hard and thick as he could ever remember it being. Yet he continued to lap at the juices that flowed from her as her hips undulated and her thighs tensed.

"Please!" he heard her whisper.

A slow, crooked smile peeled his lips back and he slithered up her, sliding his body over hers, pushing her thighs farther apart with his knees and fastened his lips to hers, his tongue probing deep.

Keenan could taste herself on his tongue and her womb leapt. She brought her hands up to clutch at his back—fingers flexing beneath his shoulder blades. Her legs went around his waist and she hooked her ankles together, drawing him as close to her body as he could get, the weight of him lying atop her so divine it made her shiver.

Fallon reached down for the straining flesh that was aching to plunge between her legs and guided it to her hot core. He stroked her with the rigid cock—smearing the pre-cum along her vaginal lips—and lifted his mouth from hers. He gazed down into her face, watched as she moistened her lips with her sweet little pink tongue, took in the need glowing in her hazel eyes then thrust slowly into her body. Once the tip was past her wet folds, he slipped both his hands beneath her firm ass and lifted her toward him, settling their groins tightly together as he buried his cock as far as it would go inside her.

Oh God, how he filled her! she thought as her nails dug into his back. He was stretching her so possessively—not moving, just lying there looking down at her, waiting for her to adjust to his thickness, his length.

"Okay?" he asked in a voice so soft he didn't recognize it.

She nodded, unable to speak past the lump lodged in her throat. Her eyes were on his handsome face, her breath coming in ragged gasps, her need so great she wanted to writhe against him as though she were an eel.

Very slowly at first he began to ease in and out of her moist channel. She knew he was gauging the discomfort she might be feeling and tightened her legs even more around him, wanting—no, *needing*—him to be more forceful with his pushes. He seemed to sense that and increased his speed, the length of his strokes until she thought the head of his cock was pushing against her very womb. It was a wondrously heavy feeling, slightly painful but completely fulfilling and she sighed as she buried her head against his shoulder.

Fallon's ass tightened with each thrust into her velvety heat. The smell of their juices was driving him mad and it was all he could do not to plunge into her like a man possessed. Her body was perfect for him. She felt right beneath him, fitting him as no woman ever had before. Strange thoughts began to flit through his mind as his need increased along with his speed. He was losing himself in this gorgeous female, handing something into her keeping that he had never planned to give to any woman. He was stunned at his reaction to her since it had not been his intention to do anything but scare her when he'd come to her door. Now he was experiencing feelings that damned well should never have been brought into the light of day. That not only worried him, it scared the hell out of him.

Keenan was amazed at the emotions rocketing through her with each thrust of Mikhail Fallon's body into hers. She was clinging to him, striving to merge their two bodies into one and that stunned her. She'd never wanted to belong to a man, never wanted to give up her freedom. Love 'em and leave 'em had been her motto up until then, but this man filling her to the brim with his powerful flesh was doing wicked things to her control. She suspected she was handing herself over to him, offering herself up, expecting him to take charge of her, and that frightened her badly. That wasn't what she wanted.

"Stop thinking," he growled at her. He was pumping into her with such fierce intent she could do no more than hold on to him and be taken along for the ride.

The bed beneath them was bouncing with the force of his thrusts, the headboard kicking against the wall. The patchwork coverlet was bunching under Keenan's body and one pillow had fallen to the floor. Overhead, the fan's blade began to spin faster. It seemed to be a goad for Fallon for his plunges became frenzied pumping that brought small grunts from Keenan's lips.

With a suddenness that stunned them both, her vaginal muscles began quivering, drawing, pulling, sucking at his flesh and his cock spurted thickly, hotly, deeply into her cunt. They were both straining as their combined releases raced through them—seeming to go on and on and on—with a fevered intensity that had them shouting with the pure, intense pleasure of the joint climaxes. His head was thrown back as he howled with ecstasy. Her fingernails were stapled into his back as she drove her hips from the bed to press brutally into his, her mouth open as she panted. They shuddered at the same time and both went limp, his weight crushing down upon her, his head turned so his cheek rested on her shoulder. With hearts thundering, blood pounding, breaths ragged and shallow, they lay exhausted with eyes closed, brows furrowed and limbs tangled.

For what seemed like hours they lay like that until Keenan finally became aware of the sticky seeping of their mixed juices down her thigh and beneath her rump. She shifted uncomfortably and heard him grunt, wondered if he'd been dozing, wondered if she had. When he lifted his head to look down at her, she felt something pluck at her heartstrings for there was a fall of dark hair covering his forehead and she ached to reach up and smooth it back.

He stared at her for a long time then rolled off her to stretch out on his back beside her. He brought one knee up and flung an arm over his eyes to block out the late afternoon sun. He had a wicked headache above his right temple and that wasn't a good sign.

"What the *hell* just happened?" he asked, his voice strained.

"I don't know," she lied. She knew perfectly well what had happened and she suspected he did too. His next words confirmed her suspicion.

"I sure as hell wasn't expecting that. Goddamn."

The scent of their combined juices embarrassed her and she sat up, swung her legs from the bed.

He reached out to run a finger across the small of her back where a dark blue tattoo of a Celtic knotwork butterfly had been drawn. "This is pretty. I like it."

She couldn't look at him, so without another word, she got up and padded into the bathroom, closing the door. Going to the sink, she braced her hands on the vanity and just stood there with her head down for several moments, staring at the drain. Slowly, she lifted her head to look in the mirror and was surprised at what she saw looking back at her.

Her eyes were glazed with spent lust. Her lips were swollen from his fierce kisses. There was a slight beard burn on her chin. Her hair was escaping the once-tight constriction of her French braid and was spiking around her head. There was a dull flush to her cheeks and upon her breasts. Her entire body held his scent.

"Bonded," she whispered. "Goddamn it, we fucking bonded!"

That was the last thing she had ever wanted or needed.

And with a man like Fallon?

She hissed and pushed away from the vanity, reaching over to pull open the glass door to the shower. She turned the water on, adjusted the temperature then went inside, closing the door tightly behind her. Vaguely, she heard the bathroom door open, but already the steam was clouding the glass, hiding her from him. She could see him standing at the toilet, bending over to lift the lid. It was on the tip of her tongue to tell him to be sure to lower the seat when he was finished but thought better of it.

Instead, she reached for the bottle of mango-scented body wash and the net scrubby.

Though she expected him to flush the toilet, he didn't, and when she heard the bathroom door close, felt slightly disappointed. A part of her had wanted him to come into the shower with her while another part had been screaming against such an intimate invasion. She knew why he hadn't flushed — he hadn't wanted the water in the shower to change temperatures. That small consideration made her smile.

When she came out of the shower with her fluffy white terrycloth bathrobe belted around her and a towel wrapped around her wet hair, he was gone. The bed had been straightened — or at least as much as any male could straighten a bed. It surprised her that he'd been that thoughtful.

Sighing, she walked out into the great room half expecting to find him lurking about but he had left her quarters and...

"Shit!" she said, her eyes narrowing. "He took my book!"

Twenty minutes later, Fallon came out of his own shower with a towel wrapped around his lean flanks. Barefoot, he strolled over to the bed and plopped down on his back, picked up the romance novel he'd spied lying on the floor as he'd left McCullough's apartment. Some perverse little imp had prodded him into pilfering it and now he was curious to see what women found so damned entertaining. He opened the book to the place held by the bookmark, held it open with one hand and shoved the other under his head as he began reading. What he read surprised him at first then made him howl with laughter. He went back a few pages to the beginning of the scene, and when he had read to the end of the chapter, slowly lowered the book and grinned.

"Now I know why you were horny as hell, babe," he said aloud.

He shifted on the bed. No wonder she'd lit into him as though she hadn't had a good fuck in months. He eyed the book with a quirk of his lips.

"Maybe you trashy bitches serve a useful purpose after all," he begrudgingly complimented the author then tossed the book aside.

He lay there scratching his bare belly then his balls for a moment before resting his free hand on his chest. He drew his knees up and stared at the ceiling, wondering why she hadn't admitted she knew what had transpired between them. She knew. He knew she knew and it had shocked her as much as it had him.

What transpired had not been foreseen by either of them and it sure as hell hadn't been what he'd wanted. Things had changed, would never be the same again, and he didn't really know how he felt about that.

"Bonded," he mused aloud. "Ain't that a fucking kick in the ass?"

Chapter Two

ℬ

The phone rang at a little past six in the morning and Keenan groaned, turning over to pluck the receiver from the base. "McCullough," she answered.

"Good morning, Agent McCullough. This is Jonas Cobb, the Supervisor's EA. He requests your presence in his office at 0730 this morning."

Keenan frowned as the connection was broken. She groaned again and hung up the receiver, lay there a moment staring up at the slowly revolving fan that was once more barely moving the air about the room then swept the covers aside. For just a moment she wondered why she was sore as she walked into the bathroom, but then memory washed over her and she felt herself blushing.

Had she really torn into that stranger, that hateful man like a starved vixen? she wondered as she lifted the lid on the toilet. Sitting down, she buried her face in her hands and moaned. What must he think of her this morning? Would that smirk of his be in place when she laid eyes on him again?

"Idiot. Idiot. Idiot," she called herself.

All the way through brushing her teeth, washing her face and braiding her hair, she considered the impossibility of what the two of them had done the afternoon before and felt her cheeks burning again.

What the hell had possessed her to give in to him? Why hadn't she fought him tooth and nail? Scratched his eyes out? Maimed him?

Instead, she had thrown her arms around him and let him screw the living daylights out of her. She had *bonded* with the bastard!

"Great God Almighty," she whimpered. "What the hell have I done?"

Her mother's words came at her from the past…

"Bonding is to be avoided at all costs, Keenan Tarryn. Do you understand? Bonding to a psychic is a hindrance, a nuisance. Sleep with whomever you choose but—for the love of God—do *not* bond with the bastard!"

As if she'd been given a choice with Fallon.

Bonding was pretty powerful stuff. When two people bonded, their souls were linked together for all time. Unbonded, a person could be married to a man for fifty years, love him dearly, yet if he died first, carry on until it was it was their time to die. But if the two had bonded, chances were good the woman would follow him into death within a short period of time, her soul torn asunder by his passing.

"Shit," she hissed. "Shit, shit, shit, shit, *shit!*"

She tried to push all thought of him out of her mind as she dressed in a loose white pullover and dark gray cotton slacks. Slipping on a pair of charcoal gray loafers, she walked out of the bedroom and into the great room, frowning once again when she thought about the paperback novel with which he'd absconded.

Thinking she'd get a cup of coffee at the commissary before going up to the Supervisor's office, she unhooked her shoulder bag from the clothes tree, swung it over her shoulder and left her quarters. She nodded to a couple of fellow women agents who passed her in the corridor, but they did not return her greeting. None of them seemed inclined to want to welcome her or stop long enough to introduce themselves. When she reached the central area where the east and west corridors met, she noticed none of the male agents coming from the east corridor spoke to the female agents coming from the west side of the building. No one spoke or seemed to be interested in anyone other than themselves as they stood waiting for the elevator. The silence was unnerving and when they got on the elevator—staring straight ahead—she was vividly reminded of robots from an old B movie. That image solidified itself when the elevator stopped and everyone piled off, going to stand on the monorail platform with the same eerie quiet.

Disturbed by such behavior, Keenan decided she'd rather walk to the Exchange than climb onboard the monorail with the automatons so she took the stairs down to the ground floor and walked out into the bright early morning sunlight. Glancing at her watch, she realized she had half an hour to kill before she was due to report to the Supervisor's office so she took her time walking to the main building.

Once inside the huge complex, she headed for the commissary and the black coffee she so desperately needed to stay awake. She hadn't slept that well—unable to get the image of Mikhail Fallon out of her mind—and kept yawning as she plodded down the thickly carpeted corridors.

"It's Agent McCullough, isn't it?"

The friendly voice behind her turned Keenan around and she found herself staring into the very handsome face of a man whose white smile held a million kilowatts of warmth. His blue eyes were crinkled at the corner and his hand was out. She took it.

"Dr. Matthew Groves," he said. "My friends call me Matty."

"You're joking," she said with a grin. "Matty Groves? As in the old folk song?"

"I'm afraid so. My mother had a wicked sense of humor," he said. "My father's name was Darnell and my mother's name was Gay."

Keenan couldn't keep the laugh from erupting. Her hand tightened in his. "Well, little Matty Groves, my friends call me Keenan," she replied. His hand was warm, filled with strength and held hers just a little bit longer than was polite before releasing it.

"Welcome to the Exchange, Keenan," he told her, his gaze roaming over her. "Ready to start the first day of the rest of your life?"

With hair as ebon as pitch and a pair of devastatingly clear sapphire blue eyes, he had Black Irish stamped all over him. Tall, broad-shouldered with a flat waist, he seemed to possess in spades the unique Celtic charm that was so very dangerous to the opposite sex. His grin was contagious and Keenan answered in

50

kind, forming an instant liking of this good-looking man named after a tragic lover's ballad.

"I have a meeting first thing this morning with the Supervisor so I'd better be ready," she told him.

He swiveled his head around to look up at a clock hanging on the wall. "Sweetie, the old man starts office hours at 0500," he stated. "Your first thing is most likely his fifth meeting of the new day."

Keenan groaned. "Oh Lord. Do I have phone calls at 4 a.m. to look forward to?"

"Not unless you're one of his Alphas," he answered. "I imagine your Alpha has been with the Supervisor since the crack of dawn seeing as he wasn't in his quarters when I stopped by to annoy him this morning."

"You and Agent Fallon are friends?" she inquired.

"Misha and I are more like pleasant enemies. We've known each other a long, long time," he said. He nudged his chin toward the commissary. "May I buy you some breakfast before your command performance?"

"I don't normally eat breakfast," she replied, "but I'm dying for a cup of coffee."

They walked into the commissary and he insisted she find a seat while he got their order. Finding a place by a sunny window, she hooked her purse over the back of the chair and settled back, yawning again. The rich smell of coffee and the pungent odors of bacon, eggs and waffles wafted through the air around her. When Groves brought his tray over to the table, she stared at the massive amount of food piled upon it.

"Surely you can't eat all that!" she said as he placed her lone cup of coffee in front of her.

"Down to the last greasy globule," he assured her, throwing a leg over the back of his chair and sliding down into the seat. "I'm a growing boy who needs loads of carbs and fatty foods to start his motor running every morning."

"Not a very healthy outlook for a physician," she teased.

"I'm Gaelic," he said then shrugged. "What can I tell ya?"

"Are you in charge of the med unit here?"

He shook his head. "No, I do research when I'm not doing the Doctors Without Borders thing. I am one helluva plastic surgeon in my spare time."

"That's wonderful," she said. "I really admire you guys."

He shrugged. "I just want to help. It's rewarding to reconstruct the face of a child born with a harelip or a deformity that hinders them from a normal life."

"Again, I truly admire you for that," she said.

As he dove into the large breakfast before him, she leaned back in her chair with both hands wrapped around her mug of coffee and sipped the piping-hot liquid.

"So you're from Georgia," he said in between mouthfuls of egg and jam-smeared toast. "Where exactly?"

"Albany," she replied, and at his nod, she asked if he'd ever been there.

"I was there to attend the funeral of a college friend," he said.

"Are you from Iowa?" she asked.

"God, no!" he stated with a snort. "I was born and raised in South Carolina but grew up in Florida."

"A Southern boy," she said, liking him better with each passing moment.

"Yeppers," he agreed, and slathered raspberry jam on another slice of toast. He motioned toward her with his bread. "The one thing they don't have in this place is grits. Do you like grits?"

"I love grits," she said with a smile. "With lots of butter and salt and preferably mixed with cut-up patty sausage." When he frowned sharply, she asked why.

"Another thing they don't have here is good sausage. Iowa food tends to be bland and their sausage sucks." He looked down into his plate. "That's why I order bacon or ham steak with my breakfast."

"How 'bout boiled peanuts?"

"Nectar of the gods," he said with a sigh then arched his brows. "Collard greens?"

"Only with a very healthy dollop of pepper sauce."

"Fried okry?"

"You betcha," she answered.

"Rutabagas, fried eggplant?"

"Egg pie?" she countered, and he sighed loudly. "I'll take that as a yes."

"I haven't had egg pie in years," he told her then shot out a hand to grip her upper arm lightly. "Tell me you know how to bake one and I'll marry you this very day!"

"I do, but let's forego the marriage until you see if my cooking is any good or not," she warned.

"You're a Georgia woman and you're Celtic," he said. "You were born to cook."

Keenan laughed. "Then what time should I reserve the reception hall for?"

Her teasing seemed to please him and he grinned around the gob of food in his mouth. His eyes were sparkling, assessing her with an intensity she found both complimentary and a bit unsettling. She had to look away from his handsome face for heat was climbing into her cheeks.

"He's not a bad guy, but he's gonna give you as much grief as you'll allow him to," Groves said, and she looked back around.

"Who?"

"Misha," Groves answered. "He can be a mean son of a bitch."

It took her a moment to realize he meant Mikhail Fallon. "Is his mother Russian?" she asked.

Groves nodded. "Yeah. I guess with a nickname like that it was fairly obvious." He scraped the last of his eggs onto a piece of bacon then popped them into his mouth. "He never knew his father. All he was ever told about him was that his last name was Fallon and he'd been a hit man for the I.R.A."

"Are his parents still alive?"

"Mother is. Father was murdered before Misha was born. Mom was married to a captain in the Spetsnaz unit of the MVD when she had her little fling with Fallon. Word is his stepfather was a truly evil son of a bitch. Rumor has it he was responsible for Fallon's death. He used to beat the holy hell out of Misha—kept it up until the day Misha put the bastard down hard, nearly killed him actually. Misha was put in a special detention center for the next seven years of his life so there has never been any love lost between the two. I hear when they are in the same room together, Misha and the Russkie can't keep their hands off each other's throats."

"Ouch," Keenan observed. "Must make family reunions a real blast."

"He rarely sees his mom for that very reason," Groves told her. "Though he calls her every Sunday when he's not on assignment."

"That almost makes him sound human."

Groves chuckled and reached for his orange juice. "I know he isn't happy about this Extension thing, so he's gonna push the limits with you. Just go with the flow and he'll eventually lose interest in annoying you if he realizes it won't make you crazy. He's more bark than bite unless you really piss him off, but since you're a woman, he'll use the venom of that wicked tongue of his instead of those meaty fists to get his point across."

"I'm not happy about the Extension either, but I don't guess either of us has a choice," she said.

"You work for the Exchange, you do what they tell you," he said. "That's the downside of our employment. May I give you a piece of advice about Misha?"

"Please."

"He's very good at hiding his thoughts. The mental block that man has developed is like trying to pry the lid off Ft. Knox. You won't be able to read him—even sense him—unless he allows it, so my advice would be to keep your own thoughts carefully hidden as well. He's bad about using other people's feelings against them."

"That's encouraging," she said, her shoulders slumping.

He leaned forward. "I tell you what—you're gonna be bone-tired by the time evening rolls around. How 'bout letting me take you to supper? There's a neat little barbeque place over in Altoona and I'm friends with the owner. We can go over and pig out—pardon the pun—and swill down good sweetened tea with lemon."

"Southern-style sweet tea?" she asked.

He nodded. "I taught him how to make it and the bastard was hooked from the first taste."

"What time?"

"Seven?"

"You've got a date!"

*　*　*　*　*

When Keenan was shown into the Supervisor's office at exactly 7:30, Fallon was already there as Groves had predicted. He didn't even look over at her when she was told to take the chair beside his. He was clutching a sheaf of papers, apparently absorbed with whatever he was reading.

"I trust you had a good night's rest, Keenan," the Supervisor said from the windows where he stood with his back to the room, hands clasped loosely behind him.

"No, sir, not really, but thank you for asking," she answered, and since she was looking past Fallon to her boss, she saw her fellow agent's lips quirk with what could only be amusement. She didn't think it was his reading material that had caused the smirk.

"Strange that neither of you slept well last evening," the Supervisor commented, turning around to face his agents. "Must have been something you ate, eh, Fallon?"

Fallon raised his head and swiveled it toward Keenan. "Guess so," he replied, his gaze raking down Keenan in such a way she ached to lash out and slap the half grin from his chiseled lips.

"Well, let's get down to business," the Supervisor stated, and came around his desk to perch on one end of it. "Tell me what you know about *drochtáirs*, Keenan."

Keenan blinked. "*Drochtáirs?*" she repeated, her brows drawing together before they shot up, her eyes widening. "I've been sensing something, but *drochtáirs?* They are mythological creatures." She felt Fallon staring avidly at her.

"One of our mediums believes seven of them are already here," the Supervisor answered.

"Does she have any proof *drochtáirs* are real though?" Keenan challenged.

"Madame Gregorovich has a very keen understanding of the preternatural world and she assures me they are," the Supervisor said, throwing Fallon a quelling look. "She believes the *drochtáirs* were on Earth long ago but were destroyed in the Great Flood. Now she believes they have come back to colonize again and that we cannot allow." He lifted a hand and pointed to the papers Fallon was holding. "Those are her notes to us on the matter."

Fallon held the papers out to Keenan. "Not a romance novel but a fairly entertaining read," he quipped.

Keenan snatched the papers from him with a glare from her narrowed eyes. "I want my bloody book back, Fallon," she snapped under her breath, low enough she hoped the Supervisor hadn't heard her.

"Haven't finished reading it yet," Fallon said. "I'm on the part where Rogue is fingering Sharyn while they are…"

"That's enough!" Keenan hissed, her face flaming. She glanced at the Supervisor who was looking at her with a bland expression on his lined face. She lowered her head, embarrassment flooding her very soul.

"Do you have something that belongs to her, Fallon?" the Supervisor inquired.

Fallon shrugged. "A trashy romance novel."

"Give it back."

Another fatalistic shrug and Fallon peeled himself out of the chair, stood then reached behind him to the pocket of his jeans where he had stuck the book. He tugged it out and extended it to Keenan.

Loath to touch something the odious man had been sitting on, Keenan nevertheless took it then opened her shoulder bag and dropped it inside without a word of thanks.

"You're welcome," Fallon said as he took his seat again.

"Don't filch anything else of hers," the Supervisor ordered. "Is that clear?"

"Wouldn't dream of it," Fallon agreed, and shot his long legs out in front of him, threaded his fingers together over his belly and laid his head on the back of the chair.

"You were going to tell me what you know about *drochtáirs*, Keenan," the Supervisor encouraged.

"Well, if I remember what I read about them, they are a species of blood fiends. A bite from their serrated fangs will make you one of them since they inject you with some kind of venom when they attack. Bite victims will in turn infect others. The creatures completely drain the blood from their victims until the body is nothing more than a decimated husk. They spend the daylight hours in the ground and can only move around after sunset. Wherever the corpses of their victims are buried, nothing will grow around the site. The land will be barren and scorched for a hundred feet or so. The same holds true concerning any land over which the creatures move. It is believed the destruction of plant life is due to the poisons given off by the *drochtáirs*. According to what I've read, they leave a noxious slime in their wake that is particularly vile." She shifted in her chair. "They live in lairs deep beneath the ground in viper shape. When they emerge, they slither swiftly across the landscape in that form, but when they are ready to attack, they assume an animal shape. What kind of animal hasn't been recorded, but whatever it is has to be big enough to overpower a full-grown man."

"One theory is they merge with whatever animal they come into contact with so there is no one specific shape," Fallon put in. "They don't shape-shift but rather invade. They can't tolerate heat. Forty degrees to them is like a hundred to humans."

Keenan shuffled through the papers she held, reading quickly through the paragraphs. "And the only way to kill them is by incineration," Keenan said. "Their victims too."

"Burning is the only sure-fire way to destroy pure evil," Fallon stated. He stared into her eyes. "Could you use your pyrokinetics to obliterate a human target, *leanabh*?"

"What does *leanabh* mean?" Keenan demanded, thinking he was insulting her.

"It is baby in Scots Gaelic," the Supervisor replied. He gave Fallon a hard look. "Stop calling her that. It is disrespectful."

Fallon sighed loudly and the Supervisor moved from his desk to the windows. "In the papers Madame Gregorovich suggests *drochtáirs* are the seed from which Raphian, the Destroyer of Men's Souls, sprang." He clasped his hands behind him once more as he looked out across the landscape. "That will make this enemy you are to seek out and put down a very formidable foe."

"I've fought minions of Raphian in the past," Fallon said. "They went down easy enough, but she didn't answer my question. Is she going to be able to wiggle her little finger or her nose or whatever else she wiggles and burn up an infected civilian?"

"Yes," Keenan said.

"How many kills do you have to your credit?"

"My share," she stated.

Fallon snorted at her answer, shaking his head as though he didn't believe her capable of such a thing.

Keenan ignored him, concentrating instead on finishing her perusal of the notes from Madame Gregorovich. "It says here, she believes the creatures have gone to ground somewhere in a cold region where they will hibernate until winter."

"We believe that means Canada," the Supervisor said. "That is supposedly where they were before the Great Flood, so they'll most likely return to the original site."

"Well, that sure as hell covers a lot of ground," Fallon scoffed. "Do we just climb aboard a couple of dog sleds and start sectioning off each province?"

"I should be able to detect them easily enough. We look for contaminated land," Keenan suggested. "It's just a matter of where to start looking."

"My idea was to have Fallon pilot a chopper over specific grids across the provinces, working your way east to west over the entire expanse. Any place that strikes you as being a potential lair can be marked from the air and then reconnoitered on foot later."

"I could eliminate it from the air," Keenan stated. "It's just a matter of concentrating fire at their lair."

"And take out a few innocent fuzzy-wuzzy little beasties in the bargain," Fallon said with a snort. "We'll go in to reconnoiter before you start frying defenseless little creatures that never hurt anyone."

Keenan turned her gaze on her new partner to give him a narrowed look. "I would never hurt an animal just for the hell of it."

"But you'd fire bomb their little condos without a second thought," he countered.

"I would not! That's not what I…"

"We'll go down and scope out the burrows. If there's a blood fiend there, you can blast away 'til your heart is content," he told her. "I won't even try to stop you."

"And what if one of those blood fiends decides to a take a bite out of us, Fallon?" she snapped.

"I'll bite him first," he said with a nasty grin that grew wider when he allowed his fangs to erupt.

Keenan nearly broke her ankle springing from the chair and putting distance between her and her new partner. Her face drained of color, her eyes were huge as she stared at the double rows of viciousness that filled Fallon's mouth.

"You're a…" She put up a defensive hand to keep him at bay. "You're a…" She couldn't get the word out.

"He's a Reaper," the Supervisor said.

"I prefer the term hell hound," Fallon quipped with a wag of his brows.

"I…" She shook her head as though to clear it of the sight of those wicked teeth. "Those fangs can't be real!"

"They are very real, Keenan," the Supervisor assured her. "And quite lethal." He looked to Fallon. "Retract them. Now!"

Fallon grinned again and the fangs were gone. He winked at Keenan, his eyes flashing a red glow that stunned her.

"What *are* you?" she hissed.

"As I said, he's a Reaper," the Supervisor told her. "Part human, part wolf and…"

"I beg to differ. I am part hound, not wolf," Fallon clarified, "although most Reapers Transition to wolflike beings. I, on the other hand, Transition to a hell hound. There are one or two other differences between me and my lupine cousins."

"Are shape-shifters who are capable of finding their prey through blood scent," the Supervisor continued as though he hadn't been interrupted.

"In other words they drink blood like vampires," she said, her top lip quirking distastefully. "I thought that was a myth too."

"'There are more things in heaven and earth, little girl, than are dreamt of in your philosophy'," Fallon drawled. "If you can throw fire from your fingertips, astral-project yourself, I can change into a hell hound when the mood strikes." He wagged his brows. "The rest of the time I'm just a horny little devil, but then you know that, don't you?" His eyes glowed scarlet red for a moment.

"Please sit down, Keenan," the Supervisor said. "He isn't going to pounce."

"Not when we've got company anyway," Fallon said.

Keenan's chest was rising and falling rapidly as she returned to her chair. A vein beat quickly at the base of her throat.

"Stop giving off those potent pheromones, McCullough, or I might not care if he watches me jump your bones," Fallon warned.

"You aren't going to touch me again," she hissed under her breath.

"We're bonded, *myneeast caillagh*, whether you like it or not."

"What does *that* mean?" she demanded.

"It means we get to screw like bunnies when…"

"No, you idiot! That word you used!"

"*Myneeast caillagh?*" He grinned nastily. "Little witch."

"You go to hell," she snarled.

"Right back at you, babe."

"So you bonded last evening," the Supervisor said with obvious satisfaction.

"Isn't that why you picked her for me?" Fallon asked. "You said you went to a lot of trouble to pick the right woman. You knew damned well once we were together, the hormones would kick in."

"Is that true?" Keenan asked. "Is that why you assigned me as his Extension? You knew we'd bond?"

"You bet your sweet ass that's why he did it," Fallon drawled. "Reapers mate for life. The lupines can't mess around on their mates, and their mates damned well better not try to mess around on them. We canines aren't as cut and dried about it, but nevertheless, we are mated for life, and you'll never be able to make it with another man. Ever."

Keenan gasped, eyes flaring. "*What?*"

"I didn't stutter, baby," Fallon grumbled.

"Oh my God!" She turned an angry glower to the Supervisor. "You could have warned us," she accused.

"If I had, both of you would have gone out of your way to avoid the other."

"Fucking A I would have," Fallon stated. "I never had any intention of taking a mate and you goddamned well knew it."

"I had my reasons," the Supervisor stated.

"But you should have given us the choice," Keenan insisted.

"Not when he's in his playing God mode, baby," Fallon told her.

"*Drochtàirs,*" the Supervisor said sharply to bring their attention back to the matter at hand. "They pose a potentially devastating threat to this world." He leaned back in his chair. "I will arrange to have a chopper placed on standby for later today. I'll also have quadrant maps pulled up for each province. I think we can safely rule out those provinces closer to the Arctic Circle such as the Yukon and Northwest Territories and Nunavut, as well as those along the eastern coastline for now. Concentrate on BASMOQ."

"British Columbia, Alberta, Saskatchewan, Manitoba, Ontario and Quebec," Fallon told her, pronouncing the last province as Keebeck.

"I know the names of the damned provinces, Fallon," Keenan said between clenched teeth.

"Just wanted to clarify," Fallon said, linking his fingers, stretching his arms above him and then cupping his neck.

"We're going to provide you both with laser pistols and whatever firepower the boys in provisions think you'll need. If there's anything else you might want to take along, just let my assistant know. Otherwise, you can go pack and I'll see you when you return."

"Pack?" Keenan questioned.

"You think this is only gonna take a few hours and then we'll be home for catfish tonight at the cafeteria?" Fallon asked.

She turned an eager grin to him. "Tonight's catfish night?" she gushed then batted her lashes. "Do they have coleslaw and French fries too, Billy Joe Bob Cletus?"

"And hushpuppies with minced onions, Betty Sue-Ann June," he growled, his lips twitching.

"Get the hell out of here, you two!" the Supervisor ordered. "And Fallon, don't aggravate the woman!"

Walking down the corridor together, Keenan and Fallon didn't speak. When they reached the monorail platform, they stood staring down the track, not looking at one another. The air was electric from the tension between them.

A young man came hurrying toward them, an apologetic smile on his freckled face. "The train is going to be a few minutes, Mr. Fallon," the young man said. "We're having a minor problem."

Fallon nodded.

"Thank you," Keenan acknowledged for the both of them.

Five minutes passed in silence. Keenan sat on one of the benches under the platform roof while Fallon stood staring down at the rail system.

"She's never wrong," Fallon finally said.

"Who?"

"My mother."

It took Keenan a moment before she realized who he meant. "Madame Gregorovich, the medium, is your mother?"

He nodded. "If she says the fiends are coming, they're coming." He leaned a shoulder against a column and folded his arms. "When I was growing up, I hated that she was a psychic. I hated what I was. I fought it tooth and nail for what little good it did me."

"From which parent did you inherit your abilities?"

He shrugged. "Both, but since Mom doesn't sprout fur and howl at the moon every three months, that part of me came from dear old Dad although she hasn't ever admitted to him having been a Reaper."

"I really know nothing of your kind," she admitted.

"What's to know? My kind—as you so sweetly put it—have supernatural strength and speed and can disappear at will. We have strong psychic abilities. Like our canine and lupine brothers, we are strong trackers and hunters. We hunt by scent, blood taste, or sound, and never fail to bring back whoever or whatever we were sent to retrieve." He cocked a shoulder. "Though our preference is to kill the quarry."

She put a protective hand to her belly. The sex they'd had the night before had been unprotected. The thought of a supernatural being lurking inside her body made her queasy.

"Don't worry. There won't be a pup from our encounter, *leanabh*," he told her through gritted teeth. "They made sure of that."

"What do you mean?"

63

"They snipped me," he said.

"You had a vasectomy?"

"I was *given* a vasectomy. There's a difference."

Keenan saw the anger in his gaze before he looked away. The monorail was approaching at last and he pushed away from the column, digging his hands into the pockets of his worn jeans.

"The Exchange did that?" she asked, surprised.

He shook his head. "It was done when I was eleven."

"Eleven?"

"Yes, ma'am," he said as the train came to a stop before them. "Before I Transitioned for the first time."

She watched him saunter into the car as though he owned it. The doors shushed closed and the monorail jerked as it started its return trip.

Keenan reached up to take hold of the bar above her. He wasn't looking at her so she studied his face where a muscle was grinding in his cheek. Handsome didn't begin to describe Mikhail Fallon. His dark looks drew the eye like a magnet. When she continued to stare at him, he turned his head and scowled at her. Having been caught, she said the first thing that came to mind.

"How come you don't have an accent?"

He was standing with his hands wrapped around a horizontal support pole as he regarded her. "I work at not having one unless it's needed. If I'm in Russia, I speak Russian. If I'm in Germany, I speak German. I have a talent for mimicry so I have the accents of the different languages down pat. You should hear my Scots burr. When I'm here, I can blend in with a generic Midwestern accent."

"Oh." She tore her gaze from the steady amber stare locked upon her.

"Go ahead and ask," he said. "I can see the questions flitting around inside your mind like fireflies."

She felt heat flooding her cheeks. "I don't have the right to..."

"Whether we like it or not, we bonded, *myneeast caillagh,* with all that implies. Ask."

Keenan hesitated. She didn't know how he'd take being told that she and Matty Groves had been discussing him behind his back. He solved the problem for her.

"My stepfather saw my mother and wanted her. He followed her and the man with whom she was living—my father—and in the course of the tail discovered my father wasn't human. Thinking him a vampire, he laid in wait and beheaded him though he didn't tell his superiors what he'd uncovered or what he'd done. He forced my mother into marrying him by threatening her unborn child. After I was born, he kept waiting for me to show signs of changing and when I didn't, he sought out some scientist in Ireland who worked with Reapers. The bastard told him I wouldn't change until I'd had a hellion implanted inside me. He refused to give Gregorovich a fledgling so my stepfather was forced to dig up my father's body and extract one."

Keenan shook her head. "I'm not following. What is a hellion?"

"A Revenant worm, a hellion, a fledgling. Different names for the same evil," he explained. "It's a parasite that gives a Reaper his powers."

She shivered. "And he put that inside you?" Her tone held her unease.

Fallon grinned nastily. "The scientist in Ireland—Daniel Dunne—wouldn't help Gregorovich, but he told him exactly what to do to create his own little Reaper. What sane man would tell someone to harvest anything from a man long dead and buried then put it in a child? I don't think Dunne actually believed my stepfather had access to a Reaper and was just pulling Gregorovich's chain. He also told Gregorovich that the first thing he should do was to make sure I couldn't reproduce." He scissored his index and middle fingers together. "So my stepfather took me to a clinic outside St. Petersburg and that was that." He shrugged. "If they were to do that to me today, I'd heal. The cut vessels would grow back together, but since it was done before my first Transition, I will remain sterile."

"Did your mother know what he'd done?"

"She had been sick for several days and we know now he had been drugging her so she couldn't stop what he was planning. She tried but was too weak and I was too little. She's never forgiven him and I've never understood why she stays with the bastard."

"Maybe she loves him."

Fallon snorted. "She hates him as much as I do. No, there's another reason but she won't tell me what it is."

"What happened after he put the hellion inside you?"

"Nothing," he said. "The fledgling doesn't come out of stasis until the host goes through puberty. It's the hormones that start the change but Dunne didn't explain that to Gregorovich so the old bastard thought the procedure had failed. After all, my father had been lying in his grave for over ten years and the hellion my stepfather harvested had been inert. Gregorovich thought it was in suspended animation, but when I didn't Transition after the Transference, he believed the fledgling was dead. Imagine his surprise when he found out he was wrong again."

"The hellion wasn't dead."

"I Transitioned for the first time on my thirteenth birthday and that's when hell opened up and I fell into it."

The monorail came to a stop and the doors peeled back. He held his hand out to indicate she was to precede him onto the platform. They started walking slowly toward the dormitory. He walked with his hands in his pockets and his head down.

"I'd been feeling strange all day," he continued. "Mean strange with my body twitching and my nerves raw. I couldn't sit still. I couldn't lie down. I itched and ached. About half an hour before the fateful introduction to what I am began, my mother's husband came home, decided he didn't like the way I was looking at him and backhanded me hard enough to break my nose— again. I'd had that kind of treatment from him all my life. That day, I'd had enough. It was like someone had waved a red flag in front of a bull. I remember thinking how much I hated him. The moment he touched me something exploded inside and I went after him." He snorted. "Surprised the shit out of the old bastard.

I'd never fought back before. If my mother hadn't come home and pulled me off him, I would have killed him that night." He lifted his head. "God knows I wanted to."

"Did you change during the fight?"

He shook his head. "No, I ran out of the house, into the woods, and it happened there. I don't remember much about it except there was this ungodly pain and then a bright flash of light. I woke up the next morning buck-naked in a pile of sopping-wet leaves with the sound of dogs baying and heavy boots trampling toward me."

"Your stepfather had called the authorities."

"No, he didn't. He was unconscious, stayed unconscious for nearly a week. I'd beaten him so badly my mother had no choice but to take him to the military doctor on the base where we lived. She didn't want him to die and have me executed for his murder. His general was the one who sent the soldiers after me. He wanted to see what a thirteen-year-old boy who could do that much damage to one of his elite Spetsnaz looked like."

They reached the elevator and he punched the Up button. She noticed his hand shook and he seemed suddenly edgy.

"You were sent to a detention camp."

"Information courtesy of good old Matty Groves," he mumbled. "It wasn't a detention camp. It was a secret research facility in Siberia."

"The general found out what you were."

His smile was brutal. "I don't think he was prepared for what happened during his interrogation. He couldn't get me off his base fast enough. Some sinister-looking men came in, shot me full of joy juice and when I woke up, I was in the frozen north."

Despite his words she saw deep pain registering in his gaze and knew without being told they'd done worse things to him in that place. He had been tortured.

The elevator arrived and the doors opened. He ushered her inside, seemed to hesitate for a moment then joined her in the cage.

"You were there for seven years," she said, turning around to face the door.

"Until I managed to escape. Ran as fast as I could to Moscow, infiltrated the American Embassy. Pierced their security like it wasn't there, asked for asylum then showed 'em what I could do when they tried to throw me out. Once they saw what a talented little freak I was, they invited me to stay. Snuck me out of the country and brought me here. I wound up at the Exchange." He shrugged, shifting from one foot to the other. "Out of the frying pan and into the fire."

The elevator stopped, settled and the doors slid back. She preceded him out of the cage. Since her room was one way and his the other, he stopped, took her arm to keep her from leaving him.

"Pack enough for a week. We can always buy more up there if we need it. Bring along warm, comfortable clothing and sturdy boots."

She didn't think he was aware he was running his thumb sensuously up and down the inside of her arm just above the elbow.

"And don't forget to cancel your date tonight with little Matty."

Her eyebrows shot up. "You know about that?"

"I know everything, *myneeast caillagh*." The glint in his eyes tightened along with the hold he had on her arm. "I know I'm the only man you'll be seeing from now on."

"You think so?" she challenged, and found herself falling into the amber glow of his gaze.

He pulled her to him and slanted his mouth recklessly across hers, claiming her with a kiss that made her toes curl. When he pulled back, there was molten heat staring back at her.

"I know so, baby," he said. He released her and turned away, striding down the corridor without a backward glance.

"Conceited prick," she said, but the words were soft and spoken in a tone that surprised her.

Shaking her head, she headed for her own apartment. Once inside, she leaned against the door and put her fingers to her lips. Her flesh was tingling as though he'd branded her.

She thought that might well have been what he'd done.

Chapter Three

ℬ

In the copilot seat, Keenan was mesmerized as she watched the shadow of the helo undulating across the ground. They were cruising along at 133 knots with a perfect blue sky above them and green farmlands stretching out like a crazy quilt below. They'd been in the air about half an hour and she was more relaxed than she could ever remembering being in a chopper. Her faith in Fallon's abilities surprised her as she relaxed as much as she could in the safety harness.

"So, tell me how you came to be with the Exchange." His voice through the headset was slightly lower than his normal tone.

Pulling her gaze from the scenery beneath them, she looked over at him. The dark aviator glasses he was wearing made him look even more handsome and she felt a tight little squeeze in her lower belly.

"I volunteered," she said. "Took the tests and here I am."

"Just like that?"

"I'd been thinking about it for nearly a year before I made the plunge, but yeah, just like that."

"You obviously didn't know what you were getting into."

"I knew," she said. "The group I was with has a dossier on the Exchange." She turned to watch a flock of Canada geese winging their way through the sky. "I learned about it through a case I was working. I felt I had abilities I could better utilize with the Exchange than through the group I was with at that time." She smoothed away a piece of lint from her pant leg. "They didn't like me using my woo-woo shit as they called it, even though my partner was an empath, he didn't have other psi powers."

Fallon grinned then chuckled.

"What's so funny?"

"I wasn't sure your woo-woo shit was gonna help me do my job either," he replied. "What about that partner you had? Were you close?"

She ducked her head. "We were lovers, but that's all in the past. It ended badly."

"How come?"

"We got into an argument once and he drew back his hand to hit me. I told him if he let that fist fly, I'd emasculate him and I meant it. I can't stand the sight of him now."

"That's good because now we're bonded and stuck with one another."

"About that..." she said, shifting in the seat so she could face him. "I'm not comfortable with what you seem to think bonding means."

He glanced at her. "What exactly do you think it means, *myneeast caillagh*?"

She frowned. "I wish you wouldn't call me that, Fallon."

"I wish you wouldn't call me a conceited prick, but that seems to be your particular endearment for me."

Keenan sighed. She wasn't going to debate him. "To me bonding means forming a close relationship and..."

"Can't get much closer than me being inside you, sweetness," he reminded her.

She let that pass. "It means one partner caring for the other, having the other partner's back."

"Physically, psychologically and professionally," he amended.

"Well, yes. I suppose so."

He cut his gaze over to her. "It also means developing a strong emotional attachment."

"All right," she agreed. "I can accept that, but it doesn't mean exclusivity."

"Bonding is the psychic version of a marriage commitment, McCullough. You may not want to acknowledge it yet, but that's just the way it is." He banked the chopper to the coordinates that

71

would take them into Canadian airspace. "And legally married or not, I don't share my woman with any man."

She groaned. "Surely that's not what you wanted."

"It wasn't, but then I didn't have any plans of ever bonding with anyone," he admitted. "The choice was taken out of my hands."

Keenan listened to him talking to air traffic control and slumped in her seat with her arms folded over her chest. She had known she was to be assigned as an Extension—an operative assigned to magnify, sharpen and augment the psi powers of another operative with similar or complimenting abilities—when she'd signed on. She'd been told that sex could act as an amplification of her powers and might be required during the course of an assignment, but that hadn't bothered her. She was no prude when it came to sex and had enjoyed a satisfied, varied love life since graduating from high school.

Although it had been months since her last sexual encounter, she hadn't really missed it. She had even stopped taking her birth control shots because she'd decided to try celibacy for a while. After her fateful encounter with Fallon, she knew she'd have to make an appointment with medical to get those shots started again.

"No, you don't," he said, interrupting her reverie. "I told you I can't get you pregnant."

Defiantly she snapped her head toward him. "What if I want to screw somebody else?"

"You can't," he said. "You won't." He shrugged without looking her way. "You'd better not. I told you that already."

Fuming, she ground her teeth together.

"Accept it, *myneeast caillagh*." He smiled. "Personally, I'm starting to warm to the idea." At her stunned look, his smile widened. "Yeah, it surprises me too."

"It's not fair," she said. "This wasn't ever supposed to happen."

"My feelings exactly, baby, but feces occurs."

For the remainder of their trip into Canada, Keenan remained silent. She couldn't say he wasn't her type because he was. Arrogance and ego aside, the man had everything she'd always considered necessary in a lover. He was handsome, tall, dark-haired and muscular. She strongly suspected there were deep, deep layers beneath the ruddy complexion that would surprise her. Peeling them away to get to the creamy center might take some doing, but chances were good the expedition would never be boring. Watching him out of the corner of her eye, she imagined he was assessing her just as carefully.

"I am."

"Stop reading my mind."

"Stop broadcasting so loudly."

She drew in a long breath and let it out slowly. Life with Mikhail Fallon was never going to be ordinary.

* * * * *

The lodging into which the Supervisor's personal assistant had booked them in Duparquet was a quaint Northern Quebec cottage with its own private, secluded lakefront and an area to land the chopper. It would be their base while they searched that province for signs of *drochtáir* presence. They'd move on to Ontario once they were satisfied there was no infestation in Quebec.

"All the comforts of home," Fallon said as he surveyed the chalet-style cottage. "Minus the need to pick up the clutter."

Keenan liked the heavy oak furniture, overstuffed sofa, comfortable-looking chairs in front of a tin-faced fireplace. The thick braided rug underfoot was lovely and the gingham curtains at the windows added a touch of femininity to an otherwise masculine room. Sticking her head in the lone bedroom, she was a bit disappointed to see only one full-sized bed, but if need be, she could make the long sofa her retreat for the night.

"You'll sleep where you belong, baby," he stated as he opened the fridge to inspect the contents. He nodded—seeming to approve the selection inside—then closed the door. "Beside me."

"Fallon..." she started to protest, but he disappeared into what she thought must be the bathroom.

"Beside me," he said again as she heard the unmistakable sound of a toilet lid hitting the back of the porcelain receptacle. A moment later, she heard him urinating.

"At least you could close the damned door!" she called out to him. "And flush the toilet this time."

"Nag, nag, nag," he mumbled.

The flushing noise made her smile as she sat down on the sofa and bent forward to untie her thick-soled utility boots.

"What do you feel like for supper?" he asked when he returned. "They've provided us with steaks, a bucket of chicken with a couple of sides and a big plate of veggies."

"Chicken is fine."

"Works for me too," he said, and plopped down in one of the chairs. He shot out his long legs, crossed them at the ankle and threaded his hands over his flat belly.

Keenan arched a brow. "Yes?"

He grinned. "You're the domestic one, sweetie. Be domestic."

She returned his grin, heaved herself up from the sofa and padded into the kitchen.

Fallon lowered his head to the back of the chair to look up at the exposed beams of the ceiling. In the kitchen the microwave came on and then the delicious smell of chicken heating wafted through the air. When she returned, he sat up and frowned.

"What are you doing?" he asked.

Keenan resumed her seat, curled her legs beside her, and with the plate balanced on the arm of the sofa, began to eat her supper. She picked up a chicken leg, bit into it and chewed, grinning.

Fallon's eyes narrowed and he uncrossed his legs, drew them in. "That's just plain mean, McCullough," he said.

Her grin widened as she took another bite. "I'm not your maid, Fallon," she told him.

He got to his feet, giving her a look that made her stop chewing and stare up at him with unease.

"Just wait," was all he said as he stomped into the kitchen.

Keenan felt her heart thud hard against her rib cage and she had difficulty swallowing the food in her mouth. Watching him warily when he came back with his own plate, she was unnerved with the way he just stared at her. She squirmed under that silent, steady regard but refused to give him the satisfaction of complaining. Even when he was finished and went to take his plate back to the kitchen, she felt even more on edge. In the back of her mind she couldn't stop thinking she'd pried open a big can of worms by not fixing him a plate when she'd done her own. Hearing him running water in the sink had an ominous sound to it.

Fallon came back into the great room, went over to the desk in the corner and opened the briefcase he'd brought with him without saying a word. He sat in the desk chair and began going over the grid maps of the Quebec Province, no doubt planning the next morning's flybys.

After finishing the rest of her food, Keenan carried her plate to the sink and washed it in the water he'd left. She cleaned up the kitchen, let the water out and then came to the door with a kitchen towel in hand.

"Do you want something to drink?" she asked. "There's Pepsi in the fridge."

He shook his head, not looking up from the maps.

"You want some coffee? I could make a pot."

"I don't drink coffee at night," he replied. "Reapers don't sleep all that well to begin with."

She turned back to the sink, laid the towel over the rim to dry then turned off the kitchen light. Coming back to the sofa, she fished in her carryall for the romance novel he had lifted from her apartment the day before and settled down to read with her legs tucked under her.

Fallon glanced at her, saw what she was doing and secretly smiled.

* * * * *

The clock said ten minutes after eleven and Keenan tried to hide her yawn. Fallon was still poring over the maps—this time of the Manitoba Province—but her eyes were growing heavy. She'd been putting off going to bed because she didn't want to think about lying beside him on the full-size mattress, his big body pressed against hers. That he would refuse to sleep on the sofa was a given, and despite the fact it looked comfortable enough, she really didn't want to sleep there either.

"We'll start at first light and that seems to be roughly 5:25 tomorrow." He began folding the maps. "I suggest you get that cute little ass of yours to bed before you break your jaw yawning."

"What about you?" she asked then blushed heatedly as he looked over at her. She felt tongue-tied, her mouth dry. "I mean, you'll be piloting. Don't you need your rest?"

He locked his gaze on her. "I'll get what I need, *myneeast caillagh*," he said softly as he stuffed the map into the briefcase and closed the lid, snapped the latches shut.

"Ah, you weren't really serious about us…" Her gaze moved to the bedroom. "You know."

"Sleeping together?"

She bobbed her head slowly up and down, chewing on her lip as she did, angry at herself for being so hesitant to speak her mind. She had never been a coy, demure woman, but this man intimidated her, made her feel so weak. To a small degree, she feared him.

And she wanted him so badly her teeth ached.

"Go to bed, McCullough."

"But…"

He turned away toward the front door, opened it and walked out, closing it gently behind him.

For a moment she stood there staring at the closed portal then her anger rose—hot with insult. "What the fuck?" she snapped, and actually took a step toward the door only to come up short.

Not only weak but indecisive as well, she labeled herself. And unsure of her ability to control Mikhail Fallon.

"But do you want to control him?" a sly little voice inside her head whispered. *"He's a bad boy, Keenan, and you know how you love bad boys."*

She stood there undecided for a moment or two longer then went to the door and opened it to find Fallon standing against the porch rail, his hands hooked over the header that ran between two columns.

"What do you hear?" he asked.

Keenan turned her attention to the moonlit forest beyond the gravel driveway. The forest was awash in a soft gray blanket and there wasn't a hint of air movement, no insect noise or furtive critter pattering.

"I don't hear anything."

"Neither do I," he said quietly, "but I can feel it."

Tuning in to her surroundings, Keenan let her psychic talent flow out over the forest. What she discovered drew her brows together. "It's not the same thing I have been feeling."

"Not the *drochtáirs*?"

"No. This is oily," she said. "The air feels oily."

"Oily and heavy," he agreed. "And that weight is sitting on my shoulders like a fucking albatross."

She shifted her own shoulders, knowing exactly what he meant. It felt as though a greasy blanket were clinging to her back. She put a hand to her chest. "Someone is watching us and it's making me very anxious. My heart is actually racing."

"Some*thing* is watching us," he corrected, and lowered his hands. "Go back inside, baby."

"Not without you," she said. "If there's something out there…"

"I'm perfectly capable of taking care of whatever it is."

"But…"

He reached out to drag her into his arms, lashing his mouth over hers, parting her lips with his tongue. The kiss was hard, thorough, and when it ended, Keenan's heart was thudding against her rib cage.

"Go. Inside," he ordered, his tone brooking no challenge. "I don't need my mind divided right now."

There was resolution in the way he stared back at her. Powerful, authoritative, rejection of his words was not an option. She did as he demanded, watching him from the doorway as he stepped off the porch and into the night.

"Close and lock the door, *myneeast caillagh.*"

She shut the door but defiantly did not lock it. Her eyes widened when the lock secured itself with a firm snap and she heard the faint sound of laughter coming from the man for whom she was beginning to develop deep feelings—against all odds and good sense, she thought.

"Conceited prick," she whispered.

"*But I'm* your *conceited prick,*" a soft voice came back to her.

"Maybe," she acknowledged.

Pulling aside the window curtain, she looked out into the streaming moonlight and realized a rolling fog had developed low to the ground. It was undulating like a restless sea creature over the oyster shell driveway and reaching its ghostly tentacles into the forest. So eerily quiet that she could hear the breath rasping in her chest, she strained to get a glimpse of Fallon, to pick up any hint of sound coming from him. Putting a thumb nail to her mouth, she nibbled on a loose cuticle—a habit she had often tried to break but could not shake. To those who knew her well it was a sign of how acutely she was stressed.

"Where are you, Fallon?" she asked, her breath fogging the glass.

By the time she saw him striding toward the cottage, an hour had passed—an hour in which she had imagined all manner of terrible things befalling him. The sight of him climbing the three short steps, his boot heels scuffing on the porch floor were such a relief, she snatched back the lock and bolted out the door, flinging her arms around him as he reached the doorway.

"Don't you *ever* do that again!" she hissed.

His arms wrapped her. "Do what?"

"Scare me like that, Fallon!" she said in a voice that said he should have known what had upset her. "I was worried about you."

Her body was pressed tightly to his and she was shaking, so he bent his knees and scooped her up in his arms, took her into the cottage and kicked the door shut. Once more the lock engaged on its own.

He carried her to the bedroom without another word between them. There was no need for words and both knew it. Once at the bed, he let her feet touch the floor then took his time undressing her. He tugged off the pullover, unbuckled the trendy belt circling her waist, unsnapped her fly then released the zipper. Tucking his fingers beneath the waistband, he hunkered down before her as he peeled the slacks down her long legs, reveling in her hand on his shoulder as she steadied herself while she stepped out of the garment. His gaze lingered on the lace and silk panties that molded to her shapely hips as he removed her socks then he stood, reaching behind her to unhook her bra. The weight of her breasts caught and held his attention as they were released. Drawing the straps of her bra down her arms, he kept his attention riveted on those lush globes and their dusky areolas. He tossed the bra aside and molded his hands to her breasts.

"Beautiful," he said quietly. He fanned his thumbs over her nipples and smiled when they swelled instantly.

"Are we taking it slow this time?" she asked, running her fingers up and down his right forearm.

He lifted his gaze from her breasts to her smiling eyes. "Unless you want it differently."

She was standing there in only her panties but she didn't seem self-conscious or inhibited by her near nakedness. Her body was toned and silky without a blemish or scar in sight. Not one stretch mark or red mole or broken vein marred her beauty, but it was enhanced by a small, heart-shaped birthmark that rode low on her left hipbone.

"I like you best when you go all caveman on me, Fallon," she admitted. "No man has ever dared do that before, and I never expected to allow one to, but with you…" She slid her hand up his arm, across his shoulder and spiked it through his dark hair. "With you, I like the edginess, the danger."

His lips stretched into a knowing smile. "Do you now?"

She brought his head to hers and kissed him, slipping her tongue along the seam of his lips, licking at the corners then thrusting it slowly inside to taste the warmth of his mouth. She ground her hips against his groin.

"What do you think?" she growled.

Fallon snaked out a hand, grabbed the waistband of her fragile panties and ripped them off her. Despite her frown at the destruction of her undergarment, he slipped his fingers into her hot channel and cupped her sex, making her lift to her toes as he tugged at the soft haven.

"I think I'm gonna fuck your brains out, McCullough," he warned. He rubbed vigorously between her legs then released her, slipping his hands beneath her rump to lift her, grinning evilly as she wrapped her legs around his waist and locked her arms around his neck. He backed her up to the wall and held her there with his body as he brought one hand between them to undo his jeans.

"I've never been taken against a wall," she told him.

"It won't be the last time," he said then thrust his cock deep inside her.

Keenan grunted with the force, feeling him stretching her, filling her, bumping up against her womb as he pulled out and shoved his shaft into her again. With each stroke, her back scraped up the wall and she knew she'd have bruises come morning.

Using his strong, powerful legs, he arched his body into hers, locking his teeth lightly into the soft flesh along her collarbone. He rubbed hard against her so that her sensitive breasts were being abraded by the material of his shirt. Her fingernails dug into his shoulders for a moment then she grabbed his head and brought his mouth to hers, wanting the thrusting of his tongue in rhythm to the thrusting of his cock, and Fallon obliged her.

His cock was larger and longer than any that had ever been inside her and she was caught up in the pleasure-pain by the way he wielded it. Him slamming roughly into her was what she'd wanted, and he was accommodating her wishes. The pressure was building so intensely she thought she might well pass out when she came.

Grunting with each upward flex of his hips, Fallon lost himself inside her silken heat. Her inner muscles were grabbing him with quick little clutches that were driving him out of his mind with need. His cock was so hard, burning so brutally he felt tears gathering in his eyes. The bonding between them was taking its toll not only on his body but his soul as well.

"Come for me, Fallon," she murmured against his mouth. "Come hard for me!"

Her voice was a silken purr and it was all the encouragement he needed to release. Hard and hot and savagely he shot into her, his head going back as he roared with the sheer force of the pleasure claiming him. Almost instantly he felt her answering spasms, and like a man possessed, rammed into her in a frenzy he worried might well unhinge his hips.

"Yes!" she cried out as her cunt muscles quivered around him. "Yes, Fallon. *Yes!*"

The last spurt of juices trickled from him and he slumped against her, breathing hard, gasping to bring air into his lungs. His heart was racing and he was covered in sweat.

"Shower," she mumbled.

"Yeah."

Without breaking contact and while they both still had a modicum of energy left in their depleted bodies, he carried her—still clinging to his hips and neck—into the bathroom and plopped against the wall. With one hand still cupped under her ass, he used the other to fumble with the shower controls.

"Hot," she said against his neck. "I like it hot."

"Me too," he said, and thought of course that would be the way she liked it for the Exchange had provided the perfect woman to him for his mate.

He smiled as he nudged aside the vinyl shower curtain and lifted his leg to step into the tub, still carrying her in his arms.

"Umm," she said with a sigh as he backed her under the flow of the steaming, cascading water.

He wanted to bathe her, put his hands on every part of her. He didn't even notice he was still fully clothed or that his boots were filling with water.

* * * * *

"So what was it?" she asked as she lightly traced a pattern upon his naked chest. "Whatever was out there?"

"I have no idea." Her head was on his shoulder, his arm around her, his chin atop the glossy sleekness of her hair. A glance at the clock on the bedside table revealed it was three in the morning. "I followed it until I lost the godawful scent." He ran his fingers up and down her bare arm. "I got the feeling whatever it was it was laughing at me."

"Did you get a sense of evil emanating from it?"

"No, did you?" he asked.

"Not really. To tell you the truth, I couldn't read it at all, but I did feel very apprehensive," she said.

"It was whistling," he told her.

"Whistling?"

"Or crooning. I really couldn't tell which." He sighed. "We've got enough on our plate that we don't need another entity to have to worry about. We..."

The entire room shook as something slammed brutally into the ceiling. There was another loud hit then maniacal laughter so deafening, so unnatural it made both Fallon and Keenan slap their hands to their ears in agony. The cottage vibrated, every windowpane cracked and all the light bulbs as well as the dresser and bathroom mirrors shattered.

"Holy shit, what the hell *is* that?" Keenan yelled.

Fallon shot off the bed, dragging on his jeans, hopping into them as he stumbled to the bedroom door. Cursing as he stepped on the broken glass in his bare feet. He jerked open the door and came face-to-face with something he'd only glimpsed in his worst nightmares.

An oversized hand with sharp talons shot forth and poked Fallon's naked chest. "You're it!" a gruff, rasping hiss of a voice said.

Shock lanced through Fallon's brain and he yelped, staggering back, clutching his chest and falling to the floor on his ass in an attempt to get away from the immense threat looming into the room.

Filling the doorway was a huge figure swathed in clumps of ragged gray fur that reeked to high heaven. Large pointed ears were crowned with spiky tufts and an overhanging brow that shadowed its red eyes. So tall it had to bend down to lean into the room, the creature shot out one long arm and thick digits capped with deadly looking claws waved childlike at Keenan.

"Greetings, Mate of the hound!" the creature said in its garbled voice, and chuckled. It snorted wetly, ran the back of its shaggy arm under its broad black snout of a nose then moved backward through the door, lumbering so heavily the floor shook beneath its weight. Its last words were slurred. "Olly, olly oxen free!"

For a moment neither Keenan nor Fallon moved or spoke. Both were staring wide-eyed at the empty doorway. When at last she found her voice, it was high-pitched and unsure.

"Fallon?" Keenan whispered.

Fallon was still on the floor with his mouth hanging open. His knees were bent, hands braced behind him to keep him from falling flat on his back. His face was pale, his legs shaking.

"Are you all right?" she asked, and realized she was sitting up on the bed as naked as the day she'd been born. She grabbed the sheet and tucked it around her.

"I don't believe I just saw what I saw," he said with awe.

"You know what it is?" She scrambled off the bed, wrapping the sheet.

"Stay where you are!" Fallon snapped. "The floor's covered in glass."

Keenan looked down to see a large shard right in front of her. She bent to pick it up. "What was that thing, Fallon?"

"*An Fear Liath Mor*—The Big Gray Man. It is the Guardian of the Gateway into the Other World," he said, slowly turning his head from the doorway. "I've never heard of it being anywhere outside Ben Macdhui."

"The mountain in Scotland?"

"Yeah," he answered. "Mama used to tell me about it when I was a child along with the Yeti and Sasquatch and Bigfoot. She was always fascinated by cryptozoology, the search for animals thought to be extinct or hypothesized to exist. I thought *An Fear Liath Mor* was just an old folk's tale."

"Just as I though *drochtáirs* were," she countered as he got to his feet, wincing. "Did you get cut?"

"Yeah I got cut," he said, and lifted one foot to brace its ankle on his knee. There were slivers of glass along his instep. He began to pull them out. "Son of a bitch."

"Come sit down and let me do that," she told him.

He hopped over to the bed and sat down on the edge. "Put your boots on, woman, before you slash your feet to ribbons," he grumbled.

"My boots are in the other room, Fallon," she reminded him. "You carried me in here, remember?"

Cursing, he got up and limped from the bedroom, coming back with her overnight bag as well as her boots. Where he walked, he left bloody footprints on the polished hardwood floor.

After she put on her boots, she went into the bathroom to rummage through the medicine chest, coming back with the things needed to see to his cuts. Kicking aside a few shards of glass, she knelt down in front of him and picked up his foot to support it on her thigh.

"What do you think it meant when it said you're it?"

"The fucking retard wants to play tag," he groused. "How the fuck would I know what he meant?"

Plucking the slivers from the sole of his foot with a pair of tweezers, she couldn't help but smile. "If it had meant us any harm, it could have pulverized us with one swipe of those claws."

"You don't think bursting our eardrums with that laugh wasn't harmful?" he questioned. He put a hand to his temple and rubbed. "I've got a bitching headache."

She glanced up at him before using the washcloth she'd brought to wipe the bottom of his foot. "Do you always get migraines when you encounter other psychics using their powers? You got one yesterday after we bonded, remember?"

He shrugged. "Yeah, I guess." He sucked in a harsh breath when she applied an astringent to his wounds.

"Do you think he'll come back?"

Fallon groaned. "I hope not."

"But we don't know what he wants. If he was inviting you to play with him—"

"I don't play with other men, *myneeast caillagh*," he growled.

"He looked like an overgrown teddy bear," she said as she applied a Band-Aid to the deepest of his cuts. "A shaggy, stinky teddy bear with a butt-ugly face, but still a teddy bear." She tilted her head to one side. "You have pretty feet for a guy."

Fallon drew himself up indignantly. "I have a man's feet, McCullough. Manly feet."

"They're still pretty," she said, stroking the arch. "Most men have ugly feet with misshapen toes and nasty nails. Your toes are straight and your nails are clean and shaped." She smiled. "Pretty feet."

"Manly feet," he protested.

"They are pretty manly feet," she compromised.

He reached out for her, took her by the arms and dragged her toward him, falling to his back on the bed as he stretched her atop him, wrapping his arms around her waist.

"Thank you for doctoring me," he said.

She lowered her head and kissed his chin. "You are welcome."

He yawned, weariness showing in his pale amber gaze.

"If you don't think Sasquatch will return, perhaps we should try to get some sleep," she told him.

"Works for me," he said, "but first..." He arched his hips for her to feel the growing erection between his legs.

"Fallon..."

"Hey. You gotta get it while it's hot," he growled, dragging the sheet from her body to bare her to his gaze.

Chapter Four

ഇ

"Hound, stop!"

Fallon halted dead in his tracks, shuddered at the imperious, gruff command.

His boots squelching wetly, his self-castigation goading him that he hadn't brought along another pair, feeling foolish that he'd gotten them soaked in the first place, he grimaced with every step. It was just after sunrise and Keenan had been sleeping when he had quietly left the cottage to search for the creature who had appeared the evening before. Now that Fallon had found it—or rather the beast had found him—he felt a keen rush of unease.

Slowly he turned to face the twenty-foot-tall creature who came lumbering out of the forest toward him, craning his neck back to look up at *An Fear Liath Mor.* "Yes, *Vainshtyr*," he said, giving the respectful title of Master to the being.

"I will have a word with you, pup," the Guardian stated then waved a massive paw at a rock. "Sit your scrawny ass down!"

Since the day he had first Transitioned, Fallon had thought himself in control of his life, immune to being intimidated by anyone or anything, yet the being hulking before him brought out intense disquiet bordering on actual fear. It wasn't the same disquiet he felt around the Supervisor—who controlled Fallon's professional life—but was rather out-and-out dread. He did as he was told as though he were a boy still in short pants, ashamed of his own reaction to the creature.

"June berries," the Guardian said as it backed against a thick tree and began scratching its shaggy back.

"Excuse me?" Fallon inquired, brow furrowing.

"I said June berries, hound! What part of that did you not understand?"

Glancing around him, Fallon saw nothing that even remotely looked like a berry, but since he had no idea what a June berry was, he could be looking at it without knowing.

"Ah, if you'll tell me where to get them for you..."

"*By the grace of the gods you'll do no such thing!*" the entity roared loud enough to nearly shatter Fallon's eardrums—again.

Fallon cringed beneath the onslaught of the command but managed not to bolt from the rock when the creature leaned toward him—broad face set into lines of fury and stare glittering dangerously. The breath coming from the beast was so rank it nearly knocked him from his perch, but he held steady, eyes watering from the stench.

"And you will forget my indiscretion and never repeat said indiscretion to another living soul," the Guardian snapped. "Is that clear?"

Completely lost, Fallon just stared at *An Fear Liath Mor*. "*Vainshtyr*, what is it I'm not to repeat?"

The creature waved a dismissive hand and straightened up to full height. "They are tasty, those gods-be-damned June berries," it said. "All ripe and plump and juicy." It lowered its beetle-brow and gave Fallon a steady look. "Much like I imagine are the teats of your mate. I would not mind comparing them."

Fallon bristled at that but knew better than to say anything to the provocative words. He dug his fingernails into the palms of his hands.

An Fear Liath Mor grinned mercilessly. "Wise choice, hound," it complimented. "Very wise." Once again it waved its giant paw. "But I digress."

The ground shook when the creature plopped down to sit cross-legged in front of Fallon. It placed its shaggy paws on its knees and curled the lethal talons downward.

"I could not resist a taste of those June berries though I know I should have left them be. I reasoned a handful would not hurt and a handful most likely would not have." It pursed its thick lips then gave a mighty sigh. "But one handful led to two then three then four until I had cleared an entire bush of its fruit." It sighed again. "And that is where my troubles began."

Staring down at a huge foot that was bobbing with irritation, Fallon vaguely remembered his mother telling him he should never look The Big Gray Man in the face for it was considered not only rude but challenging.

"I like canines so I will allow it."

Fallon looked up, realizing his thoughts had been plucked from the air. A dull pain drove through his skull at the invasion but he pushed it aside.

"Canines are good, loyal creatures." The beast shrugged. "Lupines? I can tolerate them even if they are a bit snappish. Felines?" It shook its head. "Well, that's a different kettle of pike. I hate felines although…" He chuckled. "They are easy to peel and taste fair to middling if you stew them long enough."

A shudder of revulsion went through Fallon and he tore his gaze from the creature, gritting his teeth.

"It was a joke, hound. A *joke!*" the Guardian said. "I am a vegetarian."

This strange conversation puzzled Fallon and he had almost screwed up the courage to ask *An Fear Liath Mor* what this was all about when the creature spoke again.

"They fermented in my belly and produced an intoxication I knew would happen, and just as with the inferior races such as your human part, I became drunk off those gods-be-damned little June berries." It wobbled that huge foot again. "And like any drunken man who places a lampshade atop his head, I made a fool of myself by intruding upon you and your mate and," it winced, "behaving as I did." It dipped its head. "And for that, I express to you my sincere apologies and ask that you not speak of my indiscretion. If it is any consolation to you, I have a mother of a hangover."

"I'm sorry, *Vainshtyr,*" Fallon replied.

"Coim," the Guardian said. "You have earned the right to call me Coim." It grinned. "I have seen your woman naked." It wagged its brows and wiggled its snout to let Fallon know it was another joke. "So call me Coim."

"I am honored," Fallon said. "Thank you, Coim." He couldn't wait to tell his mother of this encounter.

"Now bring me up to speed about these nasties for which you are searching in my bailiwick," came the demand.

"My apologies, Coim, but isn't Scotland where…?"

"This entire world is my jurisdiction, pup. I can go wherever I like. The Doorways open here, there, wherever I need them to. Once every three years I go home for the span of a few months' time." Sadness flitted through the creature's alien eyes. "My masters grant me that boon and this is the year I may go." It seemed to mentally shake itself then asked the hell hound to continue.

"Okay," Fallon said. He lifted his right leg and crossed it at the ankle on his left knee. "The entities we're looking for are called *drochtáirs*. They are blood fiends from beyond our galaxy that prey on humans. Their bite will change a human into an undead creature who will in turn seek out other humans."

"Distasteful," the Guardian pronounced with a lift of his rubbery lip. "And not on my watch will this happen!"

"They live in lairs, burrows under the ground where it is fairly cold but not frozen. Heat is anathema to them and fire is the only true way to destroy them."

Ad Fear Liath Mor rose gracefully to its feet and began pacing with its long arms clasped behind its shaggy back. "What should I look for in order to find these abominations?"

"The burrows would have no vegetation growing around them. Wherever the creatures pass, they kill the grasses and plants, melt the snow. We will look for them from the air, mark their burrows then go down and destroy them."

"You believe them in this province then?"

"They may be in several provinces and the chances are good that they are."

An Fear Liath Mor frowned deeply. "How large are these nasties?"

"In their natural form it is believed they are like serpents. They can take over other creatures like badgers, wolverines and the like in order to attack humans."

The Guardian stopped pacing, lifted a giant foot then slammed it to the ground. The ground shook. "I could make paste of them, eh?"

"I suppose you could, if you were of a mind to help us hunt."

Massive shoulders hitched upward. "What else do I have on my plate?" it inquired with a twinkle of its unusual eyes.

"But they must be reduced to ash so they won't resurrect. Stomping on them might be fun, but then you will need to incinerate the puddle."

"I can call fire from the Doorway if needs be. That should suffice."

"If you could take the three western provinces, Keenan and I could search these three."

"Consider it done."

"I..." Fallon began, but the creature simply vanished, leaving behind a rank smell and a low whistle.

For a moment longer, Fallon sat on the rock and thought about the strange conversation. It was good to know there was no threat coming at them from *An Fear Liath Mor*. It was even better to know the Guardian would be helping them eradicate the menace to humankind. Rising, he grimaced as his feet squished in the wet boots. He sighed heavily and started back to the cabin.

He should have been concentrating on eradicating the latest menace to his world, but instead, he found himself thinking of Keenan's lush breasts and willing body.

"You've thrown me way off kilter, *myneeast caillagh,*" he said to himself. "What are you doing to me?"

As he cut through the dampness of the new morning, he hunkered into the comfort of his faded denim jacket and thought of how quickly his life had so drastically changed. He had gone from adamant fury about not having an Extension foisted off on him to eagerness to be with her again. Gone was the anger that had made him snap at her that first day to be replaced with a growing affection he could neither adequately explain nor understand.

"It's the bonding," he said aloud, and knew that was part of it. The other part was simply Keenan.

He jammed his hands into the pockets of his worn jeans and let his mind touch lightly upon hers. In his mind's eye he saw her. She was up and about, sitting on the sofa with a mug of steaming coffee held in both hands. As soon as his consciousness touched hers, she smiled and looked up.

"*Good morning,*" she whispered.

"*Good morning,*" he sent back to her, though the contact made his head throb. "*Pour me a cup?*"

He saw her put her mug aside, go into the kitchen and take another mug from the cupboard. By the time he entered the cottage, she was seated again and his mug was on the end table beside one of the chairs.

"I thought we'd be leaving at first light."

"I had something to do," he said.

"I sensed you were with our night visitor. Where did you find him?"

"It found me," he answered. He told her what had transpired and she shook her head.

"Poor thing. He must have been very embarrassed by his behavior."

Then he told her the Guardian would be aiding them in finding the *drochtáirs*.

"That should cut down on our tracking time," she said. "How soon do you want to leave?"

"We can leave now," he said.

"I could make you breakfast."

He paused with the mug halfway to his lips. "You're offering to cook for me?"

"If you're hungry."

"*Can* you cook?" he queried.

She thought of what Matty Groves had said to her and repeated it. "I'm a Georgia woman and I'm Celtic. I was born to cook."

Fallon had a glimpse of Matty's face flitting through her mind and frowned. "Keep him out of your thoughts, *myneeast caillagh*. I'm the jealous sort."

"Are you really?" she countered over her shoulder as she walked into the bedroom.

"I didn't think so, but apparently I am," he admitted, following her as far as the door. "So don't let that idiot's face drift through your head again."

Keenan laughed and finished the remainder of her coffee. "I'll strip the bed and..."

"No need," he said. "The staff will send someone to see to the cleaning." He glanced at his watch and frowned. "It's almost nine o'clock. I didn't realize I'd been with the Guardian that long."

"Time flies when you're having fun," she said as she stuffed a shirt into her bag. She paused. "I didn't have any fear for your safety this morning. I had a feeling the big guy would be looking out for you."

"Else you would have come looking for me."

She bobbed her head. "You betcha I would have. You want breakfast?"

Fallon didn't know if that pleased him or scared him. Either way, he thought it best to let the matter ride for the time being. "Nah."

Before another half hour had passed they were airborne and flying low over the tundra to the north of the cottage. Following the ecotone—the delineating boundary between the forest and the stark landscape of the tundra—Fallon began to expand the search area along the set grid lines he'd drawn on the maps. Within another four hours they had marked three suspicious-looking areas along the grid and were headed back that way to put down nearby to inspect the spots. The first two proved to be nothing of value, and other than the sharp, buffeting thirty-five-mile-hour winds hitting them as they inspected the indentions on the site, there was no problem.

The third site proved to be an entirely different can of worms. They landed just as the sun was riding the ridge of mountains and the air was grower colder. Keenan switched on the flashlight and swept the beam toward the burrow.

"Do you smell that?"

Fallon nodded. "Putrid," he said as they neared a spot in the ground around which the close-cropped sedges, mosses and lichens were dark brown.

"No trails leading away from the burrow," she said.

"That's a good sign. It means it hasn't been out since it got here."

They were being very careful on their approach. The sky was a deep magenta color as the sun lowered behind the ridge, and the wind was biting cold despite it being summer. There wasn't a hint of moisture in the air but dark gray clouds were roiling overhead.

Keenan stopped. "Movement."

Fallon halted as well. He too had felt the shifting of the land beneath his boots. The stench intensified. "It's coming up," he said quietly. He motioned her back and well away from the rim of the burrow.

A greenish vapor oozed from the center of the burrow and filled the air with the noxious stench of sulfur. Fallon fingered the handle of the experimental laser pistol that the Supervisor had provided for him.

"You most likely won't need it with Keenan's pyrokinetic powers, but I'd rather err on the side of safety."

Slipping his finger into the trigger guard, he withdrew the heavy weapon and thumbed off the safety. Even as he leveled the weapon at the burrow, he could feel the air around him change, an electrical charge building. He didn't need to look Keenan's way to know the change was coming from where she stood.

"Here it comes," she said, and from the corner of his eye he watched her wave her hands in a strange, complex pattern. Her fingers began to glow as though she had dipped them in phosphorescent powder. Trickles of tiny embers fell from her fingertips like floating fireflies.

Fallon flexed his knees, the pistol held firm in a two-handed grip, but when the slithering mass of ugly-ass creatures came shooting out of the burrow, he was too stunned to pull the trigger.

Not that he needed to for Keenan concentrated the thrust of her growing power at the serpent-like beings and twin balls of sizzling flame shot from her hands and directly into the path of the vipers. A wild shriek of ungodly pain split the early evening air and a stink more powerful than before blasted through the air.

Fallon lowered his pistol—his attention riveted on Keenan as she concentrated the flame on the disintegrating heap. Around her there was a dark orange aura that shimmered like a heat mirage. As the flames diminished, the aura began to waver until it was nothing more than a pale misty shape around her. When that too faded, Keenan staggered then dropped to her knees.

"Keenan!" Fallon shouted, and raced to her. His head was throbbing like a bass drum.

"I'm all right," she said, but he could sense the drain on her life force and scooped her up in his arms, hurrying back to the chopper.

Over his shoulder, he glanced at the curl of blackened forms that lay clumped just beyond the burrow.

"Did I get them all?"

"You fried them, baby," he said. "They are fucking toast."

"I counted three."

"Well, that leaves four wriggling around somewhere."

"*I sautéed three as well, pup.*"

The voice was faint but both Fallon and Keenan heard it clearly as he lifted her into the chopper.

"Shit! That means they may travel in threes, Fallon," Keenan said, her voice weak.

"*That is my thought as well,*" An Fear Liath Mor stated. "*You are well, Mate of the hound?*"

"I will be. Using fire really takes it out of me."

"*Then rest. Look after her, pup. I'm off to hunt.*" The voice faded away.

95

"If we're dealing with three of those little shits per burrow, that means there may be twenty-one of them," Fallon said as he buckled her into her seat.

"If they'd gotten away from us, they could have contaminated six people," Keenan said. She stared into his eyes. "My God, Fallon. That leaves fifteen of those things out there!"

"Yeah," he said grimly. "And potentially that many people infected."

They both looked at the charred bodies of the *drochtáirs* as the chopper began to lift from the ground.

"Fallon, look!" she said, leaning toward the window. "There's a phosphorescent glow along the burrow's edge."

He pushed the control stick to the right and swung the chopper around so he could see what she meant.

"If they all leave that kind of residue behind them, we can easily pick up their trails even in the dark," she proposed.

"I found another hole and have destroyed the inhabitants. There was a cluster of three each time in the far western provinces," An Fear Liath Mor's voice whispered to them. *"I am rapidly losing strength and need to rest."*

"Then rest, Coim," Fallon told the creature. "We'll take it from here."

"It is my belief the seven landed in that many provinces, hound. Look to Ontario now. I have the far western two under control." Once more the gruff voice faded.

"That leaves twelve in Ontario, Manitoba and Saskatchewan," Keenan mused.

Chapter Five

ဢ

Fallon and Keenan trudged up the slight incline to the little cabin where they would be spending the night in Manitoba. They had not slept or rested since starting out from the lakeside cottage the night before. Flyovers of Ontario had finally netted them a glowing trail from another burrow and they had tracked the *drochtáirs* to a small farm. Too late to help the five people slaughtered by the insatiable beasts, they had managed between them to incinerate their quarries but had then been forced to do the same with the victims. As a result, Keenan was dead on her feet, exhausted, completely drained.

It was just past eight in the morning when they entered the cabin. Fallon set the alarm clock for 2 p.m. then he and Keenan flopped down—fully clothed, still wearing their boots—on their bellies. Within seconds, both were sound asleep.

"Wake up, hound!"

Fallon sat straight up in the bed with a gasp. The loud command that had shot through his sleeping brain had caused his heart to thud wickedly in his chest and a brutal ache over his right eye. For a moment he had no idea where he was. At the movement beside him, he looked down to find Keenan struggling to push herself up.

"He's got to stop invading our minds like that," she mumbled as she turned over to her back.

Sometime during their sleep, Fallon had flipped over and dragged a pillow beneath his head. Keenan had been lying flat and now had a crick in her neck, which she rubbed vigorously as she sat up.

"I have taken out the nasties in Saskatchewan while you were taking your beauty rest," the Guardian grumbled. *"Must I come over there and do the same in Manitoba?"*

"We'll handle it," Fallon growled back at the creature.

"Hop to, hound!"

"I think I'm beginning to hate that thing," Fallon mumbled.

* * * * *

The trip back to the States was uneventful if tiring and by the time the car from the Exchange dropped them off at the dormitory, Fallon and Keenan were exhausted and feeling grungy. They parted at the elevator, going to their separate suites.

As she undressed and reached in to turn the shower on, Keenan thought about the conversation they'd had in the elevator.

"You don't like elevators, do you?" she'd asked.

He'd shaken his head. "I wouldn't have gotten into this thing alone. With you, I can handle it." He shifted his shoulders. "Up to a point."

"Are you claustrophobic?"

His amber eyes flicked to her. "Yeah. All Reapers are. The containment cell is a hell unto itself."

"What's a containment cell?"

"Where they put me when I go through my quarterly Transition cycle," he said. "That's three to four lovely days of pure agony. No tenerse, no Sustenance. Nothing but sheer torment."

She'd had no idea what tenerse was, but she was fairly sure Sustenance meant blood, though she had yet to see him drink anything that resembled it.

"I inject a vac-syringe of tenerse into me every morning to keep my cycles on schedule. Without it, I'd be a jibbering idiot. Reapers get addicted to the stuff. The Sustenance, I take as I want it. If you'd looked carefully in the fridges in the places where we stayed, you'd have found the plastibags of it in the vegetable drawer."

Keenan pushed the glass shower door aside and climbed in, letting the full force of the hot water hit her chest and belly. The thought of Fallon swilling down blood didn't sicken her in the least, although before she'd met the man, such a thing would have made her stomach heave. Things were certainly moving along at the speed of light.

She smiled.

"I don't remember inviting you into my shower."

His arms came around her and he pulled her tight to his chest.

"I don't remember you saying I couldn't join you," he countered, nuzzling her neck.

"Ah, how did you get in here anyway?" she questioned.

His right hand slid down her belly and his fingers spiked through the wet curls at the apex of her thighs. "Memorized your code when you punched it in."

"In other words, you were skipping through my mind."

"Skipping, slithering..." He bumped her ass with a rock-hard erection. "Writhing, wriggling." He rubbed himself against her and his tongue flicked at the opening of her ear, his voice going low and throaty. "Probing."

"Pervert," she labeled him, and moved so she could turn to face him. Bringing her arms up to encircle his neck, she pulled her body up, wrapping her legs around his lean hips then tilted her head to one side as she gazed at him. "So show me what you got, lineman." She pronounced the word as two — line man.

One ebony brow quirked upward as he molded his hands to her bottom. "Lineman?"

"Well, you are working with a pretty stiff pole there, aren't you?"

He nodded and took a step forward, putting them both under the very warm cascade of the water. Expertly, he dipped his knees and aimed his stiff rod at her velvety folds. With one thrust of his hips, he was buried inside the slick sheath and her back was against the tiled wall.

"You have a shower fetish, don't you?" she asked.

"Cleanliness is next to godliness," he mumbled as he trailed hot kisses down her neck. The rasp of his five o'clock shadow on her tender flesh made mincemeat of her flesh.

With him seated deep inside her and beginning a slow yet forceful upward push with his hips as she rode his cock, Keenan closed her eyes and inhaled the scent of his thick, wet hair rubbing her against her cheek. She cradled him to her, reveling in the slick slide of their wet flesh upon one another. The steam was rising along with the lustful arches of his body, and she clung to him, her lips against his ear.

"Fuck me, Fallon," she whispered. "Fuck your woman."

A low growl of acceptance rumbled from his throat and he began slamming into her with even more force, his hard shaft thrusting to the very core of her cunt.

Distantly, she heard the phone ringing but it didn't matter. Nothing mattered at that moment except satisfying the immense itch his rod was causing inside her. She gripped him tighter with her legs, pulsed her inner muscles around him and smiled when he hissed at the sensation. She clenched him again and they both came hard and long—his spurts seeming to fill her as he rocked her up and down the wall until with one last quiver of his muscles, his head sank to her shoulder and his warm breath fanned over her breasts.

"I love you," she heard him say.

"Right back at you," she whispered into his wet hair.

Fallon raised his head and looked at her. The love he had expressed was glowing in his amber eyes.

"I mean it."

She brought one hand around to run her fingertips over his lips. "I know, baby. I know you do."

He kissed her fingers, speaking past them. "I never thought to ever tell a woman that." He grinned wickedly. "Or a man for that matter."

Keenan's brows shot up. "You're bisexual?"

"Some Reapers are," he said. "It's rare but it happens." He shook his head. "I'm not one of them though. I was joking."

"Well, I don't share my toys with other girls or boys," she said. "So you'd best be content with me, Fallon. I'm all you're gonna have."

100

"You're all I'm ever gonna want," he said, and slanted his lips over hers.

Chapter Six

ℬ

"He is not in a very good mood," Cobb, the Supervisor's executive assistant, quipped. "You've kept him waiting and he doesn't like that." He narrowed his eyes. "Where were the two of you? Neither of you answered your dorm or cell phones."

"Must have been problems on the line," Keenan said.

"Or on the lineman," Fallon mumbled then grunted when Keenan drove her elbow into his side.

Cobb sniffed. "Don't let it happen again. You both know you are to be contactable at all times."

"We *were* contacting, Jonas," Fallon said with a sly grin. "As a matter of fact, we couldn't have been contacting more if…"

"Will you stop?" Keenan asked, face turning crimson. Fallon chuckled.

"Just go on in," Cobb snapped, "before I too wind up bearing the brunt of the Supervisor's ire."

Fallon opened the Supervisor's door and ushered Keenan in ahead of him, looking back at Cobb to give the officious little man a broad wink. Since he wasn't looking where he was going, he plowed in his partner's back, not realizing she'd come to an abrupt stop. When he looked around, his gaze went past her to a stranger bending over the Supervisor, pointing to something on the desk. The moment the stranger looked up and his eyes met Fallon's, the Reaper knew who he was even before Keenan spoke.

"What are you doing here, Zack?"

Breslin—Keenan's ex-partner—straightened, folded his arms over a broad chest and smiled nastily. "Going over plans with my new boss, Kiki," he drawled, never taking his smirk from Fallon. "Happy to see me?"

Keenan swiveled her head to look at Fallon. "I had no idea he would do this," she said, pleading in the way she was staring at him not to cause trouble.

"There is to be no trouble between the two of you," the Supervisor said. "The Extension stands. Agent Breslin is not here as a field agent but as a trainer."

"In what?" Fallon inquired. "How to hit women?"

Breslin's gaze narrowed. "I never laid a hand on her or any other woman."

"Not from lacking of wanting to though, was it?" Fallon challenged.

Breslin shrugged. "Once you've been around her long enough, you might find yourself wanting to smack her around too."

Fallon started toward the smirking man, but Keenan caught his arm.

"He's baiting you," she said under her breath. "Don't buy into it."

His hands clenching and unclenching at his side, Fallon swung an angry look to the Supervisor. "You must be scraping the barrel if you can't find trainers any better than this one."

"Why you..." Breslin snarled, and started to skirt the desk, but the Supervisor barked an order for the man to stay where he was.

"I am not going to have any pissing contests between you two!" the Supervisor grated. "Is that clear?" He waved Keenan and her partner to chairs in front of his desk. "Sit down and let me tell you why Breslin has been hired."

"And before you think I followed you here, Keenan, you are welcome to look at my employment papers so you can see the date I put in to work here. It was long before you did," Breslin informed her.

Fallon turned to Keenan. "Didn't you say he was an empath?" At her nod, he swung a glower back to Breslin. "Then he knew what you were planning."

"That's neither here nor there," the Supervisor said, obviously wanting to forestall any argument. "We have a situation and Breslin was the right man to bring onboard to help us contain it. He has extensive knowledge of faith healers and psychic surgeons, is an expert on the subject actually."

"What has that got to do with what the Exchange does?" Fallon asked. "We go after brutal things that go bump in the night, not Aunt Tildy's psychic healer."

"Because there's a new kid on the block," Breslin said, "and she's not above having anyone who investigates her or tries to stop her or her people murdered."

"You're talking about Mignon Bolivar," Keenan said.

"The woman based down in Georgia?" Fallon queried.

The Supervisor nodded. "She has what she calls Healing Centers in all fifty states and one on Guam. She's applied for licenses in Puerto Rico and the Virgin Islands. The men and women who perform the psychic surgeries and faith healings are called Sensitives and she has over a hundred of them on her payroll, two per Healing Center — one man, one woman."

"The Healing Centers are actually huge circus tents from which her Sensitives bilk people of their hard-earned money," Breslin scoffed.

"She came up on our radar just before I left the agency," she answered. "What we were hearing wasn't good, but I had no idea she had resorted to having people killed."

"Worse than killed, Kiki," Breslin said softly. "Tortured and mutilated as a warning to others. I've seen some of the bodies." He shuddered. "It wasn't pretty."

"The rumored murders are only the tip of the iceberg with this Bolivar woman," the Supervisor injected. "Hundreds of thousands of dollars are lost every year by people devoid of hope who buy into the promises these charlatans offer. Most of those conned out of their money can ill afford to lose it. Many go into debt trying to come up with the money necessary to pay these deceivers. We're talking old folks, young couples with very ill children, husbands who are forced to watch their wives battling excruciating cancers. These are the kind of people Bolivar preys on and I want it stopped."

"But that's what the agency we worked for was designed to do," Keenan said, glancing at Breslin. "I'm like Fallon—why is the Exchange getting involved in what is essentially a con game?"

"Because she has something," Breslin said. "Some *thing* she sends after these people. It isn't human. It couldn't be. The corpses I saw could not have been brutalized in the manner they were by anything human. They were literally torn apart, organs pulled out, heads twisted completely around."

"What kind of *thing* are you talking about?" Fallon challenged.

"The savage kind," Breslin stated.

"The kind of thing I usually send you to take out," the Supervisor added. "The kind of thing the average Joe doesn't know exists in our world."

"And slap-happy boy here is supposed to train me how to do that?" Fallon scoffed with a snort. "Gimme a break."

"No, Agent Breslin is here to train our operatives in the techniques Bolivar and her Sensitives are using to bamboozle the unsuspecting. We want to infiltrate her organization with our own people and at the right moment put a stop to this nefarious business of hers, shut her down and bring her to justice, find out what she's using to commit those murders and eliminate it. Agent McCullough, with your talents you should have no trouble convincing her to hire you as a Sensitive. Your objective is to become her number one healer." The Supervisor turned to Fallon. "Finding the entity she's controlling and destroying it is your assignment. In order to do that, getting close to Bolivar is the first order of business. We want you closer to her than glue on a book binding. We need her to rely on you completely."

"She likes her men tall, dark and hands-on," Breslin stated. "You should do all right."

"If I remember correctly, she has a huge security force and never travels without being surrounded by four personal bodyguards," Keenan said.

"Her Protectors," Breslin supplied.

"If Fallon can convince her he's the next best thing to sliced bread when it comes to security…"

"I *am* the next best thing to sliced bread, *myneeast caillagh*," Fallon said with a leer.

"Little witch, eh?" Breslin questioned with an arched brow. "How quaint."

Fallon gave the other man a narrowed look. "Not as quaint as Kiki. *Ta Gaelg eu myrgeddin?*" *You also speak Manx?*

"*Cadjoor rish Dooinney loayrt rish y gheay,*" Breslin replied. *Like a man talking to the wind.*

Fallon grunted disdainfully.

The Supervisor leaned back in his chair. "You three will need to work together to set this up. Fallon, you know the best operatives so pick six you think will do—three men and three women, preferably among those who have Extensions. They need to have strong psi powers and impenetrable mind shields."

"There are only three who fit that bill—two men and one woman. Mind shielding is not as easy as it sounds," Fallon replied. He put a hand to his temple, knowing Breslin was trying to slip past his guards. He gave the new man a nasty scowl but Breslin merely grinned.

"Three would be enough. If we flood Bolivar with too many candidates, she'll know something is up," Breslin suggested.

"He's right," Keenan agreed. "And we can't introduce those three too closely together."

"They've got to be trained anyway," Breslin reminded her. "Psychic surgery is nothing more than sleight of hand, but in order to do it effectively, you have to be damned good at it. I can teach them that along with the customary rhetoric that goes with the faith healing." He locked gazes with Keenan. "I'm looking forward to working with you again."

Keenan pursed her lips but said nothing. Fallon ground his teeth and also refrained from commenting. They glanced at one another, and the look that passed between them said everything either needed to say to the other.

"We'll start first thing in the morning and you'll leave for Georgia next Tuesday, Fallon," the Supervisor said. "Agent Breslin will be setting up what he needs to teach the operatives and I'll contact the agents you think can handle the assignment."

Fallon nodded. "Roursch, Eddings and Lanier," he supplied. "As far as I know, they are all here unless you've sent them on assignments within the last few days."

"No, I haven't." The Supervisor switched his attention to Keenan. "I want Fallon well in place before you come on the scene, so we won't be sending you down to Georgia for a couple of weeks. For now, I need you to go to Procurement and have them supply you with some down-home-type dresses made from calico and gingham. Something shapeless and old-fashioned. You will also need worn-down shoes, stockings that have seen better days and some raggedy undergarments."

"Like a girl from the hills of Kentucky would wear," Breslin put in.

"That's my cover? A girl from Butcher Hollow?" she inquired, brows elevated.

"We've chosen a really out-of-the-way place called Regis Cove and your new name is Tandy Lynch," the Supervisor told her. "If Bolivar does any checking, she'll find your family's been at the Cove for generations and that the good people up there have nothing but wondrous things to say about little Tandy and the miracles she wielded.

"Tandy is fey and she has the healing touch. She's very shy and easily led by her older brother Nathan, who is a real scoundrel. He's always run off any potential boyfriends up at the Cove so she's still a virgin. He's looking for the right man to hand her over to. Seeing a way to make money with her God-given gift, he's brought her down out of the mountains and will be offering her services to Bolivar—for a price of course. She's terrified of Nathan and looks to him before she ever opens her mouth. We'll need to find an agent to…"

"I would be happy to play the part of Keenan's dastardly brother," Breslin said.

Keenan looked at Fallon. "I don't know. I thought you weren't going to be out in the field, Zack."

"I think he'll fit the bill perfectly," Fallon surprised the others by saying. "Bring him on. I think he and I will play real well together."

"What will the relationship be between Tandy and Fallon?" Keenan asked, chewing on her lip. The idea of Fallon and Breslin at each other's throats sent chills down her spine. "Surely a man like him would frighten an innocent girl like her."

The Supervisor actually smiled, something he rarely did. "She's so starved for affection, ripe, a moonstruck romantic at heart, so when she meets Fallon, she will take to him like a pig to slop."

"Delightful imagery," Keenan mumbled.

"*Lhiannan*, I'll let you wallow on me all you want," Fallon teased.

"This isn't a joke," Breslin snapped, eyes flashing. "Bolivar is cheating people, bilking them of money they need to exist on, destroying them financially or murdering them, and she needs her ass kicked back into yesterday!"

"And she'll get it handed to her on a silver platter," Keenan said. "So don't go all high and mighty on us, Zack. We know how to do our jobs."

Breslin's upper lip quirked as though he had reservations but he didn't argue the point. "I'll see you in the morning."

With that, he marched across the room and exited, shutting the door just a bit too forcefully behind him. Before either the Supervisor or Keenan could stop him, Fallon was out of his chair and jerking open the door, leaving it wide in his wake.

"I should go after him and..." Keenan began as she pushed from her chair.

"Which one?" the Supervisor inquired.

"Fallon," she replied.

The Supervisor shook his head. "No. You should let them work it out between them," he insisted.

"But..."

"I said no." The denial was firm and brooked no argument. "You've got your assignment so I suggest you stop at Procurement, get your wardrobe together—and be sure to tell them to provide you with a battered cardboard suitcase—then make a stop at the Library to learn what you can about Regis Cove and the people who live there."

"Yes sir, but…"

"And do it now, Agent McCullough," the Supervisor interrupted. "Without the benefit of any side trips to see how those two men are handling their differences."

Keenan did as she was ordered, though her mind was not on her assignment but the mayhem she feared was about to erupt.

As Keenan made her way to Procurement, Fallon caught up with Breslin and snaked out a hand to grab the other man by the collar, jerking him around and slamming him against the corridor wall. Before Breslin could react, Fallon had his forearm pressed brutally across Breslin's throat and his well-honed body jammed against his opponent.

"You so much as look like you're going to raise your hand to her and I promise you I'll break that sucker off at the root and shove it so far up your ass you'll be able to brush your teeth from the inside," Fallon snarled, his lips drew back, eyes pinpoints of red light. "Do you understand?"

Breslin tried to push out of the hold but stilled as Fallon leaned in even harder, fangs erupting.

"Do. You. Understand?" Fallon asked, stressing each word with a fierce growl.

Slowly the other man nodded. He was staring wide-eyed at the glistening fangs and beginning to tremble. Fear rolled off him with a musky stench that caused Fallon's nostrils to quiver.

"Did you soil yourself, human?" he queried. He pressed his arm more firmly on Breslin's windpipe.

"N-No," Breslin croaked, trying to swallow.

Fallon held him for just a heartbeat longer then stepped back, giving Keenan's ex-partner a disdainful snort before pivoting on his heel and stalking off, not even bothering to look back as Breslin slumped down the wall to hunker on the floor.

Chapter Seven

ॐ

It had been a long day for Keenan and she was drained, her feet dragging as she made her way to the monorail platform. Far too much information had been crowded into her head in a short period of time and had settled there to throb brutally between her temples. Absently, she put a hand up to rub at the pain.

"It can't be that bad."

She looked around to find Matty Groves falling into step beside her.

"Oh yes it can," she replied tiredly.

"I heard about the assignment and the preparations for it. How 'bout letting me take you to supper this evening before you start tackling anything more? You can relax, unwind." He shrugged. "You gotta eat anyway."

Keenan hesitated. Fallon had warned her away from Matty, but Fallon was busy doing something the Supervisor had assigned him and wouldn't be back until after ten that evening. She hated eating alone, but the thought of Fallon getting possessive and quarrelsome made her leery.

"Afraid of the big bad hound?" Matty asked, halting his steps.

There was something almost insulting in the way he asked. "No," she replied defensively as she too stopped walking.

"Then you must be afraid of pissing off the hound," he countered, folding his arms across his chest.

"I'm not," she stated then raised her chin. "Give me half an hour to shower and change, and I'll meet you at the monorail."

Matty smiled. "All righty then. I'll be waiting."

She watched him turn back toward the administrative building and took a deep breath. With every step she took toward her quarters, she worried that she had made a huge mistake by accepting Matty's supper invitation.

"He's giving you the old possessive Reaper shit, huh?" Matty asked as they dove into their salads.

"You could say that," she muttered.

"Don't let him snow you, Keenan. He's not a lupine Reaper. He's a canine Reaper and they are a whole other can of worms." He laughed at his own words and speared a black olive.

"In what way?"

Matty chewed around a wide grin, swallowed then picked up his napkin to wipe his lips. "Think about what hound dog usually means when a woman applies that insult to a man."

Keenan frowned. "When I was in college that term meant an insatiable guy who jumps every woman he sees." She shook her head. "Fallon isn't like that."

Matty took a drink of his tea, speaking to her over the rim of the glass. "What do you actually know about Reapers, sweetie?"

"Very little except for what he's told me."

Matty shoveled a large forkful of lettuce into his mouth and devoured it before pushing the bowl aside. "Well, you see it's like this. Lupine Reapers were created by the goddess Morrigunia to champion humankind. She wanted them single-minded in that pursuit, but She also knew they'd need to have gentleness in their lives to counterbalance the brutality that is their lot. But She is also a defender of womanhood so She put a geis, a magical prohibition, on Her Reapers that keeps them from actually having intercourse with a woman they don't intend to bond with. Once they do the nasty with a lady, that's it. They are mated for life and he won't ever touch another female."

"Like wolves."

"Yeah, like wolves," he agreed. "But hounds are a different matter altogether. Why She created them is anyone's guess, but She didn't put that particular geis on them and She didn't create all that many. As a matter of fact, other than Fallon, I don't know of another canine Reaper in existence."

112

"So what you're telling me is he can screw all the women he wants to," she said, eyes hard and mouth tight.

"No, I'm saying that he's screwed more than his share over the years. Hell, I think he got most of *my* share, but who's counting?" He chuckled. "As he views it, he'll be faithful to you, Keenan, but if he needs to jump in the sack with someone for an assignment, he won't think twice about it." When she opened her mouth to let out the angry words that were mirrored on her face, he held up a hand. "I'm not saying he'll want it, but he will do it."

Her appetite gone, Keenan pushed her salad aside as well. "Well, that sucks," she said.

The waitress came to take their bowls away so Matty said nothing to Keenan's statement. When the server was gone, he leaned toward her over the table.

"Are you the jealous kind, darling?" he asked.

Keenan toyed with her tea glass. "I didn't think I was, but the thought of Fallon climbing into bed with another woman makes my damned blood boil." She lifted the glass and took a long drink.

"If you're worried about him giving you something he picks up from someone, don't. His parasite would kill any infection that came into contact with him so he wouldn't pass it along."

"Contracting an STD from him doesn't piss me off half as much as him being with a woman in the first place," she admitted. "He got all high and mighty telling me I couldn't make it with other men, and now to find out the good old double standard is hard at work here just fries my okry."

Matty grinned at her expression. "If you need someone to tweak his nose for you, I'll volunteer to climb in bed with you any time you need me, darling."

Looking up from staring at the tablecloth, Keenan caught the twinkle in Matty's blue eyes. She smiled and reached over to pat his arm. "I'll get back to you on that."

There was a moment of uneasy silence then Matty sighed. "Here's comes supper. Rabbit food is okay, but I'm a steak and taters kinda guy." He rubbed his hands together as the waitress placed his Porterhouse before him.

The food was excellent—cooked to perfection, and by the time the last French fry dredged through ketchup had been plucked from Keenan's plate and the last chunk of baked potato with sour cream had been lifted from Matty's, the offer of dessert was declined.

"I'm as full as a tick," Matty commented, rubbing his flat abdomen, "but I could sure use a drink. Have you been to the lounge yet?" He shot out his right leg and reached into his pocket.

"There's a lounge?" she asked, folding her napkin before placing it atop the table. "I haven't had a chance to go over the employment package to find out what all we have on the installation."

"We have a great little lounge with a dance floor. They serve the best margaritas I've ever had. Want to give it a try?" He picked up the guest check presenter and slid his personal ID card down a groove in the side.

"That's a handy little device," Keenan observed.

"An Exchange invention. It automatically adds in the tip and takes the money out of my personal checking account," he said. "So are we gonna get a nightcap?"

She started to shake her head but thought better of it. "Yeah. I could use a drink. Sure, let's go."

The lounge was darkly lit with a long bar on one end of the room with tables and booths on the other, the two areas separated by a parquet dance floor with a spectacularly beautiful old-fashioned jukebox, its classic dome shape framing the bubble tubes that were pulsing red, orange and green.

"Oh man!" Keenan exclaimed as she headed straight for the machine. Like a child in a candy shop, she put her palms to the control panel to take a look at the list of songs. "Man!"

"I think its all sixties music this go 'round," he told her. "They change eras every month. Hank, the barman, told me the jukebox will hold twelve hundred songs, so the music you'll find there is from all the musical genres of that decade—pop, country, classical, foreign, Broadway, motion picture and TV themes, you name it."

"Just look at these songs!" she whispered. "Some of them I haven't heard in years!"

"Three plays for a quarter," he told her, digging into his pocket for the coin. "You choose and I'll go get our drinks. What's your poison?"

"A Bloody Maria," she said.

"With tequila instead of vodka, heavy on the lime and hot sauce."

She glanced up at him and smiled. "I knew I liked you. If they throw in a handful of olives, I'll be in seventh heaven."

"You got it," he said, and headed toward the bar.

A few minutes later, the bartender brought their drinks, introduced himself as Hank Levins and welcomed Keenan to the Exchange.

"Our tavern wench is out with the flu," Matty said when Hank left. "But it's a slow night." He looked around, nodded at the only other two customers in the lounge. "A real slow night."

Keenan relaxed in the booth, her first sip of the Bloody Maria soothing and hitting just the right spot as it went down. The music had changed, further easing the tenseness from her shoulders and neck.

"Don't let it worry you, sweetie," Matty said. He was sipping on what looked like a tequila sunrise. In the dim corner where they were sitting, she couldn't really tell.

"What?"

"That he might be required to sleep with another woman," Matty replied diplomatically. "Since the two of you have bonded, his heart won't be in it. It'll be strictly business to him."

She cupped her hands around the tall hurricane glass. "You know him that well?"

"I'm the closest thing to a buddy he has," was the reply. "He's kinda choosey about whom he hangs with—if you know what I mean." He grinned. "I've never been a threat to him."

She turned her head and looked out across the darkened room. "I've never considered myself the jealous sort, you know? If a man wanted out of a relationship, if he strayed, that was okay. It was love 'em and leave 'em, no strings attached—especially not heartstrings. I moved on and never looked back, but now..." She shrugged, sighed deeply and slumped in the booth. "Damn but this bonding thing has put a kibosh to that carefree lifestyle."

"I haven't spoken to him since you two bonded, but I've heard he didn't go shrieking through the halls cursing the Fates, beating his chest and tearing out his hair. He seems to have accepted it better than I would have thought."

"He's dealing with it better than I am," she admitted.

"Sometimes Groves' mouth spews out more trash than a garbage truck."

Both turned to find Fallon standing beside the booth. He was looking at Keenan so intently the temperature in the room seemed to have dipped.

"You got through early," Keenan said, her voice unnaturally high as though she were a child caught doing what she knew she shouldn't.

Clearing his throat, Matty moved over, unconsciously putting himself closer to Keenan. "Ah, you wanna join us, Misha?" Matty queried.

Fallon turned the full brunt of his stare to the doctor. "Ah, you wanna leave while you can still walk and talk and take nourishment, Matthew?" he countered.

"Fallon, we..." Keenan began, but already Matty was sliding out of the booth.

"Nothing was going on," Matty told Fallon.

"Except your big mouth," Fallon said, crowding Matty so he could sit down in the booth with Keenan.

Matty gave Keenan an apologetic look. "I'll see you later," he said, and hurried away.

For a long moment Keenan just looked at Fallon. He was sitting across from her with his arms folded over his chest, his eyes locked on hers. Finally she could stand the silence no longer.

"Are you going to be an ass about this?" she questioned.

He shook his head. "Nope." He unfolded his arms and braced them on the tabletop, leaning toward her with that fixated stare locked on her face. "But I am going to be a real cur about it, *myneeast caillagh*. A very territorial cur who isn't in a very good frame of mind right now."

"Nothing happened," she defended. "We had supper and came in for a drink." She too leaned forward, her voice tight and her gaze filled with resentment. "Let's get something straight between us right here and now, Fallon. I am not your private property to be ordered about. If I want to have supper and-or a drink with a friend, I will do so. You are not going to tell me what I can and can't do. Is that clear?"

One black brow swept upward. "So long as you understand that if I need to fuck another woman, I will," he returned.

Keenan blinked then moved back as though he'd slapped her. Her eyes narrowed. "Well, I guess you can fuck whomever you please," she snarled.

"Did you happen to notice I said fuck and not make love to?" he asked.

"You think there's a difference?" she countered, not appeased.

"I know goddamned well there is," he stated. "I would never fuck you, Keenan. Fucking is simply a part of the job. Making love is part of the bonding." Before she could comment on that statement, he scooted out of the booth. "You want another drink?"

She shook her head. She hadn't finished the first one. As he sauntered over to the bar, she thought of getting up and leaving. Her anger was like a red-hot prod poking at her heart, but when he turned from the bar and headed for the jukebox, she remained seated, curious about what music he might choose. Watching him come back toward the table after he'd made his selection, she felt her body responding to his long-legged strut and the powerful span of his broad shoulders.

He reached the booth just as the music began playing. He held out his hand.

"Dance with me," he said.

Though she was tempted to refuse him, the song was a particular favorite, seemed so apropos, so she threw caution to the wind and reached out her hand to take his. He led her onto the parquet dance floor and swept her gently into his arms, holding her firmly, moving so seductively to the rhythm it made her ache.

"You know I'm the jealous sort," he said, looking down at her. "You're gonna have to accept that, Keenan."

His lower body was pressed to hers, his hips stroking her with every turn, the bulge between his legs sweeping across the juncture of her thighs as he slow danced her around the floor to the strains of The Righteous Brothers singing "Soul and Inspiration".

"And I'm the independent sort," she declared. "You're gonna have to accept that, Fallon."

His slow, easy smile took her breath away. "Okay," he agreed. "I'll try to be less restrictive if you'll be more understanding."

"Understanding of...?"

"What I might have to do has nothing to do with us, Keenan," he said, his hand tightening around hers. "It won't be because I want to do it. It will be because it's necessary. That would be the *only* reason it would happen."

"And I'm expected to like you slipping between the sheets with another woman?" she demanded.

"No, but I do expect you to know I won't like it any better than you will."

She snorted. "Taking absolutely no enjoyment from the act whatsoever."

"I can't prevent my body from deriving pleasure from sex, *lhiannan*. That's biological."

"What about the jealousy part?" she inquired. "Are you going to work on that?"

"I doubt it," he said, swinging her around again. "That you'll have to live with."

"Then you'll have to live with it too," she said. "I'm not going to stop having a life just because you staked a claim to my body, and remember there's always the old what's sauce for the goose is sauce for the gander idiom."

He frowned. "What's that supposed to mean?"

"If it's acceptable for one of us to do, it should be acceptable for the other," she replied. "You're not the only operative in this partnership. It might fall on me one day to use my body just as you might use yours." She gave him a thin smile. "Or should I say someone might fall on me just as you might fall on someone else."

He stopped moving to the music, his body tensing, and his handsome face suddenly hard as stone. "Try it and see what happens to that someone, McCullough."

Before she could respond, he spun around and started from the lounge, his hand brutally tight on hers as he pulled her behind him as he dug his other hand into his pocket. Detouring to the bar, he slapped a ten-dollar bill down on the top and told the bartender to keep the change.

"You're hurting me," Keenan complained, stumbling along in his wake.

He ignored her as his long stride ate up the distance to the door. Once out in the corridor, he came to an abrupt stop, pivoted around and pushed her against the wall, bracing her there with his hard body.

"You are *mine!*" he said from between clenched teeth. "Fuck some other man, Keenan, and I'll gut him right before your eyes and make you watch while I shove his intestines down his thieving throat!"

Savagely he covered her mouth with his—the kiss so powerful, so potent it made her heart hammer against her ribs. He was grinding against her with one leg thrust roughly between hers. Her breasts were flattened against his muscular chest, her back aching from the force of his body weight.

But none of that mattered for he had ignited a fierce passion within her and her hands crawled up his body to bury themselves in his hair, holding his head so she could match his kiss with a hard one of her own. She rubbed her core along his thigh, heat raging in her lower body. Her tongue dueled with his, swept over his teeth.

"Bed," he mumbled as he tore his mouth from hers.

"Yeah," she agreed, panting as once more he reached for her hand and tugged her along in his wake, half running to keep up with his pace. She barely noticed the people they passed or the second looks that were wide with surprise and speculation.

Fallon disdained waiting for the monorail and pushed through the door to the outside, hurrying along the walkway toward the dorm. He said nothing. She was equally silent, muttering a garbled greeting to the doorman as Fallon jerked open the dorm's main door and thrust her through. She didn't question his decision to take the stairs and followed behind him with her hand still clutched tightly in his.

It was to his room he led her.

If the starkness of his quarters shocked her as the motion detectors controlling the overhead lights came on, she didn't let it show. He all but dragged her through the nearly empty living area and into a bedroom the same size as her own but furnished with only a full-size bed beside which stood a single nightstand devoid of everything save a shadeless lamp and a small chest of drawers. To say the room was utilitarian would have put it mildly. It was austere to the point of being monastic. Not even a rug covered the floor or a drape the windows. She frowned at the harshness of the glaring light as he swung her up and onto the mattress—as hard as any upon which she'd ever had the misfortune to recline. Without either headboard or footboard, the bed springs squeaked as he bumped his legs against it in his hurry to rid himself of his clothing.

"Fallon," she said, glancing at the bare window. Although they were several floors up, she didn't feel comfortable with the light on.

"Huh," he grunted, and reached over to turn off the lamp— the only source of light in the room.

Plunged into near total darkness since the lights had gone out in the living area now that no one was moving, she could just barely make out his silhouette as he stripped off his shirt, kicked off his loafers and began working on his pants. She watched him bend over as he removed his underwear and then he was atop her, covering her like a quilt, his mouth seeking hers as his hands pulled at her clothing, ripping open her blouse despite her gasp of protest, pushing up her bra to expose her breast, tugging her skirt up to thrust his fingers under the silk of her panties and into her heated center.

She arched upward—her hips offering her sex to his quest. He delved deep, stretching her with three fingers that twisted gently but firmly inside her slick core. His cock was rock-hard against her thigh as his mouth trailed kisses down her chin and neck until his lips took possession of her nipple. His hard suckle made her squirm and she twisted her fingers in his thick hair, closing her eyes to the delicious feel of his mouth and the deep penetration. The moment his thumb touched her clit, she hissed like a cat and bucked on the mattress.

"Do it!" she snarled.

He didn't need another invitation. He pulled his fingers from her, pushed up so he could grab the waistband with both hands and tore the panties from her, flinging the flimsy garment aside. With a growl, he covered her again, guiding his cock into her.

Keenan brought one leg up and hooked it around his hip, straining her body from the mattress to meet the frenzied thrusts that had set the bed beneath them to shaking. Her hands went to his neck and she pulled his mouth down to hers, their tongues mating as he slammed into her wet sheath with force. She brought her other leg up and snared him between them, riding him as he was her.

Beyond the windows lightning flared in the night sky and a heavy, low rumble echoed across the Iowa countryside. As they lost themselves in tearing lust, rain began to pound heavily against the glass and the heavens strobed with spidery webs of electrical discharge that flickered from one side of the horizon to the other.

Fallon's powerful plunges into her soft body were greeted with ragged breaths and fingernails digging into his shoulder. His mouth slid away so he was pressing his cheek to hers. With his eyes tightly squeezed in order to concentrate on the delicious tightening of his balls, the raging thrust of his cock as fire built deep in his groin, he managed to jab his hands beneath her ass and jerk her up. His cock went deeper still and she released a loud shout of encouragement, her legs squeezing him like a silken vise. He was grunting with each blind stroke. His hammering heart felt as though it were about to burst. Sweat glistened on his forehead, his upper lip, and ran in slow trickles down his chest. The scent of his body's fluids mingling with hers filled his nostrils to spur him on to a greater effort. With the sound of his flesh slapping against hers, he felt the climax rushing through his cock at the same moment the walls of her vagina began to ripple around him.

"God!" he bellowed. His cum was so violent, so intense, he thought he might well have blacked out as it rushed from his swollen shaft and spurted thickly inside her willing channel. A hard shudder slithered down him. He felt her quiver. Her nails raked down his back and clamped into the flesh of his buttocks as he pistoned into her like a runaway machine. Beneath them, the bed was bouncing on the bare Terrazzo floor. With his head thrown back, he bayed—there was no other way to describe it—and she screamed as the last wave of satisfaction moved through their bodies.

Heaving for breath, shivering like a man with the ague, he fell from her to his back and lay there slick with sweat, semen and vaginal juices coating his shrinking cock.

"Dear lord, Fallon," he heard her gasp. "Are you trying to kill us both?"

Her voice was hoarse from her piercing scream and her gulps for air would have been comical had he not been too drained to even smile. It took what waning strength he had just to turn his head on the pillow to gaze at her. His eyelids heavy, he stared at her.

"You are so goddamn beautiful," he told her softly.

Keenan managed to turn over on her side to face him. "I'm glad you think so."

"Know so," he said. His eyes closed and just that quickly he was asleep.

"Wore your ass out, didn't I, Fallon?" she whispered, content just to gaze at his handsome face—peaceful and youthful as he slept.

Mentally, she ran her fingers over those chiseled features from the tiny crow's feet beside his eyes to the light indention of symmetrical lines bracketing his full lips. Those lips were beautiful, she thought. A dark rose color, they were swollen from their kisses.

Her attention moved to the straight, fine nose and the dark growth of the five o'clock shadow shading his upper lip and jaw. His black hair was tousled so attractively—falling low over his slightly creased forehead.

"So handsome," she thought, and let her eyes wander down his muscular chest where the crisp mat of hair spread across his chiseled pecs and marched in a tiger line down to a thicker pelt between his legs. No sissified manscaping for this boy, she was thankful to see.

It was the shaft—now at rest and lying crooked over his upper thigh—that held her scrutiny the longest. He was very well endowed, thick and broad and long.

Keenan sighed. Her gaze flicked over his taut thighs then crawled back up his body to settle on his face. He was lightly snoring and for some reason that made her feel at peace, comfortable.

Easing from the mattress, she stood and removed her blouse, bra and skirt then slid back into bed with him and snuggled as close as she could. Since he was lying on his back with his head turned toward her, she pressed her forehead to his, inhaled the sweetness of his warm breath, closed her eyes and joined him in sleep.

Chapter Eight

ဢ

"Wake up, hound!"

Fallon sat straight up in the bed, his heart hammering for the loud voice had sounded right in his ear and he would have recognized it anywhere. When he realized he was in his own austere bedroom and not the Canadian wilds, he blinked.

"Coim?"

"I do not like those who prey upon the innocents."

Running a hand through his hair, the events of the night before came back to him and Fallon turned to look down at the empty space beside him. He frowned. When had the little witch left his side and how deeply had he been sleeping that he had not heard her go? Cocking an ear toward the bathroom, he did not hear water—of any kind—running and that deepened his frown. It was barely six o'clock. She should still be lying beside him.

"You are a lazy hound, but then all hounds are lazy. Get up, stop thinking of your mate and attend to my words!"

"All right already," Fallon grumbled, swinging his bare legs from the mattress. "Can I at least take a piss first?"

"Such a puny thing with which to take a piss but, aye, go ahead," came the begrudging reply.

Fallon looked down at his morning woody and winced, wondering since the creature could invade his mind if he could also remote view him.

"How else would I know the size of your dribble?"

Ignoring the snide query, Fallon padded into the bathroom to relieve himself. The seat was down and that made him even angrier at himself. Keenan had come into the room, taken care of her own business before slipping out—unheard and unsensed. He mentally castigated himself for letting down his guard so carelessly.

"She did not wish to wake you. Our conversation was brief but pleasant."

The frown morphed into a look of surprise on the Reaper's face. "You spoke with Keenan this morning?"

"*I told you, hound!*" came the exasperated snarl. "*I do not like those who prey upon those who can not defend themselves!*" There was a snort then, "*And wash your hands!*"

Doing as he was ordered, Fallon looked up in to the mirror over the sink and he could see *An Fear Liath Mor* like a rippling ghost in the glass.

"What are you talking about, Coim?" he asked.

There was a long, loud sigh in Fallon's ears. "*Pay attention, hound. I have little to do to occupy my time so I thought to venture into your dreams to see what you were up to.*"

"Lucky me," Fallon mumbled as he dried his hands and left to make his way to the kitchen.

"*You were thinking of a female who cheats people by claiming to be a healer, who murders those who oppose her in some unknown way. I do not like such humans. I will rid my world of their ilk. Naturally, I will assist you and your mate in this.*"

That surprised Fallon. "You want to help?"

"*Did I not say I did?*" came the bark. "*Perhaps you are not as intelligent as I thought you, pup.*"

"Or maybe it's too early in the morning to be throwing this shit at me," Fallon complained as he filled the coffee pot with water. When there was a long, ominous silence, he stilled, water overflowing the pot then a loud hiss nearly deafened him.

"*Wasteful hound! Shut off the water!*"

Grinding his teeth—a muscle flexing in his jaw—Fallon filled the coffeemaker with water and opened the overhead cabinet to take out a filter and the makings for his morning coffee. He measured two scoops of coffee, a quarter cup of sugar, and dropped both into the filter. He turned the machine on and walked into the living area where a single recliner sat beside a table with a built-in lamp. Across the room stood a state-of-the-art plasma TV next to a computer desk wall unit.

"Uncomfortable room," An Fear Liath Mor observed.

"It has everything I need," Fallon defended. He slumped down in the recliner, totally unconscious of his nudity, and kicked the footrest back so his long legs shot out.

"Most pitiful accommodations," the beast stated, *"but as I was saying, I will assist you. I have already instructed your mate on what I will do for her. All you need do is bring her to me."*

That got Fallon's attention. He narrowed his eyes. "Why?"

"So I may grace her with certain skills she will need to put this charlatan out of commission."

"What certain skills?"

There was a long, metaphysical sigh that sounded like a rushing wind through Fallon's mind.

"She worried that the — what did she call it? Ah, yes! The con game. She was concerned that in pretending to be a healer, this con game would hurt the innocents. Her dreams last eve were filled with despondency about harming the gullible. I gently woke her and told her there was no need for her to agonize over this. I will grant unto her the ability to heal."

Fallon sat up so quickly, the recliner bounced under him. "You told her what?"

"It is well within the scope of my powers, hound," An Fear Liath Mor snapped. *"I take care of my wards as best I can without interfering with the Great God's plans for them. With healing, He gifts me with the option of knowing when and how to intervene. There are of course times when He overrules what I want to do, but that is His right as the Great God. When He has decided an innocent's life race is run and it is time to be brought Home, He takes the matter out of my hands."*

"You are going to give Keenan the ability to actually heal the sick?" Fallon wanted clarified.

"Is that not what I said, hound! Why are you not paying attention to my words?"

Pushing up from the recliner, Fallon stomped into the kitchen to pour his coffee. "You are playing with fire here, Coim," he warned.

"I am not." The statement sounded miffed.

"You're putting her in a bad spot. If people learn she can actually cure, they will clamor all over her to be healed."

There was silence for a moment. *"But isn't that what you were planning anyway, pup?"*

"No," Fallon said, drawing the word out. "We want to put Keenan into the organization so we can find out what kind of creature this Mignon Bolivar is using to kill those who oppose her."

"Creature. Aye, that was in your dreams. I remember now."

"Stay the heck out of my dreams, okay?" Fallon asked. As awed by the beast as he was, he still didn't want it rifling through his mind and especially not when he was asleep.

"Let me investigate this creature you mention," An Fear Liath Mor said. *"I will get back with you on it by the time you bring her to me."*

"And just when…?"

Fallon stopped, feeling the entity pulling back out of his mind. He hissed, snatching open a cabinet door to extract a coffee mug. It irritated him that Coim made no mention of his request to stay out of Fallon's dreams.

Leaning against the counter, he took a mouthful of the scalding hot coffee, winced, then with a brutal scowl on his features stomped into the bathroom, needing a long, cold shower to rid him of his anger.

* * * * *

"Good morning."

Her voice was so soft, so welcoming, so sexy he wanted to reach through the phone and cup her breasts.

"Good morning," he said softly. "Had breakfast yet?"

"I was going to give you another ten minutes and call to see if you wanted to go down to the cafeteria," she replied. "I'd offer to cook for us but I still haven't had a chance to stock the fridge or shelves."

"I'm on my way," he said, and hung up the receiver, feeling like a randy teenager eager to see his girlfriend.

127

She was waiting at her door when he walked up. Her smile made his heart ache, his body throb, and he snaked an arm around to pull her to him.

"Good morning," he said again, kissing her gently on the lips.

She returned his kiss. "Did he wake you after I left?"

Fallon snorted. "It nearly blasted my eardrums out," he complained. He stepped back as she pulled her door closed, reluctantly sliding his arm from her, and then reached down to thread his fingers through hers when she turned to face him.

"Did he tell you he wants you to drive us down to the Ozarks to meet him this weekend?" She tilted her head to one side. "Do you think he has to be in the mountains all the time?"

"Best way to stay hidden from those who it doesn't want to see it," he replied.

"Coim isn't an it," she said. "He's very masculine."

Something in her voice made Fallon glance down at her as they walked toward the elevator. "Why are you blushing?"

"He saw me naked," she said, ducking her head. "Again."

"I'm going to have to have a talk with it," he growled. "Only God knows how long it was watching us lying there in the buff."

She changed the subject, pulling him past the elevator and to the stairway door. "Do you really think he can give me the power to heal the sick?"

"It says it can." He was grateful she wasn't making him ride down in the claustrophobic cage. "How do you feel about that?"

"I'm no Aimee Semple McPherson and I don't want people thinking I am, but if during this assignment I can help people instead of conning them, I'm all for it."

They were walking slowly down the stairs, the only people in the stairwell. She stopped and gave him a worried look.

"Coim doesn't want anyone to know he's doing this. He doesn't want anyone to know about him or that we're going down there to meet him."

"I haven't told anyone," Fallon said. "I purposefully left it out of my report that we encountered anything other than the blood fiends up in Canada." He shrugged. "That would have opened a whole other can of worms for *An Fear Liath Mor.*"

"So what do we tell the Supervisor about where we're going this weekend?"

"We don't need to tell him anything," Fallon replied. "Our off time is our own. I think we're due some down time, don't you?"

She nodded and they continued down the stairs.

"There is one problem," he said as they reached the ground floor and he opened the door for her.

"What?"

"I don't have a car and unless you're into riding on the back of my motorcycle, we'll have to take yours."

"You don't have a car?" she said, eyebrows elevated.

He shook his head. "Never wanted one. I like my bike. It suits me."

She tilted her head to one side, seeing him in her mind's eye astride a bruising chopper, tearing down the highway at breakneck speed.

"It's a Harley, isn't it?" she asked.

"Is there any other?" he countered.

She leaned in to him as they walked through the lobby and out into the early morning sunlight shining down on the monorail platform.

"If you had to have a car, what kind would you buy?"

He shrugged. "I don't want a car."

"But if you were forced to buy one, what kind would it be?"

He pulled her around and encircled her with his arms as they waited for the train to arrive. "What would you have me buy, *myneeast caillagh*?"

She thought about it for a moment. "A sports car. Something sleek and black and fast and terribly decadent."

Three Exchange employees exited the dorm building and started toward them so Fallon released her, shoving his hands into his pockets and leaning his back against a stanchion. He didn't speak to the newcomers and they made no effort to speak to him or Keenan.

"Stepford drones," he said under his breath, and Keenan giggled, thinking the same thing.

Once inside the train, he held on to the pole above her head, bumping into her as the car began moving.

"So what kind of car do you have?" he asked. When she told him, he groaned. "My God, *lhiannan*, that's a granny car. I wouldn't be caught dead in one of those ugly ass things."

She raised her chin. "I like my car, and since that's what we'll be taking this weekend, you'll just have to live with it." At his grunt, she laughed.

The cafeteria was bustling with people by the time they arrived, picked out their food and found a table. Matty waved to them from across the room where he was sitting with a tall, Amazon-looking woman.

"Our medical examiner Dr. Phyllis Papadopoulos," Fallon told her. "They are on-again, off-again lovers. They are working on some kind of DNA cloning project together."

"Dolly the sheep kind of stuff?" she asked as she salted her scrambled eggs.

"I guess. That shit doesn't interest me, so when he starts spouting all that medical research mumbo-jumbo at me, I zone out," he answered.

Keenan looked down at his tray as he began off-loading his breakfast onto the table and shook her head. "I can't believe what I'm seeing."

"Hey, what can I say? I'm a growing boy."

Three fried eggs, eight pieces of bacon, two slices of ham, a huge dollop of fried potatoes, a large bowl of assorted fruit, a stack of pancakes, six sausage patties and bowl of raisin bran littered the table.

"Reapers have large appetites," he said. He nudged his chin toward the oversized glass of orange juice he'd taken instead of more coffee. "And a sweet tooth like you wouldn't believe." He salt and peppered his eggs and potatoes. "I think the love of sugar counterbalances having the Sustenance each morning."

She felt a slight wave of nausea push at the back of her throat but she tamped it down, deliberately taking a large gulp of her apple juice to aid in the process.

"Too much sugar for my kind can prove to be a problem though," he said.

"Why?"

"It works like a super-charged aphrodisiac," he replied, wagging his brows.

"Remind me to keep the candy at a minimum then," she muttered. "My mother is a diabetic so we rarely had it at home when I was growing up."

"Where does she live?" he asked as he gobbled a huge forkful of pancake slathered with blueberry syrup.

"In Colquitt, Georgia," she said. "It's near Albany." She speared a glob of egg. "I haven't seen her in two years."

"Maybe you'll get to visit her when the assignment is over."

"I don't think so," she said, looking across the room.

"I take it you don't have a close relationship then?"

She shook her head. "Far from it. She thinks I should be married to Zack and giving him a son. She knew I'd never bond with him so he posed no threat." She turned back to him. "Hell, she doesn't even like children. Why want one to dislike?"

He shoved his plate away—appetite gone, although there was very little food left to begin with. His amber eyes locked on hers. "I'm not going to allow that asshole to become a problem for us, *myneeast caillagh*," he warned. "I'll take him apart piece by bloody piece before I allow him to come between us."

Keenan laid her hand on his forearm. "There isn't going to be a problem, Fallon. I am with you, I want to be with you, and I am going to *stay* with you." She squeezed his arm. "That's the way it is."

Neither noticed the young woman who had approached the table until she cleared her throat. Both jerked their heads around and up to scowl at the intrusion.

"What?" Fallon growled.

"I'm sorry to interrupt your breakfast, Agent Fallon, but the Supervisor asks that you and Agent McCullough be in the training room by 0800," the young woman stated. A flickering smile trembled on her lips then she turned and walked away.

"I'm finished anyway," Keenan said. She pushed her chair back as Fallon got to his feet.

Since the cleaning staff would clear the table, they left the cafeteria, silent as they made their way to the third floor, taking the stairs. When they reached the third floor landing, Fallon reached out to take Keenan's arm. She turned to face him where he stood a step down from her.

"I'm possessive and you know that," he said. "And I can be a son of a bitch."

"A word of advice?" she asked, covering his hand with hers. He nodded, gaze wary. "Don't let him push your buttons. He's going to try, but the best way to get his goat is not to let him get to you."

"Okay," he said.

"Okay," she echoed, and turned to open the door.

Breslin was leaning with his hips against a desk at the front of the training room, his arms folded and his face hard as stone. He tracked Keenan's movement to a comfortable chair but seemed to ignore Fallon's taking a seat beside her. The Supervisor was already seated and going over a thick file in his lap, apparently so engrossed with the material he did not greet the new arrivals.

"Class starts at 0730 every day, Agent McCullough," Breslin said. "You're late."

"I don't remember you giving us a time to be here," Keenan responded to his harsh tone. "Do you, Misha?"

Her use of Fallon's nickname made the Supervisor look up.

"If he did, I sure as shit didn't hear him," Fallon replied.

"0730 from now on," Breslin snapped. "And not a minute after."

"And fuck you too," Fallon said in a pleasant voice as he thrust out his long legs, crossed them at the ankles and braced his head in his hands.

"Watch your language, Agent Fallon," the Supervisor warned in a low voice that did not quite hide the hint of amusement.

"Since you've already wasted a half hour of my time..."

"And it's such precious time too, isn't it?" Fallon smirked.

"Let's get to it," Breslin said, ignoring the jibe. "Keenan, did you study the information on Regis Cove last night?"

"She was with me last night," Fallon said. "All night."

Breslin squinted and a muscle worked in his cheek. "Sir, if you would ask Agent Fallon to refrain from speaking until he has been asked to do so, I would appreciate it."

"Just as I'd appreciate it if you'd drop dead, but since I doubt I'll get what I want, it's not likely you'll get what you want either," Fallon told him.

"Fallon," the Supervisor said, drawing the name out. He looked up. "Get on with it, Breslin."

"So you did not familiarize yourself with the material?" Breslin grumbled.

"I read every word of it this morning, memorized it and filed it away for use later," Keenan said. "What do you want to know, Zack?"

Two hours later, Fallon was bored out of his mind, humming to himself and staring at the ceiling. It was a relief when the Supervisor told him he could go. Not having to be told a second time, he drew his long legs in and was out of the room in a flash.

Three hours after that, he caught up with Keenan in the cafeteria just as she was about to join Matty for lunch.

"Oh shit. Here comes Attila the Hun," he heard Matty complain.

"And a merry fucking afternoon to you too, quack," Fallon said, and swung a long leg over a chair and slid down into it. He leaned over to give Keenan a peck on the cheek. "I see you survived Faith Healing 101."

"You seem in a good mood," she said, casting a quick look to Matty.

"I *am* in a good mood," he said. He aimed his attention at Matty. "Benevolent enough to overlook you consorting with the horny doctor."

"Did you fall and hit your head, Fallon?" Matty inquired as he scored the pork chop on his plate.

"You're not a threat," Fallon said then rapped his fingers on the edge of the table as he looked around the room. "Where's the asshole?"

"He and the Supervisor are having lunch together," Keenan said. She stuffed a forkful of salad — the only food she'd purchased — into her mouth. "I wasn't invited. Aren't you going to eat?"

"Had a couple of burgers and fries before I came back," was the response.

"What he means is he ate six quarter pound hamburgers, four cartons of fries and swilled down the largest pop they had at the counter then topped it off with two fried apple pies," Matty said dryly.

"I don't doubt it," Keenan said. "I've seen his eating habits."

"It was three fried apple pies, but who's counting?" Fallon sniffed.

"You'd better watch his sugar intake, Keenan," Matty warned.

Keenan smiled. "Tell me about the DNA cloning project you're working on," she said.

Matty's face lit. "We're making real progress. Can you imagine the implications if we succeed?"

"What do you mean?" she asked as she took the last bite of her salad.

"Think about it, Keenan," Matty said. "People are dying every day for want of new hearts, livers and kidneys. There just aren't enough to go around and it's become a big thing on the black market. Poor people sell their organs to feed their families. You have unscrupulous funeral home directors who clandestinely sell bone and tissue that is diseased, infecting unsuspecting transplant patients who die needlessly from someone else's illness. If cloning becomes the norm, we'll all have expendable molds from which to take the pieces-parts we need to live fifty years longer than the norm. I'm working up a facial replica right now from blood and tissue samples I received a few days ago. Sort of a living mask." He grinned broadly. "Guess who the model is."

"You'd better not," Fallon warned, eyes narrowing, his good mood disappearing in a flash.

"Who?" Keenan asked, looking from one man to the other when neither answered. She repeated her question, taking up her napkin to wipe her lips.

"You," Fallon growled.

"Me?" she gasped.

Matty waved his fork. "I'm just trying to duplicate your blood and tissue, Keenan. It's not like I'm attempting to clone you. That's years away, but if I can genetically generate a piece of living tissue, I'm more than halfway there to re-creating an entire body. We can grow replacement ears on a mouse so why not replacement faces for burn victims?"

Keenan felt chill bumps prickle her arm. "I don't think I'd like to find out I had a Stepford sister lying in a tank of embryonic fluid somewhere, Matty."

"A long way off," Matty said, scooping up a forkful of peas.

Fallon stared at the scientist-physician sitting across from him. Matty had some psi powers of his own and had always been hard to read. At that moment, Fallon found the man's mind completely sealed off and that concerned him. He thought about the people waiting for the monorail that morning—the unsmiling, single-minded worker bees, who never spoke, never smiled, were never seen taking part in any of the activities at the Exchange. He shuddered, hoping Matty wasn't doing something they would all regret.

"Leave her out of your experiments, Matty," Fallon said. "I mean it."

"All right," Matty said, and continued to eat.

"What did you do while I was being bored stiff this morning?" Keenan asked, finishing off her raspberry lemonade.

"I made good use of my time," he said. "I also went by scheduling and signed us out from 1800 Friday until 2100 Sunday."

Matty looked up. "You two going somewhere?"

"We're taking the weekend off," Fallon said. "Thought I'd take her up to the Dells."

"Man, I love the Dells," Matty said. "Neat place." His eyebrows drew together. "Are you taking your bike?"

"We'll be taking my car," Keenan said. "No way am I riding all that way on the back of a motorcycle."

"Chicken," Fallon accused.

"Responsible adult," she countered then saw Breslin motioning for her. She sighed. "Recess is over, guys." She stood. "Are you coming back to the lecture?"

Fallon shook his head. "Not on your life, *myneeast caillagh*." He too stood. "I think I'll do some more research on Bolivar."

"Then I'll see you back at the dorm after sixth period," she said with a grin.

"Unless teacher makes you stay for detention," Matty chuckled.

"He'd best not," Fallon stated.

Watching her walk away, Fallon felt a tiny squeeze to his heart. He knew he had fallen hard for the woman and life without her would never be the same. His intense feelings for her had blossomed so quickly, so thoroughly he still had trouble believing it.

"She is one terrific lady," Matty said.

Fallon looked around. "If you want to be friends with her, Matt, that's okay by me, but if you have something else in mind, I'd think again if I were you."

Matty held his hands up. "I get it," he said. "She's yours. There's no need to belabor the point, Misha."

Yet there was something in Matty's gaze that belied the acceptance of the situation.

And that worried Fallon.

Chapter Nine

ຄ

"Oh my God!" Keenan said, walking around the low-slung sports car. She shot Fallon an open-mouthed look of surprise. "This is what you were doing this morning? Buying this?"

"Like it?"

She ran her hand over the sleek black metallic finish from front headlight to taillight before she answered. "Yes," she whispered. "Oh God, yes!"

He dangled the keys on the tip of his index finger. "Wanna take her for a spin?"

Keenan snatched the keys. "Get in, lineman!"

Fallon laughed as she practically ran around to the driver's side. "I hope you can drive a stick."

"Do Canada geese poop in flight?" she asked, sliding behind the wheel.

He got in and shut the door, smiling broadly as he watched her run the palms of her hands up and down the outside of the braided leather steering wheel cover as though it were a lover's body.

Keenan took them off the Exchange and onto the highway that led to Marshalltown, dropping the convertible roof so the wind could whip their hair. He settled back in the luxurious leather seat as she put the car through its paces, getting it up to a hundred on one flat stretch then letting it slow to the requisite fifty-five, cruising along as though she owned the road.

"She handles like a dream," she pronounced.

"Consider her yours any time you want to drive her," he said. "Otherwise, she'll just sit in the garage alongside my bike."

"And that would be a waste of a prime lady," she said. She scowled as a car shot past them as though they were standing still. For a moment Fallon thought she'd retaliate, but then she sighed.

"There you go being a responsible adult again," he teased.

"Are you going to take your bike down to Georgia?" she asked.

"It would fit the persona of a lone badass better than this piece of fluff," he said.

"Fluff," she said with a snort. "This beauty is so far above that description it ain't funny. This is pure evil on a stick shift, Fallon."

"Even so, the bike will be better."

"Yeah, you're probably right."

"How 'bout we eat supper up in Marshalltown tonight?" he asked. "I know this really great little Mexican restaurant that serves the best fajitas this side of Acapulco and their frozen margaritas are sinful."

"Sure, but I need to get back fairly early. Breslin loaded me down with all kinds of mountain-related stuff he wants me to learn." She flicked him a glance. "You don't have to worry about setting up a persona. You've got the badass part down pat, lineman."

He leaned toward her and cupped her between the legs with his right hand. "You think?" He kneaded her, pressing his thumb over the spot in her pants where he knew her clit was located.

"You're as evil as your new car, Fallon," she said, her breath quickening. She glanced behind them then whipped the car into a nearly ninety degree turn as she took it down a narrow gravel road. White dust flew behind them until she discovered a grass-streaked farm lane and jerked the wheel—fishtailing the sports car—onto it. A quarter of a mile down the potholed, almost nonexistent path, the lane petered out. Slamming on the brakes, the Porsche jolted to a stop and she turned off the engine and popped open her seat belt.

Fallon dragged her over the console and onto his lap, his hands molding to her breasts as their mouths clashed. Hard as stone beneath her shapely ass, he arched his hips up, grinding against her.

"Umm," she said into his mouth, and pushed herself up on her knees so she could wedge a hand between them and free him from his black denim jeans. Tearing her mouth free, she slid onto the floorboard and, before he could stop her, had her lips around his cock, suckling him hard.

"Damn, baby," he gasped, one hand slapped to the edge of the door and the other grabbed hold of the stick shift as her mouth devoured him. His hips were flexing upward with every draw of her lips.

Getting a blowjob was nothing new for Fallon, but one this intense, so *hungry*, both baffled and made him proud as hell that he'd found a woman who enjoyed doing him. From the way she moved her tongue under the head of his cock, this wasn't her first time at oral sex, but he intended to make sure he was the last man she pleasured in that way. Just the thought of her doing this with another man brought a red haze to his vision and he moved his hand from the stick shift to her hair to hold her head against him. He saw her look up through her eyelashes at him then she squeezed him so tight with her lips he nearly came. Grinding his teeth, he shoved his hands under her armpits and pulled her off him.

"I want inside you," he growled.

Keenan's eyes glittered as he threw open the door. She scrambled off him and into the nearly knee-high weeds to either side of the car. He swung his legs off the seat with his cock thrust straight out through the opened fly of his jeans and snatched at her pants. Thankful she was wearing slacks that had an elastic waistband, he yanked them down her long legs and she kicked them away. He tore off her panties and grabbed her, lifting her onto his cock in one smooth, fluid movement.

"Goddamn," he whispered. "I can't keep my cock outta you, woman."

She wrapped her legs around him as he pushed her up against the open car door and began to thrust his hips upward, impaling her deeply upon his shaft. Clinging to his neck, she sank her teeth into the strong column, unaware she'd drawn blood until she tasted the saltiness on her tongue.

Not that it bothered Fallon. If anything the sting of her bite spurred him to a more frenzied movement, and his hips became like jackhammers driving into her. The car shook from the force of his movements, and when they came, they came together in a blinding rush of release that brought a howl from his throat and a low growl of satisfaction from hers. The ripples of her vaginal walls around his pulsing cock seemed to go on forever, and when the last little squeeze came, they were both soaked with sweat.

Spent, his head on her shoulder, his knees shaking from the intensity of his climax and the force of his thrusts, he struggled to breathe. She was wrapped around him like an anaconda and he never wanted to break free.

"That's. What. You. Get. For. Touching me there," she managed to say.

"I'll try to restrain myself from now on," he replied on a long, satiated sigh.

"Don't," she said.

They stood that way for a while longer until they heard rustling in the grass around them.

"Snakes," he said. "I can smell them."

"I don't like snakes, lineman," she said, craning her neck back and forth in an attempt to see the sneaky varmints.

He turned so he could lower her into the seat and retrieve her pants. "They don't bother me unless they're ghorets. Then I'd have a real problem with them."

"Ghorets?" she questioned, flinching as his semen oozed from her and onto the leather seat. She squirmed, not liking the sensation at all.

He stuffed himself back into his pants, zipped up his fly and then bent down to pick up her pants.

"They are a type of serpent I hope to God we don't have on Earth," he said. "They are the only thing Reapers truly fear. A single drop of their venom would be enough to kill a human, but it would only make me so sick I would wish I could die." He handed her pants to her. "Sorry, I don't have anything for you to clean up with."

"Where's my panties?"

He looked on the ground, found the undergarment and picked it up. As she cleaned herself, he went around to the driver's side.

"Try to keep your hands off my package while I'm driving," he said as he opened the door and got behind the wheel. "I don't drive a car all that well to begin with."

"I'll try, but I'm making no promises," she said as she wiggled into her pants, having tossed her soiled panties into the weeds.

Clothed, she pulled the seat belt around her then looked at him. "Seat belt," she said. He'd not been wearing his while she drove, but she hadn't noticed until they'd stopped.

"I hate seat belts."

"Seat belt," she insisted.

"Nag, nag, nag," he complained, but did as she ordered.

All the way to the restaurant and back that evening they were unusually quiet, simply content to be with one another. When they arrived back at the Exchange, they reluctantly parted. She had studying to do and he had a cold shower with his name on it waiting.

* * * * *

"And then you let the entrails drop from your palm and onto the mark's belly, sweeping it aside so no one will get a good look at them," Breslin instructed.

"People actually believe this stuff was growing inside them?" she asked, marveling at the piece of sheep's intestine in the palm of her hand.

"They want to believe, Keenan," Breslin said. "That's how Bolivar hoodwinks them so completely."

Keenan yawned then mumbled an apology.

"Another late night with lover boy?" Breslin smirked.

"No," she said. "I spent the evening alone."

"After you got back from Marshalltown," he stated.

Bristling under his angry look, she dropped the entrails into a container and went over to the sink to wash her hands. "My private life is my own, Zack," she reminded him. "What I do with it is none of your business."

"It's my business if your hanky panky jeopardizes the mission," he replied, coming over to the sink. "You've got to keep your mind on the assignment or Bolivar is going to eat you alive." He reached for her but she sidestepped him. That didn't deter him and he tried again, this time managing to get a grip on her arm. "Listen, Kiki. I want you back. I know I..."

"Let go," she said, eyes hard as she stared into his face. "I mean it."

"We could make it work. It got a bit out of hand back then, but that was only because you were driving me crazy with not accepting my proposal. Your mom and I..."

"Leave my mother out of this!" she said, savagely breaking free of his hold. "That was most of the problem to begin with!"

"I can't help it that she liked me," he said. "She thought we were good together."

"*She* didn't know *you!*" Keenan snapped, and jerked a paper towel from the dispenser to dry her hands.

"We're going to be working closely together down in Georgia," he said, his voice full of wheedling. "Why can't we just patch things up and go back to the way it was? You know I love you. I've always loved you."

"Well, I don't love *you*," Keenan said. "I don't think I ever did."

Breslin shook his head. "You don't mean that. We were good together."

"No, we really weren't," she said, and tossed the used paper towel forcefully into the trashcan. She turned her back on him and started away.

"I'm going to get you back," he told her. "I will!"

"Dream on," she said as she shoved the training room door open and walked out.

All the way to the lounge she cursed the Fates that had brought Zack Breslin to the Exchange. In her heart of hearts she'd known she hadn't seen the last of him. To have him here now was driving her crazy. Having to work with him again was driving her to drink.

"A tequila setup," she told the barman as she approached the bar.

"Bad day, Agent McCullough?" he asked, not surprising her that he knew her name.

"It's Keenan and yep, Hank, it's been a bitch of a day," she said, handing over her ID card for him to swipe down the register. She looked around. "Your bar waitress still out?"

"She'll be in around five," he replied as he handed back her card. "Drop some money in the jukebox, Keenan. I'll bring your order over to you."

She thanked him and headed for the jukebox, selecting slow, melancholy songs that matched her mood. Taking a seat in the same booth she and Matty had shared, she kicked off her shoes and put her feet up on the seat, leaning into the V between the booth's back and the wall, and closed her eyes. She heard the heavy thud of glass on the table and mumbled another "Thank you" without so much as cracking an eyelid. After a few moments, she opened her eyes and took three consecutive shots of tequila—wincing as each after burn scorched a pathway down her throat. One more shot and she leaned back again, closing her eyes, her thoughts so morose a fierce grimace settled on her face.

How long she sat that way, she didn't know, but when she opened her eyes, Fallon was sitting across from her, nursing a beer straight from the bottle.

"Hey you," she said.

"Hey." He slowly smiled. "Do you know you snore?"

"I wasn't asleep."

"Yes you were, and you were snoring."

"No, I wasn't. You must be having trouble with your hearing," she said, reaching out to pour another shot of tequila.

Fallon watched her complete the ritual with the salt and lime and shook his head. "You'll get wasted like that, *lhiannan*."

"It's Hump Day, lineman," she said. "I need to unwind a bit before I head up to my lonely, horny little room."

"Is that an invitation to join you in your lonely, horny little room to hump you?" he inquired politely.

"Well," she said, pouring another shot. "You did say you couldn't keep your cock outta me, remember?" Her words were beginning to slur.

"Only too well." He took a swig of his beer then leaned forward with his elbows on the table. "What's wrong?"

She poured a third shot, but before she knocked it back, he shot out a hand to cover hers and keep the glass on the table.

"What's wrong?" he repeated, caressing her slender hand.

"Memories," she sang. "Light the corners of my mind…"

"What did asshole do?"

She snorted. "You've got to stop calling him that."

"No, I don't. What'd he do?"

She sighed and slumped back in the booth. "Reminded me of a time I'd just as soon forget."

"Which was…?"

Her mouth tightened. "When he asked me to marry him."

That surprised Fallon and he slid his hand from hers. "What did you tell him?"

"I told him no," she stated then emphatically repeated it. "I told him *no*."

He watched her fling back the third shot. "Why?" he asked, and jumped when she slammed the shot glass on the table.

"Because I didn't want to marry him, Fallon," she snapped.

"Him or anyone?"

"Him!" she spat. "I didn't want to marry him because he was pushing me into it. My mother was pushing me into it. Hell, even

145

my priest was pushing me into it and Breslin is a fucking lapsed Catholic with two ex-wives!"

Fallon whistled. "Boy gets around, don't he?"

"My mother had the wedding all planned. She had the engagement party already booked at the country club. She was consulting wedding dress designers." She glared at him. "Designers, for shitsake! Do you hear what I'm saying?"

"I think so. You don't like designer wedding gowns."

She continued as though she hadn't heard him. "She had swaths of material for the attendants' gowns. She had a photographer on standby and a caterer and a fucking limousine service, and she'd booked us a suite at a fancy-schmancy resort down in the Caribbean!"

"Sounds like she was living vicariously through you," he said gently.

"She fucking nailed him, Fallon!" she shouted.

"Keenan, shush!" Fallon hissed at her.

Heads turned toward them but thankfully there were only a few people in the lounge. Both the bartender and the waitress were studiously avoiding looking at Keenan.

Keenan lowered her voice but her eyes were ferocious as she spoke.

"Don't you understand? She fucked him! My own mother fucked the man I was dating! In my fucking room on my fucking bed! Now do you see?"

"More than I wanted to," he mumbled.

"I didn't love the son of a bitch," she said, shaking her head. "I really didn't, but he was my partner and the sex was good — really, really good."

"A little more info there than I wanted to hear, McCullough," he grumbled.

"But for my own mother to hump him?" Tears filled her eyes. "How could she do that, Fallon? How could she do that to her own daughter?"

"You know for a fact that this happened?" he queried.

"I saw them!" she yelled.

Fallon winced. He knew matters were only going to get worse and she was only going to get louder if she kept drinking. He swiped the bottle of tequila from the table and scooted out of the booth.

"What the fuck you doing?" she demanded. "Gimmee back that goddamned bottle."

"Let's take this back to your place, okay?" he said in a low voice. "You don't need to air your dirty laundry in here."

Where she was finally registered with Keenan and her face took on a pinched look. "Oh shit," she muttered, looking around shamefully.

"Come on," he prompted, and waited for her to slide out of the booth. She had to snake out an arm to catch herself since she stumbled when she stood up.

"Sorry," she apologized.

"You're not used to drinking, are you, baby?" he asked, sliding his arm around her. The liquor had gone straight to her head.

"One-drink Kiki," she said. "That's what they used to call me."

"And how many shots did you have before I joined you?"

"Donknow." She wiped the back of her mouth with her hand, she wavered, then let her head fall back to look at him. She grinned lasciviously. "Hot damn, boy. You are one mouthful, you know?"

He shook his head. "You're drunk, baby."

She put up a hand and poked him in the chest with her index finger. Lowering her voice, she gazed at him through her eyelashes. "Actually, you're more than a mouthful, but that ain't a polite thing to say, you know?" She giggled. "And right tasty too."

He grinned. "Let's go, *lhiannan.*"

"Go where?" she asked in a suspicious voice.

"To your room."

Her face brightened. "You gonna fuck me, Fallon?" she asked so loud people laughed.

Fallon felt the heat from his blush and shushed her again, but she swatted at his chest — her lips pursed — and told him not to tell her to hush.

"If you ain't gonna fuck me, I ain't going nowhere with you," she said then went still, eyes puzzled.

She frowned, smacked her lips.

She burped, smacked her lips again.

Then her eyes rolled up in her head and he barely caught her before she hit the floor. Fumbling with her and striving to put the tequila bottle down on the table, he swore under his breath. He managed to rid himself of the bottle and sling Keenan over his shoulder, grunting from the effort. Limp as an eel, her arms and head swung down his back, she was out cold. With an arm wrapped around her legs, he started out of the bar.

Those he passed on the way to the dormitory studiously avoided looking his way as he carried his unconscious burden along the walkway. The doorman saw him coming and rushed over to open the door for him. Fallon nodded his thanks and headed for the elevator, already beginning to sweat before the metal doors even slid open. The doorman pushed the button for him then went back to his kiosk since the look on the agent's face was brutal.

Stepping inside the cage never failed to unnerve Fallon. His throat always tightened and his chest burned. Even having Keenan with him did not dispel the claustrophobia that weighted him down. He breathed a deep sigh of relief when the doors opened again and he was free of the confinement.

He carried her to her quarters, punched in the code then went straight to the bedroom. After laying her down on the bed, he gently removed her clothing, found a nightgown in the dresser and clothed her in it. Then he turned her to her side, stood there for a moment looking down at her before leaving the room, quietly closing the door behind him.

He went into the kitchen, rummaged through her nearly empty fridge and decided there was nothing there that interested him. After trying the cupboards and swearing viciously at her lack of food, he stomped to the phone and called the restaurant since the cafeteria would be closed at this time of evening.

"Yeah, this is Fallon. What's the special tonight?" He listened then ordered double of everything and asked that it be delivered to Keenan's quarters ASAP. When he hung up, he made a mental note to take her shopping right after work the next day.

With nothing to do until his supper arrived, he went to the sofa and sat. Glancing down at the array of paperbacks under her coffee table, he bent over and picked up the first one he saw.

"Probably *How Ripe is My Valley* or *The Clit Also Rises*," he said aloud. The actual title made him snort. He laid it on the sofa seat, took off his boots, stood up and pulled his shirttail from his jeans then stretched out to see if the actual story was as purple as the title. He was deeply engrossed in the paranormal romance when the doorbell chimed.

The young man with the cart was nervous as he rolled it into Keenan's apartment. His hand actually trembled when he took the five-dollar tip Fallon gave him after having his ID card swiped down the check presenter.

"I don't bite, you know," Fallon said in a droll voice.

"No, sir, Mr. F-Fallon," the young man stammered.

After the delivery man left, Fallon dove into the food with one hand while he kept the romance novel in the other. As he ate, he read feverishly, completely immersed in the storyline. When he'd finished everything he'd ordered, he rolled the cart out into the corridor and with a beer in hand, went back to the sofa, stretched out and continued to read.

By four o'clock the next morning he was on his second romance, and when he heard Keenan stirring in the bedroom, reluctantly bookmarked his place, laid the book on the coffee table and went in to check on her — as he'd done many times during the night.

She was pulling the nightgown over her head and getting into the shower when he came to the bathroom door. She'd barely glanced at him as he entered her bedroom.

"You okay?" he asked.

149

"My head feels like someone is playing ping-pong in there." Her voice sounded hollow inside the shower.

"Where's your aspirin?"

"Medicine cabinet," she mumbled as she ducked her head under the water.

He went into the kitchen for a glass of water then came back, found the aspirin and had it waiting for her when the shower turned off. He also had an oversized towel in his hands when she stepped onto the bathmat. Wrapping her in it, he held her as she laid her head on his chest.

"I feel like shit," she said.

"Take your aspirin," he advised, reaching for the tablets.

She plucked them from his palm, took the glass of water and downed the medicine. Without a protest, she let him sweep her into his arms and carry her back into the bedroom.

"You hungry?" he asked.

She grimaced. "I may never eat again."

"Perhaps you should never drink again," he suggested as he sat her down on the bed. He wrapped his arm around her as she leaned on his shoulder once more.

"How big a fool did I make of myself last night, Fallon?" she asked.

"Well, the entire Exchange knows you can't hold your liquor and that I carried you back here slung over my shoulder," he said.

"Oh God," she groaned. "How embarrassing!"

"Ah, it gets worse," he warned her.

She lifted her head to look at him, searching his eyes. "How much worse?"

He cocked a shoulder. "They also know your mother slept with asshole."

He didn't think it was possible for her face to get any paler. He was wrong.

"Shit." Her face screwed up and she said it again.

"Just act like you don't care and in a couple of days, no one will even remember," he told her.

"Breslin is going to…"

"Asshole isn't going to do anything," Fallon said. "Not if he wants to keep his teeth."

Keenan released a long sigh. "Did you get any sleep last night or were you taking care of me the whole time?"

"Reapers don't need much sleep," he said. "I read all night."

She shot him a suspicious look. "Read what?"

"Well, first it was *Love's Dark Master*," he said, "and now I'm almost finished with *Tie Me To You Forever*." He wagged his brows. "Kinky stuff that."

"Pervert," she said, and pushed away from him. She stood and walked over to her closet. "I might as well get dressed. If I lie back down, I might not get up again before noontime."

"What's asshole got planned for you today?" he inquired since his presence in the training room hadn't been requested.

"We're going to work on the mountain girl persona," she said, taking out a pair of jeans and a pullover.

Fallon leaned back on his elbows on the bed and watched her dress. It pleased him she wasn't in the least self-conscious around him as she dropped the towel and stepped into her panties.

"What are you going to do today?" she asked as she hooked her bra.

"Thursdays are generally my gym days," he said. "I'll be working out until around two, break for lunch, then run ten miles before calling it a day."

"Sounds sweaty," she said.

He liked the way she pulled the jeans up her long legs. They fit snuggly across her delicious little upturned rump and he realized the sight of her zipping up was giving him a helluva hard-on.

"Come here," he said.

Keenan looked around at him and her gaze went to the bulge between his legs. She shook her head. "No sex this morning," she said. "It's bad enough everyone is going to know I got shitfaced last night. I don't want to go into the training room smelling of semen."

"Come here," he said again, sitting up.

"Fallon…"

"I just want to kiss you," he said. "Nothing more. I swear."

She went to him and he pulled her down to sit sideways on his lap with his left arm behind her and his right hand cupping her cheek to draw her mouth to his.

The kiss was soft and sweet, but for all its innocence, as heady as summer wine.

"Good morning," he said when he released her lips and she could feel his erection flex beneath her.

"Good morning," she whispered.

"Do you know I love you?"

She nodded. "Yes, I do. Do you know I love you?"

His smile was slow and so endearing. "Yes, *tarrishagh,* I do."

"What does that mean?"

"Beloved," he said, and kissed her gently again.

Keenan started to say something but the ringing phone made them both jump.

"The Supervisor's assistant," Fallon prophesied.

Keenan slid off his lap and went to her nightstand. "Hello?" She listened for a moment then winced. "Yes, we'll be right there." When she hung up, she looked around at Fallon. "I think we're both in deep doodoo."

"I stay in deep doodoo with him, sweetie," he said. He stood and went into the bathroom to relieve himself as she finished dressing.

* * * * *

"That went well," Keenan mumbled after two hours of being screamed at by the most important man at the Exchange.

"Yeah, I like having my ass handed to me at five o'clock in the morning too," Fallon said through clenched teeth.

They were walking side by side down the corridor but would soon part—Keenan going on to the training room where an irate Zack Breslin was awaiting her and Fallon to the gymnasium.

"I'm surprised he gave in about us having the weekend off," she commented. She glanced at him. "Did you use a bit of psi persuasion on him?"

"Wouldn't have done me any good. I've tried it in the past and it doesn't work with him for some reason. From this bitch of a headache I've got right now, I'd say he was scanning my mind even though I had clamped a tight shield around it, and he's not supposed to have psi abilities." He rubbed at his temple. "He's not what he seems, goddamn it, and I'd be willing to bet he knows we're not going to the Dells but to the Ozarks and why."

"You think he knows about Coim?" she asked.

"Yeah, but if it surprised him, I didn't sense it." He was walking with his hands in his back pockets. "What if he knows about *An Fear Liath Mor*?"

"Naturally he knows of me. He is a Shadowlord, hound. He has many powers," came the voice from far away, bringing Fallon to a stop.

"Shadowlord?" Fallon repeated. "What the hell is…?"

Keenan stopped walking too. "Are you talking to Coim again?"

"Greetings, Mate of the hound," Coim said congenially, but in a soft voice so unlike his usual booming bray. *"Feeling better now?"*

"What is a Shadowlord?" Fallon repeated.

"Nothing you need to concern yourself about!" another voice—that of the Supervisor—snapped in their minds. *"Get your ass to the gym, Fallon. McCullough, don't keep Breslin waiting!"*

Fallon felt Coim drawing back but heard the beast cackling humorously as it fled. Having his suspicions about the Supervisor's powers proved correct made him realize he needed to start being more circumspect around the man.

"I'll see you tonight," Keenan told him as she hurried away.

"Yeah," he mumbled.

If it was the last thing he did, he was determined to find out what a Shadowlord was and what powers he could wield.

Chapter Ten

ಐ

Fallon looked around the forest to which Coim's instructions the night before had led them in the high Ozarks. It was a beautiful spot off the beaten track with tall, stately trees and a meandering stream that bubbled over rocks that glistened in the late afternoon sun.

"He's coming," Keenan said, wrapping her arms around her and rubbing them. "I feel that strange sense of foreboding that always accompanies him it seems."

"I would no more harm you than I would my own lady, Mate of the hound," Coim said softly.

And there it stood, Fallon thought, right behind them. He could sense Keenan steeling herself to turn around to face the creature she'd only seen once before. He reached for her hand. Together, they turned.

An Fear Liath Mor's big mouth stretched into a cumbersome smile as it bowed slightly to Keenan.

"How goes it, hound?" it inquired.

"Fair to middling," Fallon acknowledged.

"And Mate of the hound? Are you healed of your June berry intoxication?" Its dark eyes twinkled and its big lips twitched with mirth.

Keenan's forehead crinkled at the strange question but she agreed that she was feeling fine now.

"Then you will wait here, hound, and your mate will accompany me."

Fallon stiffened. "Now wait a minute. I..."

"You will wait here," the beast stated firmly, and in a flash both he and Keenan had disappeared into thin air.

For just a split second Fallon stood stock still with his mouth dropped open then he howled with fury and went tearing through the woods, searching for his woman.

He did not find her, and long after the sun had set he was still roaming the forest, crashing through the underbrush, calling her name and feeling the first uneasy ripples of fear coming at him like poisoned blow darts. At moonrise, he was sitting dejectedly on a fallen log with his head in his hands, cursing *An Fear Liath Mor* and his own gullibility in trusting anyone or anything other than himself. The moment the heavy hand fell upon his shoulder, he knew a murderous rage upon which he would have acted had he not raised his head to find Keenan standing in front of him, none the worse for wear.

He shot to his feet and grabbed her in an embrace that drove the wind from her lungs. Her laughter as she returned his hug was the most wonderful thing he'd ever heard.

"You need to learn to trust your friends, hound," Coim told him. "You could not go where I led your mate. You would not have survived the journey."

Fallon wasn't listening. He pushed Keenan back from him and swept his scrutiny over every inch of her, looking for any sign she'd been hurt. "Are you all right?" he asked.

"I am fine, lineman," she said, placing a palm to his cheek.

He crushed her to him again then turned enraged eyes to the beast. "Don't you *ever* do that again!"

"Chill, hound," Coim said sternly. "You are a heart attack waiting to happen." It switched its gaze to Keenan, its eyes soft and filled with affection. "Take care, Kiki. Call upon me if you have need of my services."

With that, the creature was gone once more, only the leaves overhead stirring at its passing.

"And don't call her Kiki!" Fallon shouted.

* * * * *

Since they hadn't been able to leave the Exchange until early Saturday morning, they wouldn't have as much time in the

Ozarks as Keenan would have liked. After spending the night at Lake of the Ozarks, she insisted they drive to Branson where she clocked over a thousand dollars worth of charges on her credit card before they left town. All but one of the purchases she'd made — nearly every one an antique of some sort — would be sent to her via parcel post. All, that is, except what rested securely in the boot of the Porsche, lovingly placed there by Keenan.

"It'll look so pretty over my dining room table," she'd said of the chandelier.

They spent the entire day in Branson and vowed they would come back to explore the amusement parks and take in the shows that looked so entertaining.

Having found a shop that sold crispy fried pastries called funnel cakes, Fallon bought two dozen of the large confections and was content to sit in the passenger seat while she started home and munch as the wind blew the powdered sugar from his cheeks. Within an hour he'd consumed all but one of the greasy treats and was growling low in his throat, eyeing Keenan with what she realized was intense lust.

"What's your problem, Fallon?" she asked, sweeping her attention down to the hard bulge at the juncture of his legs.

"Sugar," he said, eyes narrowed. "Too much sugar."

She tightened her hands on the steering wheel. "Oh," she said, eyebrows raised. "And you're just now realizing that?"

"Pull over," he said.

They were on the interstate. "Where?" she asked.

"I don't care where, woman. Just pull over!"

Keenan sighed and flipped on the turn signal, grateful the sun had already set. Reluctantly she hit the switch to raise the ragtop.

Twenty minutes later she was not a happy camper though her Reaper was sound asleep. He'd gone at her as though she were a bitch in heat, and while the experience had been fulfilling, she had kept an eye on the road, expecting a Missouri State Patrolman to come cruising up at any moment. Making love in a

Porsche took some doing, some acrobatic maneuvering, and she had strained a muscle or two during the process.

She swore to watch Fallon's sugar consumption from that day on.

Chapter Eleven

ဆာ

He slammed his booted heel into the kickstand and leaned the bike to the right. His gaze wandering the congested area in front of him, he turned off the ignition, took the key out then reached up to remove his black helmet. Shaking out his hair, he swung his long leg over the seat and stood, slid the helmet down the sissy bar and pulled the black leather gloves from his hands. Unzipping his tank bag, he stuffed the gloves inside then peeled out of his leather jacket and stepped to the back of his bike where he unlocked one of the saddlebags to slip the folded jacket inside before locking it again.

The grounds around him were thronged with people of every age, color and size. The farm field was packed with noisy, sweaty humanity all headed to the huge tent about five hundred yards away. Surveying the cars being directed into the makeshift parking area, he saw there were expensive foreign jobs and neatly washed and waxed family cars crammed amidst the rusted-out buckets that were badly in need of new suspension systems and mud-encrusted pickup trucks. Crying children, squalling infants, coughing old folks and arguing husbands with their meek-looking wives passed him as though he weren't standing there.

Beyond the tent on a rise of ground stood a fleet of semi-trailers and at least two dozen very expensive motor homes.

The sound of a band revving up to play an old-time revival song amused him as he started toward the tent at a leisurely stroll. Somewhere among the rolling tide of unwashed and over-perfumed bodies were several Exchange operatives sent ahead to be there for his arrival. He would meet them when the time was right, and in the mood he was in at that moment, that time wouldn't come fast enough.

As he walked—his harness boots kicking up the dry Georgia red clay—his thoughts went to Keenan. He hadn't wanted to

159

leave her behind. Just knowing she was there with Breslin rankled like nothing ever had and he clenched his hands into fists, unaware his jaw had tightened and his eyes turned hard.

"He wants to get back together," she'd told him as she'd watched him packing his things into the soft saddlebags he'd strap to the sissy bar of his bike.

"Ain't gonna happen," he'd declared.

"I told him as much," she'd agreed.

She'd walked with him down to the garage, carrying his sleeping bag roll. While he secured his belongings to the bike, she had looked worried, but she hadn't looked afraid. He knew she could — and would — handle Breslin.

Her worry was for him.

"You'll be careful?" she asked as he slipped his arms around her.

"Just as careful as you will," he'd replied, kissing her.

They'd both known not to let the kiss get out of hand. Not that it should have since Monday night had passed without either of them getting a wink of sleep. They had made love four times and both were worn out from the intensity of their passion.

"Don't think of anything but your assignment," she'd ordered.

His last sight was her standing there waving to him as he sped away, and that image would stay with him all the way from Iowa to Macon, Georgia.

He wove his way around slower-moving people and past many who simply stepped aside to let him by when they noticed his black T-shirt, black jeans and black biker boots. Fifty feet out from the red and white tent, the ground had been padded with wood shavings and the air was redolent with its musky scent. The air was barely moving, the afternoon sun beating down with a vengeance. People were trying to cool themselves with the cardboard fans being handed out by the two white-clad young women who stood to either side of the tent flap, ushering the faithful inside. One tried to hand Fallon a fan and he shook his head, but not before getting a look at what was on the front of the fan—Mignon Bolivar's smiling face, a halo behind her midnight black hair.

As he made his way into the tent, he was amazed at how many people were already packed onto the folding chairs that ringed the center stage in a tight U. There was barely enough room to sidestep between the chairs so he chose to stand among those who loitered at the back of the tent, edging himself as close to the flap as he could. It seemed cooler there and with his Reaper's naturally high body temp, he wasn't quite as uncomfortable as he knew he'd have been sardined in with the teeming masses occupying the chairs.

Or as claustrophobic.

For nearly another hour, the faithful continued to move into the tent until there didn't appear to be a solid inch of ground or seating that was not occupied. The empty section down front that had been reserved for the crippled, the infirm and the ambulatory was now filled and a few gurneys were laid next to each other off to one side. The band continued to play old revival songs with more jubilance than skill and the cardboard fans snapped back and forth, back and forth.

Then with a suddenness that caught him by surprise the music stopped and everyone around him went deathly silent. He noticed a tall, cadaverous-looking man walking to the center of the stage, a single spotlight lighting his nearly bald pate.

"Brothers and Sisters," he said in an ominous voice, "Mother Mignon Bolivar."

Every head snapped toward the back of the tent and the spotlight crawled from the center of the stage down the pathway to the flaps and hung there, causing Fallon to squint from its intensity.

And then she walked past him and he knew beyond any shadow of a doubt that this woman was sheer evil without a single drop of redeeming quality in her shapely body. Though she was clad in a soft shimmering gold silk sheath that covered her from neck to ankle, he could feel the wickedness rolling off her in waves. In her wake, he caught a whiff of a very expensive perfume.

No one made a sound — not even the children, who had been bawling throughout the band's performance. No one reached out to touch her as she passed. Every eye followed her progress down the aisle, two very muscular bodyguards in pristine white suits right behind her. The moment she took the stage, she turned lazily and bestowed upon her followers a smile that seemed loving and benevolent, but to Fallon was rigid with loathing and so predatory it made the hair on his arms stand up. He watched her slowly raise her arms to the heavens, let her head fall back, and when she spoke, he felt a shaft of repugnance travel through his body.

"My children, I am here by the Grace of God," she said then demurely lowered her head. The spotlight that had followed her every step up the aisle now shone upon her rich, black hair that fell well past her slender waist. "I am at His command to do His bidding."

All hell broke loose and the crowd went wild, whistling and cheering, stomping and clapping, arms waving in the air as the band struck up another rousing revival song. From the back of the stage came a line of singers in pale blue robes to begin singing the lyrics.

With his arms folded over his chest, Fallon watched the spectacle unfold before him. Her voice was soft, mesmerizing and filled with power as she looked down at the rows of people who were wearing round phosphorescent orange stickers on their shirts or bodices. As the light from the spotlight grew more intense, a fine sheen of sweat began to coat her face and stain the front of her lovely gold silk sheath. At one point as the sick kept coming, she seemed to sway and a white-clad bodyguard stepped forward to catch her. She nodded as though to say she was all right and *healed* three more people before she began to sag gracefully to the floor. Once again, the bodyguard came to her rescue, sweeping her up in his arms then kneeling on the floor with her as a pretty young woman in a long pale green dress stepped forward to wash Bolivar's face with a white cloth.

Oh you're good, baby, Fallon thought as he watched the crowd go still until Bolivar was once more on her feet, bravely continuing to minister to her followers as the two bodyguards stood close should she fall again. Carney people had a term for someone like her. They called them sky grafters, and watching Bolivar do her thing, Fallon knew that was exactly what she was—a grafter of the particularly mercenary sort.

As the last limping old man left the stage—two hours after the pageant began—Bolivar held up her hands again, silencing the crowd.

"I am weary, my Brothers and Sisters. So weary and ill at heart at seeing all the tragedy and evil that has befallen my beloved ones." A crystal tear tracked down her lovely cheek. "It grieves the heart inside my breast to see such travail thrust upon the believers, but I will strive until my last to bring health back to these sorely put-upon children of God."

"Amen." The chorus was low and heartfelt and handkerchiefs were plied throughout the crowd.

"But, my Brothers and Sisters, it takes a lot of love offerings to keep the word out here," he heard Bolivar say. "Nothing in this life is free except the blessings of our Savior, Jesus Christ."

"Amen!" the crowd responded.

"I hate to ask you to help me forward my ministry to those who are most in need of it, but without your help and aid it could not be done."

Heads nodded as hands moved to pockets and pocketbooks. The faithful knew what was needed.

"So dig deep, I beg you, so I can continue to spread His word and His healing among you."

The choir broke into an upbeat tune as Bolivar slumped against one of her bodyguards and he carried her to the only chair on the stage—a gilt-framed, red velvet monstrosity that more closely resembled an electric chair than a throne. There she slumped with a hand to her forehead, seeming to gasp for breath as her followers filled the collection plates being passed among them.

Fallon snorted and left, walking out into the hot Georgia night. There were workers milling around the tent and he thought they were most likely fifty-milers, green help who hadn't made a fifty-mile jump beyond where the tent was at that moment. That he thought of them in carney language seemed right for that was exactly what this was—a carnival with Bolivar talking up the marks, drawing them in to the show.

If he had thought the noise had been loud before the revival, the volume and excitement had surely doubled as the marks made for their cars and trucks. The joy of the Holy Spirit was upon their faces, the jubilation coming through in their voices. They had seen the power of the Lord at work in the healings and they were still misty-eyed from watching the fallen being redeemed once they'd professed their belief in God. Just watching them made Fallon physically ill for he knew they were being bilked, duped, and there had been nothing holy that had happened inside that tent. Bolivar was simply using them and that rankled him so badly he wanted to spit.

He had not grown up with religion as a central part of his life, but he had come to it late. His Irish heritage had taken him to a Catholic church and to a priest who had given him one-on-one instructions in the faith of his father. At the age of twenty-five he had been confirmed in that faith. He had embraced it wholeheartedly, but that faith was constantly at war with the killing side of him. He had learned over the years to compartmentalize the things he knew to be outside the realm of organized religion—like *An Fear Liath Mor*—because he needed the peace and serenity only his adopted faith could offer him. He knew there was never peace in a Reaper's soul unless he embraced something much larger than himself and overlooked the true evil that existed all around him.

What Bolivar was doing was twisting the emotions and the needs of her flock for her own personal gain and that pissed him off to no end.

And there she was coming toward him with her four white-suited bodyguards walking one in front, one behind and one to either side of her to keep the faithful from coming near her. Those among the faithful who wanted to touch her, speak to her, profess their love and respect for her were being stiff-armed aside as she walked with head down and hands clasped demurely in front of her, the long skirt of her gold sheath swinging gracefully with each step she took. Behind walked her Sensitives—one beautiful girl in her twenties and a handsome young man about the same age, both dressed in white.

Fallon pulled his hands from his pockets since he'd already spotted the operatives from the Exchange making their way toward Bolivar and her entourage. He recognized both of the men since they were often his sparring partners at the gym. A wicked smile plucked at his lips.

"'The coming of the lawless one will be in accordance with the work of Satan displayed in all kinds of counterfeit miracles, signs and wonders'," the burlier of the two yelled at Bolivar. "Second Thessalonians, chapter two, verse nine!"

Bolivar winced but continued on, surreptitiously glancing at the bodyguard on her right.

"And in second Timothy, chapter four, verse three, it says, 'For the time will come when they will not endure sound doctrine; but after their own lusts shall they heap to themselves teachers, having itching ears'," the second man quoted from the bible. "More like itchy palms with you. You are a harlot, a deceiver, a false prophet, Mignon Bolivar!"

Three of the bodyguards broke away from Bolivar and started toward the shouting men. Fallon stopped and folded his arms over his chest. This was going to be good.

One by one the bodyguards were soundly trounced by the two operatives, thrown about the ground as though they were no more than chaff from wheat in a mighty wind. Noses were bloodied, eyes blackened and not a single punch landed upon the operatives who used their burly strength to break arms and jaws and severely roust the next two bodyguards sent in to accost them.

"'Beloved, do not believe every spirit, but test the spirits, whether they are of God...' That comes from the first verse of first John, chapter four," the first man shouted to the group of horrified onlookers who had congregated around the fight. "This woman is evil. She is not what you think she is. She is fleecing you!"

Several workers rushed forward but they fell like dominoes before the two bible-verse-spouting men clad in plaid shirts and dirty blue jeans. A whirlwind of fists met anyone who dared come too close or even looked as though they wanted to take umbrage with what the men were shouting.

"'And he doeth great wonders, so that he maketh fire come down from heaven on the earth in the sight of men, and deceiveth them that dwell on the earth by the means of those miracles which he had power to do in the sight of the beast.' Revelations, chapter thirteen, verses thirteen and fourteen!'" the second man said, pointing a rigid finger at Bolivar. "You will burn in hell for deceiving these good people!"

Bolivar was staring wide-eyed at the men, her remaining bodyguard blocking their approach to her. She was looking about frantically, no doubt searching for one of her people to put a stop to the taunts. Her gaze passed over Fallon, stopped then came back to him and held.

Just as he knew it would since the subliminal message that he would be her savior, her protector, that he had been sent, was even then weaving its way through her mind.

"Be careful using your powers," the Supervisor had warned him. "There could be a receiver among her people. When you send, send only to your target and shield that transmission carefully."

"You need me and only me. You can trust me and only me," Fallon directed to her.

She gave him a pleading look as she clung to her remaining bodyguard.

Fallon nodded slightly and headed toward the larger of the two disruptors.

"'To the law and to the testimony—if they speak not according to this word, it is because there is no light in them'," the first man shouted, arms raised to the heavens.

"That's enough," Fallon said.

The burly man spun around to face Fallon. A mean look entered the man's pale gray eyes and he took a powerhouse swing at Fallon, who ducked beneath the punch and drove his fist into the man's solar plexus. A loud whomp of sound accompanied the jab and the burly man bent over, stumbling back from the power of the hit.

What followed was a spectacle of pure masculine strength as Fallon used every boxing, martial arts and street brawling technique he'd ever learned to take the two men down. They rushed him and he stepped aside with a savage jab to a jaw or a wicked kick. He used his fists like bludgeons to meet their own punches, blocking each except one that landed brutally to the side of his face, staggering him.

But he didn't go down beneath the dual onslaught. He executed the superb training he had learned at the hands and feet of the burly man to defeat him — although the outcome of the fight was a foregone conclusion even before it began.

Fallon was enjoying himself and his opponents were taking a beating that sprayed blood and darkened eyes. He was working off the anger he felt toward Bolivar and her sideshow, and the anxiety he felt at having left Keenan with Breslin. Toward the end, he wasn't pulling his punches and neither were they yet he still managed to put them down — the last one with a roundhouse kick that sent the man to the ground.

From out of the crowd rushed six men he knew were operatives who waved away Bolivar's workers. They picked up the beaten men and started dragging them away.

"They're not right in the head," one man told Bolivar. "They're our kin. We'll see to them!"

"Where is the law when you need it?" a woman yelled from the crowd. "Them men need to be put in jail!"

That was the last thing the operatives needed, Fallon thought, and if they were left to Bolivar's people, might not survive the night.

"The law is out there on the highway directing traffic," someone said with a snort. "That's more important to them than seeing to Mother Bolivar's safety!"

"Somebody run get a policeman," a young African-American woman told them. "You men leave those rabble rousers right where they are!" Her words were ignored.

The men who were taking the unconscious fighters away looked big and powerful enough to make mincemeat out of anyone who tried to stop them, so people simply moved out of the way, wedging back in a silent wave.

Fallon's knuckles were bleeding, aching savagely and he shook them, put a hand up to his cheek, knowing the skin had split when he'd been hit. He hoped no one noticed the wound had healed almost instantly or would wonder when no bruise formed. He couldn't let anyone see his knuckles either, for in a matter of moments, they too would show no signs of being injured thanks to his Reaper constitution. Looking around, he didn't see Bolivar, her untouched bodyguard or the two Sensitives. Gritting his teeth for he hoped his performance with the two operatives hadn't been in vain, he dusted off the legs of his jeans and started for the parking lot.

A heavy hand fell on his shoulder and he whipped around— shrugging it off as he brought his fists up.

"Easy there, dude. I'm just here to deliver a message," the man stated, hands up and out to the side.

"Yeah, like what?" Fallon snapped.

"Mother Bolivar would like to see you."

Fallon narrowed his eyes suspiciously. "Why?"

"I expect she wants to thank you for your help and to see if you're all right," the man gave Fallon a quick once-over. "You seem fine to me, but you know how women are."

Fallon pretended to think it over—turning his head toward the parking lot for a long moment. He looked back at the man then shrugged. "I ain't got nowhere to be and no time to be there."

"Right this way," the man said, sweeping a hand toward the backyard.

Sauntering behind and to the right of his guide, Fallon swept his hooded gaze back and forth, watching everything, taking in all that was around him. Those he passed nodded respectfully to him and he knew already word of him was filtering through the workers. A few men stepped well away, but every woman he passed batted her eyes and licked her lips as though he were the main course at the evening meal.

"Damned lot lizards," the man beside him quipped. "More trouble than they'll ever be worth."

"Some look to be possum belly queens to me," Fallon replied. "Wouldn't touch one of 'em with a titanium-lined Johnny bag."

"Where was your last show?"

"Out in cornhusker land," Fallon replied. "Worked the motordrome circuit." He snorted disgustedly. "Last place was in Altoona, Iowa."

"Well, now I would have pegged you for something different altogether."

"I filled in on the goon squad if that's what you mean, but I damned sure wasn't wearing no fucking white suits."

The man laughed, stopped and offered his hand. "Ollie," he said. "Ollie Rankin." He slapped Fallon on the back with his free hand. "I knew you were one of us. Could smell the sawdust in your blood."

Fallon half smiled as he shook Ollie's hand but didn't let it reach his eyes, which he kept cold and lethal.

"Mother Bolivar lost her right-hand man a few nights ago, and the goons she's got shadowing her now are next to worthless," Ollie reported, releasing Fallon's hand.

"So I noticed. Anyone who could let a rube beat the shit out of him ain't worth much in my book." He fell into step beside Ollie as the older man began walking again. "What happened to her main man?"

"Nipped by the cops on a concealed weapons charge. Stupid fuck. He knew better. Swears he wasn't carrying, but it was his Glock he was carrying on him. Says he don't know how it got there." Ollie hawked up a glob of phlegm and spat it out. "Stupid dumb fuck."

"So what's the gig here? She walking on water down there at the creek?"

Ollie's congenial grin slipped. "Don't be smarting off about Mother Bolivar. That is not a wise thing to do, my friend. Watch your mouth with her. She might offer you a position, and if you're smart, you'll take it."

"How's the end?"

"You can pull down a G-note a week as her primary shadow," Ollie said. "Second string rakes in half that much."

Fallon whistled. "She must be scoring it big to shell out that kind of money."

"This is a legit operation. Mother Bolivar is doing the Lord's work."

"Sure she is," Fallon scoffed. "That's why those two rubes were here tonight. They were thanking her for her evangelism."

"She has her detractors, her enemies," Ollie admitted. "Even Christ had those who called him a charlatan."

"How often does she get attacked like that?"

"Let's just say you'll earn your take..." He frowned. "I didn't catch your name."

"Didn't pitch it to you," Fallon said. "It's Robin Marks."

Ollie chuckled. "Yeah, and I'm the Prince of Siam."

"That's my name, like it or not. You can blame my mama," Fallon said with a shrug. It was a utility name among carnies, used when a man didn't want to give his real name.

They had arrived at the most expensive motor home in the backyard—the one he'd known would belong to Bolivar. Ollie rapped lightly and the white-clad bodyguard who had accompanied Bolivar to the motor home opened the door. He stepped back to allow the two men in.

She was sitting barefoot on the sofa with her long, smooth legs stretched out in front of her. Gone was the gold silk sheath and in its place was a short white terrycloth robe. Her rich black hair had been plaited into one long braid that rested over her left shoulder. In her hand was a tall glass of amber-colored liquid. She smiled at him to show straight, very white teeth.

"Mother Bolivar, this is Robin Marks," Ollie introduced.

Bolivar's eyes twinkled at hearing the name. "My knight in shining armor," she said, raising the glass to him. "Thank you."

"My pleasure, ma'am," Fallon said.

"Rob's a fellow showman," Ollie said then quickly added, "like me."

"Is that so?" she asked before taking a small sip of her beverage.

Fallon stared into eyes the color of dark, rich coffee, framed by stunningly beautiful features set in a café au lait face, and could hear the wheels turning in her head. He used a strong psychic nudge to push past any reservations she might have concerning him, and when she ran her tongue over her upper lip, he knew he was successful. Her mind was tight but he found a crack and slipped inside as smoothly and easily as water through a sieve. She reached out to pat the chair that stood at a ninety-degree angle to the sofa.

"Come sit by me, Sir Robin," she said in a throaty voice, "and let's talk a spell."

Fallon walked to the chair and took a seat, lifting one long leg to cross it at the knee of the other. He rested his hands on the chair arms and gave her a steady look.

"Sweet operation you have here," he said.

She thrust her lips out in a slight pout. "I enjoy doing the Lord's work," she said.

"Very lucratively if the surroundings are any indication."

Her eyes turned glacial. "I'll have you know I'm..."

"Raking in money hand over fist, but you need a man at your back to shadow you, baby, and if you work your cards right, you can have him," Fallon interrupted. "For a price." He grinned nastily. "I'm not cheap, but I can be had."

There was residual suspicion in her mind and he let his psychic fingers do the walking through that suspicious organ, opening a slight furrow to drop in the seeds of trust, covered them with a thin layer of belief then gently watered them with a fine sprinkle of certainty that he was exactly what he appeared to be. While he was roaming the garden of her subconscious, he looked for any signs that she might have psi powers of her own, but he found nothing to indicate she did. Neither did he find any image of whatever it was she had sent to kill those who went up against her.

"Where were you before you came here?" she asked, and he knew the matter had been settled in her mind that he was one of them, though he also knew she'd check on his story, one from the Exchange that was airtight.

"Altoona, Iowa, at a little Podunk amusement park," he answered.

She frowned. "Why?"

He shrugged. "Got D.Q.'d at my last gig. Needed the money and it was there."

"What did you do to get disqualified?"

"Fucking the boss's wife is not the best way to win friends and influence enemies, and before you ask, I'm not saying who, where or when that happened. You don't need to know."

Her dark eyes roamed over him. "I can see where you might tempt a woman to cheat on her wedding vows."

The right side of his mouth quirked up. "I'm very good at what I do."

She wet her lips again. "I just bet you are."

He watched her lean over and put her glass on the coffee table in front of the sofa, and then she scooted down on the sofa, the white terrycloth robe rucking up her firm thighs.

"Why don't you come over here and show me how good you really are, Sir Robin," she said.

Fallon shook his head. "I'm not looking to be laid, *cannyssagh*. All I want is a job."

One perfectly sculpted black brown arched. "What if you could have both, but it took one to get the other?" She raised one knee and the edge of the robe slid down to the crease of her legs to barely hide the V shadowed there. Idly, she stroked her long, caramel-colored fingers along the inside of her thigh.

Fallon lowered his leg to the floor, stood and moved over to the couch. "You want me?"

172

Bolivar reached out to run a fingernail down the fly of his jeans, her eyes never leaving his. "What do you think?" She turned her hand so she could slide her fingers between his legs to cup him.

"I think an evangelical preacher-woman shouldn't be groping a strange man in her trailer. What would the faithful say?"

She tugged at his crotch, which had thickened noticeably. "They'd say she was a horny as hell preacher-woman who had a right to some enjoyment in life."

He batted her hand away and leaned over to untie the belt of her robe, flicking the two sides apart. His gaze slithered over her nakedness and he had to admit she was a gorgeous woman with a killer body. Firm and taut, her café au lait skin was as smooth as silk. Her breasts were small—almost conical—but the nipples were large, a dark chocolate color. With a small, neatly tucked waist and gently flaring hips to go with the long legs, she was a prime specimen of dusky womanhood.

"Well?" she asked, resting her hands to either side of her head on the sofa pillow. "What do you think?"

"I think you're a beautiful woman and you damned well know it," he replied.

She raised her other knee and then let them fall wide apart in invitation. "Then what are you waiting for?"

He looked away from the manicured curls at the apex of her thighs. "Like I said, I'm not cheap, but I can be had. It'll take fifteen hundred a week and my own trailer. I don't bunk with anyone."

"Not even the boss lady?" she asked, flicking her tongue along her top lip.

"After the shit I stepped in?" He shook his head. "No thanks."

"Show me what you got, stud, and we'll see about the amenities," she said, writhing seductively to tempt him.

"Business up front," he said then placed his hand over her crotch, his middle finger grazing the opening he wasn't surprised to find oozing juices. He slid his hand farther under her so the tip of his finger touched her anus. "Pleasure later."

"Twelve hundred and..."

"Fifteen," he corrected, "and my own trailer." He rubbed his finger around her opening. "And the ride of your life."

She held her arms up to him. "Show me and it's a deal."

"Uh-uh. Deal first."

Bolivar lowered her arms and stared at him for a long moment. "You'd better be worth every goddamned cent, stud," she warned. "Fifteen and your own place."

Fallon's face didn't change by even a flicker of an eyelash as he withdrew his hand from between her legs and reached up to unbutton his shirt halfway down before tugging it free of his jeans. He shrugged it from his shoulders and watched her eyes widened as she took in the heavily muscled and furred chest. Working his belt open, he unhooked the waistband of his jeans, unzipped them then sat down on the sofa beside her.

"Move over, babe," he said, wriggling back so he'd have room to take off his boots. When he stood, he watched her avid gaze lower to his crotch. As he pushed his jeans down his hips and his cock sprang free, she groaned.

"Now that is a helluva bargaining tool," she said, licking her lips.

He kicked his jeans aside, said nothing to her remark and simply covered her body with his, slamming his mouth over hers in a kiss that made her tremble beneath him. While she was wrapping her arms around him, he slipped once more into her mind—the part where the libido held sway—and sought out the best way to proceed with her. He wasn't at all surprised to find her interest, what turned her on, was rough sex and that was what he intended to give her.

* * * * *

Keenan read the paragraph again—just as she had read it the five other times—but it made no sense to her and she pitched the book aside, releasing a long, irritated sigh as she unfolded her legs and propelled herself from the sofa. She was antsy, uneasy and her chest felt as though a ton of bricks were crushing her. Going into the kitchen, she snatched open the fridge door and stood there looking at the shelves.

"Shit," she said, and slammed the door, but after opening the pantry, she realized there was nothing in it she really felt like eating either.

Glancing at her wristwatch, she saw that it was after 9 p.m. A trip into town might clear her head and shopping always perked her up. So after slipping on her loafers and grabbing her purse, she started out the door.

"*Keenan.*"

His voice was soft but as clear as though he were standing right beside her, whispering into her ear.

"Yeah, lineman," she answered.

"*I love you.*"

In those three words she heard a world of guilt and grief and knew. She put her forehead to the door panel, squeezed her eyelids closed.

"I love you too," she said, her heart breaking, a sob catching in her throat.

There was a soft touch against her mind as though he had reached out to stroke her head and then he was gone.

A single tear fell from Keenan's eye.

It mirrored a tear that at that very moment was sliding down another cheek in Georgia.

Chapter Twelve

ත

"Hell no," Fallon stated when Bolivar laid the white linen suit over the chair. "I'm not wearing that piece of shit."

"All my security men wear…"

"I said no," he snapped, eyes flashing and jaw clenched.

Bolivar lifted her chin. "And if I insist?"

"If you do, I'm outta here, baby," he told her.

He was standing in the living room of his new accommodations that had belonged to her ex-head of security wearing nothing but a pair of tight black boxer shorts that hugged him like a second skin.

"Just what do you expect to wear? I have an image to maintain and I'll not have you walking ahead of me…"

"I walk beside you, not ahead of you," he said, cutting her off. "I want to be where I can protect you. If I'm ahead of you, someone could grab you from the back or the side."

Her lips peeled back from her teeth. "All right, but you are *not* going to wear those dirty, torn jeans I saw you in yesterday!"

"I clean up nicely, baby," he drawled. "And I'll be on your doorstep just before the sun goes down."

He had learned that she usually slept until noon but rarely came out of her motor home before two or three in the afternoon. Today she'd made an exception by personally bringing over the hideous suit for him to wear as he escorted her to the creek at sunset for the mass baptisms of her newly professed faithful. He knew she had another reason for coming to his trailer, but he had no intention of allowing her to paw him as he knew she had planned.

"Don't forget who's the man here, *Robin*," she said, underscoring the name.

176

"I won't, Mother Bolivar," he said, and reached out to grab her, jerk her to him. "*I* am the man, baby."

Before she could protest, he kissed her long and hard, rubbing his lower body against hers lewdly, thrusting his thigh between her legs to slide it along her crotch as he swept his tongue deep into her mouth. She clung to him as though he were a lifesaver, seemingly greedy for his kiss and anything he was willing to give her. When he moved back from her, took her arms and pulled them from his neck, he gave her a brutal grin.

"Now scat so I can shower and shave. You want me to look presentable to your followers, don't you?"

Heavy-lidded, she rubbed her palms over his chest. "I could join you in that shower," she suggested.

"Yeah, and we both know what else will get joined," he said. He shook his head. "Not now." He turned her around and swatted her shapely ass. "Now get."

She reluctantly went to the door, stopping to look around at him with such blatant lust glittering in her eyes it shocked him.

"You're mine after the show," she said. "All night long. I'm going to wear your tight little ass out, boy."

Fallon let nothing show on his face as she blew him a kiss and left, but the moment the door closed, he put a hand to his mouth to wipe away her kiss.

* * * * *

The faithful were standing twenty deep on the banks of the creek as the sun lowered in the western sky. Fans were being plied vigorously for the heat was stifling, the air so thick and clammy it scorched the lungs. Torches were being lit by the workers and the pathway that led from the creek to the backyard where Bolivar's motor home was being zealously guarded by a quartet of brawny men in white suits was also lined with flickering torches, the smoke from which barely moved in the still night.

Fallon straightened his tie, turned his head sideways to look at the earring dangling in his left ear and nodded approvingly. He was dressed in an outfit he knew she'd never have approved had

177

he told her of it, but he also knew once she saw him in it, she would melt just as every other woman who saw did. Sensing her growing anger that he had yet to appear at her doorstep, he closed his eyes and cloaked himself in the invisibility that was second nature to his kind. He could pass by hundreds of people and not a single one would notice him. Easing the door open, he slipped out, his boot heels making no sound at all on the compacted earth as he made his way to her trailer.

"Where the hell is he?" Bolivar snarled, shooting her furious glower on a hapless Ollie.

Ollie opened the door and nearly fainted when he found the man he'd been waiting for standing on the top step. He jumped back, eyes wide as he took in what Marks was wearing. Guiltily, he looked behind him. "Ah, Mother Bolivar? He's here."

Bolivar opened her mouth to shout again, but the object of her ire strolled into the trailer and the words died in her throat. She gaped at the ruggedly handsome, supremely virile and overpoweringly male vision who came to stand before her.

"My God," she whispered.

From the toes of his brightly polished black leather boots, up the matte finish of the tight black leather pants, past the black belt with the pewter rectangular Celtic hound knotwork buckle, over the long-sleeved black silk shirt buttoned at the neck and accentuated with a thin black leather tie, to the silver grim reaper with crossed scythes earring dangling in his ear and the black felt western hat with its silver braided band, the brim cocked low over his forehead, the man was breathtaking. He exuded sensuality and power, and the unrelieved vista of black clothing made the amber of his eyes glow like lanterns in his chiseled face. He looked tough and he looked perfectly capable of breaking a man in half if the need arose.

"Do you approve?" he asked in a low, silky voice.

Bolivar had to swallow before she could answer. Her eyes were devouring him, roaming over him like newly hatched vipers. Her breathing was so loud he could hear it, and the scent her body was giving off made his nostrils flare.

"Yes," she whispered. "Oh yes."

He went to her and crooked his arm. "Ready?"

She slid her hand over his silk sleeve to link her arm with his. Staring into his mesmerizing gaze, she felt her womb clench. "Yes."

"There won't be any trouble tonight," he said. "I guarantee it."

"Who would dare mess with you?" she asked.

"Only a fool," he replied, "or someone with a death wish."

She drew in a breath. "You would kill for me, Robin?"

He didn't hesitate. "In a heartbeat."

One look at the hard glint in his eyes and it was easy to see a man such as this could take — and most likely had — someone's life. There was a brutal set to his jawline, and the way his full bottom lip stretched taut suggested he could be as savage as necessary when violence was required. His eyes moved constantly as he surveyed the crowd — lingering now and then on an individual before moving on. There was an aggressive sense about him that he was on guard, primed, and only a hair trigger away from erupting.

"I feel safe with you," she whispered.

Two hours later, naked before him, the evangelical leader of tens of thousands of devout followers sank to the floor at his feet and put her hands to the buttons of his pants, staring up at him with a rapt expression that echoed those of the faithful she had only moments before baptized in the creek.

Fallon stared down at her for a moment, but when she freed him from his pants, he raised his head and stared across the living room of the motor home. His eyelids flickered as her mouth encircled him and he put his hands to either side of her head as she plied her lips upon his hardening shaft. The only thought going through his mind was a single word — unfaithful — and it ate away at his soul as her mouth nibbled on his flesh.

* * * * *

Keenan turned over to turn out the light and her gaze went to the bedside clock. It was well past midnight and she had not heard from Fallon since the evening before. She had thought he would at least touch her with his mind to let her know he was all right, that he loved her. With the light out, she lay there in the darkness and stared up at the ceiling, sending her thoughts to him.

"Fallon?" she whispered.

There was no answer, but there came back to her a heavy sense of shame and guilt and overpowering remorse.

"I know, lineman," she said, sensing his hurt. "I know."

She could feel his wounded pride and understood that it cut deep into his very soul. He was like a lost, confused child, but he refused to cry out for help. She had the sensation that he was striving to hold it together so she slowly slipped out of his subconscious and turned over to her side.

There would be no sleep for her that night.

Chapter Thirteen

ନ୍ଦ

Fallon was restless and in a foul mood as he leaned with his ankles crossed against his bike in the parking lot of the I-75 rest area near Gainesville, Florida. He'd been with Bolivar for over a week and the subtle psychic pushes he kept pressing on her had made him indispensable in her eyes. Wherever she went, she insisted he be right beside her, dressed in unrelieved black outfits she told him made him look meaner than a junk yard dog.

"I am meaner than a junk yard dog," he'd growled.

"No one would dare accost me with you at my side," she said, and that proved to be true. Despite the faithful venturing forward to bestow love and adoration on her, they kept their distance, the tall, muscular man beside her a strong deterrent not to come too close.

The ministry—as Bolivar referred to it—had stayed in Macon for three more days after Robin Marks had joined it. Now the cavalcade of motor homes and semis and deuce-and-a-half trucks were on the highway, making the next jump—carnie talk for the move to the next engagement—to Ocala, Florida, where they would spend a week before heading to Dothan, Alabama.

"I'm going to buy a trailer for your bike when we get to Kissimmee," Bolivar said as she walked up and handed him a cold bottle of spring water. "I want you in the trailer with me."

He unscrewed the top of the bottle, tipped it up and took a long swallow, keenly aware of her avid gaze locked on his neck. When he lowered the bottle, he wiped the back of his hand across his mouth.

"Why?" he asked in a hard tone, looking over the top of his dark Ray-Bans. "So you can fuck me at every twenty-mile marker?"

181

Bolivar frowned. "Don't use language like that out in public, Robin," she ordered.

Fallon glanced around. The only people near enough to hear were all part of their group. He snorted, showing his contempt of her demand.

"I mean it," she snapped. "Show me the respect I'm due."

One of the things he'd learned about Mignon Bolivar was that she liked him to talk dirty to her while they were screwing, but only then. She also liked the sex rough and thought nothing of handcuffing him to her bed and riding him for hours on end. The woman was an expert at getting a man hard and keeping him there until he was begging for release. So far, he'd been able to refrain from doing so after the one and only time at the beginning of their relationship that he'd shamed himself by pleading. Now he stoically endured her prolonged bouts of what she considered love play, refusing to beg for her to end the sexual abuse. Sooner or later she lost interest and would allow him to come.

"Did you hear me, Robin? And take those sunglasses off so I can see your eyes!"

Pushing the shades to the top of his head, he sighed. "Yeah, baby, I heard you," he said, screwing the top back on the bottle. He uncrossed his legs, straightened then turned to stow the bottle in the tank bag.

Bolivar ran a hand over the black T-shirt that was molded to his broad back. "Why don't I ride with you for a while?" she asked.

"I don't have another helmet," he said, not wanting her with him.

"Florida doesn't have a helmet law for anyone over twenty-one," she said. "I checked."

"You would," he mumbled, knowing the choice had been taken from him.

"What?"

"I said you could if you want to."

She slipped an arm around his waist and leaned against him. "I could do you right here, right now, you look so hot," she whispered.

"I am hot," he said, shrugging her away. "It's over ninety out here."

She looked hurt that he could dismiss her so easily, but he just stared at her, not giving an inch.

"I just heard on the radio that hurricane made landfall in Miami," Ollie said as he came strolling up. "Best we get on down the road before the weather starts getting persnickety."

"I'm gonna ride with Robbie for a bit," Bolivar stated.

"Suit yourself, ma'am," Ollie agreed. He gave Fallon a commiserating look since every man and woman in the ministry knew what was going on. "But we could run into some rain."

"I won't melt," she stated.

"No, ma'am, but what about your hair?"

Fallon's lips twitched with barely suppressed amusement. He hadn't thought about that. Bolivar's pride and joy were the expensive human hair wigs she wore over her own short-cropped tight curls. He'd only seen her once without a wig, and after running his palm over the soft curls had made the mistake of telling her he liked the nappy texture. She'd slapped him so hard she'd split his bottom lip then slapped him even harder a second time, screaming that he was never to use that word again.

"My hair?" she repeated, putting a hand to the waist-length weave of crocheted curls. She glanced at Fallon, registered the mocking look on his face. "What's so funny, Robin?"

"I didn't think about your wig-hat, baby," he said in a smooth voice. "The wind will take that thing off before we're five miles down the interstate."

"So I can't ride with you," she said.

"Guess not," he said with a nonchalant shrug then threw a long leg over his bike and heeled up the kickstand.

"That's what you think, you bastard," she snarled, and whipped off the wig, tossing it savagely to Ollie.

Those among the caravan who were watching tried to hide their shock at seeing Mother Bolivar as she really was. They were gawking with mouths dropped open, but when she climbed onto the back of the motorcycle, there was stunned silence.

Fallon felt her fingernails digging into his sides and twisted around to give her a brutal look. "Stop it. Right now."

She drove her nails deeper into his flesh. "Make me."

His eyes turned glacial. "I don't think you want me to snatch you off this bike and beat the shit out of you right here in front of everyone, but if you don't take your fucking claws out of me, bitch, I fucking will, even if I go to jail for it!" he hissed.

She raised her chin. "And you think the men here would let you do something like that?" she challenged.

"They might take me down, but not before I break your nose, your jaw and knock out a few teeth," he stated. His eyes narrowed into lethal slits. "You wanna see just how fast I can move after you let loose a single scream for help? See how much damage I can do before they stop me? I've never hit a woman in my life, but for you, I'd make an exception."

She held his malevolent glare for a second or two longer then relaxed her fingers. "You're going to pay for this tonight, Robbie. I promise you, you will," she swore.

"Yeah, like I'm shaking in my goddamned boots," he shot back, lowering his sunglasses and turning around to switch on the motor. He revved the engine loudly, backed the bike out of the parking slot and peeled out of the rest area, zipping narrowly ahead of a sixteen-wheeler as he melded onto the interstate. A blast of the semi's horn brought Fallon's hand up in a nasty salute before the bike shot forward with a vengeance.

"You're going to get us killed!" Bolivar screamed in his ear. Her arms were locked around his waist, her chest pressed tight to his back.

"We all gotta die someday," he said under his breath.

* * * * *

Four Days Later

184

Keenan was just as restless—if not as angry as her partner—for she'd just learned it would be another week before she would be allowed to join Fallon. Between them, the Supervisor and Breslin had decided that speaking in tongues was something they needed to add to the repertoire of strange and mysterious abilities Tandy Lynch possessed and only Breslin would be able to translate her words. Coming up with a pseudo-language that would allow Keenan and Breslin to communicate when she was "filled with the Holy Spirit" had seemed like a good idea at the time but was proving to be harder than she could have imagined.

"You aren't concentrating," Breslin complained as he threw down his notebook of words and phrases they'd created.

"I'm tired, Zack," she replied. "We've been at this for hours and I'm just tired."

"There can't be any room for error, Kiki," Breslin reminded her. "These people are dangerous. If they find out we're playing them, they won't hesitate to sic whatever that thing is they've got on us." He narrowed his eyes. "I don't know about you, but I'm not ready to meet my maker yet."

Keenan released a long, weary breath. She had a headache, her stomach was growling and she was nervous because she hadn't heard from Fallon in six days. The last communication anyone at the Exchange received from him had come just before the ministry left Georgia and that had been several days past. A quick phone call to a number in New York had been rerouted to the Exchange in Iowa. All Fallon had said was they were on their way to Florida and nothing more. She was worried about him and concerned that he hadn't sent her at least a reassuring touch from his mind to hers for nearly a week.

"All right. Obviously your mind is on the prick," Breslin said, showing his irritation. "Get the hell out of here. We'll take this up again tomorrow." He slammed his briefcase shut, snatched it up and stalked out of the room.

Keenan winced as he slammed the training room door shut behind him. Sometimes she forgot he could read her thoughts as easily as Fallon could, and she knew she had to work on that. It

185

wouldn't do to have Breslin privy to the inner turmoil roiling around inside her. When the door opened again, she put a tight clamp on her thoughts and turned, expecting Breslin.

"Matty," she said, relieved. "When did you get back?"

"About an hour ago," he said, coming over to give her a hug. He'd been at a convention in Las Vegas since Fallon had been gone and she'd missed talking to him.

"I'm glad you're back," she told him. "I could really use a friend right now."

Matty's eyebrows shot up. "What happened? Is Misha all right?"

"Yeah, as far as I know. I haven't heard from him in days but he checked in with command and things appear okay."

"But you're not so sure."

"The last contact I had from him, he wasn't in a good place mentally," she said. "I think the assignment is getting to him."

"You mean getting close to his target is getting to him," Matty suggested, searching her eyes.

"I think he believed he could handle it, but the bonding…" She cocked a shoulder.

"Well, well, well," Matty said, grinning. "You think the big dog is feeling the tether and not coping well with the limitations?"

"Maybe," she mumbled, wanting to tell Matty she was getting feelings of shame from Fallon but knowing her partner wouldn't want her saying such a thing about him.

"He'll maintain, Kiki," Matty said, using the nickname Breslin had given her. "No need to worry about him." He looked around. "Are you through for the day, or is the big, bad taskmaster coming back?"

"No, I'm through," she said, and started gathering up her notebooks.

"Then let's go get some supper and I'll take you to the show in Grinnell. That new space pirate flick is playing."

"I don't know…"

"It'll take your mind off everything. All work and no play and all that," Matty insisted.

She'd been working hard over the last week and it would be another week before she'd see Fallon. Worrying about him was all she could do at the moment, and that was taking its toll on her. She hadn't been sleeping very well and couldn't concentrate. Perhaps what she needed was to relax and unwind for a few hours.

"Okay," she said. "Let me go ditch this stuff in my locker and I'll be ready to go."

"Fantastic!" Matty said. "I'll meet you in the lobby. How's that?"

"That'll work," she said.

When she met him later in the lobby, he was standing there with one hand behind his back. As she came up to him, he brought his hand around and in it was a single deep red rose.

"For you, my beauty," he said, extending it to her.

Keenan accepted the rose then gasped as a thorn pricked her thumb.

"Oh sweetie, I'm sorry!" Matty said. He took out his handkerchief. "Let me see."

"It's nothing," she said, but he reached for her injured finger and blotted the drop of blood.

"Damned florist," Matty said. "They're supposed to snap off the thorns."

"They just missed one, that's all," she said. Her thumb was stinging so she drew on the injury again. "No harm done."

"Well, I intend to give them a piece of what's left of my mind tomorrow," he told her. He stuffed the handkerchief in his pocket then draped his arm around her. "I promise I won't let anything else hurt you tonight."

Uncomfortable with his arm around her, Keenan started to move away but his hold tightened and he started walking, chatting a mile a minute about the movie they would be seeing that evening. As he led her out of the building and to his car, she realized the man walking beside her was acting as though this were a date and not two friends having supper and taking in a flick.

"Matty," she said when he opened the car door for her. "This isn't going to lead to anything. You know that, don't you?"

She watched some strange emotion flicker across his face but then he grinned.

"You're off limits," he said. "The hound dog made that very clear."

"Just so there's no misunderstanding," she said, still uneasy with the way he was looking at her.

"Nope. I see things very clearly, sweetie." He shut her door then walked around the front of the car to the driver's side.

Keenan looked down at the rose. It was beautiful — floral perfection — and the color was vibrant and the petals as soft as velvet, but that lone thorn had marred the flawlessness of the flower and her thumb still stung from the bite.

"Okay, so what do you feel in the mood for?" Matty asked as he got into the car. "Chinese, Mexican, Italian, American, what?"

"I had pizza for supper last night," she replied. "How 'bout that new Thai place in Grinnell?"

"Sounds good," he said. "The spicier the better!"

Keenan asked about his conference in Vegas and he began to wax enthusiastically about the biogenic innovations he'd been shown. As he talked, she put a hand up to her temple. Her headache had increased and she knew it was because she'd skipped lunch — not something she normally did. Her stomach was growling so loudly Matty heard it.

"Are you starving yourself, darling?" he asked.

"Breslin worked us all the way through lunch and I am famished," she admitted.

"Good," he said, nodding. "I like to take my women out on an empty stomach."

"Why's that?"

"Makes me look like a hero when I feed 'em," he said with a laugh.

She laughed and they talked about this and that until he asked her if they'd learned anything new about Mignon Bolivar.

"Oh, she's a piece of work," Keenan said. "Her real name is Francine Cook. Her grandmother Yvette was a white woman who worked kooch shows back in the forties and fifties. According to police records from Oklahoma City, she was raped by a black man and nine months later gave birth to her only child, a daughter she named Jonelle. Jonelle is Bolivar's mother."

"Still alive?"

"Yes. She and the grandmother live in Gibsontown, Florida."

"What about Bolivar's father? Do you know who he was?"

"It's a pretty good assumption that he was one of the carnival workers though Jonelle never named him. It could have been one of many although she did have a carnie marriage with a man named Bud Tolliver for about four years." She rubbed her temple where the headache had become a stabbing agony. "Francine was born to the carnie way of life and later became a talker for one of the game booths."

"Talker?"

"What most people call a carnival barker. Anyway, by the time she was twenty-four, she owned her own joint and it's a safe bet she was pulling down somewhere around a hundred grand a year, bilking unsuspecting customers—or rubes as they call them—out of thousands of dollars from rigged game booths."

Matty whistled. "Man, I'm in the wrong business."

"You and me both," Keenan agreed.

"I didn't realize carnival people made that kind of money."

"The ones good at their job do all right. You ever notice the motor homes at the fairs? Those things don't come cheap."

"No, I don't suppose they do," Matty replied. He flipped on his turn signal. "So why did she leave the carnie and become a faith healer?"

"More money obviously," Keenan said, "but African-American people in the carnies have a tough row to hoe. Carnival goers make it rough for them and the local authorities do the good old racial profiling thing to the max when a man or woman of color arrives in their town."

"So she moved on to a profession where color obviously doesn't matter."

"Desperate people who are quickly losing hope don't care about the color of your skin if you can lay your hands on them and heal," Keenan said. She put her thumb up to her mouth, annoyed that the wound was still burning. "In the guise of religion where there should be no color boundaries, Bolivar has found a perfect avenue to steal from those who are too weak, too old and too helpless to know she's conning them."

"Are you going to be okay with doing the same thing?" Matty asked quietly, flicking her a side glance as he stopped for a red light.

Keenan couldn't tell him about the powers she had been given in the Ozarks. Only three people knew. Fallon would say nothing and she was sure the Supervisor would never reveal what had transpired down there.

"I guess I'll have to be," she said. "It's better to hurt a few now than to allow Bolivar to keep on bilking hundreds more."

"And killing those who oppose her."

Keenan nodded. "Yeah. That's the most important thing." She twisted around in the seat. "What could it be she uses to do those killings, Matty? Breslin said the victims looked like they'd been put through a meat grinder. Every bone in their bodies had been broken, every organ flattened."

"Breslin thinks its some kind of supernatural entity she's controlling," Matty said. "I've seen and heard enough at the Exchange to know that's not as farfetched as an outsider would think. I mean, look at Fallon. He's not altogether human, you know?" He snapped his fingers. "Hey, that may be why you haven't heard from him in a few days."

"Why?" she asked as he pulled into the Thai restaurant.

"I'd have to look at his records to be sure, but he could be going through that three-day Transition cycle he undergoes four times a year. If that's the case, he's holed up somewhere."

"He told me about that," she said. "About the containment cell here." Her face mirrored her worry. "Do you think he'll be all right?"

"Yeah, sure. If I know Misha—and I do—he'll pretend he went on a bender. No way he'd let anyone see him like that."

Keenan shivered. "He said he never wanted me to see that side of him."

"Believe me, darling, you don't want to," Matty told her. He turned off the engine and opened his door. "Okay, let's go fill that growling tummy of yours!"

As they sat eating the spicy Thai food, Matty thought back to a very enlightening phone call he'd made a few hours earlier. Over the course of that long conversation, he had discovered a kindred soul whose objectives could be made to mesh quite well with his own. Plans had been set into motion, an agreement made, and if everything worked as Matty hoped, the woman sitting across from him would be his—and his alone—before too many months passed.

Chapter Fourteen

ౠ

He took the slap without saying a word. Took still another stinging slap, but when she drew back to hit him a third time, he'd reached his limit and caught her wrist, gripping it tightly as he jerked it to one side.

"Woman, I'm in no fucking mood for your shit," he said, shoving her away from him.

"Where the hell have you been?" Bolivar shouted.

Fallon ran a dirty hand through his dirt-streaked hair. He so wanted to tell her he'd been in a burrow underground hiding, riding out a particularly brutal Transition that had left him weak and itching to kill something. He hadn't slept in three days, he was hungry and his blood-lust was overbearing. The rabbit he'd caught earlier that morning hadn't satisfied the need for Sustenance nor had the mellow-eyed milk cow that had stood docilely while he sank his fangs into her neck and fed. He needed human blood to assuage the craving that was making him itch as though he were having a bad allergic reaction.

He also needed the vial of tenerse that would make him look—if not feel—more human. At the moment he knew he looked gaunt and hollow-eyed, pale and his hands were shaking.

"Answer me, Robbie. Where have you been?" Bolivar screeched, and doubled her fist to slam it into his back as he walked past her.

That was all he could take. The killer inside him, the savage beast that was almost always close to the surface came roaring out and he grabbed her, threw her across the room. Luckily she landed on the sofa, her eyes wide, lips parted, fear turning her caramel skin lighter still.

"Don't you fucking ever hit me again, bitch!" he warned her, stalking to the sofa and leaning over her, his lips drawn back, hands clenched in the front of her dressing gown. "I'll fucking strangle you if you do!"

He had gone to ground for his Transition with violent thoughts of beating the shit out of Bolivar crowding his head. The night after the motorcycle ride, she had scratched him so savagely he had to knock her out with a punishing psychic push to her subconscious so she wouldn't remember her attack on him or the fact his injuries healed within seconds of her delivering them. She had slapped him the moment they were alone in her motor home that evening. She'd pulled his hair, kicked and kneed him, slammed her balled fist into the side of his head and—adding insult to injury—had spat on him.

Storming out of her trailer, he had vanished in the deluge that was part of the hurricane crawling up the peninsula. He knew he was close to Transition, but the fury lightning through him had brought the cycle on earlier than it should have come. Lying naked in the ground after tearing off his clothing with only violent thoughts of sinking his fangs into Bolivar's slender throat, he had rode out the pain and the overwhelming sense of despair that always accompanied Transition. When at last he'd come back to what little humanity he had, he had crawled out of the burrow, dragging his torn and muddy clothes with him, and stood in the dying sunlight with tears running down his cheeks.

"*Keenan!*" he had screamed, dropping to his knees, burying his face in the clothing. His keening and the predatory scent of him had scared away all the nearby animals so when he was forced to hunt, only the one rabbit had not been quick enough.

And the sweet-faced cow who had wrapped her long tongue around his arm as he drank for her neck.

Now he was hovering over Bolivar and wanting nothing more than to smash her lovely face and feed from her corpse, drain her as dry as a husk, root through her organs to pilfer every last drop of blood. He could see the realization in her fearful eyes that he might well kill her then and there. He barely felt her trembling hand as she put it on his forearm.

"I'm sorry," she said. "I'm really sorry, Robbie." She stroked his arms, her lips quivering as she tried to smile at him. "I was just so worried about you."

The killing rage that had claimed him began to settle to a low simmer and he let go of her dressing gown, straightened. He desperately needed a bath for he stank to high heaven, but he needed the tenerse even more. He stumbled away from her and snatched open a drawer, pulled out a vial and a vac-syringe.

Bolivar sat up, watching him as he loaded the vac-syringe then plunged the needle into his neck. He saw her wince at the same time he did for the drug burned like liquid fire through his jugular and spread down his shoulder and chest with raking claws that made him twitch with the pain of it.

"W-What was that you took?" she asked.

"Leave me the fuck alone," he mumbled—still clutching the vial and the vac-syringe—and went lurching down the short hallway to the bedroom then into the bathroom at the rear of the motor home.

"Was it heroin?" she persisted, foolish enough to come after him. "Cocaine?" She stood framed in the doorway as he stripped out of his torn and filthy clothing. "Was it some kind of steroid?"

He reached into the large corner shower and turned the water on as hot as he could get it, steam beginning to build behind the glass door before he jerked it open and stepped inside, carrying the tenerse with him. He knew he didn't dare leave it where she could get her hands on it. He would need to hide it securely when he got out of the shower.

"Damn it, Robbie! What did you take?" she shouted.

"None of your fucking business!" he screamed at her so loud the glass door shook.

Bolivar backed away from the shower. For a long time she stood watching him bathing then walked out of the bathroom—kicking his dirty clothes aside—and started rummaging through his drawers for clean ones.

"Son of a whoring bitch," she muttered to herself. "You'd better not have been with another woman!"

She was sitting on his bed when he came out of the bath, dripping wet. Ignoring her, he flopped facedown on the silk coverlet with his hands to either side of his head and closed his eyes.

"If I find out you…" she began

"Don't accuse me of anything or I swear I'll walk out that door right now," he hissed.

Bolivar stared at his back as she always did when it was bare. There were deep crisscrossed lines marring the broad expanse and extending down onto his buttocks and upper thighs.

"Love taps from my stepfather," he'd told her when she'd demanded to know who had hurt him so badly.

Knowing all too well the abuses a stepfather could dish out, Bolivar moved up the bed and lay down beside him, for once keeping her hands to herself.

"What was that you took?"

"It was a painkiller." He sighed deeply. "Just let me sleep, will ya?"

"We're going to talk when you wake up," she said.

"Yeah, yeah, yeah."

"I had to postpone the revival for tonight. Everyone has been out looking for you."

He sighed again and lifted his head so he could turn to look at her. "One more word out of you and I'm going to throw you out of this trailer."

She clamped her mouth shut and shot from the bed, stomping down the hall and out of the motor home with a vile, unladylike curse.

"*Hound?*"

Fallon groaned. All he needed was Coim intruding at that moment. The tenerse was beginning to work and the itching was subsiding, but he still felt terrible. "Not now, please?" he pleaded.

"*Your mate is worried about you. Do you wish me to contact her and let her know you are well?*"

As he had driven his bike at breakneck speed down the interstate with Bolivar clinging like a parasitic vine to his back, *An Fear Liath Mor* had used the same quiet voice it was using now to speak to Fallon.

"There is one among those with you who has powers, pup," Coim had warned. *"He is a powerful mind-shielder but I scented him as I searched for the creature you tell me the woman is using to kill her foes. This man knows you are not what you seem so be very careful. Do not use your powers to communicate with your mate for he may intercept them. This is why I have not contacted you before now."*

Fallon turned over, flinging an arm over his eyes. "Why are you now breaking the silence you imposed?" he questioned.

"The one who has the powers is among those she sent out to look for you. I will know when he returns."

"Which one is he?"

"The one with the red hair and beard."

There was only one man among the ministry who fit that description. He was Bolivar's manager of operations, a man named Mizhak Roland.

"Is Keenan okay?"

"Tired but well," Coim reported. *"She will join you next week, but I think you will not be happy when you see her."*

Fallon's eyes opened. "Why not?"

"She has lost weight worrying about you." The beast lowered its voice even more. *"Just as you have lost weight worrying about her."*

"I miss her, Coim."

"I know, pup." The voice was sad and filled with commiseration.

"Tell her…" Fallon squeezed his eyes shut again. "Tell her I love her and miss her, and tell her why I haven't contacted her. Let her know I just came out of Transition."

"I will do this," An Fear Liath Mor stated then slowly withdrew.

Fallon heard the door to the motor home open and groaned. He knew who it was for she was broadcasting her thoughts as she came toward the bedroom. Knowing she'd give him no peace until he'd explained things to her satisfaction, he reminded himself he was there to be her right-hand man, to get as close to her as her skin so he could bring her down. Snarling, he swung his legs over the side of the bed and sat up.

She stopped in the doorway when she saw him sitting up. "I demand to know what you took," she said.

He didn't bother to look around. "It was a painkiller."

"For a real pain or recreation?"

He snorted then twisted his head to give her a steady glower. "Do I look like I'm having fun?"

Her chin came up. "You look like shit."

"Well, that's exactly how I feel."

Perhaps encouraged by his softer tone, she ventured farther into the bedroom. "What kind of pain?"

He scrubbed his hands over his face, wincing as his palms encountered the prickle of a three-day growth of beard. Also feeling the sweat dripping from his brow, he armed it away then flung a carelessly hand toward a chair in the corner of the room.

Bolivar's lips pursed but she sat down, crossing her long legs and curling her hands over the padded arms of the chair.

"I have bad headaches," he said without preamble as he stared down at the floor. "Vicious, brutal headaches." That was true for all Reapers did.

"You mean migraines."

He shook his head. "Worse. Mine don't just cause pain, they cause personality changes."

Bolivar's eyebrows drew together. "What kind of changes?"

"I get mean, and when I get mean, I get dangerous."

"And that's why you threatened me the other night?" she demanded.

"I get them like clockwork about four times a year but stress or anger can bring one on early. When that happens, I have to get as far away from other people as I can."

"Why?"

He looked up. "Because if I don't, I'll hurt them." He held her stare. "Or kill them."

Bolivar blinked, opened her mouth no doubt to scoff at his words, but she must have seen something in his eyes for she only said, "Go on."

"I wasn't due to have a bout until a week or so from now, but when you jumped on my ass and started hitting me, when you slammed your fist into my skull, you brought the damned thing on early. I knew if I didn't get away from you right then and stay away until the cycle passed, I'd most likely cripple you." He lowered his head again. "Or worse."

From the corner of his eye, he saw her leg jump and could feel her agitation. He slipped gently into her mind to read her thoughts, careful to direct the psi energy only to her and to shield it so no one else could detect the retrieval. He wasn't surprised to learn she was reconsidering their relationship and though she was keenly attracted to the sexual part, she had a healthy fear of him. He intended to deepen that fear.

"I've killed people when they pushed me too far," he said. "Most of the time I wasn't even aware I'd done it until I found myself covered in their blood."

Bolivar shuddered and tore her gaze from his.

Fallon grinned inwardly. There had been a reason to get physical with her—both sexually and violently—and both had served his purpose. Though he could have implanted the idea that they'd had mind-blowing sex in her brain, the chemicals in her body and the body itself would know differently. He'd had no choice but to join their bodies, mingle their fluids so all of her would remember the intimacy. Now it was time to sever the link that he had found so disgusting and shameful—much to his surprise.

He sent her a revealing thought.

"You bring out the worst in me and I bring out the worst in you," she said.

"You think?" he countered, knowing his sublim had taken root.

"I don't want to end up a statistic," she said, unknowingly repeating his psi push.

"And I don't want you to."

"As much as I enjoy our physical interludes, I think we should limit our working relationship to you protecting me and leave the...ah...intimate side out of the equation."

He nodded. "I think you're right."

He added another subtle but important nudge.

"I know you have your needs, Robin, but I don't want you fucking the girls in the ministry. Do you understand?" Her eyes flared with jealousy.

"I haven't seen one I'd have," he said sarcastically.

"If you need to do that, then you can fuck a townie, but don't you dare bring her here to this trailer. Understood?"

He shrugged. "I don't piss in my own yard, baby."

One more strong push that was vitally important.

"Maybe one day I'll find you a nice girl I wouldn't mind you keeping around," she said, and from the look on her face, her words had surprised her.

He glanced over at the clothing she had laid out for him earlier. The black T-shirt and black jeans were folded neatly on the top of the dresser along with a pair of tight black boxers and black socks.

"Why don't I take you out to supper tonight?" he suggested, testing the sublims to see if they took. "Let me make it up to you for being such a rat bastard."

Bolivar stood. "No, Robbie. I don't think so. Like I said, let's just keep this strictly professional from here on out."

"Okay," he agreed. He watched her walk out of the bedroom and a slow, merciless smile tugged at his chiseled features.

He'd played her just like a cheap guitar.

Chapter Fifteen

∽

Sitting in the motor home galley's custom-built dining booth with one leg stretched out and the other crooked at the knee, Fallon was chomping contentedly on a large red apple as he listened to Mizhak Roland giving his weekly report to Bolivar. The motor home being driven by Ollie was tooling along I-10 in the Florida Panhandle near Marianna, Florida, on its way to Dothan, Alabama—almost a six-hour trip from Kissimmee—and would soon be taking U.S. 131 north into the Wiregrass region of the Heart of Dixie state. They were about half an hour from their destination.

"Not bad," Bolivar said of what they'd taken in from the Kissimmee revival. "Let's hope Dothan does as well."

Roland pulled at his thick red beard. "We may run into a slight problem."

"What kind of problem?"

"We have some competition I'm afraid."

Bolivar was reclining on the sofa, Roland in the chair adjacent. She scowled. "What kind of competition?"

"There's a berg across the Alabama-Georgia line called Colquitt and I've been told a brother-sister act has been making the rounds of small Baptist churches in the area—a mini-revival if you will. Seems the sister has healing powers and people are flocking to the churches on Saturday nights instead of out to bars and movie theaters."

"Healing powers?" Bolivar questioned with a snort. "Are you shitting me?"

Roland shook his head. "No, I'm not, and it seems her following is growing. People are starting to talk about her, and when I sent Purvis into Dothan, he called to tell me the duo had just been in to get their stuff from the county. They'll be setting up shop about a mile from the fairgrounds where we'll be and they'll be having their revival while we're still there."

Fallon took another bite of his apple. He knew Steve Purvis was Bolivar's advance man—an employee who went ahead of the group to handle such details as licenses and bribes to local offices so the group would be left alone while in the area.

"Get somebody over there and take a look at these grifters," Bolivar snapped. "Run them out of the area."

"You want me to do it?" Fallon inquired.

"No, Robbie, I need you with me," Bolivar said. She put a hand on Roland's arm. "If you need to send Martiya, do so."

"Who's Martiya?" Fallon asked.

"No one you need to concern yourself with, *rikono*," Roland replied.

Fallon didn't move a muscle or acknowledge in any way he knew what the Romany word meant. If he had any doubt the man knew what he was, he no longer did. He held the older man's suspicious glower and tried to slip past the shield around Roland's mind but it was locked tight—just as his own was.

"Not a problem," Fallon said, and took another bite of apple, grinning broadly as he chewed.

"Pray you never meet Martiya," Roland told him. "Or have reason to have her come after you."

"Bad ass, is she?" Fallon quipped.

Roland never blinked. "The baddest of the bad."

Bolivar got up from the sofa and walked past Fallon to the refrigerator. "Perhaps you should go get dressed now, Robbie," she told him. "Your stuff is on the bed. I want to make a good impression when we arrive at the fairgrounds. There will be reporters there."

"Okey-dokey," Fallon told her, and slid out of the booth. Now that he was no longer forced to service her carnal needs, he didn't mind acting halfway human with her. He still didn't show her the groveling respect her other employees did, but he had mellowed to a great degree.

The carpet beneath his bare feet was so plush he made no sound as he walked down to her bedroom and shut the door. He stood still and directed his psi powers to the conversation going on in the living area.

"I'm telling you I don't trust him, *Day*," Roland said, using the Romany word for mother. "There is darkness surrounding him. He is not what he seems."

"Yes, so you've said time and again," Bolivar grumbled.

"He's a dangerous man."

"Oh, I agree with you on that," Bolivar replied, "and calling him a dog to his face won't make him any less dangerous if he finds out what *rikono* means."

"He won't," Roland said with a snort. "Irish Travelers aren't the brightest bulbs in the pack. What psychic ability he has is minimal so he didn't pick up on my meaning."

In the bedroom Fallon silently repeated the word minimal then chuckled to himself. He shook his head. "I think all the filaments in *your* bulb pack may have snapped apart, Roland, my man," he mused.

So they'd checked with the amusement park in Altoona and discovered the Irish daredevil named Danny Burke who'd performed in the Wall of Death, he thought. He knew they'd then learned that Burke had been arrested by the Des Moines police for being part of a scheme to bilk homeowners out of thousands of dollars in phony driveway paving scams. Burke—a member of the infamous Irish Travelers, an alleged band of wandering con artists who roamed the country fleecing the populace—had jumped bail and was now in the wind. They would also have learned that there were several outstanding federal warrants circulating on Daniel Michael Burke aka Burke Daniels aka Danny Michaels and that he was wanted for questioning as a person of interest in two murder cases.

"All the same," he heard Roland say. "I'm gonna keep a close watch on him because I don't trust him any farther than I can see him. Sammy should have the cameras and bugs installed by now in Burke's trailer."

Fallon laughed and pulled his T-shirt over his head. He already knew about the bugging for when Sammy's wife Riley came to tell Fallon that Bolivar wanted him to ride with her this trip instead of driving his own motor home, he'd read the information in Riley's weak mind. His laughter stopped abruptly when he heard Bolivar's next words.

"I don't give a shit about those cameras, but I want this yokel over in Georgia taken care of. Send Martiya over there tonight. We don't need any competition."

Blind fury lashed across his face and he reached for the doorknob, but stilled before he jerked open the door. He knew the beast Breslin mentioned had to be this Martiya. He also knew he had to keep Roland from sending whoever or whatever Martiya was after Keenan, convincing Bolivar it wasn't in her best interest. No matter what, he had to protect Keenan. He couldn't, however, push sublims on Bolivar with Roland in the same room. He would have to wait until they arrived in Dothan and the Rom was out of the motor home. Stepping away from the door, he closed his eyes and tried once again to intercept Roland's thoughts, to determine if the Rom might even then be trying to contact the beast.

But Roland's mind was an iron vault into which Fallon could not break. The man's safeguards were strong, powerful. He knew the only way he would be able to penetrate that locked barrier would be when Roland used his abilities to psychically communicate with another. While Roland was transmitting—his concentration centered—Fallon could slip unnoticed past the blockade and create an avenue he could later use to travel through Roland's subconscious undetected. Until Roland opened his mind, Fallon could do nothing.

Or he's where he can't hold his safeguards in place, Fallon thought and a sly smile tugged at the corners of his mouth.

Closing his eyes again, he slipped into Ollie's mind and placed a suggestion that Ollie was to pay no attention to what was about to happen.

Fallon then opened the bedroom door and headed for the living area. Bolivar and Roland stopped talking at his approach. When they saw the look on his face, Bolivar put up a hand to forestall him and Roland lurched out of the chair, his fists coming up.

"*Rikono*, huh?" Fallon said, and before Roland could block him, plowed a hard, brutal fist into the older man's gut then sent a left hook directly into the Rom's face. The sickening sound of a nose breaking and the spray of blood sent Bolivar scrambling back as Roland pitched sideways to the floor.

"What the hell are you doing?" she demanded.

"Bastard called me a fucking dog!" Fallon snarled, sensing Roland was out cold.

"You..."

He held up his hand and Bolivar froze, the force of his psi powers hitting her like a sledge hammer so her mind blanked out and she stood there with her mouth ajar, eyes glazed, unable to move with her thought processes temporarily shut down. With her completely under his control, he turned his attention to Roland, slithering easily past the man's mental roadblocks. He searched for the entity called Martiya, but all he encountered was a seething cauldron of pure evil that made Fallon shudder. The beast was enclosed with darkness but Fallon had an impression of savage strength, immense powers and a straining desire to maim and mutilate. When unleashed, whatever the thing was, Fallon sensed it would be formidable.

He took three steps over to Bolivar and grabbed her upper arms, staring down into her lax face.

"You will rescind the order you gave Roland. You will not send Martiya after the woman in Georgia. What you will do is send Ollie over there to bring the Lynches back for you to meet. You will be cordial and you will offer Tandy Lynch a position with the ministry. You will take her under your wing, protect her at all costs and make her the centerpiece of your show. Understood?"

Bolivar nodded, a thin stream of drool falling from her open mouth, her pupils dilated.

"Tandy Lynch will become the daughter you never had, and you will groom her to take over your ministry so you can retire.

There will be no more phony healings." He pushed that sublim hard, anchoring it tightly in Bolivar's brain. "Understood?"

Once more Bolivar's head moved slowly up and down.

That done, Fallon let go of Bolivar's arms and hunkered down beside Roland. He closed his eyes and slipped once more into the man's twisted brain. After he'd learned all he needed, he paved his pathway into the Rom's subconscious then stood. He looked over at Bolivar.

"You will also tell Roland he is not to retaliate for the punch I gave him. I don't need any more shit from him today. Tell him he deserved it."

Bolivar nodded still again.

Walking up to the cockpit, Fallon put a hand on Ollie's shoulder.

"I want you to pull over into the breakdown lane, but before you do, contact the man driving Roland's motor home and tell him he's to pull off behind us. Roland will be getting out."

Ollie reached for the mike on the dashboard and brought it to his mouth. "Carl? You need to pull in behind me when I stop. Mizhak needs to get out."

"Copy that, Oll," came the reply.

Ollie flicked on his turn signal.

"Good man," Fallon said, clapping Ollie on the shoulder then he turned and went back into the living area where Roland was moaning and trying to regain consciousness. Fallon glanced down at him and kept walking, heading for the bedroom and the clothing Bolivar had laid out for him to wear.

* * * * *

Keenan patted a handkerchief across her forehead. It was sweltering hot now that the hurricane had blown itself. The old-fashioned, outdated calico dress she was wearing fell midway down her calves and allowed very little cooling air to reach her legs. With the long sleeves buttoned tight at the wrist and the high collar, she was roasting and feeling as confined as if she were wearing a steel corset beneath the loose, unflattering garment.

Breslin — with his threadbare wool suit, wide sixties-era loud tie and scuffed boots — wasn't faring much better. His face was slick with sweat, his cheeks red from the oppressive heat, and he was fanning his straw Panama fedora in an attempt to get some relief. He mopped his own handkerchief down his chin and neck.

"Goddamn it's hot," he complained as he watched the Exchange personnel as they set up the shoddy tent that would be Tandy's stage.

"You don't miss having air conditioning in a car until you don't have it, do you?" Keenan asked as she glanced at the 1963 coupe with its severe case of body cancer and dirty wide whitewall tires. "Having a radio in that thing would have made the trip at least bearable."

Breslin laughed. "Yeah, it would have, but at least we had some interesting conversations."

Matty Groves — who had been ordered by the Supervisor to join in on this leg of the operation — came ambling up. He looked just as uncomfortable as Keenan and Breslin with his short-sleeve white shirt stained under the arms and his clip-on bow tie cocked at an angle at his neck.

"I am really beginning to regret being chosen for this assignment," he stated.

"I still don't know why the Supervisor thought we needed you," Breslin complained.

Keenan knew for Matty and she had been called in for a secret meeting with the Supervisor. What they had learned had been sobering, scary, and Matty was now giving Keenan surreptitious looks that made her uneasy.

"I guess that will manifest itself to you in due time," Matty said. It was obvious he didn't like Breslin and the feeling appeared to be mutual. "If he'd wanted you to know, he'd have told you."

"Don't wax smart with me, Groves," Breslin snapped.

"Quinn," Keenan corrected. "His name is Dr. Regis Quinn, our third cousin from the Cove."

"Yeah, *Nate*," Matty said, stressing Breslin's undercover name. "I'm the one in the family who went to the big city and studied medicine, made something of myself. Remember?"

"And you lost your fucking license because you were an incompetent alcoholic with an addiction for gambling," Breslin grated. "I know the scenario, asswipe."

"Zack, please stop," Keenan said. "This isn't a game."

"Don't think for a minute I don't know what you're up to, Reggie," Breslin hissed.

"That makes two of us," Matty threw back at him.

"Gentlemen," Keenan said with exasperation. "This isn't helping. We..."

"Truck coming," one of the Exchange workers called out to them.

"An expensive truck," Breslin observed as the three of them turned to look at the bright red truck headed toward them. "And lookee at the emblem on the door."

"Mother Bolivar's Mission," Matty read. "Well now, ain't that right neighborly of them to come calling?"

"Into character, people. It's showtime," Breslin said unnecessarily, and Keenan saw Matty stick out his tongue behind the agent's back.

* * * * *

"Oh my God, will you look at that piece of shit clunker?" Bolivar quipped as the rusted-out blue and white coupe pulled up before her motor home. "Talk about yokels!"

Fallon was sitting on the steps of the trailer, leaning back on his elbows. His heart was thudding wildly in his chest. It had been nearly three weeks since he'd last seen Keenan, and though he couldn't see her clearly through the dirty windshield of the car, he could feel her presence as sharply as the air he was breathing. He wished with all his being he could communicate with her but Roland was standing only a few feet away. Fallon knew Coim would have warned Keenan about the man so he couldn't expect her to send him a mental message either.

Breslin got out of the car first, pushing open the driver's door that squealed loudly.

"Lord, help us," Bolivar muttered under her breath, and rolled her eyes.

"Be nice," Fallon told her. He was surprised to see Matty exit the car next from the backseat. His gaze locked with the physician's and he saw Matty shrug slightly.

"Mother Bolivar!" Breslin said, hurrying forward with his hand outstretched. "What an honor! What a real honor!"

Bolivar flinched as her hand was engulfed in the tall man's and squeezed firmly. Her upper body shook as he enthusiastically pumped her hand up and down.

"A real honor!" Breslin said again, his face eager, eyes open wide. "I am tickled you sent your man to see me!"

"This is Nathan Lynch, Mother," Ollie introduced. "And his sister Tandy. The other gentleman there is their cousin Dr. Quinn."

"Dr. Quinn, medicine man?" Fallon questioned with a quirk of his lips. He made no effort to get up, barely glanced at Breslin and completely ignored Keenan.

"That would be me," Matty said, stepping forward to shoot out a hand, jabbing it right at Fallon who had no choice but to sit up and take it.

"This is my head of security, Robin Marks," Bolivar offered.

"And do you?" Matty inquired.

Fallon's eyes narrowed. "Do I what?" he asked as Matty kept possession of his hand.

"Go about robbing marks?"

"Let go," Fallon growled, wresting his hand from Matty's grip.

"Reggie thinks he's one of them comedians you see on the television," Breslin said. "He's right clownful that's a fact." He shot Matty a warning look.

Bolivar took a step toward Keenan and held out her hand. "Hello, Tandy."

Keenan bobbed a curtsy. "How do, ma'am," she said, and looked to Breslin. At his nod, she shyly took Bolivar's hand limply in hers.

"I'm told you have been graced with the gift of the Laying on of Hands," Bolivar said gently.

"Mark 16:18 says, 'Lay your hands on the sick and they shall be healed'," Breslin quoted. "That's what she does. She touches them sick folk and they get well. The Lord has been good to us, praise Jesus."

"I'm sure," Bolivar mumbled, refusing to look at the man. Her gaze was on Keenan. "Where are you from, Tandy?"

"I'm from Regis Cove," Breslin answered. "Up Kentuck way, in the mountains." He laughed. "Reggie here was named after our birthplace."

Fallon braced his elbows on his knees, threaded his fingers together and stared at Breslin although every fiber in his body was aware of Keenan standing not more than three feet away.

"How long have you been healing people, Tandy?" Bolivar asked.

"She started when she was about ten, as I recall," Breslin interrupted again. "There was a cave-in up to one of the mines, and when they brought them miners out, most was dead or a'dying. Tandy went over to one who hailed from the Cove and put her hands on him and he made it through just like that!" He snapped his fingers. "I realized she had been given the Gift and knew I had to share it with the world one day."

Bolivar reached out to take Keenan's hand and was stunned when Keenan jerked away, putting up an arm as though she expected to be hit. Everyone except Breslin, Matty and Fallon gasped.

"Honey, I'm not going to hurt you," Bolivar said, looking to Fallon for help.

"Oh, she ain't always right in the head," Breslin said in a hard voice, his face suddenly turning red. It was obvious the agent had his obnoxious persona down pat, and when he lurched toward Keenan to grab her, Fallon shot between them, moving so fast he was little more than a blur, coming chest to chest with the other man.

"Back off," Fallon said.

"Now you look here, mister..." Breslin said, anger making his eyes glitter.

Fallon brought up a hand and shoved Breslin. "I said back off."

"Tandy, honey, come with me," Bolivar said, holding out her hand.

Watching Keenan from the corner of his eye, Fallon saw she was making herself tremble violently and her fingers were twisting in the skirt of her shapeless gown. He had to dig his fingernails into his palms to keep from grinning at her frightened appearance.

"Look here now, Mother Bolivar," Breslin said, "I didn't come here to be treated disrespectful by one of your hired guns. I thought I was here to talk about joining my revival with yourn."

"Your revival?" Fallon questioned sarcastically. He moved so he was standing almost nose to nose with Breslin, glaring into the other man's face. "You a healer too or just a loud-mouth prick who likes to beat on women?"

"Get outta my face, bubba, or I'm gonna..." Breslin snapped, made the mistake of shoving Fallon back, and before anyone could react, took a roundhouse swing at his opponent. Fallon ducked then drove a meaty fist into Breslin's gut, knocking the air out of him and sending him staggering back to land on his ass in the dirt.

"Tandy, come in the trailer. Now!" Bolivar said in a firm voice. She slipped her arm around Keenan to lead her.

Keenan stumbled along in Bolivar's wake, tossing fearful glances at her "brother" as he scrambled to get to his feet.

"Don't let 'em fight, ma'am," she pleaded. "Don't want to be no cause for Nate shedding that gentleman's blood."

"I don't think you have to worry about that," Bolivar said with a satisfied grin.

210

"But ye don't want 'em to fight fist to skull, ma'am. Ain't Christian and Nate be a ornery one when hit comes to fightin'. He don't do it fair-like," Keenan protested as Bolivar opened the motor home door and pushed her gently inside.

"You let Robbie take care of your brother, Tandy," Bolivar said, closing the door behind them. "Why don't you take a seat and let's get acquainted."

Keenan had both hands buried in the skirt of her dress and was looking about her as though she expected bogeymen to jump out at her at any moment.

"Go on, sit," Bolivar insisted, and took a seat on the sofa.

"But, ma'am..."

"Honey, sit. That's man stuff out there. In here, we're ladies."

Keenan hesitated a few beats. Letting go of her skirt long enough to brush the back of it several times as though she didn't want to soil the upholstery, she eased down into one of the overstuffed chairs sitting at angles to the sofa. Her lips parted.

"Lordy be!" she said. "Hit's like sittin' on a toadie stool!" She wiped her hand on her skirt then ran it along the velvet arm of the chair as though in wonder.

"You don't have soft chairs where you live, Tandy?" Bolivar questioned.

"No, ma'am," Keenan said in an awed, hushed voice. "T'weren't nothin' nowhere as nice as this here cheer."

Bolivar winced at the mountain twang and vocabulary. "I see we will need to get you a language instructor," she observed.

Keenan blushed. "Beggin' yer pardon, but I allow how I don't talk too good, ma'am. I dint get me much ed'cation like Nate and Reggie done."

"I don't speak well," Bolivar corrected.

"Oh no'm! You speak real good, ma'am."

"I mean the correct English for what you said is I don't speak well," Bolivar told her, smiling encouragingly.

Keenan's lips quivered as though she were trying to answer the smile then she took a deep breath. "I don't speak well," she repeated.

Bolivar clapped soundlessly. "Now tell me all about you. How old are you, Tandy?"

"I be…"

"I am," Bolivar cut in.

Keenan nodded emphatically. "I am twenty and nine."

"Just twenty-nine."

"Oh," Keenan said brightly. "I am just twenty-nine."

Bolivar laughed. "You are a breath of fresh air, Tandy. You truly are."

Keenan ducked her head, blushing beneath the compliment.

"Do you have a boyfriend back in Regis Cove?"

Keenan drew her shoulders up as though she were a turtle trying to hide its head and didn't look up as she spoke.

"No'm," she said. "Me, I was just a little bit choicey when it come to them boys what was a'tryin' to court me." Her hands went to her lap and tangled themselves in her skirt again. "I knowed all the families in the kentry and all their chillen. Most of them I be kin to, you see? Them what I weren't kin to didn't interest me none 'cause they was rough types and all." One shoulder rose higher than the other. "I wanted to pick me out the handsomest boy in the Cove, but he got took by my friend Anise and the only other one he went and left to jine the Army."

"So you've never dated?" Bolivar asked.

Keenan shook her head. "No'm unless you count the times Reggie took me to the pitcher show since we left the Cove."

"Reggie's your cousin though, so that wouldn't be a date."

"He's my cousin three times down the ladder," Keenan said. "My ma and pa was three times cousins."

"Well, outside Kentucky, people don't generally marry their cousins—three times removed or not," Bolivar explained.

"Oh, I ain't gonna marry Reggie!" she said with a laugh. "He's like a brother to me, you see?"

212

The door opened and Fallon came into the motor home. He looked none the worse for wear as he walked nonchalantly over to the fridge, opened it and took out a soft drink, popping the tab.

"You two getting acquainted?" he asked, taking a long swig of the beverage.

"Yes, we are. Tandy, would you like a soda?"

Keenan looked up shyly, glanced at Fallon then quickly looked away again. "You mean a coh-cola, ma'am?"

Bolivar exchanged an amused smile with Fallon. "Yes, dear, that's what I mean."

"Yes'm, I wouldn't mind somethin' cold right along now. It sure be hot out there."

Fallon arched a brow, and at Bolivar's nod, brought two cans of pop over to the two women. He opened both and handed one to Bolivar then leaned toward Keenan to hand her the other. The moment the younger woman pressed back in the chair and her hands came up defensively, he cursed beneath his breath and squatted on the floor in front of her.

"Darling, let's me and you get something straight right off the bat, okay?" he said, both sodas in his hands. When she didn't look at him but kept her chin tucked against her chest, he craned his head down so he could see her face. "Will you look at me, Tandy?"

Hesitantly, she lifted her head a little, met his eyes then looked away again.

"Sweetie, I'm not going to hurt you," he said gently.

Once more her eyes met his, skipped away then came back. They held a bit longer this time then leapt away again. Color rose in her pale cheeks.

"Not all men hit women, Tandy," Bolivar said quietly. "Robbie has never hit a woman in his life. Have you, Robbie?"

"Nope."

Keenan lifted her chin a fraction of an inch, looked at the soft drink in his hand, and when he extended it toward her this time, she took it, cupping both hands around the cold aluminum can, bringing it to her chest as though it were a child.

"Thank you kindly, Mr. Robbie," she said.

"It's just Robbie," he told her then stood, took the chair beside her, stretched his legs out and crossed his booted ankles. "Don't let me interrupt you ladies."

"How did you come to be doing the Lord's work over there in Georgia, Tandy?" Bolivar inquired.

"Nate, he heard tell you helped sick folk and the like, and he think to himself I could do that too, so we lit out with Reggie and we starts doing the Lord's work for Him. I wouldn't have knowed no better if'n he hadn't recalled it to me."

Fallon sipped his soda as Keenan went on with the same spiel he'd heard at the Exchange. He marveled that her voice at first was hesitant, shy, but with each encouragement from Bolivar, the narration became more detailed, had more animation, so that by the time she was finished with the contrived tale of how she, her brother and cousin had arrived in Georgia, she was relaxed yet excited.

"So's you can see hit's been handed down to me that I be one of the healing women up to the Cove, but I come up the hard way, you see. There be people who think healing women is..." She lowered her voice. "Witches and the like." She shook head. "I ain't no setch thang. I be a good girl."

"Well, it sounds to me as though you've had a tough time of it," Bolivar commented when the tale was done.

Keenan nodded. "Yes'm." She wiped the bottom of the can on her sleeve to rid it of the beads of moisture. "I was borned in the kentry and ain't never been out o' hit a'fore now. Sometimes we'uns has had the awfullest times. Tar busted one of them times and we'uns don't got no spare. Didn't have no extra money when we got to Augusta so we's slept in the car after paying them officials for the licenses and all."

"In this heat?" Bolivar gasped.

"Yes'm. We'uns didn't get no rest that night. We'uns was just wore teetotally plumb out from that there heat." She closed her eyes and smiled. "Ain't used to this here air conditioning." She opened her eyes. "A body could get used to it though."

As Bolivar continued to question Keenan, Fallon watched the woman he loved. As Coim had said, she'd lost weight, but he'd bet a silver dollar she'd done so to better fit the role she was playing instead of having been pining away for him. He looked down at her scuffed shoes — the seams of which had popped loose along the big toe — and saw that she was continuously scraping one foot over the other as a nervous adolescent girl would do. He noticed the hem of her dress was frayed and even though he knew it was a costume she was wearing, it hurt him for some inexplicable reason. He wanted her in fine silks and rich satins and plush velvets and tailored corduroys. He wanted her in designer clothing with the most sensual lingerie lovingly molding her body. He wanted diamonds and pearls and links of gold on her slender neck and fingers and in her earlobes.

"Robbie?"

He shook himself and forced his attention to Bolivar. "I'm sorry. What?"

"Would you have Roland go into town and purchase a new motor home for Tandy? Something really nice."

"Ma'am, I can't let you do that!" Keenan gasped. "That wouldn't be right!"

"And tell him to find a used one for her brother and cousin since it seems they will be joining us as well."

"But, ma'am!" Keenan protested. "We got folks workin' with us over in Georgia and they got nowheres to go. We..."

"I'll pay your brother for your tent and the equipment you have and whatever I can use, I'll just incorporate it with mine. Any of your people who would like to work for me, I'll gladly hire. How's that?"

Keenan shook her head. "Ma'am, you're a kindly passel of folks to share like this and all, but this be moving too fast for the likes of me to catch a grasp of it. I don't..." She looked up as though sudden realization had hit her, fear stamped on her features. "Nate, he takes care of the business ends of thangs. If'n he thought I was a'goin' behind his back..."

"You let us worry about your brother," Bolivar said. "Isn't that right, Robbie?"

215

Fallon uncrossed his legs and stood. "I'll see to it," he said. He moved toward the door.

"And ask Johnny Mae to come see us," Bolivar instructed. "She used to teach third grade before she married Ollie. I'm sure she'll be happy to teach Tandy better English."

As he went out the door, he heard Bolivar telling Keenan about all the good things that would be coming her way soon and he smiled.

Chapter Sixteen

ഔ

"So what do you think of her?" Bolivar asked as she and Fallon had a late lunch.

"Mousy little thing," he said as he scored the slice of ham on his plate. "Afraid of her own shadow."

"I expect her brother is the cause of that." Bolivar took a bite of bread. "Did you let him know in no uncertain terms that if he dares raise a hand to her again, you'll make him wish he hadn't?"

Fallon smiled. "I believe my exact words were if he did, I'd break that sucker off at the root and shove it so far up his ass he'd be able to brush his teeth from the inside out."

Bolivar laughed. "Oh Robbie, I like that!" She scooped up a forkful of creamed potatoes, still chuckling. "What other impression did you get from her?"

He shrugged. "Well, she could be almost pretty given the right clothes and a bit of makeup," he replied. "Right now she looks like a drowned rat with that godawful dress and ratty hair."

"I think she's lovely," Bolivar said. "She has perfect features. Her eyes are beautiful and beneath that sack of a dress, I believe she has a striking little figure."

"If you say so," he said as though the subject didn't interest him. "Oh, by the way, I found out why they brought the cousin along."

"And that is?"

He reached for his glass of iced tea, took a sip before answering. "When she uses her so-called powers, she has a tendency to get nose and ear bleeds."

That news had startled him when Matty had informed him. They had been in the company of Roland and another ministry worker so he'd been unable to question Matty as he'd needed to.

"She's also collapsed into unconsciousness and on occasion has had violent seizures."

And that scared him even more. If any of it was true, he was not going to be a happy camper when she used the powers Coim had bestowed on her.

"I don't like the sound of that," Bolivar said, and Fallon was pleased the protective instinct toward Keenan he had instilled in Bolivar had taken firm root. "So Quinn was brought along to take care of her."

"Yeah. Unlike that fucker of a brother of hers, he isn't a bad sort, although I've got a feeling he's a bit too fond of the drink taken, as my grandma used to say."

"Why doesn't that surprise me?" She wiped her lips with her napkin. "What did the brother say when you told him she had agreed to come work with us?"

Fallon snorted. "He didn't like that he hadn't been consulted and involved in the discussion. According to him, he's her manager and he's also the one who interprets for her."

Bolivar's eyebrows shot up. "She speaks in Tongues?"

Fallon nodded. "He says she does and he swears he's the only one who can interpret what she's saying so he's vital to the ministry."

"This just keeps getting better and better," she said. "I've been looking for someone to pass the torch to and I believe I've found her in Tandy."

"You're thinking of retiring?"

"Well, I hadn't been actively thinking about it until the last few days, but I've had my eye out," she said, unknowingly repeating the very words he'd implanted in her mind. "Tandy just seems right to me."

"You should know," he said.

"I'm going to work with her while we're here in Alabama, train her every day. Johnny Mae will also be working with her. She can read and write but that's about the extent of her education." She got up and started clearing the table of the dishes although normally one of the girls in her employ did that. "I think by the time we get over into Louisiana, she'll be ready for her first revival. Until then, I'll just have her mingle in with the choir, keep a very low profile. That way she can see what's going on but she won't be where the public will notice her."

"As plain as she is, I don't think that's going to be a problem," Fallon said.

Bolivar smiled in such a way he knew another of his sublims had dropped into place.

* * * * *

For the next three weeks Fallon stayed as far away from Keenan as space would allow. Whenever she was with Bolivar, he made himself scarce. He couldn't be near her without wanting to touch her, to hold her, to kiss her, and he was afraid he'd accidentally give away his feelings. He ached to take her in his arms and make love to her all night. Every time he saw her, his body clenched with desperate need and he would push himself in whatever he was doing—taking to running five miles every day in an effort to tire himself out so his cock wouldn't flex every time he was within eyesight of her. He lay awake at night so stiff he was in agony and had to take matters in hand in order to get some rest. In the morning he was usually surly and gruff, but since everyone accepted that kind of behavior from him, no one questioned it.

Thankfully, he saw little of Breslin who had fallen in with Roland as though they'd been best buds all their lives. Keenan's ex-partner-lover was insinuating himself in with almost all the ministry workers who weren't smart enough to know they were being used. Those who suspected the brawny man had ulterior motives stayed clear of him. One of them—a former circus roughneck named Sammy Pyle—seemed to have developed an intense dislike of Breslin and the two had gone a few rounds before Fallon stepped in to put a stop to it.

"He's learning the ropes from Roland," Bolivar had told Fallon. "Mizhak says he's a quick study."

"He's a born conman," Fallon quipped. "It's written all over his ugly ass face."

"You really don't like him, do you?"

"He's a coward," Fallon stated. "Any man who would hit a woman is nothing more than that in my book."

"You threatened to hit me," she reminded him.

"I wouldn't have," he said then grinned nastily. "But you didn't know that, did you?"

Matty—as the self-appointed physician for the ministry—was making himself useful in treating everyday injuries and suturing the occasional work-related wound. Though he couldn't prescribe medications because his license had been revoked, that didn't stop him from procuring drugs when they were needed.

"Don't ask," Fallon warned Bolivar. "If he gets caught, it's his ass, not ours. We'll just say we didn't know what he was up to, and since you didn't hire him on as a sawbones, no one can prove otherwise."

Fallon knew the drugs were legal, had been provided by the Exchange and had no worries that Matty would ever be investigated by any of the law enforcement agencies they encountered in whatever state they would happen to be in.

It was Saturday night, their last week in Alabama, and they would be moving on to Metairie, Louisiana, after the mass baptism on Sunday evening. The next revival wouldn't begin until Friday and everyone was looking forward to tearing down the tent and moving on, setting up Tuesday and having Wednesday and Thursday off since the ten days in a row after that would be working days.

Keenan was in her motor home watching TV and munching popcorn when a knock came at the door. Her heart accelerated for she was hoping against hope it was Fallon. Being near him but unable to speak to him beyond a few words in passing or shooting him the occasional look was proving to be sheer hell for her.

"I'm coming!" she said, and scrambled off the sofa, running barefoot to the door. When she threw it open, her face fell. "Oh, it's you."

Matty grimaced. "Well, hello to you too, little cousin." He fanned her back with his hands. "Scoot."

Keenan moved back to allow him to enter then shut the door.

"Look what I brought you," Matty said, and reached inside his coat pocket. He brought out a CD.

Keenan knew the CD would block any listening devices should there be any in the motor home and Breslin had already swept the entire vehicle for hidden cameras and found none. She smiled broadly when she read the title. "Celtic ballads? Oh Reggie, thank you!" she said, kissing him on the cheek before turning to load the CD. She turned the volume up then came over to hook her arm through his and led him to the sofa.

To everyone in the ministry, Tandy had a playful, loving relationship with Reggie, but it was clear she was fearful of her brother and stayed out of his way as much as possible. Thankfully, Mother Bolivar kept her well away from Nate Lynch during the day, and at night he was usually playing poker with several of the men and left her alone. Rarely did he come to visit and when he did, he wasn't in the motor home alone with her for more than a minute or two before company arrived—usually in the person of Johnny Mae or Ollie if not Bolivar herself.

Once they were seated, Keenan drew her legs up on the sofa, snuggled up to Matty as he tossed an arm over her shoulder, threaded her fingers through his then began to speak to him in a very soft voice.

"Have you had a chance to talk to him?" she asked.

"Yeppers. He's doing good," Matty replied. "He rode into town yesterday and I drove in after him. Managed to hook up with him at a burger joint. We got in a few words before a couple of Bolivar's men showed up. He has a name for the creature Breslin says kills for Bolivar, but he still doesn't know what it is or how to find it."

"What kind of name?"

"Martiya. He believed it was a Rom name but since he's being watched carefully, his trailer is wired for sight and sound, and he's fairly sure they check on where he's been on the computer, he hasn't had a chance to research. So your future Nobel Prize recip ventured over to the local liberry, typed in the name and came back with an interesting meaning."

"Which is?"

"Spirit of the night."

"Huh," she said then gazed up at him. "Nobel Prize recip for what?"

"Biogenetics," he said. "I am going to be the first man to clone you, m'dear."

"Lucky me," she said, and laid her head on his chest. "Did he ask about me?"

Matty sighed heavily and seemed to be grinding his teeth before he finally answered her. "Of course he asked about you," he said. "He's worried about you and though he didn't say so, he walks around with a constant erection unless he really was that happy to see me—which I doubt."

Keenan grinned. Matty had become a dear friend. She suspected he'd like to be much more to her so she'd been careful not to lead him on or encourage him in that way. Were it not necessary to sit as close to him as she was for fear of any stray information leaking out to their targets, she would not be pressed to him at that moment.

"Will you tell him I miss him and I'm looking forward to Louisiana?"

"Horny little witch," Matty said. "As if he doesn't know that already! Yeah, I'll tell him. Anything else you want me to pass along? Your undying devotion and sappy love for him for all eternity? Should I tell him your womb weeps with need for his strong, stiff..."

"Watch it!" she growled, digging her elbow into his side.

Matty laughed. "I gotta get going before I throw you down on this sofa and have my cousinly way with you." He unwound his arm from around her neck and pulled his fingers free. Before he got up, he told her Breslin needed to talk to her without there being witnesses around.

"I don't know if that's possible," she said as she stood. "Bolivar doesn't trust him with me. Zack has played his role too well. Did he say what it was about?"

"Nope. Just that it's important." He wrapped her in a brief bear hug then headed for the door. "Enjoy your music, cuz!"

"I will," she replied.

After Matty left, Keenan lay down on the sofa and listened to the haunting music coming from the CD player. The only trouble was it made her want Fallon even more. Her body longed for his, her hands itched to roam freely over his beautiful body. Though they'd never spoken of it, she thought of the scars on his back and clenched her teeth. He hadn't told her it was his stepfather's doing—he hadn't needed to. Those scars had simply been the elephant in their bed about which they did not speak since she sensed he was very sensitive about it. He was always so careful about not turning his bare back to her, but there had been a few times when he'd forgotten and she'd had a good look at the carnage streaking his back.

There were so many things about Fallon that were a mystery to her. They hadn't been together long enough for her to learn all the secrets she knew his life held. More than anything she wanted to spend time alone with him when there was nothing for them to do, to worry about—time just to be together without a care in the world.

"Alone on a beach where there's crystal-clear turquoise water and sea gulls sweeping past overhead," she said then sighed.

She fell into a light doze thinking of Fallon's arms wrapped securely around her and the warm sun beating down on their naked, entwined bodies. She sat up with a start when the door opened again and Breslin slipped in. He put a finger to his lips then came over to the sofa.

"What's up?"

Breslin didn't waste any time. "When I called in to the Exchange to give them a progress report this afternoon, they said your mother had been trying to get in touch with you."

"Why?" she asked, brows furrowed.

"Your Aunt Marjorie passed away early this morning. Lily wants you home for the funeral on Monday," he answered.

Keenan had always been fond of her mother's sister who had been more of a mother to her than Lily Doyle McCullough had ever been. Her heart ached at hearing of Marjie's passing.

"Oh Zack, no! There's no way I can leave here now." Tears filled her eyes. "What am I going to do? Mama will never forgive me if I don't show up."

"I'll call Lily and tell her you're on assignment and it's impossible to contact you. She'll just have to accept that." He put an arm around her as tears began falling down her cheeks and drew her to him. "Baby, I'm sorry. I know how much you loved Marjie."

"She was such a sweet woman," Keenan said, and broke down, her shoulder shaking.

Breslin put his other arm around her and rocked her, crooning to her as she poured out her grief on his shoulder. Bolivar took that moment to enter the motor home without knocking, her eyes blazing with fury.

"What did you do to her, you slimy bastard?" she demanded, advancing on the sofa.

Breslin noticed Fallon right behind her and tensed.

"I ain't done nothing to her, Mother Bolivar!" he was quick to say. "I called up to home to see how our ma was a'doing and found out our aunt had passed on. I came to tell Tandy 'cause they was real close. That's why she's crying." He glanced at Fallon who was surprised Breslin allowed him to slip easily into his mind to read the truth.

"Is what he saying true, Tandy?" Bolivar asked, going to sit on the other side of Tandy on the sofa. "He didn't hit you, did he? Look up at me and let me see your face."

"He didn't hit me, ma'am," Keenan said, running a hand under her nose. She lifted her face to reveal red, tear-swollen eyes.

"Robbie, get her some tissues," Bolivar ordered.

Fallon walked into the kitchen and plucked several from a cute little dispenser on the counter then brought them over to her.

"Thank you, Mr. Robbie," Keenan said, taking them with a trembling hand.

"Sorry about your aunt," Fallon said.

"Is there anything we can do?" Bolivar said.

"The funeral's on Monday and she wants to go," Breslin said, "but I told her how that can't be."

"Why the hell not?" Bolivar snapped. "If she wants to go, she can damned well go. She's not a prisoner here."

"Well, in that case, I'll take..."

"You aren't taking her anywhere!" Bolivar declared. "Reggie can take her."

"Reggie can't go," Fallon was quick to say, causing both Breslin and Keenan to give him a strange look, but he was staring hard at Bolivar. "He's shit-faced drunk in his trailer."

Bolivar put a hand to her head as though it were suddenly hurting. She wavered for a moment then turned to Fallon. "Then you take her."

"Me? Why me?" Fallon asked in a frustrated tone.

"Because I trust you and there's no one else I'd allow to do it," Bolivar said. "You can take my car."

"Mignon, I have no desire to..."

"You'll take her up there, Robbie, and that's that!" Bolivar ordered.

Fallon pretended to display a look of aggravation then nodded.

"Thank you, Mr. Robbie," Bolivar said sweetly, and patted him on the cheek, but Fallon jerked his face away as though he were angry.

"*Oh man, you're a piece of work, aren't you?*" Breslin sent, but at Fallon's warning look, remembered they weren't supposed to communicate that way. He blanched as Keenan stiffened in his hold.

"Tandy, pack a few of your new things. I think I have a black dress that will fit you." She turned to Fallon as Keenan left the room. "I want you to drive straight through and call me as soon as you get up there. Be back by Wednesday. You know where to meet us in Metairie?"

"Yeah, yeah," Fallon snapped. "If I'm gonna do this, I need to pack a bag."

"You *are* going to do this, Robbie," Bolivar told him.

"Yeah, well, I don't have to like it," Fallon snapped. He spun around and stormed out of the trailer.

"Testy little fella, ain't he?" Breslin quipped.

"He'll take care of your sister. That's all that matters," Bolivar replied.

"If'n he lays one hand to her…"

Bolivar snorted. "He knows better."

Breslin got up from the sofa and came to stand directly beside Bolivar even though the woman stiffened.

"You don't see the way he looks at her when you ain't watching, Mother Bolivar," he said slyly. "That man ain't what you think he is."

Bolivar raised her chin. "So people keep telling me but I trust him."

"Well, don't you blame me none if Tandy comes back with her cherry busted. I don't trust that Marks no longer I can see 'im."

With a disgusted quirk of her lip, Bolivar turned her back on him and also left, her footsteps taking her directly to Fallon's motor home. She entered just as imperiously as she had Keenan's and walked through to the bedroom.

Fallon looked up from stuffing clothes into an overnight bag. "No, I won't lay a hand to her," he said before she could speak. "She's not my type."

"Her brother seems to think she is."

"He wants to take her up there, so if he can make me look bad, that's what he'll do." He gave her a steady look, implanted another quick psychic suggestion then returned to his packing.

"He says she's a virgin."

"I don't believe it," Fallon said. "I told you she's afraid of her own shadow. Somebody made her that way."

226

Bolivar chewed on her thumbnail. "You think Nate has abused her?"

Fallon shrugged then zipped up his bag. "Who knows?"

"The keys to my car are with Ollie. You'd damned well better take care of it, Robbie. One scratch and you'll owe me a new paint job."

Fallon grunted. Bolivar felt about her silver BMW the same way he did his bike so he couldn't fault her there. The car was in an enclosed eight-foot hauler that was towed behind one of the bunkhouse motor homes where the female ministry workers slept. It was lovingly cared for by Ollie, washed once a week whether it had been driven or not and inspected daily for scratches and road dings.

"Any other instructions, Mom?" he grumbled as he lifted the bag and slung it over his shoulder.

"Be nice to her."

He rolled his eyes. "I'll be as nice as I know how to be."

"I mean it, Robbie. She's afraid of you so don't get all hard-assed on her. Okay?"

"Afraid of me?" he said with a blink. "Why the hell would she be afraid of me?"

Bolivar's left eyebrow shot up. "I believe she said something like, 'I ain't got nothin' agin him but Mr. Robbie, he don't look right to me.'"

He snorted. "Yeah, well, that could mean she thinks I'm crazy," he scoffed, "and apparently I am to be driving her up to Coon Balls, Kentucky."

"She meant she's afraid of you. Nate says I don't see you looking at her but I do. You're always scowling at her. Why do you do that?"

"I don't. You're seeing things," he said, and walked past her out of the bedroom.

"Just be nice to her, Robbie. Please? For me?"

He ignored her as he went out the door and into the hot, humid night. Spying one of the young male workers, he told him

227

to fetch Ollie. "Tell him to bring Mother Bolivar's car keys with him. I'll be needing it tonight."

The young man's eyes widened. "You're gonna drive it?" he questioned.

"Just do what I told you, Spivey. Now!" Fallon snapped. He was anxious to get on the road, to be alone at last with Keenan. His palms were sweating he was so excited and striving hard to conceal it. The moment he saw Keenan coming toward him, his heart slammed hard against his chest but he managed to turn his back on her and keep walking toward the bunkhouse motor home where the car was being hauled.

Ollie came jogging up, glancing at Bolivar to make sure it was all right to drive her car off the hauler.

"There isn't much gas in the tank, is there, Oll?" Bolivar asked.

"No, ma'am," Ollie replied as he began to unfasten the rear ramp door. "Don't like to transport it with its tank full. Ain't safe."

"I'll fill up before we leave," Fallon said, and turned to look at Keenan. "You've had supper haven't you?"

"Yes sir," she said as she came to stand a few feet away.

Breslin was standing beside her, his face tight, eyes narrowed. The look he shot Fallon was filled with venom. "You'd best be respectful of my sister, Marks," he said in a harsh tone.

"Or what?" Fallon asked. "You gonna spread some more shit about me?"

"Cool it. Both of you," Bolivar reprimanded them.

"Thank you for allowing me to go to the funeral, ma'am," Keenan said, deliberately putting herself between the two men who were glaring daggers at one another. "I really appreciate it."

Bolivar smiled and reached out to hug Keenan. "You just take care and hurry back." She shook a finger at Keenan. "And don't come back to us speaking mountain twang, okay?"

Keenan laughed. "No, ma'am. I won't."

They all moved back as Ollie turned the car on and the brake lights pulsed. When the ex-carney drove the sports car out of the hauler, Fallon rapped on the trunk, Ollie hit the interior trunk release and the lid popped up. He tossed in his overnight bag then turned to take Keenan's from her.

"You watch yourself, girl," Breslin growled.

"Don't worry none, bubba," Fallon sneered. "She's safer with me than she'll ever be with you."

"Prick," Breslin spat.

"Asswipe," Fallon returned as he traded places with Ollie behind the wheel.

Keenan hurried around to the passenger side and smiled at Fallon as he leaned over the console to push the door open for her.

"Put your seat belt on," Fallon said.

She started to reach for the seat-belt strap behind her but stopped, realizing Tandy wouldn't know about such things since the old car in which she'd arrived had only a lap belt. She slid her hand behind her as though searching for the lap belt.

"On the door," Fallon said. "Just pull it across you."

Keenan gave him a bewildered look though her eyes were twinkling. "Sir?" she questioned.

With a heavy, put-upon sigh, Fallon unsnapped his own and leaned over—his shoulder brushing her breast as he retrieved the belt and tugged it across her body, pushed the tongue down into the cable buckle then straightened.

"Like that," he informed her.

"Oh all right," she said sweetly. "Thank you, Mr. Robbie."

"You be welcome and such, Miss Tandy," he said in a twangy voice, and heard her trying to stifle a giggle.

As he backed away from the small group of people gathered behind the bunkhouse motor home, he saw Roland among them, watching every move he made. It occurred to him the car might be bugged with some kind of listening device—not to mention a GPS tracker—and he frowned. Reaching over, he switched on the radio, turning it as loud as was humanly possible to endure. He was aware of Keenan staring at him and he shook his head slightly. When he found a convenience store far enough away from the caravan, he pulled in and switched off the radio.

"Did you say you had to pee?" he asked.

Keenan pursed her lips. "No sir. I said I had to wee."

"Then get 'er done while I'm pumping the gas," he said, motioning for her to go inside the convenience store.

"Yes sir," she replied, and opened her door.

"And don't wander off!" he called out to her, sending her a mental image of standing by the drink coolers.

After he'd filled up the car, he pulled over in front of the store and went in, passing Keenan who was meandering along the candy aisle. He went into the restroom and when he came out, she was standing at the coolers as though trying to decide which soft drink she wanted.

"We're going to have to change cars," he said in a low voice as he opened the cooler door and took out a root beer. "There's a GPS on this one and it damned sure needs to go to Kentucky."

"How are we going to do that?" she asked, pointing to a bottle of raspberry tea.

"I need to call the Exchange and have them meet us where I-55 meets up with I-40. Someone else is going to have to drive this baby up to Regis Cove. I'll have them fly us down to Albany or we won't get there in time. That is where the funeral is going to be, isn't it?"

"Yes, but I need to stop somewhere and call my mother to let her know I'm coming or she'll be hounding them at HQ."

"We'll do that once we're on the road," he said, and motioned her toward the checkout counter as though impatient with her.

"I don't think anyone's watching us, lineman," she mumbled.

"I hope not," he said, "but once we get back in the car, we can transmit without having to worry about it being intercepted."

She nodded.

Once more on the road, he seemed to relax. They were far enough along I-55 that there were no overhead lights to illuminate the interior of the car and no vehicles following them. He reached for her hand and brought it to his lips.

"I've missed you like you wouldn't believe," he told her.

"Oh yes, I would," she admitted. *"I've felt the same way."*

He glanced over at her. *"You wait until we're in bed again and I'll show you how much I missed you,* myneeast caillagh.*"*

Keenan tightened her fingers around his as he kissed her hand again, lowering it to rest on his thigh. He was quiet for a moment, but when he sent her his next thought, she could hear the anguish in it.

"Never again, Keenan," he said. *"Never with another woman. It hurt too much."*

"I know."

"Then what's worrying you? I can feel your anxiety."

"It's not you, lineman. It's me. As much as I loved Aunt Marjie, I dread seeing my mother even if it's only for the funeral. She's going to make the whole thing about her. She always does."

"I'll be right there with you," he said then hissed.

"What?"

"I'll need a suit. Remind me to tell Jonas to go to my quarters and pick up a suit. He can have whoever is going to fly us down to Albany bring it with him." He took his left hand off the steering wheel and mimicked talking.

Keenan understood. "I really appreciate you doing this, Mr. Robbie," she said aloud.

Fallon smiled. "Yeah, well, why don't you try to get some sleep? It's gonna be a long night."

"And you don't want me disturbing you," she said in a forlorn voice.

"I don't like jabbering when I'm on the road," he said. "That's why I drive a bike."

"All right, sir. I'll leave you alone."

"I hope not."

"Wait until I get you in bed," Keenan purred.

* * * * *

231

They were at a large, busy truck stop just south of the Tennessee border. It was well past midnight but Keenan had insisted on calling her mother and getting it out of the way. Fallon was standing outside one of the phone booths, leaning against the doorjamb with his arms crossed. He knew the exact moment the phone call was answered on the other end for Keenan's jaw clenched.

"Hello, Mama," she said then sat there with her features tight, lips pursed as her mother apparently berated her. When she spoke again, he noticed her voice was softer than he'd ever heard it.

"I am on an assignment, Mama. Didn't Zack tell you?"

A long pause.

"Well, then you know I can't just drop what I'm doing and call you right back. That's not the kind of job I have."

Another long pause and Fallon watched the knuckles of her right hand turn white from the force with which she was gripping the phone.

"I *am* on my way home to Albany, Mama. I should be there after lunchtime tomorrow. When is the rosary going to be...?"

The longest pause, and when Keenan's head lowered, he put a hand on her shoulder and squeezed lightly.

"Yes, Mama, I know she loved me. I loved her too."

He saw Keenan's head come up and there were two bright spots of color in her cheeks.

"*No*, he's not with me! Why the heck would you think he would be?"

A very short pause then Keenan shot to her feet.

"Look, I've got to go. I'll see you tomorrow at the rosary."

Just a second before she slammed the receiver on the hook, Fallon distinctly heard the voice at the other end yelling for her not to hang up.

"Rosary is at 6 p.m. Let's go," Keenan said, shoving past him, her shoulders hunched.

He had to run to catch up with her.

232

"That bad?"

"Yeah," she snapped. "That bad."

* * * * *

Fallon handed over the keys of the BMW to the young woman who would be driving it to Regis Cove. He received instructions from her on which number to call so a phone call from Georgia would be routed through the Cove and then down to Louisiana. Since there was only one phone at the Cove, the Exchange was in control of the landline. After driving them to the airfield where a Lear jet was awaiting them, the driver bid them a safe trip and said she'd meet them back there on Tuesday.

Once the jet was airborne and the seat belt sign was off, Fallon took Keenan's hand and led her through the plane, ignoring the attendant, and to the restroom. Closing and locking the door behind him.

"I couldn't wait," he said, grabbing the skirt of her dress and jerking it upward.

"And you said I was impatient," she said, fumbling with her bra as he unbuttoned his jeans, shot the zipper down then shoved her panties down her legs.

"You are impatient," he said, and wrapped his arms around her to lift her. Those sweet long legs of hers going around him to clamp tightly about his waist. He wedged his hand between their bodies and guided himself into her velvety warmth, backing her against the lavatory, thrusting upward with a long, hard arch of his pelvis.

"Ah, Fallon," she moaned, her arms draped around his neck, pulling his mouth to hers.

Their tongues collided just as their lower bodies were doing. He growled low in his throat with every push into her hot body. She was like a velvet glove clenching his cock, sliding down it, pulsing around it, and he was a man possessed as he drove into her. His legs were like steel pistons and he bounced her on his shaft, grinding against her, thrusting into her so powerfully she grunted with each push.

He tore his mouth from hers to press his lips to her throat. He wasn't even aware he was sinking his fangs into the soft muscle at the side of her neck until he tasted her blood. By then it was too late to stop and the climax that spiraled out of control shot through his body like lava from an erupting volcano. As soon as her sheath began to undulate, vibrate around him, he bucked against her violently, drawing her essence deep into his mouth, swallowing convulsively.

Keenan was aware of what he was doing. She had felt the sting as the sharpness pierced her flesh, but it seemed right. It seemed natural that he feed from her. Though her head swam and she felt weak, she knew he would not take more than he should and so she clung to him—wondering what it would be like to be as he was.

The last ripple of her cunt around him subsided and he felt drained. He sagged against her, his fangs retracting as his forehead fell to her shoulder. He was breathing heavily, gasping for breath, and his hearing was muffled for the blood rushing through his ears. Her arms were holding him fiercely but her lips were on his cheek, kissing him over and over again—soft little busses that sent a shiver down his spine.

"Too long," he managed to say.

"Yes," she answered.

"Next time in a bed," he said then lifted his head to lock gazes with her. "In your bed. In your mother's house."

She opened her mouth to protest but then realized what he was doing. He was laying to rest the ghost of Zack Breslin and Lily McCullough defiling her room, and she nodded.

"Yes."

She unhooked her ankles and slid her legs down his. His arms were still around her, hers around him, and she pressed her cheek to his chest, listening to the rapid tattoo of his heart beneath the cotton of his black T-shirt.

"I love you, lineman," she said.

"I love you, *tarrishagh*," he whispered.

The plane shook as it hit a bit of turbulence and they eased apart from one another. They stood forehead to forehead for a moment then he squatted down to retrieve her panties, held them for her to step into as her hand rested on his shoulders. After their clothing was once more in place, he opened the door and they went to their seats, the attendant pretending he hadn't noticed their abrupt disappearance.

Chapter Seventeen

છ૦

She rounded a lazy curve and her mother's house came into view.

"Shit!" Fallon whispered, bending down to look up through the windshield at the immense red brick structure that set on a slight rise. The Early Classical Revival was ablaze with sedate lighting in all the tall windows and the two long single-story wings flanking the main portion of the house were bracketed by two large live oaks festooned with twinkling lights. The curving driveway that passed in front of the house was lined with copper-shaded path lights and upon the great expanse of lawn were accent lights that shone up into the oaks and lit many of the shrubs that adorned lush floral islands here and there.

"My mother likes plants," Keenan mumbled, and turned the car onto another part of the driveway that led to the back of the opulent structure.

"A six-car garage?" Fallon questioned as they neared the detached structure.

"That was for Daddy's collection of antique cars," she said. "His hobby was restoring them." She pointed to another wing jutting off the back of the house. "That's the regular garage."

"With only four bays," he snorted.

As they neared the garage, one of the doors slid up and Keenan pulled into the brightly lit interior. An older Afro-American gentleman in a dove gray suit was waiting as she parked and turned off the ignition.

"Jessie," she said. "He's as old as Methuselah but he can run rings around me walking the perimeter of the property."

Opening the door for her, the butler smiled warmly. "Welcome home, Miss Kiki," he said, holding out a hand to help her from the car. "It is so nice to have you with us again."

Keenan returned his smile and drew him into her arms. "How've you been, Jess?"

"Fair to middling," he reported, patting her gently on the back. "Your mama didn't say how long you'll be staying with us but I hope it will be awhile."

"Just tonight," Keenan said, and turned to Fallon as he joined them. "Jess, this is the man I'm going to spend the rest of my life with." She took Fallon's hand. "This is Misha Fallon."

"Welcome to Heartstone, Mr. Fallon," Jessie said with a graceful bow of his white head. "Mrs. McCullough failed to mention you had a guest with you, Miss Kiki."

"That's because I'm about as welcome to her as a case of the quick-steps, Jessie," Fallon told the older man. He held out his hand. "It's nice to meet you."

Jessie's lips quirked. "Ah, I see," he said, taking the proffered hand. He looked at Keenan with love. "I do believe I am going to like this young man of yours."

"You will," Keenan said. "He's nothing like that other asshole I brought here."

"I'm a lower class of asshole," Fallon said, "but I'm harmless."

"Don't you believe it," Keenan said. "He's about as dangerous as they come."

Jessie inclined his head. "I imagine he is." He held out his hand for Keenan to precede him. "I'll get your bags for you." One thick white brow shot up. "Shall I put Mr. Fallon in the..."

"Misha," Fallon corrected. "Not even my father was Mr. Fallon, and I'll be bunking with the tart here."

Jessie laughed, his eyes dancing. "Well, I suppose that answered my question. His bags will accompany yours into your old room."

"Yep," Keenan said with a decisive nod, and started for the door into the house.

Fallon glanced back at Jessie and winked. He liked the man and he had a feeling Jessie more than likely had provided the brighter moments in Keenan's troubled past.

The route Keenan took through the house landed them first in the kitchen where she stopped to talk to the cook, a jovial Afro-American woman who had to weigh at least three hundred pounds.

"Are you wanting some supper, young lady?" the woman whose name was Peaches inquired.

"Yes, ma'am," Keenan answered. "At lunch I told Fallon we had to save room for supper because I knew you'd fix something heavenly."

Peaches folded her arms over her massive chest and squinted angrily. "Well, your mama didn't tell me nothing about you being here to eat. If I'd known you was going to be here, I'd have made all your favorites. As it is, leftovers is gonna have to do."

"Your leftovers are better than any five-star restaurant I've ever been in," Keenan told her. "Just pile it on and I'll be happy."

"Miss Lily won't be here so you can enjoy your food, sugar," Peaches declared. "Eat it however you see fit."

"She has an engagement, huh?" Keenan asked. "Did this come up before or after she told you I wasn't alone?"

Peaches shot Fallon an apologetic look. "After."

"I am wounded to the core," Fallon said, hand to his heart. "She neglects to tell the good Jess about me because I'm not worth wasting the breath over then she runs off so she won't have to eat with me. Could Lily love me any less?"

The black woman chuckled. "I got a feeling you give as good as you get, son. Now shoo." She waved her hands at them. "Get outta my kitchen and let me work."

Leading him into the den, Keenan went to the bar. "What's your poison tonight, lineman?" she asked.

"I'm a cheap date, McCullough. Give me whatever you've got the most of." He sat on one of four loveseats scattered about the spacious room.

Keenan smiled as she rooted among the bottles and found the most expensive Scotch. She poured him two fingers of the rare vintage and poured herself a glass of plum wine. She brought the libations over to him and kicked off her shoes before joining him on the loveseat.

"Well, at least we won't have to put up with Mama's shit tonight," she said.

"Don't count on it," he said, and nodded toward the doorway where a well-dressed woman stood watching them.

"Keenan, I would like a word with you," her mother said then looked pointedly at Fallon. "In private."

Keenan took a sip of the wine then licked her lips, enjoying the wince that action brought to her mother. "Anything you have to say to me can be said in front of Fallon. We are after all partners."

"Do you really want him to hear my private opinion of him, Keenan?" her mother demanded.

"I imagine he already knows your opinion of him," Keenan said. "And he doesn't give a rat's ass about how you feel."

"That's true," Fallon said happily. "I really don't." He grinned brutally. "And thanks for making yourself scarce tonight, Lil." He draped his arm behind Keenan and squeezed her to him. "It might get a bit loud later on this evening."

"You son of a bitch!" Lily shouted, eyes flaring. "I want you out of my house this instant!"

"He's not going anywhere, Mama," Keenan said firmly. "This is my house more than it is yours since Daddy left it to me. Whom I invite to my house is not your concern. After supper, he and I are going up to my room and to bed..."

"You will not play the whore in your father's house!" her mother practically screamed. "That man will sleep in one of the guest rooms!"

"He's sleeping with me."

"The hell he is! He..."

"You didn't have a problem with Zack Breslin sleeping in my bed," Keenan countered.

"Or you humping him in your daughter's bed," Fallon commented. "Don't worry though. You aren't my type, so the only humping that's gonna be done in that room tonight will be between me and Keenan."

Her mother's mouth dropped open. "You *told* him?" When Keenan didn't answer, her mother pivoted on her heel and stormed from the room. The sound of doors slamming followed in her wake.

"I think you hurt her feelings, *lhiannan*," Fallon laughed.

Keenan rubbed a hand over her face. "I hope she stays away all night. I know she's got a man she sees on the sly." She laid her head on his shoulder. "A married man."

"Ouch," he said. "She's into taking what's not hers, isn't she?"

"My mother is a barracuda," she said, tucking her legs beneath her. "She'll do whatever it takes to get her way. There was a rumor the death of a woman with whom she was having a brutal feud wasn't an accident."

"You think she's capable of murder?" he asked, brows drawn together.

"I've learned not to put anything past my mother. I think she's perfectly capable of ordering someone to kill for her, yes. I've never wanted to know for sure."

"Lovely," he muttered.

"Y'all come on and get your supper now," Peaches called to them from the kitchen. "Miss Lily done pulled out of the garage."

Keenan patted his leg. "Come on, lineman. You're in for a real treat!"

* * * * *

After a truly delicious meal that had him yawning and rubbing his stomach like an old man, Fallon trooped wearily up the stairs with Keenan after he'd made the obligatory call to Bolivar. The call—rerouted through Regis Cove—was short and to the point, and he had been as gruff as Robbie Marks would have been in a similar situation.

"Yeah, she's okay," he'd snapped. "Can't keep her yap shut around the women here but she's okay."

"I can't believe this mausoleum was built for just three people," he mused as he stopped to look at a family portrait of Keenan, her mother and father. "How old were you when this was taken?"

"Twelve," she said.

"You be a cute little shit," he said, sweeping his arm around her. "So innocent-looking and sweet as a sugar cane." He nuzzled her neck.

Keenan pushed him away playfully. "Actually, when Daddy built the house, he did so with the idea of creating a dynasty of McCullough sons to follow in his footsteps. When I was born, he was a bit disappointed, but he truly expected the next child to be a boy." He reached out to touch her father's likeness. "There was no next child."

"Lily couldn't have another or what?"

"She had never wanted one in the first place," she replied. "If she hadn't been convinced of that before she went into labor with me, twenty-nine hours of what she terms excruciating agony settled the issue in her mind."

"I take it she went on the Pill without your father knowing."

"Oh no," Keenan said. "There might be a mishap with the Pill. My mother tends to be rather forgetful. She was afraid she might slip up and get knocked up again so she went up to Atlanta and had her tubes tied when Daddy was on a business trip with Grandpa." She dusted her hands together then started down the hall. "And that settled that."

"And he never knew?"

"No, I don't think he did," she replied as she stopped at a door, took a deep breath then opened it. "Voila! Welcome to teenage heaven."

And that was exactly what her room looked like. He moved past her to stand in the center of the soft pink and light green confection that had been her room when she was a girl.

"Man," he said. The frills and lace and stuffed animals amused him. The posters of the 80s heartthrobs that plastered the green gingham wallpaper amused him even more.

241

"I think of my room every time I see a bottle of Pepto-Bismol," she said with a sigh.

"Don Johnson?" he questioned with a pained look. "Harry Hamlin and Richard Grieco?"

"They were my men back in the day," she defended her choice of movie stars. "Obviously you didn't see Harry in that Olympic gods movie." She rolled her eyes and fanned her face. "Lordy, lordy, lordy! That white toga and those tanned legs? Yum!"

He walked over to a large bulletin board that was obviously her trophy wall. There were blue ribbons and medals for swimming and track as well as gymnastics.

"I'm impressed," he said then moved on to look at the stacks of records, books and whatnots that littered her room. He glanced around. "Obviously you weren't the neat freak back then that you are now."

She grinned. "No, I wasn't into housekeeping." She giggled. "He was my main crush." She pointed to a door hung with a full-length poster of Harrison Ford as Hans Solo.

"Him I understand," he said and put his arms around her. "Who's your main crush now, babe?"

All the weeks of wanting him so desperately had not truly been sated in the restroom of the plane. She wanted to be able to touch him, to run her hands all over his tall, muscular body. She wanted him to take her leisurely and she wanted to be able to feel the delicious weight of his body upon hers.

"What?" he asked as she pushed him back.

"Come with me," she said, and took his hand to lead him out of the room.

They left her room, moved down the hallway until they came to another door that she flung open without a moment's thought. As she led him through the tastefully decorated room, he knew it had to be her mother's personal inner sanctum. The salary he received in a year's time would not have replaced the expensive furnishings contained within its walls.

"What are you doing?" he asked as she headed for what he knew must be her mother's bathroom.

"I am going to rape, ravage and pillage you, lineman," she said. "In my mother's precious bathtub."

Bathtub? he questioned as she pushed open the door, reached inside to turn on the lights then took him through a large expanse of marble vanity with twin sinks, toilet and bidet, huge enclosed glass-block tiled shower and into a room nearly as big as his entire bedroom at the Exchange dormitory.

"Shit," he breathed.

The room had three floor-to-ceiling glass walls that looked out over a private, secluded garden filled with lush foliage and marble statues, effectively lit from ground level. Overhead, the ceiling was a solid pane of glass above which the stars in the night twinkled and the waning moon shone. From copper pots suspended from brass chains and attached to brackets on the windows fell lush cascades of potted plants. On each corner was a miniature palm. Under foot was a thick dark green carpet that looked like immaculately groomed grass. The lights that twinkled from strips along each window frame reflected in the glass. Beyond the windows in the garden was a tropical waterfall, and the sound of it could be heard in the bathroom along with the gentle, low clink of a bass wind chime.

But the *pièce de résistance* was the huge sunken garden bathtub that sat in the center of the room.

Carved from beige travertine marble, the fixture was twelve feet square with a brass railing and steps down into the gently bubbling water. The spigot and controls looked like real gold and when Keenan informed him they were, Fallon shook his head.

"This room cost more to build and furnish than most people's homes," he said. "Didn't it?"

"I imagine so," Keenan agreed. She was busy lighting the scores of amber-colored glass votives that sat on a long strip of mirror behind the tub. The air held the scent of gardenia as the scented candles flamed.

In a large wicker basket was a stack of plush white towels, and when she was finished lighting the candles, Keenan withdrew two, placed them at one end of the tub and told her lover to strip.

"Nice and slow, bad boy. I want to enjoy the show," she said as she took a seat tailor fashion on the floor.

Fallon grinned then slowly, inch by inch, tugged the tail of his shirt from his pants. He'd taken off his boots in the den just as his lady had kicked off her own shoes and had stuffed his socks inside. As he crossed his arms over his chest to pull the partially unbuttoned shirt over his head, he felt his groin tighten with anticipation. He could feel the heaviness building and with it the desire.

Keenan leaned back on her elbows as his shirt came off. "Stand still," she said when he dropped the garment carelessly to the floor.

He obeyed, feeling a bit foolish yet aroused with his hands at his sides, his legs slightly spread. He could feel her gaze sliding over his chest and his nipples hardened just from the thought of her touching them. Some wild part of him wanted her to pinch them hard, bite them, and at that wayward thought, his cock pulsed hard against his pants.

"Now very slowly unzip your pants," she ordered.

With infinite care, he put his hands to the button of his fly and undid it, spreading the waistband apart. He gradually tugged the slider of his zipper down inch by agonizing inch until all the teeth were separated and the slider rested on the bottom stop.

"What now, warden?" he asked in a husky tone.

"Hook your thumbs inside your waistband and slide them ever so slowly down your hips," she instructed.

Doing just that, he began to work the tight jeans over his lean hips. Down past the waistband of his black boxers, over his hipbones and onto the hard plane of his thighs.

"Stop," she said, and sat up. She walked on her knees over to him and looked up into his bemused face. "Move your hands."

He took his thumbs from the jeans and let his arms hang loosely at his sides once more.

Keenan reached up and took hold of the waistband of the jeans and began to lower them, pushing the fabric down his thighs, past his knees and onto his ankles.

"Step out," she said, and he did, watching as she tossed the garment aside.

Clad only in his boxer shorts, he remained still as she swept her eyes over him from bare feet to head, back again, and then like the needle on a scale fluctuating from one number to another before finally settling on just one. When her attention rested, it locked on the bulge between his legs. She leaned forward and pressed her lips to the swelling, blowing her warm breath through the fabric.

Fallon sucked in a breath. He hadn't felt anything as erotic in a long time. The hot, damp air issuing from her mouth spread under his balls and he shivered, his hands going to her head as she continued to exhale on his hardening flesh.

Slowly working the boxers down until she had uncovered his abdomen, she ran one hand beneath the loose leg band of the undergarment and slid it between his legs.

"Ah God, Keenan," he whispered, closing his eyes and letting his head fall back. His thigh muscles were quivering as she kneaded him in counter rhythm to the hot breath she was blowing against his cock. The cheeks of his ass tightened.

Smiling to herself, she plucked at the fabric of his boxers until his cock sprang from the fly.

"Look what I found," she said.

He could feel her staring intently at his cock and lowered his head, opened his eyes. Seeing her lick her lips was almost his undoing, he warned her with a low growl.

Keenan sat back on her heels, eased her hands from the boxers then drew them down his legs. She didn't need to tell him to step out for he did so, shunting them off to one side with the edge of his foot. He was breathing heavily, loudly, the air going in and out of his lungs much quicker than was normal.

She looked up into his beautiful male face. "Spread your legs," she whispered.

His jaw clenched. His fists clenched, but he did as told. "You're playing with fire," he cautioned her.

"I know."

Leaning forward again, she began to blow slow, hot breaths on the straining head of his cock. With each rub of her palm, her middle finger moved closer to his anus and each time it did, his ass cheeks tensed.

"Keenan," he said, drawing the name out. He was digging his nails into his palms, his legs feeling weaker by the second.

One moment she was kneeling at his feet and the next she was standing before him, ordering him into the tub.

"Now?" he asked, wanting to throw her to the floor and slam into her hot cunt.

"Into. The. Tub," she said.

Teeth clenched, he moved over to the rail, took hold of it and stepped down into the water, amazed at how hot it was and the silky feel of it lapping at his legs.

She took her time taking off her clothing. The dress had a long row of buttons down the front. She unbuttoned each one slowly, leisurely flicking the two edges of the dress apart. Once it was undone, she shrugged out of it and it slithered to the floor in a silken pool.

Fallon swallowed convulsively. "You know you're torturing me, don't you," he said in a gruff voice.

Her breasts were full and firm, the cleavage deep as she reached around behind her to unhook her bra. The push of her flesh against the cups of the bra made his shaft weep and he realized he had reached the point where he was almost panting, eager to be buried deep inside her. Staring at those beautiful globes as they came free of their confinement, Fallon heard a groan escape his lips. Beneath the water, his shaft leapt, his balls tightened and heat drove straight through his groin.

Keenan slid her hands beneath the waistband of her silk bikini briefs and pushed them down her long, shapely legs.

With regal grace she stepped down into the water and moved to sit across from him on the opposite bench.

He moved so quickly she gasped, gliding across the water and onto her. Wedging her legs apart, he settled himself atop her and grabbed a handful of hair to draw her head back, slanting his mouth ruthlessly on hers, kissing her deep and hard and thoroughly.

Keenan put her arms around him as their tongues performed a heady mating dance. He ground his lower body against hers. His lips slid to her ear, he flicked his tongue into the depths then clamped her earlobe gently between his teeth.

He trailed kisses along her cheek and down her neck, planting a long kiss to the hollow of her throat where a vein pulsed wildly. He moved on to her shoulders and across the upper part of her chest then ducked his head beneath the tumbling waters to latch his lips greedily upon her nipple.

Keenan buried her fingers in his hair and laid her head back along the tub's rim as he suckled her. His tongue was sweeping across the engorged tip and his nibbling teeth were causing wicked things to happen to her lower body. He had good breath control for he moved on to her other breast and lavished just as much attention there before popping out of the water, flinging his wet hair, droplets flying. His hands were still on her breasts, his thumbs having taken over for his tongue as he flicked them back and forth over the sensitive nubs.

Fallon pushed her back upon the ledge and spread her thighs wide as he scooted down in the water until he could position his shaft at the opening of her wet folds. With one firm thrust, he impaled her and began working his hips as her arms and legs wrapped around him. His hands beneath her rump, he increased the depth and force of his drives until they were both grunting and the water was splashing over the sides of the tub.

Though her backbone was being bruised against the tub's side from the power of his thrusts, Keenan didn't care. The pleasure was building inside her and beginning to spiral out of control. She could feel the heat flooding her belly, the itch beginning, the frantic need elevating within her lover. His fingers were digging into her buttock, but none of that mattered. She squeezed her legs tight around him, dug her own fingernails into his ravaged back then clamped her teeth onto his shoulder.

"God!" he exclaimed, and jerked. His rutting rose to a violent level as he pounded into her, his cock rigid and driving so deep she could feel it pressing against her womb. When he came, he came so hard he nearly convulsed, shuddering fiercely.

Keenan felt him pouring into her and reveled in that feeling, her cunt pulsing around him as her own climax came. She made a slight squealing noise and clung to him even more as wave after delicious wave undulated through her. His weight was solid against her, his groin slapping against hers as he tried to prolong her pleasure even as the last of his energy and lust was spent. It was good her arms were secure around him when the last spasm left her or else he would have slid boneless beneath the rippling water.

"Sweet merciful God" he mumbled, and she could feel the pounding of his heart against her chest. "Much more of that and I'll be a dead man."

She held him to her with one hand and with the other, pushed the wet hair from his eyes. "Liked that I take it?"

He grunted in answer, his eyes closed as he labored to get his breath and heartbeat under control.

"As much as I'd like us to be in here when Mama gets home, I'm starting to look like a prune," she said, holding her wrinkled palm up. "Let's take the rest of this to my room."

He forced one eye open and gave her a jaundiced look. "You're assuming I've got more left in me, *myneeast caillagh.*" He groaned. "I'm not sure I do."

"All you have to do is lie there while I drain you dry," she said. "Think you can do that, lineman?"

A long, heartfelt sigh came from his chest. "If I have to, I suppose I can."

"You have to because God only knows when we'll be able to do this again."

He yawned. "On the plane," he stated. "Again." Then released his tight hold on her. "And in the car alongside the road somewhere." He stood and held out his hand to help her up. "Again."

"You trying to wear me out, Fallon?" she asked as he pulled her to her feet.

He laughed and climbed out of the tub, drawing her in his wake. He bent over, plucked up the towels, unfolded one and wrapped it around her then cocooned himself in the other as she leaned down to retrieve their clothing.

"The floor's a mess," he said as she started out of the door. "Shouldn't we mop it up?"

"Leave it," she ordered.

After one last amused look at the mess they'd made in Lily's bathroom, he shrugged, grinned and followed his lady back to her room.

Chapter Eighteen

Keenan was still sleeping when Fallon slipped out of her room around six the next morning and padded barefoot down the stairs and into the kitchen. The funeral wasn't until 10:30 so he had plenty of time to kill before he drove her to the church.

"I gave Peaches the morning off to attend the funeral so if you want coffee you'll have to pour it yourself then join me."

Glancing around, he saw the French doors from the kitchen to the patio were standing open and Keenan's mother was sitting on the patio.

"Did you make it?" he called out.

"You see anyone else lurking about?" she countered.

After pouring himself a cup of coffee, he took it outside. "Did you put a few drops of cyanide in it for flavoring?"

She made an unladylike sound. "Poisoning would be too easy a death for a man like you," she quipped.

Keenan had not been exaggerating about the view from the patio. It was stunning and in the early morning sun, light filtered through the trees to settle upon a small pond over which a curved wooden bridge had been built.

"You have a very lovely home," he said as he sat in one of the thickly upholstered wrought iron chairs.

"My husband provided quite well for us," she said. Clothed in a gaily patterned silk caftan with gold sandals on her manicured feet, she was wearing a pair of dark sunglasses—no doubt to hide the effects of a late night with her lover. "Kiki never wanted for anything when she was growing up. Everything was given to her." She lifted her china coffee cup to her lips. "That's why she is such a spoiled brat now."

"Oh, I don't think she's spoiled at all," Fallon said. "She has a very level head on her shoulders."

Lily turned her face toward him. "Did you enjoy fucking my daughter in my bathtub, Mr. Fallon?"

Fallon crossed one leg over the other and settled back comfortably in the chair. He hadn't gotten over how much her voice sounded like Keenan's. "I don't fuck your daughter, Lil. I make love to her, but maybe you aren't familiar with the nuances of love play."

"I know a ruthless bounder when I see one," she said.

"Is that what you think I am?"

She reached up to lower the sunglasses so he could see her frosty eyes. "Perhaps bounder is too generous a word. I know all about men like you, Fallon."

He smiled nastily. "And what it is you think you know about me?"

"I know you are a crude, vulgar, grasping cad. You see this house and think of yourself as its master one day." She leaned forward. "Well, baby, I'm here to tell you that you'll never get your greedy hands on it or my daughter!"

Fallon didn't respond to her taunt. He held her angry glare for a moment then took a long drink of his coffee, gazing at her over the rim of the delicate cup. Surprised at the excellent flavor of the brew, he complimented her by raising the cup in salute.

"Did you hear what I said?" she snapped.

"Why don't you let your daughter run her own life?" he countered.

"Because my daughter cannot be trusted to do the right thing!" she said. "All her life she's had this fixation with the downtrodden, the outcasts and the dregs of society no one else would give the time of day. She befriended the most inappropriate children when she was growing up, dragging those bumpkins and white-trash children home to play with her, insisting I invite them to her birthday parties."

"And did you?"

Keenan's mother's lip crooked upward. "What do you think?"

"I think you underestimated Keenan's capacity to love when she was a child and you're underestimating it now. She looks past what's in a person's bank account to that person's real worth—if they have any—and makes her decision based on how she perceives them. I don't think designer clothes and half-million dollar automobiles have much value to her."

Lily regarded him at length with a steady, unblinking glower of pure, unadulterated revulsion, but if she thought the stare would unnerve him, intimidate him and make him turn away, Fallon knew she was going to be in for a major disappointment. He held the bristling scowl aiming daggers at him and politely smiled.

"You fucking conceited prick," she exploded, eyes flashing. "I'll see you six feet under before I let you have my daughter! She belongs with Zack Breslin!"

The smile slipped from Fallon's face to be replaced with a brutal visage that made Lily McCullough pull back.

"And that's one man I'll put six feet under if he so much as lays one hand on Keenan," he snarled. "What the hell kind of mother are you that you would want a man you spread your whoring legs for to screw your only child?"

"Zack loves her and he'll be a good father to her child," she declared.

"He isn't going to get the chance. I'll neuter him first!"

"The plans have all been made, and I can promise you Keenan and Zack will be married before the year is out even if I have to force the marriage on her!"

Fallon stared at with his brows drawn together in a savage scowl. "You're a sick, twisted bitch who should have been drowned at birth."

"And you're a dead man," Lily spat, shooting up from her chair so violently it tipped over. Without another look his way, she stormed off across the immaculately trimmed backyard.

"Get me out of this house."

Fallon snapped his head around to see Keenan standing in her bathrobe, tears streaking down her cheeks.

"Now, Fallon!" she pleaded.

He was out of his chair and at her side in an instant, sweeping her up in his arms. "You got it, babe," he said, carrying her through the kitchen and up the stairs.

* * * * *

As soon as the funeral was over and the reception line began forming, Keenan excused herself from the padded chairs in the front row under the dark green tent and took Fallon's hand. She'd already spoken to her remaining aunts and Marjorie's grieving husband—making her excuses for why she would not be at the luncheon afterward, saying her goodbyes, expressing her love for her family—but she had no intention of prolonging her visit on the chance her mother would cause an additional scene.

Once in the car, she broke down and cried miserably all the way to the airport. Fallon didn't try to comfort her for he knew her anguish and misery had as much to do with the loss of her beloved aunt as it did the death of whatever love she might have still held for her mother. There was no relief for that, no consoling and no placation. Her pain would have to play itself out and only time would cure the depression.

"I hate her," she'd said on the way to the church that morning. "I hate her so much I can't stand it, Fallon."

He understood her despair as well as her fury. His feelings for his stepfather weren't much different than those she held for her mother.

The Lear was waiting for them and took off only moments after they settled onboard. Keenan sat beside Fallon with her head on his shoulder, their hands locked together.

There was no quick trip to the restroom on the flight up to Memphis. At the airfield there, the young woman who had driven Bolivar's car to Regis Cove was waiting for them. Keenan got into the backseat and lay down with her back to the front.

"Mate of the hound, I am sorry for your loss."

"Thank you," Keenan said softly. "I have asked you to call me Keenan."

"*Keenan,*" the beast whispered then cleared its throat as though embarrassed. "*Hound? I will be leaving shortly for my world. Take care of your lady while I am gone.*"

"I will."

"*I will ask my masters about this creature you are trying to find. Though I have tried to track it, I have had no success.*"

"Tell them its name means Spirit of the Night."

"*Aye, that I will.*" The presence drew back as silently as it had come.

"You okay back there?" Fallon asked.

"Let's go, lineman," she said. "Every minute I'm here cuts like a knife."

He knew she was having a crisis but there was nothing he could do. He would leave her alone, knowing when she was ready to discuss it, she'd come to him. He also knew there would be no stopping along the road on the way to Louisiana, no chance to love her.

There would, however, be a stop for gas, a trip to the restroom to remove all traces of the smeared makeup on her face and a change back into a dowdier, looser-fitting dress as better suited the young woman known as Tandy Lynch.

Back in Albany—after the last mourner had departed her home and she had wearily climbed the stairs to her bedroom, Lily McCullough walked to the door of her garden tub room and stared at the carpet that was still sopping wet from the evening before. She stood there for a long time and when she finally shook herself free of the murderous rage she felt, she went to the phone on her bedside table and dialed a number in Atlanta.

"Royce?" she said when the call went through. "I have another job for you."

Chapter Nineteen

𝕊𝕆

Bolivar called out for Fallon to come on in. She was in the bedroom with Keenan—had been for several hours—for this was the night Tandy Lynch would make her ministry debut in Metairie, Louisiana, to a packed tent.

"We'll be ready in a minute!" Bolivar said.

"Take your time," Fallon mumbled. He knew that excuse all too well and plopped down in the chair, swiping a magazine off the coffee table. Idly thumbing through it, he found an article that looked interesting and started reading—anything to keep his mind off Keenan and the need that was growing with leaps and bounds inside his body. He heard rustling but didn't look up.

"Well, what do you think?"

Frowning, he stuck his thumb in the magazine to mark his place, lifted his head and froze.

"Well?" Bolivar prompted.

Without any other conscious thought in his mind save touching the beautiful vision standing before him, he slowly rose to his feet, so mesmerized he simply dropped the magazine to the floor. He couldn't move. He couldn't breathe. His heart was pounding so fiercely in his chest he thought he might well pass out for his blood was racing hot and thick through his veins. All he could do was stare at the magnificent creature across from him even though what he really wanted to do was kneel at her feet and offer her all that was his.

"Robbie, honestly!" Boliver snapped. "Say something!"

"She..." He had to clear his throat. "She looks nice," he managed to say.

"Nice?" Bolivar gasped with disbelief. "She looks nice?"

"Yeah," he said, flinging out a hand. "She looks nice."

Keenan's hazel eyes were locked on his.

"Oh for the love of God, Robbie," Bolivar snarled. "Shut your mouth. You look like a beached carp!" She reached out to adjust a soft brown curl that dangled over Keenan's left shoulder. "I take it you have been struck dumb by the beauty I have brought out in this sweet girl."

"Do I look all right, Mr. Robbie?" Keenan asked, her eyes twinkling.

"You know you do," he heard himself say, and had to shake his head to clear it of the urge to rush to her and drag her into his arms.

"Then I would like you to escort her to the tent tonight," Bolivar said. "I'll be in front with the old cadre surrounding me. People will be rubbernecking trying to see Tandy and figure out who she is. Don't you let some rube touch this gown, do you hear me?"

The gown in which Keenan was dressed had to be the most beautiful creation in the world. He'd never seen its like and he knew beyond a shadow of a doubt it had cost Bolivar a small fortune.

Made of shimmering copper-colored taffeta, the gown had an empire waistline and a flowing hankie-hem skirt. The edges of the hem and the bodice had been sewn with hundreds of sparkling copper beads and the short cap sleeves were made of lace in the same color as the gown. The effect of the light hitting the crystal beads was stunning.

"Show him your shoes, sweetie," Bolivar told her.

Keenan flicked the hem of her skirt back so he could see the copper-colored leather sandals embellished with crystal beads.

"Aren't they beautiful?" Keenan asked.

"You are beautiful," he whispered, lost in the hazel depths of her eyes.

Bolivar stiffened then turned to give Keenan a gentle look. "Would you go back to the bedroom and get my shawl?"

"Yes, ma'am," Keenan replied.

As soon as she was gone, Bolivar shot out a hand and grabbed Fallon's arm.

"Don't even think about it," she hissed.

Fallon blinked and his eyebrows drew together. *What was this?* he asked himself. He had instilled strong sublims regarding Keenan and himself in Bolivar's mind—sublims that would make it possible for him to be with her without suspicion. Now those sublims had been erased.

"I don't understand what you mean," he said.

"Hell yes, you do. You keep away from her, Robbie," Bolivar said, jabbing a finger into his chest. "She's off limits to you."

Trying to slip into Bolivar's mind proved to be impossible. Something—or someone—had countermanded his psychic suggestions. There were impenetrable psychic roadblocks that had been erected in the few short days he'd been gone. Roland's smirking face crossed his mind and he silently cursed the gypsy bastard.

"Are we clear on this, Robbie?" Bolivar pressed.

"Is something wrong?" Keenan asked as she came back with Bolivar's shawl.

"Nothing I can't handle, sweetie," Bolivar replied. She took the shawl and swung it around her slender shoulders, adjusted the gold folds of her dress then smiled warmly at Keenan. "Tonight's your night and I'm not got to allow anything," she glanced at Fallon, "or anyone to spoil it for you."

A light tapping at the door alerted Bolivar that the crowd was in the tent and it was time for her to make her appearance.

"All right," the evangelist said. "It's showtime!" She went to the door and waited for Fallon to open it for her. "Thank you, Robbie."

"I live to serve," Fallon mumbled as he spied Roland standing just outside with the bodyguards who would be escorting Bolivar into the tent.

"What's wrong?" Keenan questioned as she joined Fallon at the door.

"Nothing, Miss Tandy," he said, locking gazes with her. He couldn't transmit an explanation to her for Roland would intercept it. All he could do was give her a look he hoped she would translate as a warning. He was relieved when she gave him a slight nod then took the arm he proffered to her.

The crowd inside the tent went wild when they saw Bolivar, but there was also a charged atmosphere as people took in the beautiful woman walking behind her being escorted by the tall, grim-faced man in black.

"Who is she?" people were asking loud enough to be heard over the rollicking choir.

Fallon felt Keenan's hand clench on his arm and he laid his free hand over it for encouragement. One look down at her and he could see a vein beating frantically in her neck. She was terrified of this crowd — he could sense it like a cold rag slapped in his face. His savage frown made those who had thought to reach out to touch her as she passed think twice and move back. Once he had escorted her onto the stage and to the smaller throne-like chair that sat beside Bolivar's, he was being bombarded by her fear.

"My Brothers and Sisters!" Bolivar said as the music died down to a low, soothing melody. "The good Lord has seen fit to send unto me a helpmate, an innocent child of the Appalachians who has come to do His work among us. She has been graced with the Laying on of Hands and gifted with Tongues."

From out of the corner of his eye, Fallon saw Zack Breslin move toward the stage. The agent was dressed in a dark gray silk suit that fit him to perfection — accentuating his wide chest and lean flanks.

"You will be the first to witness the miracles that will come forth from this sweet child's hands. You will see firsthand the abilities our Lord and Savior in His wisdom has sent down to cure your ills and cleanse your spirits. Join with me now in welcoming to our fold Sister Tandy Lynch."

Thunderous applause met Keenan as she left her chair and walked to where Bolivar was standing. Fallon could see the panic rising in his lady's eyes and the nervous way she kept licking her lips. Her hands were clenched at her sides. She was trembling.

Bolivar slipped an arm around Keenan. "This sweet, beautiful young woman is here to serve you, has given up her personal life into the service of our Lord, Jesus Christ, opened her heart and arms to do His will. While I preach the sermon this night, I ask that you silently pray for the success of Sister Tandy's mission. Pray her task on this earth will be done in accordance with His wishes."

"Amen!" rang out among the crowd.

Fallon stood off to one side and surveyed the crowd. Eager, hopeful eyes were locked on Keenan. People were pointing at her. The uneasiness he had begun to feel was increasing. His gaze shifted to Breslin who acknowledged his look with raised eyebrows. Neither man could communicate here since Roland was only a few feet away from the stage, standing beside Matty, who was staring intently at Fallon.

You feel it too, don't you, Matty? Fallon thought to himself. There was something zinging through the air that was setting off warning signals, and all three men sensed it.

Bolivar's sermon lasted longer than usual. To Fallon's way of thinking, the older woman was prolonging the part of the revival in which she turned over the reins to Keenan. Lapping up every last bit of adoration she could squeeze from the crowd, she finally turned to the choir and the members began to hum softly.

"If you are sick of body, of mind or spirit," Bolivar said. "If illness has befallen you and taken over your life, if pain and paralysis of limb has become a way of life for you, then open your hearts and minds to the spirit of our Lord and invite Him to enter."

"Amen," the crowd said.

"Welcome Him with every fiber of your being and ask Him to heal you, Brothers and Sisters. Get down on your knees and beseech Him to allow you to be made whole once again."

"Amen!"

"Praise the Lord!"

"Search deep in your hearts and confess your innermost sins to our Lord and ask for His forgiveness. Only then can you hope to be made whole in body, mind and spirit."

"Amen, Mother! Amen!"

"Sister Tandy, come forward, child," Bolivar said, stretching out a hand to Keenan.

Fallon saw Keenan swallow hard before she left her chair once more and came to stand at Bolivar's right side. She took the older woman's hand.

"If you have made yourself known to my helpers, then let those who would seek the Lord's deliverance from the travails that have beset them now come forward," Bolivar said.

Those upon whose breasts the bright orange stickers had been placed stood and began moving into the aisles to form a long, long line that extended all the way out the doors of the tent. Even above the choir's humming Fallon heard Keenan's low whimper of apprehension. Hating what this was doing to her, he watched as she stood there quivering—unable to help her and knowing that was tearing him apart.

By the time the first of the faithful stood before her on the stage, Keenan was as pale as a ghost.

"What is your ailment, Brother?" Mother Bolivar asked.

It was a woman standing behind the man who answered.

"My boy lost his hearing when an oil rig he was working on exploded," she said. "That was four years ago."

"Does he believe in the power of the Lord?"

"Yes, ma'am. He's a good Christian boy."

"Does he believe the Lord will cure him?"

"Oh yes, ma'am!"

"Then have him kneel before Sister Tandy."

The woman motioned her son to his knees and the young man moved quickly, staring up at Tandy with a look that bordered on worship.

Her hand trembling violently, Keenan placed it upon the kneeling man's head.

Almost immediately the man jerked, flung his arms out, and Fallon realized he was one of Bolivar's men—a shill planted there to motivate those who came after.

"Lord, heal this poor man!" Bolivar cried out, lifting her arms to the heavens. "Heal him and make him whole!"

Keenan seemed to hesitate then placed her other hand on the man's head. When he jerked again, her eyes widened and she pulled her hands back as he shot to his feet.

"I can hear!" he shouted. "I can hear the choir!"

"Praise the Lord!"

The crowd cheered and Fallon felt his heart pounding brutally in his chest. He was staring at Keenan's frightened face as the next person—another shill—knelt at her feet.

"And what ails you, Sister?" Bolivar asked the woman.

"It's my left hand," the woman said of the limb that hung limply at her side. "I had a stroke and can't lift it."

"Kneel, Sister, and let the power of the Lord work through Sister Tandy," Bolivar said.

It was no surprise that as soon as Keenan touched the woman she was cured, raising her supposedly lifeless arm in praise to God. This time the crowd went wild and those in line pushed forward, eager to know the touch of the angel whose eyes were bright with unshed tears.

"I don't like this."

Fallon turned to find Matty standing beside him.

"Yeah, well, neither do I," Fallon said.

"She's scared half to death up there," Matty complained.

Fallon didn't need to be told. He could see the terror stamped on Keenan's face, the tremor in her hand each time she touched a new person.

"That one isn't one of ours," Matty said of the next faithful to kneel at Keenan's feet. "I noticed him on the way over here. He's got some kind of rash all over his body. Just the idea of her touching him…" He shuddered.

And then something strange happened that silenced every man, woman and child in the tent. Sister Tandy placed her hands on the man's head. Her head went back, her throat arched. A strangled cry came from her parted lips and she stiffened as

261

though struck by lightning. From her lips came words from a language no one understood — not even Breslin, who was frowning sharply as he gaped up at her.

"I don't think those are words they rehearsed," Matty muttered to Fallon. "Zack looks like he's been poleaxed."

Complete silence filled the tent as Keenan's voice rang out over the crowd. The man touched by her hands moaned, shook and then pitched to one side, crumpling to the floor.

"Look at him!" a woman sitting in the front row shouted. "She cured him. The disease is leaving his body!"

People shot to their feet and craned their necks to see. Those close by gasped as they watched the redness fading from the man's face, neck and arms.

Fallon and Matty moved closer so they could see, coming to stand by Breslin.

"What's she saying?" Bolivar asked from above them.

Breslin looked up at her. "She's calling down the power of the Lord to heal him," he lied.

"Oh my God," Matty whispered, and sprang up onto the stage. He barely made it to Keenan's side before she began to fall. He caught her as both Fallon and Breslin vaulted onto the stage.

Fallon stared down at the woman he loved and felt cold dread shoot him. There was a slight trickle of blood coming from her left ear as she lay in Matty's arms. Her eyes were glazed and she was so pale she looked like a ghost.

"Did I cure him?" she asked, her voice weak.

"Yes," Bolivar said. She was looking down at the man who was sitting up, staring at his arms. "Yes, Tandy, you did." There was awe in her voice for she knew the man wasn't one of hers.

"Then help me up," Keenan said. When Matty would have prevented her from doing so, she leveled her gaze on him. "Help me up."

Fallon wanted to deny her as he knew Matty did, but he saw determination stamped on her lovely face. Whatever she was feeling now, it was no longer fear and there was a radiance about her that was pushing aside the paleness.

"I think you should go lie down," Matty said. "You've..."

"I've work to do," Keenan said, pushing against his chest. "Now help me up."

Reluctantly Matty drew her to her feet and stepped back, shooting Fallon a beseeching look to which Fallon slightly shook his head. There was nothing either of them could do at that moment. Even Breslin seemed stunned by the turn of events.

"Come forward," he heard Keenan tell the next person in line. She held out her hand. "How may I help you, my friend?"

Fallon blinked. The voice coming from Keenan's mouth was different, stronger and shaded with a light accent he couldn't place.

"Get off the stage," Bolivar hissed to Fallon and Matty. "Now!"

Though both men were loath to do so, they complied, jumping down to stand beside Breslin.

"What the hell is going on here?" Breslin whispered urgently.

"I don't know," Fallon said.

Before Keenan laid her hands to the kneeling person's brow, she turned to face Bolivar and in a clear, carrying voice that brooked no objection said, "You have worked long and hard for our Lord, Mother. It is time you rested. I will take your burden now."

Without so much as a flicker of protest, Bolivar smiled knowingly, turned and walked to her chair, sat down with her hands folded primly in her lap.

One by one the faithful came to kneel at Keenan's feet. Though she wavered from time to time and seemed to be weakening, she would rally with each new ailment laid before her and gently lay her hands to the heads of the seekers. Whether her touch cured them, no one could tell for there were no more pilgrims with brilliant rashes or limp arms. Those who came to her left with beaming faces and tears streaking their faces, but they did not shout their healing or make a spectacle of themselves before the crowd.

Fallon looked about him and marveled at the stillness, the silence that had fallen upon the crowd. It was unnerving, eerie, and the faces staring up at Keenan were filled with adulation.

"I don't like this," Breslin said at one point. "Not one goddamn bit. Look at them! They're eating this shit up!"

"She's healing them," Matty said quietly. "By all that is holy, that's what she's doing."

"Bullshit," Breslin snapped. "They just think she is."

But Fallon knew better and he knew Bolivar and her people knew it too. This was no con job being pulled here. This was the real thing.

At last the final faithful came forward—being rolled in a wheelchair—and as the helpers struggled to push the wheelchair onto the stage, Keenan shook her head.

"I will come to him," she said, and moved toward the step.

It was Roland who rushed forward and took her hand to help her down the steps, and it was Roland who stood at her side with something akin to reverence on his craggy features.

"How long have you been afflicted this way, my friend?" Keenan asked, squatting down before the wheelchair-bound man.

"Since I was a boy," the man replied. "I haven't walked since grade school, Sister Tandy."

"If you believe in the power of God, I promise you that you will walk this night," Keenan said, and there was a gasp that ran like wildfire through the crowd.

"Goddamn it!" Breslin hissed. "She shouldn't make claims like that. This crowd will chew her up and spit her out when that bastard doesn't get up and do a jig!"

"I believe," Fallon heard the man say in a breaking voice. "I do believe."

Keenan rose to her feet and held her hands out to the man. "Then take my hands."

Reaching out for her, the man threaded his fingers through Keenan's and she stepped back, pulling him to his feet.

Every breath was held. Every heart ceased to beat. Not one person dared to blink. All attention was directed on the man who was being levered to a standing position.

"Give yourself to the Lord and He will make you whole again," Keenan said softly. "Do you give yourself to the Lord?"

"I do," the man said. He was wobbling but he was standing.

Keenan unlocked her fingers from his and took another step back. "Then come to me, my friend."

Fallon felt Matty's hand on his arm but didn't look around. His attention was glued on Keenan whose face was shining with an unearthly light and whose hazel eyes were glowing.

"What did you do to her, Coim?" he whispered. "What did you do?"

"Come to me," Keenan repeated.

The man wavered, his arms out in front of him, but then he lifted his right foot and took a single step.

"No," Matty denied. "This isn't happening."

One step more.

"Praise the Lord," Roland said as he stepped closer to the man lest he should fall.

A third step before the man lifted his head and looked directly into Keenan's eyes. "I can walk," he said. "I can walk!"

And the crowd erupted into pandemonium as people surged forward. It was plain they wanted to touch the woman who had wrought this miracle, but Roland moved in front of her, motioning frantically for the bodyguards to block the onrushing crowd.

"We've got to get her out of here!" Breslin shouted. He vaulted onto the stage and ran toward Keenan, reaching down to shove his hands under her arms and lift her onto the stage.

Fallon shoved Matty ahead of him, bellowing for Matty to help Breslin get Keenan out of harm's way. All around him people were stampeding to get to her, the noise so thunderous he wasn't sure if Matty had heard or not. Chairs were knocked over. The tent shuddered as people slammed into the tent poles.

Everywhere was sheer chaos and Fallon had to shove the faithful aside as he struggled to get to Keenan.

"This can't be happening," Matty told Breslin. "It doesn't make any sense!"

"Something is inciting the crowd," Breslin snapped. His arm was around Keenan and he was practically carrying her on his hip as Roland and Matty ran interference for him.

Fallon was thinking the same thing, and as he scrambled to get onto the stage, he felt a shiver run down his back and looked around, seeking the source. He half expected to see some monstrous shape looming out of the crowd, but he saw nothing and no one who looked as though they were a threat. But the sensation of being watched remained even as he got to his feet on the stage and ran after Breslin and Matty.

"Through there!" Roland said, pointing to a flap in the back of the tent. He hopped down and held his hand up for Keenan.

Breslin didn't hesitate but swept Keenan up into his arms then dropped her into the gypsy's. He and Matty jumped off the stage, followed closely by Fallon as Matty ran to hold the tent flap aside.

Running with Keenan cradled against him, Roland made straight for his own trailer, yelling for one of the workers to open the door. He barely decreased his speed as he bolted up the steps and inside with Matty, Breslin and Fallon close on his heels.

"Lock the door!"

Keenan seemed dazed as the Rom carried her to the sofa and set her down. She put a hand to her temple, touched her ear and then brought her hand around to look down at the red stain on her fingers. She looked up as Fallon hurried over to her.

"I'm bleeding," she said.

"I'll get a cloth," Roland said to no one in particular.

Fallon hunkered down in front of her and took her free hand. "Are you all right, *lhiannan*?" he asked softly.

"Watch your mouth!" Breslin hissed at the endearment.

"I think so," Keenan said. "What happened?"

"You don't know?" Matty inquired. All three men were hovering around her as Roland came back from wetting a washcloth.

"I remember Bolivar introducing me," she said as she put the wet cloth to her ear. "I seem to recall someone saying he could hear, but I don't remember anything after that."

Matty and Breslin exchanged a look.

"You don't remember the man with the rash?" Fallon asked.

"Or the man in the wheelchair?"

Keenan shook her head. "It's all a blank."

"Which is probably a good thing, *Bhen*," Roland said, calling her Sister.

Looking up at Matty, Keenan searched his worried gaze. "Did I heal someone?"

"Yeah," Matty said. "Several someones."

Keenan's brows drew together. "I don't remember anything."

There was a pounding on the door and Roland cursed, yelling for whoever it was to go away.

"It's me, Mizhak," Bolivar said.

Breslin turned to let her in and she did so quickly, the sound of shouting voices drowning out whatever words she said to him. She came straight to Keenan.

"Are you all right, Tandy?"

"Yes, ma'am," Keenan said, "but I've got a terrible headache."

"She needs to lie down," Bolivar said. "Out. All of you. I'll stay with her." She nudged Fallon with her knee. "Get up, Robbie."

Fallon ground his teeth but stood. Once again he tried to slip into Bolivar's mind but found it firmly barred. A glance at Roland revealed no expression on the Rom's face or on Breslin's for that matter, but Fallon knew one or the other of them had shut him out. Having no choice but to do as Bolivar ordered, he followed the others out into the oppressively hot August night.

267

"All right, who the hell did it?" Roland snarled.

"Did what?" Breslin asked.

"Both of you have the power," Roland accused in a low, hissing tone. "I know this. Which one of you worked that crowd into a frenzy tonight?" He was staring savagely at Breslin.

"I don't know what you're talking about," Breslin told him.

Roland whipped his head toward Fallon.

"It wasn't me," Fallon said.

"I know what you are," Roland said, eyes narrowed. "You can hide from the authorities, but you can not hide what you are from a Rom!"

"What's he talking about?" Breslin questioned.

"You could have gotten her killed tonight," Roland shouted at Breslin. "Don't you realize that?"

"It wasn't me," Breslin shot back. "Why would I do something to hurt her?"

"You beat her," Roland said. "I know this too. You thought to stir up the crowd so there would be an even bigger draw the next time, more money taken in!"

"Bullshit," Breslin said. "I didn't do any such thing."

"Whichever one of you did this, you had best be glad no harm came to the little one tonight. Had she been hurt, I would respond in kind to the one who caused that hurt!" Roland warned.

"I don't think Nate would have been foolish enough to do something like this," Matty said. "Tandy is his meal ticket, Mizhak. You'd better look elsewhere for the culprit."

Roland shifted his angry glower to Fallon. "I am watching you," he growled. "Stay away from the little one. Don't think I don't know what you tried to do. I stopped you then and I will stop you again."

"What's he talking about?" Breslin asked, bristling. "What did you try to do, Marks?"

"This is between him and me," Roland snapped.

Fallon didn't think Roland had any idea that a pathway had been opened into his mind and he slipped into the Rom's mind, did a quick reconnaissance, reassured by what he found. There was no hint Roland knew about Fallon's association with the Exchange or his real reason for being with the revival. The only thoughts in his head regarding Keenan were an overwhelming desire to protect her and a growing admiration for her abilities. Matty was being accepted as a bumbling fool, the gypsy liked Breslin and had bought the agent's story. As for Fallon, the gypsy hated him — but for deeper, more complex reasons Fallon could not pry from the Rom's mind.

"Go help the men disperse the crowd," Roland ordered. "They need all the help they can get."

"Let the police do it," Breslin snapped.

"You do as I say!" Roland bellowed. "You work for Mother Bolivar and you will do as I say!"

For a moment it seemed Breslin would draw back his fist and hit the gypsy, but with a nasty curse, he spun on his heel and stalked off.

"You too," Roland told Matty and Fallon.

Matty took Fallon's arm and they started toward the crowd that was milling about the back lot, trying to get through the security men and to the trailer where Keenan was.

"If Breslin didn't do it and you and I didn't do it, that only leaves Roland," Matty said softly.

"Or Bolivar," Fallon stated.

Matty stopped walking and put out a hand to stay Fallon. "You think she has psi powers?"

"I didn't think so, but I don't believe it was Roland. Who else stood to gain from Sister Tandy being overrun by an out-of-control mob?" Fallon asked him.

"What's going on here, Misha?" Matty queried.

"I don't know, but I damned sure intend to find out!"

Chapter Twenty

ℬ

Worried about Keenan all night, Fallon didn't sleep, so by the morning he was irritable, had a brutal headache and an upset stomach to boot. The tenerse seemed to hurt more than usual and the Sustenance did little to calm the hunger building within him.

He had been at the opened door to his trailer when he saw Keenan leaving Roland's trailer not long after dawn. Beside her had been Bolivar. Where the gypsy had spent the night he neither knew nor cared. Keenan had gone into her trailer without a glance his way, Bolivar into hers, so Fallon had made a beeline to his boss's motor home, entering without knocking.

"What do you want, Robbie?" Bolivar asked. "I'm in no mood to soothe your wounded male pride."

"Are you going to put her on display again today?" he asked without preamble.

"If I don't, the crowd will riot. Unless I miss my guess, ticket sales will skyrocket all through the day."

"Do you have any idea how dangerous this could be for her?" he challenged.

"You'll protect her," she replied. Her gaze swept down him. "Roland will see to it."

Fallon felt another chill gouging at his spine, but before he could question her remark, she turned and left him standing in the living area.

"Don't let the door hit your ass on the way out," she called from the bedroom.

Fallon flinched. Dismissed just that easily, he thought, and he supposed he had Roland to thank for Bolivar's abrupt change in attitude toward him. He might be useful to her, but she no longer trusted — or even liked him it seemed.

What he wanted to do was go to Keenan's trailer, but since he couldn't speak freely to her either normally or psychically, he would stay away. He stood there staring at the motor home Breslin and Matty shared and would have laid odds it was wired for sight and sound as was his. Unless he invited Matty into town with him—everyone knew how he felt regarding Breslin—there was no way to speak privately to the agents. Stymied for the moment, he went back to his trailer, stripped, put on a pair of black running shorts, socks and sneakers and headed for the road, intent on working some of the frustration out of his system.

Keenan stood at her front window, wishing she could talk to him. What had happened the night before had shaken her badly and though she had talked with Bolivar, it was Fallon she needed.

Roland sat on the steps of his motor home, knife and column of wood in hand. He paused in his whittling to follow the progress of the man for whom he had such little trust.

* * * * *

As darkness fell on that humid Louisiana night, the faithful once more lined the aisle from the stage all the way out the tent flap and even beyond. People on crutches, in wheelchairs, with walkers and canes and on litters stood quietly as the choir hummed and Sister Tandy laid her hands upon the ill and wasted. Men and women with casts on their limbs, the blind and deaf, the lame and the infirm stood patiently anticipating their moment with the healer. Each time a pilgrim was healed, a mighty cheer rose from those gathered.

Fallon and Breslin stood together on the right side of the stage with Matty and Roland on the left. Breslin was in a foul mood since he wasn't a part of what Keenan was doing. There was no talking in tongues for him to translate and that pissed him off.

"What does she think she's doing?" he asked Fallon.

"Healing the sick," Fallon snapped. "What the fuck do you think she's doing?"

"Eat shit and die," Breslin snarled.

Fallon ignored the man. He was surveying the crowd, closely watching every person who came within touching distance of Keenan. Though he could not see her face, he had the impression she was tiring, her movements becoming slower with each person who came to her. He caught Matty's eye, but the physician merely shrugged. He too was standing where he could not see Keenan that clearly because of the extra security, but Fallon knew like Breslin and Roland and himself, Matty was ready to leap to the stage at a moment's notice to help her if she needed him.

As he swept his gaze over the crowd, Fallon felt the same icy chill he had from the night before. His head suddenly throbbed and he knew somewhere in the audience there was someone or something bombarding him with psychic slams. He was vaguely aware of Breslin moving away from him, but he was searching the people in the chairs, trying to hone in on the one who was sending such punishing shots his way.

There was a collective gasp from the crowd and Fallon whipped his head around, his attention going automatically to Keenan. His eyes widened for there was blood streaming from her ears and nostrils. For a crippling moment he could not move. He saw Breslin catapulting onto the stage. Saw Matty doing the same, but he stood frozen.

Once again something slammed brutally into his head and he grunted with the force of it, bending forward with his hands slapped to his temples. Around him people were leaping to their feet and the noise was shattering, savagely accentuating the agony rippling through his head.

"*Robin!*" he heard Bolivar shout and struggled to lift his head. As he did, his gaze went to a face in the second row and he staggered beneath the onslaught of rage smashing against him. It was all he could do to tear his eyes from the one savaging him so fixedly.

Just as they had the evening before, Breslin, Matty and Roland were carrying Keenan off the stage. One look at her body and Fallon knew she was unconscious. He stumbled toward the stage, in so much pain he could barely scramble onto the platform, rolling to his feet as the other three men disappeared out the back of the tent. Staggering, he followed them as a phalanx of security closed in to keep outsiders at bay. Pushing his way past several guards, he made his way to Roland's motor home where the men had once more taken refuge.

Blundering through the door, Fallon fell to his knees and flopped to his side, the pain in his head crippling him. His own ears and nostrils were bleeding and a bright, searing haze clouded his vision.

"What the hell is wrong with *him*?" he heard Breslin ask as though from far away.

The last thing he remembered before unconsciousness swept up to claim him was Roland's face glaring down at him through the gathering darkness.

* * * * *

He woke to a brutal, pounding headache and a sick stomach that barely allowed him to twist to the side of the bed before he puked. A cool hand held his forehead as he strained to rid himself of his stomach contents. With each tensing of his gag reflexes, the agony lying between his temples sent shards of glass through his brain.

"Man, you are really sick," someone said. He thought it might have been Matty, but he wasn't sure.

"Maybe he'll die and we won't have to put up with his shit anymore."

That sounded like either Roland or Breslin, but the voice was distorted by the loud, agonizing buzzing in his ears.

"As soon as he's able to talk, send someone to get me. I don't like leaving Tandy."

That was definitely Bolivar's voice and Fallon struggled to speak to her, frantic for word on Keenan's condition, but the gagging prevented him. So forceful was his nausea, he saw stars every time he heaved and a thick wash of cold sweat was covering his entire body.

"Here, drink this."

Something fizzy was placed to his lips and Fallon tried to bat it away. By the glare of the sun coming in through the bedroom window he knew it was morning and what he needed wasn't the cure being foisted off on him but the vac-syringe. His body was beginning to itch and burn beneath the sheen of sweat.

"Come on, drink it."

Whether he wanted it or not, the liquid was poured down his unwilling throat. He gagged, choked, coughed but managed to swallow of the cherry-flavored stuff. His eyes watering, he was made to drink even more of it, but it was helping to alleviate some of the brutal nausea that was eating away at him.

"He's a piss-poor patient, ain't he?"

Roland. The buzzing was dying down.

"Do me a favor, would you, Mizhak?"

Matty. The nausea was abating and the pain in his head was easing just a tad.

"Whatcha need?"

"Go to his trailer and look in his bathroom. You'll find a syringe and a vial. Bring it to me."

"What...?"

"Don't ask any questions, okay? I think you know he needs what's in that syringe."

There was a moment of silence then the sound of receding footsteps, the closing of a door.

"All right, open your eyes," Matty ordered as he rolled up his sleeve.

Opening his eyes was easier said than done. Fallon struggled to do it as Matty pushed him back onto the bed and ran a cold cloth over his face.

"Here," Matty said, holding his arm out to Fallon.

"I can't..."

"Just do it," Matty snapped.

Fallon sank his fangs into Matty's arm, needing the Sustenance. When he'd taken enough to quench his need, he collapsed against the pillow.

"Now tell me what the hell happened to you last night."

"Lily," Fallon said. "She was in the audience."

"Her mother Lily?"

Breslin came into view, his face angry. "How the hell did she know where we were?" he demanded. "It couldn't have been Lily."

"I saw her," Fallon grated, reaching up a trembling hand to scrub at his face. He locked eyes with Breslin. "She's got psi powers. She more than likely read our destination in Keenan's mind."

Breslin shook his head. "Hell no, she doesn't," he snapped then his eyebrows clashed. "At least I don't think she does." He held Fallon's stare. "Are you sure?"

"Goddamned sure," Fallon said. "She's a very powerful sender. I kept up my guard when we were with her, but Keenan was so on edge the entire time she probably forgot to block her thoughts."

"Like mother, like daughter," Matty said. "She did this to you?"

Fallon nodded, swallowing hard. His body was in torment for need of the tenerse.

"Well, she did a number on you, son," Matty stated. "That was tenerse I gave you to stop the nausea and it hasn't helped, has it?"

"No," Fallon replied. "You've got to find her, Breslin. Stop her. She's a loose cannon and if she tells someone who Keenan really is…"

"I'm on it," Breslin said, and pivoted on his heel.

"How is she?" Fallon asked.

"Keenan?" Matty clarified. "Sleeping when I was over there last. Too much strain on her body last night. As soon as I saw the blood, I knew we had to put a stop to the show."

"We can't let that happen again," Fallon said. "It's too dangerous."

"I know, and it isn't going to happen again. You guys will have to find another way to locate that entity. What about those other agents Breslin was training?"

275

Fallon tried to sit up in the bed but was too weak. "Thirsty," he said.

"Want some water?"

Fallon nodded although the action increased the agony in his head. "The other agents are useless to us now," Fallon said. "Bolivar has a real miracle worker in her hands. She isn't going to give a damn about three would-be Sensitives."

Matty poured a glass of water and slid his hand under Fallon's neck. "As soon as Roland brings your injection, I'm going after Breslin to help look for her mother."

Gulping the entire glass, Fallon waved a weak hand at Matty. "Go ahead," he insisted. "I can give it to myself."

"You sure?"

"Yeah, go on. Finding Lily is more important. If she blows Keenan's cover, there's no telling what Bolivar or Roland will do."

Matty removed his hand from under Fallon's neck. "Okay, but you stay still until the tenerse takes hold. Understand?"

"I hear you."

Fallon thought he must have dozed off despite the pain racking his body for when Roland shook him he snapped his eyes open and growled.

"Yeah, you try biting me, Reaper, and I'll fry your fucking ass," Roland hissed. "Here!"

Fallon took the vac-syringe without even looking at it and brought it up to his neck. Thrusting the needle into the carotid artery, he depressed the plunger before he noticed the smirk on Roland's face and realized something was very wrong. The moment the payload entered his body he knew he was in deep shit.

* * * * *

Matty waited until Breslin left the grounds before he walked over to Bolivar's trailer. He rapped a couple of times then went on in, smiling as he encountered the evangelist reclining on the sofa.

"How's she doing?"

"She's still sleeping," Bolivar reported. "I don't know what you gave her but she's really out of it."

"It's called pairilis and it will help her body to heal," Matty replied. "How are you feeling?"

"Drained," Bolivar reported. "I ache all over."

"I can fix that," Matty said, and came over to the sofa. "Turn over and I'll massage your neck and shoulders. That'll help."

"Yeah, it would," she agreed, and did as he suggested. The moment his hands began kneading her tense muscles, she groaned. "I'll give you an hour to stop that."

Matty smiled, his knowledgeable fingers working magic on her stiff tendons.

"Mignon?" he asked softly.

"Yes?"

"I want you to listen to my instructions and then follow them to the letter. Do you understand?" His voice wound through her head like an uncoiling serpent.

"Yes, Reggie," she agreed.

Matty plied her muscles, and as he did, he implanted the sublims deep into her subconscious—just as he had delved there once before to erase Fallon's.

"Robin Marks is actually a man named Mikhail Fallon. He was sent here by one of your enemies to shut you down, to stop your ministry, to eventually kill you. Do you understand what I am saying?"

"He's a hired killer."

"That's right. He's a hired killer," Matty said, squeezing her shoulders. "Roland knows all about him. He knows Fallon is a very dangerous man. He will take care of Fallon for you."

"Yes," Bolivar mumbled.

"Now I am going to leave you. You will sleep as I have instructed. Is that clear?"

"Yes, Reggie."

"Good, now sleep."

Matty waited until he was sure Bolivar was deeply under then got to his feet. He went down the hallway, checked on Keenan to make sure she too was sleeping soundly—her psychic powers completely shut down. He bent over, kissed her forehead and then adjusted the covers securely around her.

"Soon, my love," he said. "Very soon."

Leaving the motor home, he saw Roland exiting his trailer and the two men swapped knowing looks. Roland nodded and Matty smiled, motioning the gypsy over.

"All done?" Matty queried.

"All done," Roland acknowledged. "What now?"

"Now we wait," Matty replied.

* * * * *

Breslin found Lily and Royce Cookson, the man she had hired, exactly where he figured they would be—the most expensive hotel in New Orleans.

"I am in the penthouse suite," Lily had informed him when he'd called on the house phone. "I'll have the manager bring you up."

As he rode up in the elevator to the palatial suite, he couldn't help but wonder what Lily was going to say. That she was enraged over her daughter's latest assignment, he had no doubt. Lily had not wanted Keenan to take the job with the Exchange—didn't want her working at all for that matter—and because Keenan had, the enmity between mother and daughter had deepened. Of course he'd had a hand in deepening that hostility, he reasoned, but that didn't concern him.

The manager stayed in the elevator when the doors shushed open on the huge expanse of black Terrazzo flooring that shone like the polished surface of a deep Arctic lake. A sweeping view of the Crescent City lay beyond the floor-to-ceiling glass walls that formed two curved half-moons from the elevator to the imposing black double doors leading into the suite. Overhead, a magnificent chandelier was suspended from the glass-domed roof.

"Sweet," Breslin said, staring at the huge brass planters filled with tropical plants that flanked the doors. He looked forward to having such luxury at hand when Keenan and he were married.

Royce opened the door and ushered Breslin in.

"She's taking a bath," Royce said with a steady look. "You're to join her."

"My pleasure," Breslin said, grinning. He had no more affection for Royce than the private detective had for him, but the two men understood one another.

Lily was reclining in a large sunken marble tub when Breslin came into the bathroom. In her hand was a fluted glass of champagne. The bottle sat on a silver tray on the floor beside the tub—a second glass beside it.

"I want him dead, Zack," she said then took a slow sip from the glass, looking at him over the rim.

"It's as good as done," Breslin said, using the toe of one shoe to slip off the heel of the other. "Any particular way you want me to do it?" He began to unbutton his shirt.

"The most painful way you can conceive," she replied. "My daughter was in agony last night because of him."

Breslin tugged the shirt from his pants. "You hurt him pretty bad too," he quipped. "He wasn't expecting that."

Lily smiled. "I've had to hide my talents from everyone over the years," she said. "I found it was necessary."

He ticked a disapproving finger at her. "Even me. How did you do that?"

"Power, Zack," she said. "Very strong power."

He shrugged out of his shirt and unbuckled his pants. "So it doesn't matter how I kill him so long as I make him suffer."

"Precisely," she said, reaching out to pour herself another glass and to pour one for him. She handed his to him as he stepped down into the tub.

"What about Kiki?" he asked.

"She'll be devastated of course, and you will console her."

"What if she still refuses to marry me?"

Lily thrust out her foot, rubbing the sole on his stiffening cock. "We'll take her to St. Brisa and have the marriage performed there. She'll be under house confinement but you can stay or go as you will. No one will ever find her there."

Breslin drained the expensive French champagne then slid across the water to press his body over hers. His arms went around her and his cock probed between the legs she'd opened wide for him.

"I'd much rather have you than her," he said in a throaty voice, his chest rubbing against her.

"You have me, sweetie," she said. "As much as you're ever going to get me." She put her arms around his neck. "Now show me what I've been missing."

Chapter Twenty-One

ᔓ

Fallon thought he had known agony in his lifetime.

He had been wrong.

Very wrong.

The pain that slithered through his body was unlike anything he'd ever experienced and he knew it was destroying the part of him that was not human, that gave him both his supernatural strength and his psi powers. He could feel the hellion whipping about under his skin—succumbing to the poison invading his system. Her fledglings were coiling over and over one another as they too yielded up their lives to the toxin.

"Ghoret venom," Roland had laughed. "Hurts like hell, don't it?"

Where the gypsy had come by the otherworldly poison was a puzzle Fallon feared he wouldn't live long enough to solve. The venom was attacking his nervous system, heating his blood to the boiling point and beginning to pulverize his internal organs. Black flecks formed on his flesh and pockets of pustules were beginning to form where the venom oozed through the skin. There was no antidote for the toxin and one drop was fatal to humans. To Reapers, it was an excruciating torment that burned so badly he wanted to scream.

But that wasn't to be the worst part of his torture, he discovered, for Roland wasn't through with him yet. He could hear the gypsy chanting in the other room and all around Fallon the walls of the motor home began to bulge and contract. The air became thick and musky, a nasty odor falling over him like a sodden cloak. His head throbbed in tempo with the rising and ebbing of the walls, and as darkness closed around him, he realized he was being drawn from the motor home and out into the beyond—a cold, impenetrable blackness that scratched at his flesh like clinging briars as he traveled through it.

"Martiya," he heard Roland chanting from a great distance and Fallon's blood ran as cold as the air surrounding him.

Sheer agony engulfed Fallon as he went crashing through the sharp brambles—feeling his flesh ripped and shredded only to land on his belly in some strange, alien landscape where nothing but varied shades of blackness prevailed. The ground beneath his cheek shook as something massive loomed on the horizon.

Pushing himself up, Fallon searched for some place to take cover, some defensive position from which he could operate, but there was no rock, no tree—nothing but a stygian vista overwhelmed with a noxious scent that clogged his nostrils.

And then *it* came at him, rushing from out of the pitch to grab him.

For the first time in his life, Mikhail Fallon screamed.

* * * * *

Breslin pulled up beside the motor home he was forced to share with Matty Groves and got out of the rust-bucket of a car that depressed him every time he slid behind the wheel. He hated being seen in the junker, hated the smell of it and couldn't wait to be rid of it.

"Did you find her?"

Glancing behind to find Matty Groves headed toward him, Breslin nodded. "Yeah. She wants me to bring Kiki to the Gallison Towers to meet with her."

"Why?" Matty asked. "Is she going to cause trouble?"

"I made her understand Kiki is undercover and just how dangerous it would be for her to interfere. I think Lily got the message." Breslin leaned against the car he hated so vehemently. "She told me to offer Mignon money to meet privately with Sister Tandy."

"How much money are we talking about?"

"One hundred thousand," Breslin replied. "Chump change to a woman like Lily."

Matty whistled. "Bolivar will jump at the chance."

"That's what I figured. Lily's on her way out here—should be here any minute so I told the security guys at the gate to expect her. She wanted me to bring Kiki to her, but I knew Mignon would never go for that and Fallon would sure as hell nix the notion." Breslin nudged his chin toward Roland's trailer. "Speaking of Fallon, how is the asshole?"

"Sleeping as far as I know," Matty replied. "I'll go with you to Bolivar's. I need to check on Keenan."

"Suit yourself," Breslin grumbled.

The stretch white limo pulled into the backyard as Breslin and Matty reached Bolivar's door. Both men turned as the vehicle rolled to a stop. A uniformed chauffeur got out and opened the door for his passenger.

"Quite an entrance," Matty said.

"The woman has more money that God," Breslin told him, "and she's not reluctant to spend it either."

Matty's attention was glued to the tall, beautiful woman who stepped out of the limo. She was dressed in a gray pinstripe suit with a pink silk blouse that seemed to shimmer beneath the roiling black clouds overhead. Her shoes and handbag screamed money.

"Mrs. McCullough," Breslin said as Lily came up to them. "This is my cousin Reggie Quinn."

"Dr. Regis Quinn," Matty corrected.

"Oh yes," Lily said. "Ned told me about you."

"Nate," Breslin stated. "My name's Nate, ma'am."

Lily's perfectly sculpted brow arched and her green eyes flashed with what could only be amusement. "Gentlemen," she said, and made the word sound like an insult, "I don't have all day. Where is this Bolivar woman and," her dark rose lips pursed, "Sister Tandy?"

"In here, ma'am," Breslin replied, sweeping a hand toward the motor home behind him.

"I'll let Mother Bolivar know she has company," Matty said, and before Breslin could stop him, rapped once on the door then went inside.

"Where is Fallon?" Lily demanded.

"Shush!" Breslin warned with a hiss. "His name is Robin Marks. Don't slip up like that or you could get us all killed!"

Lily rolled her eyes. "Then where is Marks?" she queried.

"Sleeping off whatever it was you did to him."

"I don't want that son of a bitch interfering, Zack. You make damned sure he stays away from this tacky trailer while I'm talking to Keenan."

"Mother Bolivar said to come on in," Matty called from the doorway.

"No slips, Lily," Breslin cautioned in a low voice. "Please."

Lily pushed him aside and strode regally to the motor home steps, taking the hand Matty offered her. "Thank you, doctor," she muttered.

"You are most welcome, ma'am," Matty said with a grin.

Bolivar was sitting up on the sofa but she got to her feet when Lily came in. She hurried over, putting out a hand in greeting. "Mrs. McCullough! What a pleasure to meet you," she gushed.

"Y'all excuse me. I'm going to go check on Tandy," Matty said.

"Please sit down, Mrs. McCullough," Bolivar invited her guest.

"I really don't have the time for chit-chat," Lily stated. "As I told Ned..."

"Nate," Breslin corrected once again.

"Whatever," Lily said with a dismissive flick of her wrist. "I would like to meet privately with Sister Tandy. I am willing to make a rather sizeable donation to you for the privilege."

"How sizeable?" Bolivar asked, unconsciously licking her lips.

Lily looked down her nose at the woman. "One hundred thousand dollars."

Matty grinned wickedly when he heard those words as he opened Bolivar's bedroom door. He was unprepared for the sight that greeted him.

Keenan was writhing on the bed, her hands clawing at her throat, struggling to breathe. She was making harsh gasping sounds as though she were drowning. An inky film of sweat covered her face, arms and legs as she convulsed. Her eyes bulged in a face that was beet-red.

"No!" Matty shouted. "No!"

He rushed to the bed and lifted her up to help her breathing.

"Keenan, baby, I'm sorry. I'm sorry!"

Oblivious to the three people who came running at his bellow, who crowded into the bedroom, Matty cradled Keenan to him and called on the one man he prayed could help.

"Roland! Call *it* off! Bring him back. Now! She's suffocating!"

"Suffocating?" Lily gasped, her face as white as a sheet. "Oh my God! Do something!"

Breslin pushed past Lily. "What the hell's wrong with her?" he shouted.

"Roland!" Matty screeched, but this time his words were a psychic blast that made both Breslin and Lily stagger beneath the onslaught. "*Bring him back!*"

"What have you done?" Breslin snarled. He reached out to grab Matty's shoulder. "Did you sic Martiya on Fallon?"

"Who is Martiya?" Lily demanded. She was trembling, unable to venture any closer to the bed.

"He works for me," Bolivar said. "He's my enforcer."

"*She* is a creature of the night," Matty hissed. "A demoness!"

"What?" Bolivar questioned.

"And you sent this thing after Fallon?" Lily questioned. "Then let her have him!"

"Do you see what's happening to your daughter?" Matty snarled. He was struggling to pull Keenan's hands from her throat

285

where she'd already gouged the flesh. "She and Fallon aren't just bonded, they are soul-linked. What he feels, she's feeling. If he dies, she dies!"

Lily's mouth dropped open and her eyes widened. "You can't let that happen!"

"*Roland!*" Matty shrieked.

"*I'm trying but* she *doesn't want to give him up.*"

Breslin and Lily heard the words as clearly as Matty did.

Matty twisted his head toward Breslin. "Go help him! Add your powers to his!"

"What are you people talking about?" Bolivar demanded.

"You too!" Matty ordered. "Go with Breslin! Now damn it!"

Breslin shot past Lily, grabbing Bolivar's arm as he went careening out the door.

"*I'm sending Breslin and Mignon to you. Take them,*" Matty sent privately to Roland on the link he had established with the Rom a week before. "*Take them to appease the demoness.*"

"*I will try.*"

Lily had slumped against the wall, staring tearfully at her daughter. "Please don't let her die. I'll give you anything you want, just don't let my baby die."

Keenan's face had turned from red to a deepening bluish color as she strained to draw breath into her lungs. She was burning with fever and the ebony sweat pouring from her had a stench that made it necessary for Matty to breathe through his mouth.

"Pick up the phone and dial this number," Matty ordered Lily, and was a bit surprised when she hopped into action, punching in the number as quickly as she could. "Give me the receiver."

Lily wedged the receiver between Matty's chin and shoulder, staring fearfully at Keenan as the young woman's struggles became weaker and weaker.

"This is Groves, agent number 014505680471X-ray. Our Reaper is down. I need a medivac chopper and biohazard crew dispatched to this location STAT, and a jet fueled and ready to take him to the Exchange. I repeat, I have a Reaper in need of immediate transport by a biohazard team. Do you copy?"

Lily nearly dropped the phone as her daughter convulsed violently then slumped limply against Matty.

"Never mind that shit. Just get that chopper here ASAP!" Matty shouted into the receiver then moved his chin away to let it drop.

"Biohazard?" Bolivar asked. "Is he contagious?"

"His flesh is," Matty replied. When she started to dial 9-1-1, he asked her what the hell she was doing.

"My girl needs medical attention," Lily said. "Do you think I'll let her ride in the same helicopter with an infectious...?"

"Put that phone down. All we need is the police out here," Matty snapped.

"Don't tell me what to do!" Lily shouted. "My child needs help!"

"And the only place she can get it is at the Exchange. She'll have to go in the plane with Fallon. Stay with her. I've got to get him onboard then have them come back for her."

"I don't give a damn about Fallon!" Lily told him. "Take Keenan first and come back for him."

"He's going to need medical help much faster than Keenan will," Matty snapped as he gently released Keenan and got up from the bed. "If he dies, it won't matter when we get her to the Exchange. She'll be dead before his body is even cold."

"But..."

"Listen to me!" Matty snarled, grabbing Lily's arm in a punishing grip. "Misha is a Reaper. He is the closest thing to immortal that you're ever going to get. If Keenan were to die, he'd go into a decline and eventually will himself to death. That is the way with his kind and bonding. But if he were to die before her, Keenan would follow him in a matter of hours. Do you hear what I am saying to you?" He shook her. "Your daughter is human and she has the frailty of a human. Fallon is a Reaper. Her death would kill him, but it would not be from physical causes as

Keenan's would be. If we let him die, you can kiss your daughter goodbye!"

Lily looked at Keenan. "I don't... I can't..."

"She's breathing better and she's lapsed into unconsciousness. Stay with her, make sure her air passage is unobstructed."

He didn't give her a chance to argue further with him. He released her and hurried from the room, shoving the front door open and jumping from the motor home. Even as he ran across the backyard, he could hear the chopper winging its way toward the fairgrounds.

People were crowded around Roland's motor home, drawn by the shrieks and howls coming from inside—though not a one of them dared venture into the trailer. Matty had to shove them aside in his haste.

"Get the fuck out of my way!" he shouted.

Roland opened the door for him and there was a strange look on the Rom's face.

"I don't think he's going to make it," Roland said.

"Breslin and Bolivar?" Matty snapped as he headed for the bedroom.

"Gone," was all the gypsy needed to say. "She wanted the Reaper, but she wanted the woman even more."

Matty came up short as soon as he saw the wreck of a man who lay sprawled across the bloody bed. Nausea leapt up his throat and he barely had time to turn before the bile came rushing from his throat. "God!" he croaked.

"Not a pretty sight," Roland agreed from the doorway.

Matty gagged again, bracing his hand on the wall. He couldn't look at the carnage on the bed, and when two men in full biohazard suits came bustling into the room, all he could do was point a trembling finger.

"Holy fucking shit!" one of the suited men exclaimed, setting down his equipment bag. "What the hell happened to him?"

"Just get him in the chopper, STAT!" Matty managed to say, his voice as shaky as his body. He wiped the back of his arm over his mouth. "As soon as you get him to the jet, get your asses back here. I've got another patient to transport."

"As bad off as this one?" the other suited man inquired as he leaned over the bed.

Matty shook his head. "No."

The biohazard team did a quick evaluation of the man on the bed and the taller of the two informed Matty they would need to perform a needle thoracocentesis to relieve the intrathoracic pressure inside.

"What does that mean?" Roland inquired, his head tilted to one side.

"He has a collapsed lung," Matty said. "They need to evacuate the air in the pleural cavity to relieve the pressure and allow the lung to re-inflate. They can't take him up in the chopper until that's done."

"Huh," Roland grunted.

"That's not all that's wrong with him," the shorter suited man declared. "It'll be a miracle if he survives. You told dispatch this guy is a Reaper?"

"Yeah," Matty said, sagging against the wall but still avoiding looking at the bed.

"Why isn't his Revenant worm healing him?"

"You see those pustules?" Matty snapped. "That's ghoret venom bubbling to the surface. His hellion and all the fledglings have dissolved. You touch that shit with your bare hands, get even a drop of it on you and you'll die in the blink of an eye."

Both men straightened, their eyes meeting through the plexi-shields of their suits.

"Will you hurry while we can still save him?" Matty shouted. "We need to transfuse him and transfer a fledging so it can begin building another hive. If he dies, I'll inject both of you with some of his sweat!"

The men bolted into action at the vehement threat. Not bothering with a gurney, they scooped the broken body of the Reaper up beneath his arms and legs.

"Get outside and keep anyone from coming close, and for the love of God, don't get any of this blood on you, Roland!" Matty warned and the gypsy jumped out of the way, hurrying to clear a path for the suited men.

Following the men as they carried the broken body of Mikhail Fallon from the motor home, Matty swallowed the gorge that threatened to erupt again as he saw the black blood dripping from Fallon's fingertips.

Outside, a pathway had been cleared to the chopper that had landed a few hundred feet away. Ducking down under the wash of the spinning blades, the biohazard team was met by another set of suited team members who had offloaded a gurney. The body was strapped to the gurney then lifted to be placed inside the helicopter.

"What do we need to know before we transport him, Doc?" one of the men from the chopper inquired.

Despite the sick feeling still plaguing him, Matty walked over to the chopper as the gurney was loaded into the belly of the bird. Taking a deep breath, he climbed into the chopper after it and looked down into the swollen and destroyed face of a man he had once called friend. Two feverish amber eyes filled with unspeakable pain were staring back at him.

"*They put a needle in your lung so you'll be able to breathe better now, Misha,*" he sent psychically so the others could not hear. "*You're on your way home. I couldn't let them kill you. She would have died if I had.*"

Bleeding lips tried to speak but no sound came out, just a bubble of black blood.

"*I'll be coming for her,*" Matty told Fallon. "*Keep her safe until I do.*"

Matty looked at the man he thought was the team leader. "Just keep him comfortable and get him to the Exchange as fast as you can. You have blood onboard?"

"Yes sir."

"Then feed it to him. That will help some. Give him as much as he'll drink."

The suited man swallowing convulsively. "Yes sir!"

"Now go!"

Matty jumped down from the bird and ran bent over to where Roland was standing. He put a hand on the gypsy's shoulder.

"You have a decision to make, my friend. You can either stay here or you can go with me. If you go with me, I promise you will never regret it."

"I will go where the *Bhen* goes," Roland said, the loyalty he had developed so strongly to Keenan strong in his cinnamon-colored eyes.

"That's what I was hoping you'd say. Get whatever you want to take with..."

"There is nothing I want here," Roland said.

"Okay, then get over to Mignon's and get Keenan ready to transport." At Roland's perplexed look, Matty explained that was Sister Tandy's true name. "We'll meet up at the tent once Keenan is secure."

"Fine by me," Roland acknowledged.

As the gypsy headed for Bolivar's motor home Matty looked among those gathered and sighted the team leader from the Exchange. He motioned the man over.

"Get our people out of here," Matty said. "I don't want any of them here when the shit hits the fan. Tell them to keep their mouths shut. Understand?"

"Yes sir," the team leader said. "What about Agent Breslin, sir? Where's he?"

"I don't know but I'm going to find him," Matty said. "Now get your ass in gear and don't leave anything of ours behind."

The last anyone saw of the man they knew as Reggie Quinn, he was sliding behind the wheel of the rusted coupe in which he, Nate and Tandy Lynch had arrived.

Chapter Twenty-Two

ൕ

It had been over a week since Fallon had been brought back to the Exchange. During that time, he had been restricted to an isolation ward where contamination protocol had been strictly enforced. Placed in a maximum security containment chamber within the isolation ward, access to him was granted to only a small contingent of specially trained medical personnel. For the first forty-eight hours of his confinement men and women in HAZMAT suits had meticulously and thoroughly washed away the bubbling black poison that erupted from the pustules covering every inch of his body. Contact with a single drop of the noxious fluid emitted from Fallon's pores would cause instantaneous death to the humans exposed to it. A potent salve was applied to the broken skin. All materials used either on or around his body were incinerated on the spot after utilization. Each HAZMAT suit underwent a stringent detoxification routine, the wearer hosed down with high-pressure water suffused with very strong disinfectant and sent through a final decontamination chamber before being allowed to dress and return to their normal lives.

A fledgling that had been harvested years before from Fallon's own body as a precaution against damage to his hellion was transferred into an incision made over his right kidney. The small eel-like abomination with green flesh covered in hard scales dove into the incision and disappeared. It was hoped the revenant worm was strong enough to endure any residual poisons left from the ghoret envenomation and fight them. Subsequent tests revealed the fledgling was surviving.

On the third day of his confinement, a surgical team was allowed in to connect the various tubes and catheters necessary to make him comfortable and to administer hefty antibiotics to aid in his healing. On the sixth day—when the pustules stopped forming and leakage of the ghoret venom from the wounds ceased — his arm and leg were set, pins screwed into place and his fractured jaw wired shut. It would be another day before casts could be plastered over his flesh.

Finally on the seventh day, he was taken out of containment and placed in a secure room within the isolation ward reserved for contagious patients. Only then could a full spectrum of tests be run to ascertain all the injuries suffered at the hands of the creature.

* * * * *

"You want the good news first or the bad?" the head surgeon at the Exchange asked the Supervisor.

"Let's have the bad news. What are his injuries?"

"It would be quicker to tell you what isn't wrong with him," the surgeon stated, "but we'll start at the top and work our way down."

Keenan was sitting quietly with her hands in her lap. She had insisted on coming to the Supervisor's office when they refused to allow her to see Fallon. Even though when she woke to find her mother hovering over her, she had refused to speak to the woman and had said very little at all since arriving back at the Exchange.

"He has an acute subdural hemotoma..."

"In English," the Supervisor snapped.

The surgeon coughed. "Ah, yes. Sorry. He has had a traumatic injury to the brain and the brain is bleeding from tears in the arteries. Pressure is building up inside his skull and we will need to go in to relieve that pressure. That will be done within the hour. In a human, an injury of this magnitude has a high mortality rate, but since we transferred the parasite, hopefully it will begin to secrete the necessary antigens to fight the ghoret poison."

"And if it doesn't?" Keenan asked softly.

"It will," the Supervisor said. "Go on, doctor."

"Yes, of course. Well, both eardrums were ruptured, but that is really a minor thing at this point. They should heal relatively fast when the Revenant begins to give off hatchlings."

Both the Supervisor and Keenan winced at the image those words evoked.

"Both retinas suffered tears during the beating. Luckily neither detached and if necessary we can repair these surgically with a laser or with cryotherapy. Again, these are minor injuries in the overall scheme of things."

"That is the reason his eyes are bandaged," the Supervisor said. "I was afraid he had lost an eye."

Keenan winced and hung her head, her hands tightening in her lap.

"No, no. There are petechial hemorrhages—red spots in the eyes—that suggest he was being strangled at some point, but there was no laceration or puncture to the eye."

The Supervisor put his thumb and forefinger to the bridge of his nose. "Continue."

"Ah, there is a broken jaw, which we have wired shut, a dislocated shoulder. His left arm is broken in three places and has been set. He has seven broken ribs with the cartilage separated from two of the floating ribs, a punctured lung and he has developed pericarditis, an inflammation of the lining of the heart, caused by the ghoret venom attacking that organ.

"Both kidneys were severely contused. His spleen was ruptured and we have removed it. The liver was lacerated but we were able to repair it. He has a fractured pelvis, a shattered right leg in which the knee cap was literally pulverized and the ankle on that foot was also broken. The bones in that leg are literally splintered. If we were dealing with a human, we would simply amputate the leg at the hip. Of course if we did that, the hellion would make it grow back."

"My God," the Supervisor said, squeezing his eyes closed. "It's a wonder he's survived this long."

"Exactly," the surgeon agreed. "But his chances are improving every hour. If he makes it through the night, he has a fair chance of beating back the undertaker."

"Is he in any pain?" Keenan asked.

"Well, we can't give him any tenerse at this point," the surgeon replied. "We are administering massive amounts of antibiotics in dual IVs in an attempt to take some of the burden from the fledgling hellion. We have catheterized him and there is a gastric feeding tube directly into the stomach supplying him with Sustenance. Right now that's all we can..."

"Is he in pain?" Keenan repeated, lifting her head to look at the surgeon.

"Ah yes," he answered softly. "I am sure he is."

"When can I see him?"

The surgeon glanced at the Supervisor, who nodded slightly.

"You can see him now if you'd like."

"I would," Keenan said. She got to her feet.

"Thank you, Doctor," the Supervisor said. "Please keep us apprised of his condition."

"Certainly," the surgeon said, and stood. He turned to look down at Keenan. "I understand the two of you are bonded."

"Yes," she said, tears filling her eyes.

"Then you must stay strong for him," the surgeon said. "You can't afford to get sick. He will need you during what is sure to be a long convalescence."

"I'll be there for him," she told him.

"Good girl."

Keenan glanced at the Supervisor and he indicated he no longer needed her presence so she left with the surgeon, closing the door behind her.

Alone in his office, the Supervisor rocked back in his chair and heaved a long, tired sigh. Though he had immense powers of his own, they had proved useless against whatever had almost killed Mikhail Fallon. He had been unable to do anything to protect the Reaper. In his own mind, he had failed his agent miserably and that was a bitter pill to swallow.

He had a feeling Keenan's mother knew much more about what had happened to his agents and the evangelist than she was letting on.

"Groves didn't tell me where he was going after we got Keenan into the chopper and I never saw Zack after Groves sent him and the woman to stop that dark man from hurting Fallon. What else can I tell you?" Lily McCullough had demanded when she'd been debriefed.

A lot more, the Supervisor thought, but he knew that information would not be forthcoming. It had been a shock to learn Keenan's mother possessed psi abilities of her own. There had never been any indication that was the case.

The Supervisor swiveled his chair around so he could look out the large picture window behind him. "You fooled us, didn't you, Mrs. McCullough?" he asked aloud.

For a long time, he watched the lightning stair-stepping across the heavens as a storm moved toward the Exchange. The blackness of the night matched the bleakness in his soul, and for the first time in a long, long time, he closed his eyes and prayed to a god he wasn't sure even listened to him now.

* * * * *

Keenan sat by Fallon's bedside all night and when the first gray fingers of daylight scratched through the sodden clouds, she finally released his right hand and stood, stretching the kinks out of her back as she turned to watch the rain hitting the window. She was hungry and her head ached miserably because of that hunger, but she didn't want to leave him, afraid if she did, he would succumb to the myriad injuries that assailed him.

"Did you get any sleep last evening?"

She didn't turn around. "No sir. I wasn't sleepy."

The Supervisor came to stand beside Fallon's bed. "He seems to be getting a bit of color back in his cheeks," he commented.

Keenan knew that was wishful thinking on the Supervisor's part. To her, Fallon was deathly pale and his stillness ate at her very soul. The bandages over his eyes, the casts on his left arm and right leg, the wrapping around his broken ribs, the dark purple bruises over every inch of flesh she could see, the scratches that gouged deep into muscle made her want to cry and keep crying until there were no tears left.

"Why don't you go get some breakfast? I'll stay with him until you get back."

Keenan shook her head. "I don't want to leave him."

She sensed the Supervisor wanted to argue with her, but instead, he reached for the call button and when a nurse came bustling into the room, ordered a tray be brought for Keenan.

"Yes sir. Right away."

"I failed him," Keenan said, laying her head against the cool glass of the window.

"How do you figure that?"

"I should have been watching his back. If I had, that thing wouldn't have gotten to him."

"We don't even know what that *thing* is or how it gets to this plane of existence. Until we find Roland, we won't know," the Supervisor told her. "How could you guard him against something you could neither see nor sense, Keenan?"

"I should have been watching his back," she repeated as though she hadn't heard him. "I'm his Extension. It was my mission to help him. I let him down." Her voice broke.

"You did no such thing," the Supervisor said firmly.

"I could feel his pain," she said. "He was in agony."

The Supervisor came over to put a comforting hand on her shoulder. "Do you feel it now?"

She shook her head. "All I feel is cold," she said, arms wrapped around her. "Cold and lost and alone."

"He is going to survive this," she was told. "He made it through the night and that is an encouraging sign." He squeezed her shoulder. "He's a tough son of a bitch and he's a fighter."

Keenan's head came up and she turned her face to the older man. "Did you call his mother? Has she been told?"

"She was on holiday with that bastard of a husband of hers and we had a helluva time finding her, but she's on her way here now. I sent a jet for her."

Keenan released a wavering breath. "If Coim had been here, he might have been able to help. He left this realm just before all this happened."

"Coim?" The Supervisor's brows drew together then shifted upward as memory surfaced. "Oh, you mean *An Fear Liath Mor*? I'm not sure it could have reached Fallon, but I imagine it would have tried."

"That thing has to be found and destroyed," Keenan said, eyes hard. "If it's the last thing I do this side of hell, I swear I will hunt it down."

"You and Fallon together," the Supervisor said then took his hand from shoulder. "Here's your food. I want you to sit down and eat."

She would have argued with him, but he gave her a stern, fatherly look and she half smiled, taking a seat in the chair as an orderly placed a tray on the over-bed table. "Yes sir."

But after the Supervisor and orderly had gone, she pushed the rolling table aside and went to stand by Fallon's bed.

"I'm sorry, lineman," she said, stroking the limp hair back from his forehead. "I should have been there for you."

Chapter Twenty-Three

80

"Madame, may I speak with you privately?"

Svetlana Gregorovich, Fallon's mother, nodded. "Of course, Supervisor." She released her son's hand and gently laid it on the mattress. Getting to her feet, she leaned over and kissed his brow just above the bandages then followed the Supervisor from the room.

"I know you must be tired," the Supervisor said as he ushered her down the hallway. "You should rest."

"There will be time to rest when I'm dead," she said in her fatalistic Russian fashion.

The Supervisor smiled. "Do you think he'll be all right now?"

"The hellion is growing stronger with every passing moment and she knows the necessity of birthing as many hatchlings as possible to aid her in healing the destruction inside my son's body." She pulled her fringed shawl closer around her. "I would suggest having one of your surgeons remove at least two of the new hatchlings though."

"Dr. Fitzroy wants to wait until Fallon is stronger."

"Do it now," Madame Gregorovich insisted. "You may need it for someone else." She shrugged when he shot her a surprised look. "You never know."

Unclipping his cell phone, the Supervisor contacted his personal assistant and gave the instructions as they walked. He looked down at Fallon's mother. "How does a cup of tea sound to you?"

"Heavenly," she replied as they reached the elevator bank.

After ordering his assistant to have a cup of tea ready for them when they arrived at the office, the Supervisor returned the cell phone to his belt and reached out to push the elevator button.

"I would get lost in this place were you not with me," Madame Gregorovich commented. "I thought the Pentagon large, but this facility is much larger."

The Supervisor gave her another surprised look. Most of the Exchange was deep underground, but very few people knew that. Not even Fallon, and he was the Alpha operative.

"How did you...?"

"Like you, I am more than I appear," she said enigmatically. "I was not born in Russia." She locked gazes with him. "Like you, I come from a place far, far away."

The elevator doors peeled back and the Supervisor held his hand out for her to precede him. Neither spoke until the cage was in motion.

"I take it Fallon doesn't know."

Madame Gregorovich shook her head. "No, he does not nor will he ever know."

"Understood," the Supervisor agreed.

They were silent again until they were seated in the Supervisor's office with the door closed, tea cups in hand. Outside, rain lashed at the windows and lightning stitched across the heavens.

"I love bad weather," she said. "It invigorates me."

The Supervisor looked around at the dark, wet landscape. "This is a most unusual summer for us."

She set her tea cup aside. "You wanted to speak to me about this creature called Martiya."

"What can you tell me about it?"

"Very little, I'm afraid. It is of the Romany mythos. The name as you know means Spirit of the Night. It is a female creature with immense strength and power. Where it resides, I cannot tell you nor do I know how to destroy her."

"The gypsy who called her down on Fallon cannot be found. Do you know anyone who might be able to control this creature? Who might be able to summon her?"

"It is never wise to summon the spirits of evil, Supervisor," Madame Gregorovich cautioned. "Even if I knew of someone who has dealt with this creature in the past—which I'm afraid I don't—gaining control over such a being is dangerous work. Many times such entities are linked to a certain family. I suspect it is allied to the gypsy's family and he learned to invoke it at his mother's knee. If that is the case, the creature would have some modicum of loyalty to the family—most likely through a blood oath—but anyone else who attempts to summon her might not fare as well."

"In other words you think we should leave her the hell alone?"

She inclined her head. "For now. Trust me when I tell you the creature will be dealt with in time by he who will know her weakness."

"You mean *An Fear Liath Mor*?"

"When he returns, he will not be in a good frame of mind when he learns what has happened to Misha. *An Fear Liath Mor* has chosen my son to befriend and that is indeed a great honor. He will have learned all he could about Martiya and will know how best to fight and destroy the creature." She pulled the shawl tighter around her as though a cold wind had blown down her spine. "I would not like to witness the meeting between them."

The Supervisor leaned back in his chair. "Then you don't think we have to worry about this Roland commanding the creature to come after Fallon again?"

"No," she said. "That will not happen."

"Luckily Matty Groves was there and realized Fallon's dying would cause Keenan's," the Supervisor said. "If only we could find him and the others…"

"If you are speaking of the evangelist and the man who was once Keenan's lover, they are no more."

"You think the gypsy killed them?"

"When he denied Martiya the soul she was after, he had to appease her. The gypsy gave the man and woman to her."

A hard shudder went through the Supervisor. "And what of our other man? What of Matty Groves? I've used every power in my personal arsenal and can't locate him. It's as though he dropped off the face of the earth. Could he too have been a victim of the creature?"

Madame Gregorovich considered the question for a moment, staring past the Supervisor at the rain trickling down the window. "No," she said at last. "I do not get the impression he is dead, but rather incapacitated."

The Supervisor's brows clashed. "In what way?"

"In such a way he cannot be found," she said. "Picture him in your mind then use your tactile senses and tell me what you feel."

He did as she asked then frowned sharply. "I have a strong taste of iron in my mouth."

She smiled. "Which implies what?"

"Iron is an inhibitor of psychic powers, it stops the flow," he said. "Groves has some psi abilities, and if the gypsy has him for whatever reason, he could have locked Groves in a building with iron sheathing. That would block my ability to locate him and his ability to send mental transmission or use any form of his psi powers. Is that what you think?"

"Yes, that is the impression I receive, but I have never met this man Groves. What I know of him I have taken from your mind. I would not know how strong his powers are."

"Not very," the Supervisor said. "At least I don't believe they are."

"If the Rom has taken him captive, he might be holding him as...what do you call it? Leverage?"

"Leverage, yes. You may be right." The Supervisor pinched his nose between his thumb and middle finger.

"Your head is bothering you?"

"Psi overload," was the answer.

"It happens with Misha as well," she reminded him. "The stronger the powers the worse the pain when it is wielded or perceived."

The intercom on the desk buzzed and the Supervisor leaned forward to depress the button. "Yes, Jonas."

"He is showing some signs of waking."

"We'll be right there!"

* * * * *

Fallon's chest expanded and a harsh, sucking sound came from deep down his throat. With his jaw wired shut, he could not open his mouth and began to whip his head from side to side. With his arms strapped to the bed, immobilized with IVs and casts, his right leg suspended in traction with steel rods buried into the bone, his broken pelvis and the tubes running from his body to various plastic bags, he could move nothing except his head.

"Agent Fallon?" Fitzroy said, leaning over the bed, but the woman at his side put a hand on his arm and shook her head.

It was Keenan who reacted with a calm and firm voice, stroking Fallon's head with one hand as she threaded the fingers of the other with his right hand.

"Fallon, it's all right. It's all right, baby," she said softly. "I'm here and you're safe. You're at the Exchange."

Fallon paused for just a moment then began making pitiful sounds that tore at Keenan's heart.

"No, lineman, no! You're not blind. You're not! Your eyes are covered with gauze pads because there were retinal tears." She glanced up at Fitzroy. "You'll be able to see as soon as they remove the pads. Do you hear me?"

Another pitiful moan came from him.

"Your jaw is wired shut and you have casts on your arm and your leg but they'll heal. They *will* heal," she stated. "You have a new hellion and she's working overtime to heal you. Okay?"

"I should be able to remove the wiring in about two weeks," the surgeon said. "Were you entirely human, it would be closer to six. You can talk if you try. Just move your lips."

Keenan glanced up at the surgeon. She knew—just as Fallon's mother and the Supervisor knew—the Reaper would not mumble his words. If he couldn't yet speak, he'd say nothing at all.

He quieted somewhat although he continued to move restlessly.

Keenan bent over him and placed her lips to his sweaty forehead. "I'm not going to leave you, lineman," she whispered in his ear. "Don't talk if you don't want to, okay?"

He stilled instantly then eased his cheek into her hand.

"Your mama is here," Keenan said.

Fallon's mother leaned over him too and spoke softly to him in Russian, telling him everything would be all right. "Your powers will return," his mother said. "As soon as the hellion can devote time away from bearing her young."

"We know it's hard for you not to be able to communicate with us, but try to relax. Let the hellion do her job," the Supervisor ordered gently. "It's going to take time, Misha."

"I really need to give him a thorough exam, ladies," Fitzroy told them. "Would you wait out in the hall please?"

"Ladies," the Supervisor said, holding a hand toward the door.

Fallon groaned again and Keenan squeezed his hand. "I'll be right outside the door." She unlaced her fingers from his and followed his mother from the room.

"This is going to be very hard for him," Svetlana Gregorovich said. "He is not accustomed to being an invalid."

The Supervisor's cell phone rang and he unhooked it from his belt. "Yes?"

Keenan watched as anger flitted over the Supervisor's face then his eyes met hers.

"Hold on," he said. "Your mother is asking to speak to you."

"No," Keenan said, shaking her head. "I have nothing to say to her."

"Jonas, tell her that isn't going to happen," the Supervisor told his assistant, "then make arrangements to have Mrs. McCullough taken to the airstrip. Instruct her pilot to leave immediately. I want her off Exchange property."

"Thank you," Keenan said softly.

"I don't care what she wants!" the Supervisor growled. "Make it clear to her that she has absolutely no power here. She can call all the government bigwigs she knows, but that won't cut any ice with me."

"Your mother is a very determined woman," Madame Gregorovich said.

"So is her daughter," Keenan stated.

"I've got a lot of work to catch up on, but I will be back to check on him," the Supervisor said. "I am making arrangements to send him to the Island to recuperate. Naturally you will go along with him, Keenan." He turned to Fallon's mother. "Would you like to accompany them?"

"No, I'm sorry I can't. I must go home," Madame Gregorovich replied. "There are things I too must do. Perhaps I can discover the whereabouts of the Martiya creature."

"That would be a great help, Madame," the Supervisor declared. "Let me know when you'd like to leave and I'll make the arrangements."

"I will."

Keenan and Fallon's mother were quiet for a moment, each lost in her own thoughts, then Keenan sighed deeply and leaned against the wall, scrubbing her hands over her tired face.

"You are worried about your friend Dr. Groves," Madame Gregorovich said.

Keenan nodded. "It's as though he's dropped off the face of the earth. They were friendly," she said then clarified the statement. "Matty and Roland. They were always hanging out together."

"Did you tell the Supervisor this?"

"It was in the report I wrote up the third day I was back," she replied. "In the frame of mind I was at that time, I'm lucky I was able to write anything down, but I did mention the friendship between Matty and Roland."

Madame frowned. "Could Dr. Groves have had a hand in what happened to Misha?"

"No!" Keenan said, vehemently shaking her head. "Definitely not! Matty and Fallon are friends. Matty would never have done anything to harm Fallon."

"Then let's hope wherever he is, no harm has befallen Dr. Groves."

Chapter Twenty-Four

ℬ

Matty restlessly paced the confines of the hotel room, dragging at the iron collar fastened around his neck. The heavy metal had rubbed a blister on his flesh and the weight was giving him a wicked headache.

Across the room, Mizhak Roland sat watching a news show as the local weatherman gave new coordinates for the ninth hurricane that season. He looked around, apparently not bothered by the iron collar he also wore. "It seems this one will bypass us."

"Good," Matty said.

Roland batted away a persistent fly that kept buzzing around him and cursed.

"You don't like the tropics, do you?" Matty asked.

"No," came the clipped reply. "I hate the heat. It doesn't bother you?"

"I'm from Georgia. I'm used to the humidity."

Roland grunted. "I will never grow accustomed to it. I prefer the snows of my native Romania."

The phone rang and both men jumped. There was only one person who could be calling and Matty lunged from the receiver.

"Hello?"

"She wouldn't see me so I am headed back to Georgia," the voice on the other end said.

"Did you get what I asked for?" Matty asked.

There was a derisive snort from the other end. "Of course and the woman agreed to help us just as you said she would. I will pick you up at the airport in Salvador International Airport in three days and we'll go from there."

"How is Keenan?" Matty asked, but the line had already gone dead. He growled as he replaced the receiver. "Bitch."

"She's on her way?"

"She'll pick us up in three days then take us to the private island she owns," Matty reported.

"Where exactly is this place?" Roland asked as he took up a world atlas and flipped the pages to South America.

"All I know is it's on the Dende Coast near Bahia," Matty replied. "Apparently it has as much security—if not more—than the island owned by the Exchange."

"And where exactly is that?" Roland inquired.

Matty shrugged. "I have absolutely no idea. It's somewhere in the Caribbean, but its exact location is on a need-to-know basis. Everyone is taken to and from there on a plane that has its windows shielded. Only the pilot and copilot have the coordinates."

"Then how will we find it?" Roland asked.

"We'll have to leave that up to Mrs. McCullough. She says she'll have the info by the time we need it, and we have to trust she will." He smiled nastily. "Money can buy you just about anything, Mizhak, if you have enough of it."

"I would like to experience that firsthand," Roland quipped. "It was a good thing I had with Mother Bolivar. With Sister Tan..." He shook his head. "With Keenan, it could have been even better."

"Yeah, well, Keenan wouldn't have continued healing people," Matty said.

"I am not so sure," Roland disagreed. "I saw the hunger in her eyes as she healed those who came to her."

"It was simply a desire to help, not a true calling," Matty reiterated. "Besides, her mother isn't about to allow her to continue making a spectacle of herself."

Roland laid the atlas in his lap. "No, she would keep her daughter locked in a prison for the remainder of her days. What a waste."

"A very expensive, lush prison," Matty said. "I, for one, won't mind living in such a place."

"Where you will have the research laboratory promised you," Roland accused.

"Don't forget the bankrolling," Matty said with a grin. "A well-equipped lab and all the personnel I'll ever need. What more could I ask for?"

"Spoken like a man who has never had his freedom curtailed," Roland replied. "Being permanently confined to the island may prove to be more than you bargained for, Matty." He plucked at the iron collar. "Not to mention having to wear these."

Matty threw out a dismissive hand. "A small price to pay, and I intend to come up with a better solution than these cumbersome collars. When Keenan arrives, I don't want her to be bothered by this uncomfortable clunker."

Roland laid aside the atlas, seemingly no longer interested in knowing where he would be hiding from the prying eye of the Exchange.

"I hope things work as you wish for them to, my friend," Roland told Matty.

"They will," Matty said. "Trust me, they will."

* * * * *

Dr. Fitzroy came out of Fallon's room and informed the women they could go back in. "I want him to rest though. I gave him a shot of tenerse so he is fairly relaxed. Make him understand the less he tries to speak, the better."

"Easier said than done," Keenan stated.

"May I have a few moments alone with him, Keenan?" Fallon's mother asked. "Then I must leave. I know he will be in good hands here."

"Sure, go ahead," Keenan said.

"I know from a long association with him that he is a stubborn man," the surgeon said wryly. "His convalescence is not going to be an easy one."

"You think he'll be all right down on the Island?" she asked.

"We've done all we can for him," Dr. Fitzroy said. "The rest is up to his hellion." He put a hand on her shoulder. "The catheter and feeding tube can come out tomorrow, and I'll take the bandage off his eyes then as well. The IV will remain in for a few more days. He can take Sustenance through a straw."

"But he's going to heal as good as new?" she asked.

"Oh yes. It will take awhile for all the broken bones to knit properly—the leg will be the last to heal since the bones in it were shattered and the kneecap destroyed—but I'd say in six to eight more weeks for his leg. We will need to keep him in a wheelchair for at least two weeks then on crutches for two more then a cane should suffice until the healing is done."

"He's not going to be happy about being in a wheelchair," she said.

"He doesn't have any choice. If he tries to put weight on that leg, he'll realize the truth of the matter soon enough."

Madame Gregorovich came out of Fallon's room, wiping a tear from her eye. She gave Keenan a wavering smile, a quick hug, then all but ran down the corridor.

"Make him understand that he needs to rest," the surgeon said. "He's going to want to get up and flit about, but be stern with him."

"Yes sir," Keenan said, bracing herself for the battle of wills to come.

"Good girl," Dr. Fitzroy said then ambled away.

Taking a deep, steadying breath, Keenan put her hands on the heavy hospital room door and pushed it open.

He did not turn his face toward her as she came to his bed. He lay so still that had she not known he was awake, she would have believed him unconscious again. His hands were clenched tightly into the sheet covering him. She pulled the chair up to his bedside and sat, reaching through the slats of the safety rail to hold his hand.

"I was so worried about you," she said.

He didn't move, didn't acknowledge that she was in the room with him.

"You're going to be just fine, lineman," she said, running her thumb over the knuckles of his hand.

Still he made no effort to let her know he understood what she was telling him.

She stared at his rigid profile, at the way his finely chiseled lips were locked tight together. She had come to know this man well and she could sense the anger, the irritation. She could sense the seething turmoil sizzling in his brain even if the power to express those mental thoughts had yet to return. The irrational, jumbled thought patterns were lashing out at her, but just as he was unable to send them coherently to her, she could not intercept them in an orderly way so they made sense to her. One thing though did come across loud and clear—the unrestrained fear he had for something dark and menacing hovering over him.

"It can't reach you here, Fallon," she said, knowing it was the creature—Martiya—that made him uneasy. "It can't touch you here."

A hard shudder ran through him, but when it subsided, he was again as still as death. She stood to lean over him, putting her free hand to his forehead.

"You are safe," she said. "Nothing can get to you here. You..."

He turned his face from her and that one simple action was like a slap in the face. She blinked against the sudden tears that formed in her eyes.

"You want me to go?" she asked, hurt by his turning away.

He did not make a sound, but by his very silence, his pulling back from her, she knew he wanted her to leave.

She drew in a shaky breath, hurt driving deep into her heart. "All right," she said, and could not stop herself from bending over to kiss his forehead.

She felt him stiffen and that hurt her even more. Without wasting another second, she spun around and rushed from the room with her fist pressed to her mouth to keep from sobbing aloud.

* * * * *

Fallon lay perfectly still with his face turned toward a window he could not see. Pain engulfed him in punishing waves, but it was a pain to which he had grown accustomed and it was receding slowly but surely. It bothered him that he could not see, would not speak unless he could do so clearly. His right leg was an agony unto itself, yet he knew the hellion would work ceaselessly until it was once more useful to him. He could feel her and her hatchlings scurrying around beneath the flesh of his back, and while it hurt, he could deal with that pain knowing it had a purpose.

Not so the bone-deep throbbing in his broken limbs or the burning aches in his damaged organs. The ghoret venom still pulsed through his veins and stung like holy hell, but there was nothing to be done about that. There were worse pains. His head felt as though someone were driving a wood splitter through his skull and nausea lurked in the back of this throat. He prayed that nausea would not erupt for he feared he would drown in his own vomit. The only way he could be even minutely comfortable was to lie perfectly still so the itching, burning, throbbing and aching would not grow out of hand.

And over it all hung the specter of the beast that had turned him from a man into a blob of hopeless jelly. Even there, in a place he knew he was safe from it, it loomed with a visage so hideous, so revolting he was hard-pressed not to shiver. The thought of that loathsome thing laying paws to him, slobbering its vile mouth over him, twisting his body in its repulsive grip, sent wave after wave of terror through him and he feared he would feel that way for a long time to come.

It had crippled him, he thought. It had broken him—not only in body but in spirit. It had done things to him there in the pitch black of that frigid hell that he would never be able to speak about for as long as he lived. Evil such as he had never imagined had been visited on him and it had slipped inside him to leave behind its noxious slime.

A low groan left Mikhail Fallon's throat. It was a helpless, hopeless rendering of acceptance against his will.

Unadulterated evil had entered the Reaper and it was still there.

* * * * *

"All right now. I want you to keep your eyes closed until I tell you to open them," Dr. Fitzroy said as he unwound the last inches of gauze strip from over Fallon's eyes. "The light is low in here but your eyes have been covered for..."

The surgeon might as well have saved his breath for as soon as the bandage came away, Fallon opened his eyes, blinking against the dim light. He blinked again as Fitzroy sighed with annoyance.

"How is your vision?"

From across the room Keenan watched as Fallon's eyes tracked across the ceiling, along the window—eyelids narrowed to the faint light coming through the slats—across the wall and past her only to slide back and hold.

"Agent Fallon?" the surgeon prompted. "Is there any residual blurriness? Can you...?"

Fallon nodded just once, his gaze still locked on Keenan.

"Good, then let's see about snipping the wires and removing the bands from your jaw."

For nearly an hour, Keenan observed the surgeon work. She said nothing though Fallon's stare was riveted upon her. Now and then she saw him flinch and knew the procedure had to be painful for they had given him an extra dose of tenerse. She could see dilation of his pupils as the med took hold of him.

"Well, that wasn't too bad, was it?" Fitzroy asked at last, stepping back from his patient. "You won't be able to eat anything solid for a few days, but I don't imagine you care about that right now." He shook his finger at Fallon. "I don't suppose it will do me any good to tell you not to open your mouth too wide. You'll do whatever you want."

Fallon ignored the man and flexed his jaw—opening and closing it, moving it from side to side—though his eyes revealed the pain that caused. After a moment, he stopped.

"All right then," Fitzroy said. "I'll be back in to see you later this afternoon." He shot Keenan a commiserating glance then left with his assistant.

Fallon kept his eyes on Keenan. There was deep, abiding hurt in his gaze and it cut her to the quick.

"Do you want me to go too?" she asked softly.

He stared at her for so long without speaking she took a deep breath, let it out then got up to leave.

"No."

She sat back down in her chair. He was no longer looking at her but had his face turned toward the window again.

"You want me to open the blinds?"

He nodded slowly so she stood and went to the window.

"It's been raining almost steadily since we came back," she said. "One hurricane after another has been brewing in the Gulf."

She turned to see him squinting against the harsh gray light of the storm. He seemed to be searching the heavens for anything that might be lurking there. Though his chest was rising slow and even, she had the impression he was agitated, nervous. The death-grip he had on the sheets told a story of its own.

"Where's Matty?" he asked in a low, gravelly voice.

Keenan came to stand at the foot of his bed. "We don't know."

He turned his face toward her, stare unwavering.

She wrapped her hands over the footboard and cleared her throat. "I was unconscious when they brought me here from Louisiana so I don't really know what happened down there that last day. I do know..." She shrugged. "I'm fairly sure, at any rate, that Mignon Bolivar and Zack Breslin are dead."

"I know they are," he said. "I heard their screams."

Chills ran down Keenan's arms when he spoke in such a matter-of-fact way. He was looking at her as though she were his enemy, as though he hated her or was so angry it was all he could do to speak to her.

"My mother was with us on the plane but I refused to talk to her. If she knows anything, the Supervisor hasn't disclosed it to me. She's gone back to Georgia."

314

He held her gaze for a moment longer then his eyes shifted downward and away.

"Fallon, we..."

"I'm tired," he said, and closed his eyes, shutting her out.

Keenan let go of the footboard. There was so much she wanted to say, so much she wanted to ask, but he had cut himself off from her, making it clear he wanted her to leave.

"Can I come back later?" she asked. "After lunch maybe?"

He didn't reply.

Tears filled Keenan's eyes and she stepped back. Her lips trembled but she refused to beg. If he didn't want to see her, didn't want her there, she'd abide by his wishes.

"If you need me..." she said—her voice breaking—before she turned and left the room.

The moment he knew he was alone Fallon opened his eyes. Hurt flickered in the amber depths—a hurt so deep, so intense he didn't know how he could survive it. Desperately wanting to lift his hands to his face but unable to do so, he shifted with annoyance. He felt exposed, vulnerable, defenseless, and that angered him. He wished he could break something, destroy it, vent his rage, but the option wasn't his. All he could do was bellow with fury and that he did, only to have the nurses come running.

"Get out!" he ordered them. "Leave me the fuck alone!"

But they hadn't. They had been expecting his outburst and had come prepared for it. The moment he saw the vac-syringe in the head nurse's hand, he bellowed again but they held him down and the drug was administered despite his weak struggles.

The last thing he remembered before the darkness flowed over him was Keenan standing in the doorway with tears running down her pale cheeks.

Chapter Twenty-Five

ᔕ

"Are you going to give me a ration of shit or do you want to get out of this room for a while?"

Fallon stared at the wheelchair for a hateful second then looked up at the Supervisor with narrowed eyes. "Why can't I have crutches?"

The Supervisor folded his arms over his chest. "Do you think your leg is healed sufficiently that you can take a chance falling on it? If you do, then I'll have crutches brought, but if you fall, if you re-injure the leg, you'll be in here even longer. Wanna gamble another month's stay before I have you carted off to the Island?"

Glaring once more at the wheelchair, Fallon sighed deeply, his shoulders slumped in surrender. He said nothing as the orderly lifted him from the bed and sat him in the wheelchair, hunkering down to position Fallon's leg with its cast on the leg support.

The Supervisor gently backed the wheelchair out of the room, swung it around and started down the hall. "How 'bout the solarium?"

"I don't care," Fallon said, but he was privately thrilled to be out of the claustrophobic room with its medicinal smells.

"You're the only patient up here right now," the Supervisor reported. "We had an appendectomy patient a few days ago but he's already gone back to the dorm."

"Whoopee," Fallon growled.

"I've scheduled you to leave for the Island day after tomorrow. They have state-of-the-art rehab equipment there and the very best physical therapists, so we should have you back on your feet in short order."

Because of the rainy weather, the solarium wasn't as bright and cheerful as it normally was. When the Supervisor rolled him over to the windows, the Reaper stared intently at a trickle of rainwater as it wriggled down the outside of the glass pane. He ignored the Supervisor who pulled up a plastic chair and sat beside him.

For nearly half an hour neither man spoke. They watched the rain falling, the low clouds streaking by and the Canada geese that flew through them.

"I'm sending Keenan with you."

Fallon flinched. "I wish you wouldn't."

"I know you do, but it's a done deal."

The Supervisor got up and started away.

"Where are you going?" Fallon asked.

"Talk to her," was all the Supervisor said, and despite Fallon yelling at him to come back, continued on his way.

Alone in the solarium with his right leg and left arm in casts, Fallon had no way to maneuver the wheelchair. Besides, he didn't think at that moment he had the strength to push the wheels. He was still weak and in more pain than he was prepared to admit to his caretakers. Hanging his head, he clenched his teeth, squeezed his eyes tightly shut with frustration and waited for Keenan to join him.

* * * * *

"Sit," the Supervisor ordered.

Keenan did as she was commanded. Over the course of the last two days she'd come down with a late summer-early autumn cold and felt miserable. Her head ached and every bone in her body felt as though it were being attacked with tiny little hammers.

"I left him in the solarium about an hour ago," the Supervisor said, "with instructions that no one was to go in there. He's too weak to ply the wheelchair on his own and I seriously doubt he'll start yelling for help until another hour has passed."

"The object of this exercise is to make it clear to him just how powerless he is right now," the third person in the room said softly.

"And you think he needs that brought home to him?" Keenan snapped. "You don't think he already feels powerless enough?"

"What Dr. Vardar is saying is that Fallon needs to look upon you as his savior when you arrive to take him back to his room," the Supervisor commented. "He'll be relieved and thankful and more inclined to talk to you."

"He'll be pissed," she corrected. "Believe me he will, and much less inclined to talk to me."

"I disagree," Dr. Vardar, the Exchange's psychiatrist, stated.

"Keenan, we've seen this kind of reaction before when an agent has been subjected to the kind of traumatic experience Fallon experienced. Not only do we need to rehabilitate his body, we need to heal his mind. At the moment, his mind has suffered far more damage than his body did."

"At the moment, Agent Fallon is feeling a great deal of shame. He…"

"Shame?" Keenan interrupted the psychiatrist. "Why should he be feeling shame?"

"Because he found out he wasn't as invincible as he believed himself to be," Dr. Vardar replied. "He has always viewed himself as being strong, unbeatable and indestructible—if you will—and completely in charge of every situation. He was helpless to prevent what happened to him, and helplessness to a man like Mikhail Fallon is completely unacceptable. Oh, he'd taken beatings in the past. His stepfather abused him at every turn so he was no stranger to pain, but the pain he was given by Martiya was much worse than anything he'd ever endured before and it crippled him. It drove him to his knees and in some dark place within him he believes he surrendered to it. Although the creature didn't break him, it did tear something vital inside him."

"And this perceived surrender is eating away at him," the Supervisor added.

"He is undergoing a very severe case of posttraumatic stress disorder," Dr. Vardar said. "He has most of the symptoms—depression, irritability, emotional detachment, difficulty paying attention, hypervigilance—have you seen him staring out the window as though he expects something to come at him?"

"Yes," Keenan said, looking down. "I have."

"In the last few days, he's also experienced nightmares," the Supervisor told her. "That is, when he can sleep at all."

"Loss of appetite, anxiety, being easily startled," Dr. Vardar continued. "All classic symptoms."

"And you want to make him feel even worse by leaving him alone in the solarium?" she questioned.

"You are his Extension, Keenan," the Supervisor reminded her. "These feelings of disassociation he's having should not include you. You are his lifeline and we want him to acknowledge it."

"What if he blames me for what happened to him?"

"How could he?" the Supervisor queried.

"Do you believe he does?" Dr. Vardar asked.

Keenan dug in her pocket for a tissue to wipe her runny nose. "It's the way he looks at me," she said. "He looks angry."

"Oh well, that's part and parcel of the PTSD," Dr. Vardar said.

"Just go to him," the Supervisor said. "Try to get him to talk about what happened. He won't discuss it with me or Dr. V., but he might open up to you."

"It will be good for him to get it out there," Dr. Vardar said. "Until he acknowledges what happened to him, he can't move past it."

Keenan wasn't sure it was a wise thing to open up the wounds she felt Fallon was trying to close, but she kept her thoughts to herself as she left the Supervisor's office and took the elevator up to the solarium. The soft music playing in the background aggravated her and she blew her nose noisily to block it out. When the elevator doors opened, she hurried out and away from the canned tune that had her wanting to thrust her fingers into her ears.

He was sitting in front of the windows, but she was fairly sure he was sleeping. His chin was tucked down and his hands were resting limply on the wheelchair's armrests. As quietly as she could, she took the chair positioned beside him and released a soft, wavering breath, passing her gaze lovingly over his profile.

To her, he was such an extraordinarily handsome man. With the thick black hair and the tawny complexion, the amber eyes and straight nose, full lower lip and the determined chin, he could pass for a matinee idol. There were no razor nicks to mar his flesh.

"They heal quickly," he'd once said to her when she asked if he never cut himself shaving. "The scar on my brow I got when I was four. If I'd gotten it after the Transference, my hellion would have healed it. She doesn't like imperfections."

As she sat there, she switched her attention to his back beneath the hospital pajama top and realized the scarring there would have occurred when he was young. That knowledge hurt her deeply and she clenched her hands together in her lap and looked away.

She lost track of how much time passed as she sat there beside him. At one point he whimpered and she saw his eyes moving rapidly back and forth beneath the lids and knew he was dreaming. His fingers twitched in his lap, but the moment she reached over and put her hand protectively over his, the nightmare ceased, the twitching stopped and he subsided into dreamless sleep once more. Content just to touch him, to have her skin close to his, she kept her hand there and returned her attention to the rolling Iowa hills.

A few moments later he woke with a start, drawing in a harsh gasp, blinking against the dull gray of the rainy afternoon. A vein in his neck throbbed rapidly and his chest rose and fell quickly—an indication he had been thrust from an unpleasant place into the realm of reality. He swallowed hard and looked down, eyes narrowing as he noticed her hand closed over his. Slowly he turned his head to look at her. When she smiled gently at him, he looked away again but did not attempt to move his hand from under hers.

"Do you want to talk about the dream?" she asked softly.

He closed his eyes as though in great pain, and when at last he opened them, stared straight ahead. She didn't think he would answer but he did, his voice was husky.

"I got the hell beaten out of me by that thing," he rasped.

Her hand tensed on his. "Yes, but you survived."

He didn't look at her. "Did I?"

"You're here, aren't you?"

A low snort accompanied his answer. "For what it's worth."

"It's worth a lot to me."

Some time passed before he spoke again.

"I had my ass handed to me, McCullough. That bitch stomped me good."

His gaze was roaming the dark skies constantly, and with each flash of lightning, he flinched.

"You are safe here. You do know that, don't you?"

"She's out there. Waiting. She didn't finish what she started and will try again until she is stopped."

"We will find it and…"

"*No!*" he shouted, his head snapping toward her. His eyes were glowing with fury. "*You will stay the hell out of this, Keenan!*"

"Fallon…" Keenan was almost afraid of the man sitting beside her. There was murderous rage in his steady glare and it sent ripples of unease down her spine.

"This is between me and that bitch!" he snarled. "She'll come for me again and when she does, I *will* put her fucking slimy ass down!"

She wasn't so sure Fallon could win in a fight against something as powerful as Martiya. The creature had nearly destroyed him, had hurt him in ways she knew she couldn't begin to comprehend, and the continuing influence on him was exacting a terrible revenge.

"Don't shut me out," she said. She twisted in the chair so she could place her free hand on his cheek. "I love you. Don't close yourself off to me, Fallon."

Fallon seemed to slump in the chair. "I'm tired," he said. "I need to go back to my room."

There was more that needed to be said, things that needed to be asked, but she could sense him withdrawing and knew she'd get nothing else from him. She lowered her hand, eased the other one from beneath his and stood.

"Do you want me to take you back to your room?"

He nodded.

Moving behind him, she looked down at his bent head then pulled the chair from the window, turned it and started out of the solarium.

"Did the Supervisor tell you we would be leaving for the Island in a couple of days?"

"Yeah," he acknowledged curtly, making it clear he didn't want to discuss it.

So she didn't. She pushed his chair down the hallway and into his room. His bed had been freshly made and a nurse was pouring an iced tumbler of water at the bedside table. The woman said nothing but left quietly, returning almost immediately with a burly orderly.

Knowing Fallon wouldn't want her to see him being lifted into bed like a child, Keenan bent down and kissed him on the top of the head.

"I'll see you tomorrow, okay?"

"Whatever," he mumbled.

Keenan exchanged a look with the nurse—who shook her head and shrugged—then left. Once in the hall, she collapsed against the wall and buried her face in her hands.

* * * * *

Because the orthopedic surgeon had decreed the hellion had healed Fallon's leg as well as could be expected, they removed the cast before they wheeled him out to the jet waiting to take him, Keenan, a nurse-practitioner and two operatives taking R & R to the Island. Cautioning him to use the crutches provided for him, they had admonished Keenan to make sure he put as little stress on the mending leg as possible. Thankfully, x-rays showed his broken arm had mended completely and that cast as well had been removed.

With the window shields locked into place, the interior of the jet proved to be exceedingly unnerving for the Reaper. His claustrophobia reared its ugly head so violently the nurse was forced to give him an extra dose of tenerse to calm him down. Even so, his uninjured leg bounced nervously and he plucked constantly at the arms of his chair. Unable to look out the windows, to hobble to the cockpit, he was forced to sit in his seat and stew — taking harsh breaths and wiping at the sweat that dotted his forehead — until they were airborne then he moved to the couch where he could be more comfortable.

"Did I tell you about the island my mother bought after my father died?" Keenan asked in an attempt to take his mind off the claustrophobic conditions.

He shook his head.

"She named it St. Brisa although it was called something else — still is, I think — on the maps. It's on the Dende Coast off Brazil."

He nodded as though he were listening though she was sure he wasn't. She kept talking in the hopes of distracting him.

"It really is a beautiful place," she continued. "Mama has always had this thing for books and movies about pirates. Actually, I think she did her dissertation on Blackbeard."

"Huh," he commented, and laid his head back on the seat, closed his eyes.

"The island is like an old-time pirate stronghold complete with cannon ramparts in the mountains. It's got security you wouldn't believe. The harbor is as tight as an old maid's ass." She laughed. "As much as my mother loves all things pirates, she has no use for the real thing and there are plenty of them down in the Caribbean."

"Uh-huh," he agreed. His bad leg was stretched out in front of him but his left leg was jumping briskly.

"The entire perimeter of the island is wired for sound and movement, and she has a small army of men who patrol it vigilantly. No one gets on the island or off without Mama being told. I imagine the Exchange's Island is the same way."

"Yeah," he agreed.

"Although she doesn't keep the island's whereabouts a secret as the Exchange does," she commented.

"Security measure," he mumbled, his words slurred.

She knew the tenerse was taking effect and said nothing else, hoping he'd go to sleep. When she noticed his leg had stopped bouncing and his breathing had become slower and more even, she relaxed. Quietly, she got up and moved away so as not to disturb him.

Half an hour later she heard him moan and set aside the book she'd been reading, taking a seat beside Fallon on the couch. He flinched and a low whimper came from somewhere deep inside his chest. His hands were clenched tight into fists—so tight the knuckles had bled of color.

Very softly she laid her hand atop one of his and he jerked, his eyes snapping open as he sucked in a hard gasp.

"It's all right," she said, her voice gentle and reassuring.

He wouldn't look at her. He was staring straight ahead as he drew in great gulps of air.

"Damn," he finally said, and lifted his free hand to wipe at the sweat peppering his face. He pressed his hand over his mouth then squeezed his eyes closed.

"Tell me what to do, lineman," Keenan said. She stroked his hand. "Let me help."

"There's nothing you can do," he grated, his words muffled through the fence of his fingers.

Then he surprised her by twisting around and lying down, putting his head in her lap. Awkwardly—grunting from the effort—he drew his injured leg onto the seat, crooked at the knee over his leg left. He thrust his clasped hands between his thighs.

Keenan smoothed the hair back from his forehead, frowning at the dampness of his scalp. She could feel waves of intense heat from his cheek and temple coming through the fabric of her lightweight slacks.

"I do love you," he said.

"I know you do."

"I hated every minute I was with Bolivar."

"I know, sweetie," she said.

"It will always be you."

She was looking down at his profile and watched him close his eyes.

"Always you," he repeated.

Keenan ran the backs of her fingers down the side of his face. "There's no one but you for me either," she told him. "I love you more than life itself."

She saw his eyes open and squint as though he had felt a sudden pain lancing through him.

"I'll protect you, *lhiannan*," he whispered. "I swear I will." He turned his head so he could look into her eyes. "Whatever it takes, I will protect you."

"I know you will, baby," she said, smiling.

He looked away from her.

"Whatever it takes," he said again.

She tried to psychically send a thought to him but either his powers had yet to return or he was too distracted to intercept the transmission. He just closed his eyes again and seemed to relax, although beneath her arm his body felt taut with tension.

Continuing to stroke his hair and cheek, not saying anything so he could rest, she stared across the aisle to the porthole, wishing the shields were up so she could at least see the fleecy clouds.

He mumbled something she didn't catch then began to snore lightly. The sound did her heart good to hear.

* * * * *

"He's going to be in there most of the afternoon, ma'am," the receptionist said. "If you're hungry, the cafeteria is in the south wing and its open twenty-four hours a day. Go out those doors, turn right and follow the dark yellow line on the floor."

Keenan thanked her, remembering there were different colored lines leading to and from all four wings of the large facility. The red line led to the clinic in the west wing. The green line ushered visitors to the living quarters in the north wing and the blue line led to the east wing where the shops, gym and entertainment facilities were located, including a huge indoor-outdoor pool.

"When they're through with him, would you page me?" Keenan asked, giving her the pager number that had been assigned her when they'd signed in at the main building.

"Certainly, Agent McCullough."

By the time her pager went off, she was finished with her late lunch and was ready to do a bit of sightseeing on the private island. Heading back to the clinic, she passed a few agents she knew, spoke briefly to them then continued on. As soon as she saw Fallon glaring at her, she knew she'd dawdled a bit too long in his estimation.

"Where the hell were you?" he asked.

"Flirting with every Peter, Dick and Harry Roderick I came into contact with," she replied sweetly. "And how was your day, dear?"

"Fuck you," he growled, but it was said with a mock grin.

"Promises, promises," she said. "Ready to go?"

"I was born ready to go," he replied.

"Have him here by six tomorrow morning, Agent McCullough," the receptionist said.

"Shit, I haven't even turned over by six in the morning," Fallon snarled.

"We'll be here," Keenan said, rolling him away before he could say something to embarrass her.

Following the green line on the floor, she headed for the living quarters, knowing he'd more than likely want to shower since both the back and front of his black T-shirt was soaked with sweat. She knew their luggage would have been unpacked, put in the drawers and everything they needed taken care of. The Exchange took care of their own.

"So how was old Harry Rod?" he asked as they neared the receptionist kiosk to get their room numbers.

"A little stiff," she said, deadpan.

"Good afternoon, Agents McCullough and Fallon," the receptionist said. "Agent Fallon, you are in your usual room and, Agent McCullough, you are in…"

"She'll bunk with me," Fallon said.

Keenan saw the receptionist's eyelids flicker just a fraction but the young woman's smile never wavered. After all, Fallon was the Alpha operative at the Exchange and what he wanted, he usually got.

"Of course, sir," she said without missing a beat. "I'll have her things moved immediately."

"Wait an hour or so," Fallon instructed. "I need a shower and I don't want people traipsing through the suite until I'm done."

"Yes sir," the receptionist said, handing the keycard to the room to Keenan. "Enjoy your stay on the Island."

"Thank you," Keenan replied.

The room into which Keenan wheeled Fallon was simply gorgeous. Done in tropical shades of deep butterscotch gold, dark green, vibrant burgundy and azure, the fabric on the seating arrangement, the draperies, and through the opened bedroom door, the comforter, drew the eye like a magnet. The furniture was pristine white wicker and the great room of the suite was so large it required four slowly revolving ceiling fans. Underfoot, the carpeting was sand-colored, making the room appear gardenlike. Everywhere was a profusion of live plants that added to the lush, tropical theme.

"This is scrumptious!" she said as she gently kicked the door shut behind her and pushed Fallon into the center of the room.

"Wait 'til you see the bathroom," he told her. "It's a bit like your mother's."

"Really?" she said. "Through that door?"

"Uh-huh."

She wheeled him into the bathing suite and whistled when she got a look at the whirlpool bathtub and huge walk-in shower—both set in a light blue tile with a midnight blue border. The entire room looked as though it were under water.

"The shower has twelve shower jets on the three walls, four in the floor and four in the ceiling. The ones on the wall come on automatically, but you have to manually turn on the other two," he said.

"Right now I could use all twenty jets," she said as she stooped down to lock the wheels in place. "Need help undressing?"

"Uh-huh," he said, leaning away from the chair back to pull off his T-shirt. He was wearing jeans and loafers without socks so as he unbuttoned his jeans, she hunkered down to take off his shoes.

"How's your ankle?" she asked, carefully removing his right shoe.

He shrugged. "Hurts worse than the goddamned kneecap does actually, but it's getting there."

"Can you put your weight on it?" she queried. "Maybe the bathtub would be better than the shower."

"I want the shower," he said like a petulant child. He unzipped his fly. "There are support bars in there and a seat if I need it."

"Okay," she said, drawing the word out. She stepped over to the shower and opened the large tempered glass door. She whistled again. "Seat, hell, Fallon! That's a bench big enough to lie down on."

He was struggling to push himself out of the chair, but it was obvious to her his left arm was bothering him and he had little strength after going through rehab earlier. She went to him and slipped an arm around him to lever him to his feet. With him holding on to a safety bar beside the shower, she tugged his jeans and underwear off, tossing them aside. When she looked up at him, she realized he was sweating profusely again.

"You're hurting, lineman. Maybe you should…"

"You wanna help, McCullough?" he cut her off.

She sighed. "Yes."

"Then help me into the fucking shower, okay?" he asked.

"Have you screwed somebody in there?" she demanded, eyes narrowed.

"Hell no!"

"Then it isn't a fucking shower," she stated then grinned.

"Yet."

He snorted. "I just want a shower, McCullough. I don't want to be mauled."

"So you say," she mumbled.

Knowing he was going to get his way no matter what she said, she gave in and once more looped her arm around him to assist him into the shower. He hopped on his left foot with his right leg crooked behind him, but with every bounce, she saw a muscle flex in his cheek and knew it caused him a lot of unnecessary pain.

"Stubborn man," she said, trying not to giggle at the way his cock flapped against his thigh as he hopped.

"Bench," he said through clenched teeth, "and stop gaping at my whingding."

"Yeppers," she agreed with a grin, and helped him to sit down. Once he was slumped against the cool tile, she glanced at the shower controls. "You want them all on?"

"I want you to take off your clothes and stay in here with me," he said, looking up at her.

Keenan put her hands on her hips. "You want me to bathe you, Fallon?"

"That too, but mostly I just want to see you naked," he said, and gave her one of his patented reckless grins that she had missed so dearly.

"You're bad," she said, and stepped out of the shower to undress.

"But I'm lovable."

"You have your moments," she agreed.

329

He watched every move she made as she took off her clothing. A fine sheen of sweat glistened on his brow and there was a dark ruddy color in his cheeks. The hand he put up to rake through his hair trembled.

After she closed the shower door and turned on all twenty jets—the water coming out at just the perfect programmed temperature—she took a big sponge and bar of mango-scented soap from the shelf and began working up a nice, rich lather. Her long braid was soon plastered to her back and the water skimming down her felt heavenly.

Fallon's attention hadn't wandered from her the entire time, and when she came over to him, running the soft sponge down his neck and arms, he felt every bone in his body melting—even the ones that hurt like hell.

"Feel good?" she asked.

"Like you wouldn't believe," he replied with a heartfelt sigh. "It's been a long time."

"I know the nurses gave you sponge baths, lineman," she said.

"Not the same," he told her. He opened one eye. "I like your hands on me."

"You'd better."

She worked her way down his chest and hips, along his thighs, then squatted in front of him to run the sponge down his calves. This close to his flesh, she could see the deep indentions that had yet to fill in where the steel pins had been inserted into the bones of his shattered right leg.

"It's taking too long," he said, reading her mind.

She looked up. "Getting your powers back?"

"In spurts," he replied.

"The x-rays show the bones are knitting together."

"Yeah, but there was so much venom in me, my entire system was saturated in it. It seeped into the very marrow of my bones. Sometimes I can even taste the vileness lurking in my saliva." He sighed. "That's why it's taking so long for Her to heal me."

"Everything else is all right though, isn't it?" she asked, thinking of the organs that had suffered damage during the beating he'd taken at the hands of Martiya.

"I guess so. My head still hurts and every now and then I feel a twinge in my lung," he said. He sounded so tired, but after washing his feet, she looked up to find his eyes filled with a need she remembered all too well.

She gently eased his thighs apart—very careful of his right leg—and went to her knees in front of him. Without a word, she lowered her head.

Fallon closed his eyes to the sweet warmth of her mouth as her lips closed around his limp flesh. He wanted her desperately but knew he had neither the strength nor the stamina to take her there in the shower. He wanted to. By the gods and all that was holy, he wanted to! He ached for her. Had been aching for her since he woke from the nightmarish hell into which he'd been plunged. More than just the sex, he wanted to lie with her in his arms, to keep the world at bay for at least a few hours.

Burying his hand in her wet hair, he gave himself up to the ecstasy her mouth always brought him. Her lips swept over and around him, sending chills down his spine.

Keenan swirled her tongue over the head of his cock and delved into the warm slit. Her hand cupped his balls, kneaded them, sought to give him the sweetest pleasure she knew how to give. She took him deep down her throat and worked the flat of her tongue against the underside of his shaft, milking him, rolling his cock. As his shaft hardened, she suckled him with strong pulls that made him groan and caused his hand to tighten in her hair. His breathing became shallow and quick, and he began to tilt his hips up to her.

When he came, he came hard, but he didn't make a sound. His cock leapt, his juices spurted, but not one sound came from his lips. As the last spasm left him and she let his spent cock slip from her mouth, she looked up and realized he was crying. Tears were sliding silently down his cheeks and he was staring at her with such deep, raw hurt it was like a slap across her face.

"Baby, what's wrong?" she said, straightening, putting her hands to his cheeks. "Did I hurt you?"

He shook his head and gathered her into his arms, bringing her wet body to his, holding her there as wave after wave of grief shook his body.

"I love you," he said. "God, I love you so much!"

There was ragged misery in his voice, anguish choking the words out of him. Her arms were around his waist, her face to his chest as he gave in to the emotions wreaking their havoc on him. It seemed to her he was holding on to her for dear life, his arms locking her to him.

"I'm right here, lineman," she said. "I've told you before, I'm not going anywhere."

As the water beat down on them from every direction, he continued to hold on to her. By the time his tears were spent, he was too drained to heave himself up from the shower bench and—much to his shame—Keenan was forced to call for an orderly to carry him into the bedroom.

Wrapped in a plush white terry cloth robe, she waited in the living area with her back to the bedroom door until the orderly had helped Fallon into a pair of shorts and put him to bed. After the orderly left, she went to the bedroom door. The moment he saw her, he held his hand out to her and she went to him, taking a seat beside him on the bed.

"You'll do just about anything for attention, won't you, Fallon?" she teased as she pushed a strand of wet hair from his eyes.

"I'm hungry," he said. "That crap they fed me at rehab was rabbit shit."

"Oh yum. Pellet form or pudding?" she inquired with an arched brow as he leaned over and took the receiver from the bedside phone. She watched him as he punched in a number he obviously knew by heart.

"Yeah, this is Fallon. I want an obscenely large rare steak and a humongous potato smothered in sour cream and chives, and a round of cheese bread dripping with real butter," he ordered. He listened then frowned. "No, did I ask for any fucking vegetable?"

He rolled his eyes. "Yes, I know potatoes are vegetables but they're not fucking green vegetables, now are they?"

Keenan pursed her lips together to keep from laughing. Her man was slowly rotating back to the obnoxious, entitled person he believed himself to be, and that was just fine by her. It proved his spirit was healing along with his body.

"I don't know. Hold on." He shoved the receiver at Keenan. "He wants to know if you want anything."

She took the phone. "Hi, I could use a glass of tea and a much smaller version of what Fallon ordered except I would love a nice green veggie to balance out the carbs. Make my steak medium well." She smiled. "Steamed broccoli would be great, thank you." She shook her head for Fallon was motioning he wanted the phone back. "Wait a minute. I think his lordship thought of something else." She handed Fallon the phone.

"Strawberry shortcake with lots of strawberries and globs of cream and two pitchers of iced tea." He ground his teeth. "Yes, she wants one too so make it four slices of cake." He slammed the phone down.

"You are so endearing yourself to the people in the cafeteria," she drawled.

"I'm hungry," he said then rubbed his right thigh. "And I hurt, Keenan." He frowned like a little boy with a boo-boo. "I hurt."

"Yes, I know you do." She pushed aside his hand and began rubbing his thigh. There was a long incision that ran from his hip to his knee at a slight angle and to either side of the wound were six round indentions where the pins had recently been removed. The calf and shin of the same leg looked like the railroad lines in a cattle yard.

As she massaged his leg, he reached up to tug on his left earlobe—a habit she realized long ago signaled he was ashamed of something he'd done.

"Damned bitch tore the earring out of my ear when she threw me across…" He flung out a dismissive hand. "Wherever the hell it was she threw me," he complained. "Now the hole has sealed up and I'll have to get it punched again."

"I'm surprised your hellion allows you to have a piercing of any kind," she said.

He sniffed. "She must think it's sexy on me or She wouldn't let me have it. It's bad enough She went and healed the fucking hole." He laid his hands over his flat belly and laced the fingers together as she worked her way down his calf. "I once tried to grow a mustache and that turned out real well."

She looked up at him. "She didn't like the 'stache?"

He shook his head. "All I got for my trouble were ingrown hairs." He rolled his head on his shoulders. "She doesn't mind a two- or three-day growth of beard, but anything more than that, She won't allow. I don't like beards anyway, but I wanted that fucking mustache something fierce."

Keenan smiled. He was back to the banter that had so endeared her to him in the first place. Though his eyes were still filled with dark shadows, he was relaxing at last and wasn't looking at her as though he wanted to strangle her.

"Roland has Matty," he said.

"That's my guess too," she replied.

"The question is why."

"They were pretty friendly at Bolivar's," she told him. "I used to see them together much of the time so I suspect the Supervisor assigned Matty to get tight with the gypsy." His eyes tracked every step she made.

"That sounds right," Fallon agreed. "Matty makes friends easily."

"Are you worried about him?" she asked, because for some strange reason she wasn't.

"I don't get the feeling he's in danger and *that's* what worries me," he answered.

There was a light knock at the door and Keenan went over to let room service in.

"Do you want the food laid out on the table?" the young man asked.

"No, just roll the cart into the bedroom. I think Agent Fallon would be more comfortable there."

Fallon pushed himself up on the bed, propped against the thickly padded headboard covered in the same tropical print as the coverlet, wincing as his injured leg dragged against the coverlet.

"There is a bed tray in the closet, Agent McCullough, and a folding card table," the young man said. "Would you like me to get them?"

"That would be great, Andy," she said, reading his name tag. "Thanks."

Bringing one of the rattan chairs from the dinette set into the bedroom to place beside the card table, Andy laid their food out for them then left.

"Man, this smells good," Keenan said. She took a seat the table.

"I've never had anything from the kitchen here that wasn't," he said as he began scoring his steak.

For a few moments they ate in silence, enjoying the tender steak and mouthwatering potato piled high with rich sour cream and pungent chives. One bite of the cheese bread and Keenan groaned with delight.

"I wonder what's in this that makes it so spicy?" she asked.

"Jalapeño jelly in the batter," he supplied.

"Ah."

"I have to find Matty," he said, and she realized his friend's whereabouts was never far from his mind.

"Coim should be back any time now," she said. "Maybe he'll have learned something about the creature. If we can find it, destroy it, Roland will be neutralized."

"Maybe," he mumbled around a huge glob of potato. He kept eyeing the strawberry shortcake with the same kind of lustful expression he'd given her in the shower.

"Eat your steak," she said, knowing full well he'd consume every ounce of sugar in the three oversized pieces of strawberry shortcake and exactly what that sugar overload would do to his Reaper libido.

"You hope," he growled, and when she looked over at him, he was grinning mercilessly.

Chapter Twenty-Six

❦

Matty and Roland took their seats in the luxury jet and buckled in. Lily McCullough was on her cell phone giving orders to a man she called Royce. Whatever she was saying to him seemed urgent and from the expression on her face, she was not a happy camper. When she finished the call, she threw the cell phone the length of the plane's aisle.

"Bad news?" Matty asked when she sat down.

"Eight mercenaries including him," she snapped. "That's a hell of a lot of people to keep quiet!" She slammed the two ends of the seat belt together.

Matty didn't like the sound of that, but her plans were something he didn't want her sharing with him anyway. The less he knew about the operation, the better. He had concerns of his own.

"Where's the incubator?" he asked. "Is it onboard?"

"Yes," Lily hissed. "Now shut the fuck up. I need to think! We've got trouble."

"Is something wrong?" Matty asked.

"Yes, something's wrong!" Lily snapped. "In all the planning we did we never once gave any thought to what would happen when Fallon or that bastard who runs him realize Keenan can't possibly be dead!"

"I don't follow," Roland said.

"Oh shit," Matty said, scrubbing a hand over his face. "How did we miss that?"

"Miss what?" the gypsy asked.

"The grief will cripple him for a day or two at the most," Lily said, chewing on a cuticle. "But then he's going to start putting two and two together if the Supervisor doesn't do it for him. He'll wonder why he hasn't just laid down and died. When another day or so passes, he's going to know something isn't right then he's going to know for sure!"

Matty drew in a harsh breath, afraid of what she might be considering. "If anything happens to Fallon, Keenan will…"

"Nothing *can* happen to him!" Lily shouted. "Don't you think I know what would occur if something did?" Her eyes were blazing with fury. "As much as I'd like to see that bastard with his throat slit, I've given strict orders he is not to be harmed." She pounded her fist on the seat.

Matty shrugged helplessly. "What are we going to do to keep him from coming after her?"

"There's nothing we *can* do," Lily said. "He can't get on my island. There's no way he can, so if and when he realizes she's alive, there's nothing he can do about it!"

"So why worry?" Roland asked. "He can't get to her. For a few days he will suffer the agony of the damned. Is that not what you wanted?"

Lily nodded slowly. "Yes, that is what I wanted, but I wanted that pain to last him for a long, long time."

"Knowing she's alive and there's no way he can get to her, find her," Roland said. "Won't that be bad enough?"

"It'll have to be," she muttered.

Lily said nothing more until they were airborne. Beckoning the steward over, she ordered a gin and tonic and told him to give the men whatever they wanted.

"Nothing for me," Matty said. "I get airsick if the first drop of booze hits my stomach."

"Vodka," Roland ordered. "No ice."

Swigging down her drink like a thirsty lumberjack when it came, Lily demanded another. She was staring out the window as she explained to Matty what was about to take place.

"There are two weekly flights to the Island," she said. "One brings passengers and the other brings in supplies. The supply jet will fly in day after tomorrow at 10 a.m. and will depart the Island around three in the afternoon. A flight carrying passengers is scheduled to land at 4 p.m. the same day and depart two hours later. It will be an hour late arriving."

Matty shifted uneasily in his seat. He really didn't want to listen, but it was obvious she felt the need to talk about what was going to occur.

"There are only four crewmen on the supply jet, but the passenger plane will have three crew plus seven passengers. Royce has arranged for the plane carrying the passengers to make an emergency landing at the airport we just left. He and his men posing as mechanics will board the plane, take out the crew as well as the passengers with nerve gas canisters and take control. The flight plan to the Island is stored in the jet's computer so all Royce has to do is fly the jet to its destination. Once they land, they will disperse and eliminate all the Island's inhabitants except for two."

Matty flinched. "Is that really necessary?"

"Yes, it is! I have a very personal reason for wanting to strike back at the Exchange," Lily interrupted him. "Not only did your precious Supervisor take my daughter from me, but he insulted me when I was there." She narrowed her eyes. "No one insults me, Groves, and does not feel the consequences. He won't know who his enemy is, but he will know one is out there and that the strike on the Island was as much his fault as Fallon's!"

Matty stared at the woman and realized she was not quite sane. The glow in her eyes was evil and it made him distinctly nervous. When that steady gaze fell to Roland, he shivered. The odds of the Rom living to a ripe old age were very slim.

* * * * *

He had never wanted to make love to her more than he did at that moment.

As he watched her put the dishes onto the rolling cart then push it from the room, his eyes locked on the gentle sway of her sweet ass. He loved seeing her barefoot with her hair still wet from the shower. He inhaled the fresh scent of her, the womanly scent, and when she came back into the room, he knew his lust must be broadcasting clear and strong for she halted abruptly, a hand to her lips.

"It's the sugar, isn't it?" she asked.

He lifted a hand to her. "It's the woman," he replied in a husky voice.

She smiled, shucking off the caftan. "Oh well, if that's the case..." She came to the bed, laced her fingers over his and climbed atop him, swinging one long, delicious leg over his, but then just kneeling there, not sure if she should put any pressure on his hips. She joined the fingers of her other hand with his.

"You're not going to hurt me, *lhiannan*," he told her, and barely recognized his own voice for it was filled with rampaging desire.

"Then what's the point?" she said, saucily flinging her hair over her shoulder.

His heart did a funny little flip at her challenge. She was swaying their hands back and forth playfully then brought his to her breasts.

He molded his palms over the full globes, feeling the nipples hardening. He slid his hands to her back and pulled her down to him so he could suckle one rosy tip. He nipped at the tip then drew the puckered nub into his mouth, sweeping his tongue over it.

"Were you breastfed?" she asked.

"Uh-uh," he mumbled then released that nipple with a loud pop. "Old man wouldn't allow it." He shifted his attention to the other nipple.

Keenan squirmed against him, carefully lowering her legs to either side of his. At one point he tensed and she knew she'd touched his injury, but he kept his arms tight around her, not allowing her to slide off him.

He moved his mouth from her flesh and looked up into her face. "Put him in you, babe," he asked, arching his hips toward her. His cock was hard and steely as it lay between them. "Ride your man."

Keenan felt his words like a slow stroke that ended with a fierce thrust into her cunt. It made her womb clench.

"You sure?"

"Never surer."

She sat up so she could push her body away from his. His hands went to either side of his head as she reached down to guide his thick shaft into the damp folds between her legs.

"I don't want to hurt you," she said.

"Baby, hurt me all you want," he gruffly commanded. "Ride him 'til he's sore."

His hands came down to clamp on her hips, his fingers digging into the shapely softness. As she slid her flesh over his, he closed his eyes and sighed.

"Oh yeah," he said. "Yeah."

Very slowly at first, he lifted her gently and lowered her on his cock, impaling her deeply with each upward tilt of his hips. She could feel the broad head of his shaft pushing at the entrance of her womb—it was a delicious pain that she wanted to last forever.

Fallon was guiding her strokes, and when he increased the speed of his lifts, she tightened the muscles of her cunt.

"Oh baby!" he hissed, and began rocking his hips up to meet her.

Her hands were on his biceps and she loved the hardness of them, the heavy expanse of bulging muscle that made her feel so feminine, so protected. Her fingers dug into that toned flesh and the bed bounced beneath them.

"Come for me," he ordered. "Come hard for me, Keenan."

She looked down into his face—the face she loved so dearly, had almost lost—and the first ripple of release undulated through her body.

"Fallon!" she cried out, slapping one hand to the top of the padded headboard as she pushed down hard on his cock.

He lifted his hips brutally, thrusting deep into her, then made quick little in and out pushes as her orgasm exploded around him. He could feel her tightening, releasing, tightening, releasing, and the wash of her fluids scalded him in pleasure.

Her head fell back—her long hair sweeping his thighs—and she screamed as wave after wave of unguarded delight rocketed through her.

Seeing her like that, Fallon knew nothing he'd ever done in his life was as sweet as the enjoyment he was giving her at that moment in time, and his seed shot hard and strong from him—into the wanting body of his mate.

Sated, depleted, drained, she collapsed against him. She was gasping for breath and he could feel her heart beating a wild tattoo against his.

"God, how I love you," she said, her lips against the base of his throat.

"I love you too," he said. "Do you have any idea just how much?"

She mumbled a reply he didn't catch then realized she had slipped into sleep. He placed a gentle kiss on her head and tried slipping into her mind to see if any of his power had returned. He wanted her to know just how much she meant to him, how much love he had for her.

At first he couldn't find a pathway, but he tried again and this time he was able to wind his way through the gentle corridors of her brain. He realized she was slipping into the fantasy realm where dreams are born. At first he started to pull away but then she made a little sobbing sound that stopped him. He ventured back through the otherworldly avenues and what he found in her dreaming mind disturbed him. He saw the images flitting through her memory, saw her with the Supervisor, heard her words.

"I failed him. I should have been watching his back. If I had, that thing wouldn't have gotten to him."

There was enormous guilt housed within her very soul. She blamed herself for what had happened to him.

For just a moment he wanted to shake her awake and tell her he did not blame her for what had occurred. She was not the one to blame. Roland was.

But then he realized she had given him something very useful, and though he was loath to wield the knowledge, he knew one day he must for the evil was bubbling inside him, and it was growing more powerful every day. He didn't know how long he could keep it at bay.

* * * * *

Two weeks later

Fallon lay awake all night with Keenan in his arms. He could feel her soft breath fanning across the hairs on his chest. Her head was on his shoulder, one arm flung over his waist and a leg resting on his. He was uncomfortable and much too warm despite the air conditioning and the fan circulating briskly above the bed, but he didn't want to relinquish his hold on her. His lips grazed her hair and he inhaled deeply the sweet scent of her. He wanted to remember that scent and the night that had just passed for the rest of his days.

He turned his head so he could see what time it was. It was nearly 5 a.m. and he frowned. He only had half an hour at most with her before he had to be at the clinic for more physical therapy.

More torture, he thought to himself.

But the therapy was working. Eight long, miserable hours each day from six to two with one fifteen-minute break for a shitty-tasting power drink loaded with vitamins and minerals for his breakfast and another fifteen blessed minutes in which to consume more rabbit food at noon. Could life get any more exciting? he wondered.

Keenan drew in a long breath then eased her head back so she could look up at him.

"You are broadcasting all kinds of garbage about some poor cartoon rabbit being thrown into a blender. That's sick, lineman."

"Never liked that wascally wabbit, anyway," he mumbled.

"What time is it?"

"A little after five."

"Umm," she said then rolled away from him. "I need a shower."

"I'll be here when you're through," he said, folding his hands behind his head.

"Don't want to take a shower with me?" she asked.

"Don't feel up to it," he replied. "You wore my ass out last night, woman."

"Complain, complain, complain," she said as she closed the bathroom door.

He lay there for a few moments more then turned his eyes to the crutches propped against the wall beside the bed. Lowering his arms, he sat up, and with a terrible scowl on his handsome face, swung his bad leg off the bed. Sweat broke out immediately on his forehead and upper lip, but he was determined to hobble to the crutches, make use of them to get to the closet. It took some doing and a whole lot of teeth grinding but he was dressed in all but his right deck shoe when Keenan came out of the bathroom, wrapped in one towel, drying her long hair with another. She came to a stop when she saw him.

"Well, aren't we the industrious one, Agent Fallon?" she asked, surprised to see him standing on the crutches with his injured leg crooked behind him.

"If you'll help me get my other shoe on, I'd appreciate it," he said solemnly.

She smiled. "I'm so proud of you, lineman."

"For what?" His words were curt, his eyes angry. "I've been dressing myself for years, McCullough. It's not a big accomplishment."

Keenan tossed the towel with which she was drying her hair on the bed and made no comment as she went over to retrieve his shoe from the closet. She brought it over to him then hunkered down to put it on his foot.

"I don't need you to escort me over to the clinic," he said as he started out of the bedroom. "Stay here, go sightseeing, go to the beach, whatever."

"You sure?" she asked.

"Yeah," he said as he kept moving.

She waited, and when she heard the low curse, she bit her lip to keep from laughing.

"Keenan?" There was exasperation in his tone.

"Yes?" she replied.

"Can you get the door?"

Without answering, she came into the great room, opened the door then turned her back on him to return to the bedroom.

"I can't shut it!"

"Then leave it open!" she yelled back.

There was another curse then silence.

"Stubborn man," she said for what she thought might be the hundredth time in the last two weeks.

Well, two could play that game. He was chafing to go it alone then let him. She would go sightseeing or to the beach or...

"Whatever," she grumbled as she pulled out a pair of shorts and a halter top from the dresser.

Since there was no need for money on the Island — everything was provided free to the operatives — all she had to do was stuff her keycard into the pocket of her shorts, grab a bottle of spring water from the fridge, a book from her bag and she was out of there.

* * * * *

He was bone-tired and although he would not admit it, was grateful for the low dosage of tenerse they gave him to help alleviate the pain eating away at his leg. His T-shirt and gym pants were soaked with sweat, he swung down the corridor on his crutches with his jaw clenched.

She hadn't left any messages with the receptionist, and that had pissed him off. No one knew where she was, although the girl in the boutique told him Agent McCullough had stopped in to get a straw hat.

"She had a book with her," the girl told him. "I bet she's at the beach."

345

He nodded and pivoted around clumsily to head back up the corridor, growling every step of the way. Everyone he passed spoke to him and he grimaced a greeting of sorts. That wasn't unusual for him since it was his normal salutation to his fellow operatives, so no one paid much attention to him.

Out of sorts, feeling pathetically useless, he stopped at a long bank of windows that happened to look out at the airfield and saw a jet being refueled. It was the supply jet he was fairly sure, and one glimpse at his wristwatch told him it would be leaving in an hour or two.

For a long time he stood staring at the plane. Finally he went over to a wall phone, called security and asked when the plane would be taking off.

"They're going to be a bit late today, Agent Fallon. The other flight due in today had hydraulic problems and had to make a stop at Salvador International," the head of security told him.

"How 'bout telling them I'll be hopping a ride back to the Exchange with them?" Fallon said.

"Yes sir, of course. I'll make sure they know."

No one would dare question him leaving, he thought. The security man wouldn't think twice about the request of an Alpha. There would be no checking with the Exchange to make sure Fallon had permission to leave the Island. It would be assumed that he did.

But he couldn't leave things open-ended with Keenan. He had to let her know he was going. The thought of trying to make his way through the sand was daunting but at least there was a wooden boardwalk that led out to the jetty. Maybe he could get her attention and she could come to him there if she was even at the beach.

Sweat dripping down the sides of his face and neck, he made his way to the boardwalk and paused to scan the shoreline. He saw two people in the water, a few stretched out on beach chairs or blankets and one lone jogger. Turning his attention to the pier that jutted out into the turquoise water, he saw a woman with a long brown braid and knew it had to be Keenan. Clenching his teeth, he starting moving in her direction.

The book she'd brought with her had not held Keenan's attention and she'd put it aside after a chapter or two. She couldn't seem to concentrate so she sat down under the thatched lanai roof built over the end the pier and dangled her legs in the water, sitting there with a cool ocean breeze fanning the loose hairs at the sides of her face, listening to the thatching rustling on the roof.

She heard the tap-tap-tap of the crutches and knew Fallon was coming up behind her. She could feel the turmoil in his mind coming off him in waves and wondered if he realized he was broadcasting his thoughts. Normally he was so careful to shield from her but today that wasn't the case.

"Hey," he said once he reached her.

She craned her head around. "Hey yourself. How was the session?"

"Hell," he said, and slumped against an upright that held the thatched roof over the end of the pier. "How was your day?"

"Well, Harry Rod, Peter, Dick and I had wild, unbridled sex in the pool, but that got boring after awhile so I came out here."

"You didn't get enough wild, unbridled sex last night?" he asked in a husky voice.

"I could have used some more in the shower this morning but my boyfriend didn't seem interested."

He grunted then turned his attention to the sweeping beauty of the ocean. "The beach here is almost as beautiful as the one at Mistral Cay," he commented.

Keenan snapped her head around. "You've been to Mistral Cay?" she gasped.

"Worked there for a while," he said then grinned. "While on assignment." He looked down at her. "How do you know about it? You been there?"

"No, but Mama owns a timeshare there," she answered.

"It isn't time the women share there, *myneeast caillagh*."

"Yeah, I know what they share, Fallon," she snapped. "Please tell me by worked there you don't mean as a helper."

He wagged his brows at her then looked away.

"Bastard," she grumbled.

"That was a long time ago," he said. "Before I met you, *lhiannan*."

"You let me catch you dipping your wick in some other woman's wax now and see what happens, hound!" she said with a snort.

He laughed and it was the first laugh she'd gotten from him since the beating.

Fallon longed to ease himself down beside her but knew it would be too awkward, too painful, and the getting back up again would be humiliating—if he could even do it and he doubted he could. Instead, he was content for a moment or two just to stare at the ocean and be close to the only woman he would ever love. He knew sooner or later she would give him the opening he was seeking.

"I tried contacting Coim, but either he isn't back yet or that psychic fence is blocking me," she told him.

"It doesn't block psi trans," he said, shifting the weight on his left leg. "If it was back, it would have answered."

"He," she stated emphatically. "He, lineman. Stop thinking of him as an it."

A low grunt signified he heard her.

"He thinks of you as a son," she said. "Did you know that?"

Fallon's lips twitch with amusement. "*He* does, huh?"

She didn't answer but swung her feet in the water. "Tomorrow, I think I'll go for a swim."

There it was, he thought. There was his opening.

He frowned. "I'd rather you didn't."

Keenan looked around at him. "Why not? I'm a good swimmer. I won a lot of medals for it in high school and college."

"Track too as I remember," he said, thinking of the blue ribbons, trophies and medals he'd seen in her girlhood room in Georgia.

"Then you know I'm not going to drown," she stated.

He shrugged. "Suit yourself. After today, it won't be my problem."

It was Keenan's turn to frown and she twisted around, bringing her feet up onto the pier. "What's that supposed to mean?"

For the longest time he didn't answer and the expression on his face made her heart accelerate—and not in a good way. She was beginning to feel true unease and opened her mouth to ask him again what he'd meant by what he'd said when he swung his eyes to hers.

"When I get back to the Exchange, I'm going to ask the Supervisor to disconnect the Extension."

Keenan sucked in a shocked breath, her eyes flaring. "What?" she whispered. Her expression said she didn't understand.

"You heard me," he said, pushing away from the upright and adjusting his hold on the crutches.

"But why?"

It had been there in her mind and he had absorbed it with both hurt and disappointment but it also gave him an out—an easy way to break it off with her in a way that would be as final as he could make it.

"I can't trust you to have my back," he said, and the words were spoken with no feeling, no inflection—just thrown at her like poisoned darts.

Keenan's forehead crinkled with hurt. "That's not true."

"If you had been watching my back, Roland wouldn't have been able to sic that thing on me. I wouldn't have been beaten to a pulp and I wouldn't be standing here in so much pain I can barely endure it."

Tears filled Keenan's eyes. "Fallon, I..."

"It's over, McCullough," he said. "I can't break the bond between us, but I can sever the Extension, and I'm going to. I don't need a partner I can't depend on."

"I love you," she said, putting out a hand. "Fallon, I love you. Doesn't that count for anything?"

Fallon watched a tear roll down her cheek, took in her trembling lips and hardened his heart.

"No, babe, it doesn't. I need you out of my life before you wind up getting me killed."

He swung around on the crutches, not giving her a chance to reply, and hobbled up the pier. He could feel her gaze on his back, could feel the hurt and the shame in her heart, but he didn't look around. Tears of his own clouding his vision, he kept going though his heart was breaking, his soul withering. It was the only way he knew how to protect her. If she was with him, sooner or later the evil inside him Martiya had left behind would bubble up and hurt her, or the creature would return for him and she'd get caught between them. He couldn't take that chance.

The last time Fallon saw her was as the plane was banking sharply northward over the sparkling turquoise waters. The pilot—unaccustomed to having a passenger—had forgotten to block the window and Fallon had a view of the pier. He leaned toward the window, and as soon as he saw her, rested his forehead on the glass. She was sitting where he'd left her, staring out to sea. He watched her until the shields came down.

An hour later, a sudden, terrible pain stabbed at the base of Fallon's brain and he slapped a hand to the sensation, gasping at the debilitating ache. Immediately his head was pounding furiously between the temples. It soon became the worst migraine he'd ever experienced. The shot of tenerse he injected in his neck barely calmed the throbbing agony.

* * * * *

At 5 p.m. that afternoon, the passenger jet finally arrived on the island. Nine people wearing body armor beneath their tropical clothing stepped off the jet and onto the runway in pairs. Each passenger was carrying two things—several small silver aerosol containers, the spray from which killed those not inoculated with the vaccine within seconds of inhalation, a palm-size heat-sensing unit used to find living targets and a nine millimeter automatic pistol concealed under their shirts. What the spray did not instantly kill when released into the air ducts, the hollow-point bullets would.

Methodically the mercenary team led by Royce Cookson infiltrated every room inside each of the four main buildings as well as the seven perimeter buildings. Despite the strong security the Exchange had in place, the Island fell easily. In all the contingency plans made by the security division, no one had considered the scenario that played itself out that afternoon.

When Cookson and his team of seven mercs left the Island at a little after 7 p.m., they carried with them the only survivor of the attack — lying unconscious on a gurney.

Chapter Twenty-Seven

ഔ

"Agent Fallon, we'll be landing shortly. You are under orders to remain on the plane," the copilot said.

Fallon scowled at the man. He was feeling numb—as though someone had shot him full of pairilis and that made him testy. "What the hell for?"

"Supervisor's orders, sir. Under no circumstances are we to allow you off the plane."

A hard glint entered the Reaper's eyes. "And you think you can keep me from deplaning..." His glare shifted to the copilot's name tag. "Scott?"

"I am to tell you there has been an incident, sir, and that you are to remain on the plane," the man said.

A hard chill went through Fallon. "Incident? What kind of incident?"

"We weren't given the particulars, sir. We were simply asked to make sure you remained onboard until an escort comes to retrieve you."

Without another word, the copilot returned to the cockpit.

Fallon closed his eyes and tried sending to Keenan, but there was no answer and he guessed he was too far away from her. He tried a second and third time anyway and was met with nothing more than a gray haze.

As soon as the plane touched down, Fallon felt the tension rippling through the psychic air like the aftershocks of an earthquake. The entire station was seething with activity and that sent another chill through him. Something bad had happened—an incident—and whatever had come down had the Exchange on high alert.

Even before the plane rolled to a stop on the tarmac, Fallon was scrambling out of his seat. His crutches had been stored in the forward compartment during the flight and he had to hop up the aisle to retrieve them. The cockpit door opened and the copilot appeared with a tranq gun in his hand.

"Sir..." he began, but Fallon waved him away.

"Give me my crutches, Scott, or I'll make you eat that toy pistol," he growled. "Unless you'd rather have it shoved up your tight little ass!"

The gun's barrel shook but the young man raised his chin. "Sir, I have orders to shoot you if you attempt to leave the plane."

There was a loud rapping on the plane's door and Fallon saw relief shift over the young man's face. He lowered the gun and turned to unlock the door. He barely had time to move aside as two burly security operatives barged their way onto the plane.

"Agent Fallon, you are to accompany us, sir," the beefier of the two barked.

"And just how the fuck do you think I'm going to get off the fucking..."

The burly agent grabbed Fallon's good arm, squatted and hoisted the Reaper over his shoulder, fireman fashion.

"Goddamn it, put me down!" Fallon snarled, his injured leg throbbing mercilessly as the security man looped an arm behind Fallon's knees.

Out the door and down the rollaway steps, carried unceremoniously like a sack of salt across the tarmac, into a side door of the terminal then down a jet way connecting a plane upon which Fallon was jostled, head hanging and hands clawing at the security man's ass.

"Behave, Agent Fallon," the man ordered with a chuckle. "I'm just doing my job, sir."

"*I'll have your fucking head!*" Fallon hissed, digging his nails into the man's buttocks.

"Keep that up, sir, and I'll think you want some of that ass you're mauling."

Cursing savagely, Fallon was lowered gently enough into a seat and would have taken a swing at the man who had carried him onboard if a meaty fist hadn't caught his and jerked it down.

"Give me a reason to throw you in a con cell for a month or two and I will, Fallon!"

Fallon snapped his head around to see the Supervisor glaring down at him and holding his fist in a steel grip he knew he would never break. The man's strength was unbelievable, and for the first time he saw something in the Supervisor's glare that bordered on true evil.

"What happened?" Fallon asked, sensing something dark and ugly beneath the waves of anger rolling off his boss.

"Why are you here?" the Supervisor countered. "Why the hell did you leave the Island?"

It was there in that one word—Island—that Fallon intercepted myriad emotions tumbling through the mind of his superior, but at the apex of that pyramid of feelings was grief.

"What happened?" he asked again, searching the eyes of the Supervisor.

"Forty-nine people are dead, Fallon," the Supervisor said through clenched teeth. "Forty-five died from inhalation of some kind of extremely toxic airborne poison and the other four were shot."

Fallon's face drained of color. "Keenan?"

"Dead," the Supervisor said brutally. "She took one shot to the base of her brain as she lay asleep in your bed. She never knew what hit her."

The world shifted violently around Fallon and he slapped his hands to the armrests of the chairs. "No," he said, shaking his head. "No. That can't be right. I would have felt it. I would have..." He remembered the crippling pain he'd felt on the plane and his face paled.

"She's dead!" the Supervisor shouted. "They are all dead. Every last one of them!" He leaned down to put his face in Fallon's. "Everyone but you."

"Sir, we are ready for takeoff," the pilot informed the Supervisor.

"Then get us airborne, Captain," the Supervisor snarled.

"You want the shields down, sir?"

"What the hell for? Some bastard knows where the Island is. What difference does it make now? We've been breached, fool!"

"Aye, sir," the pilot said, snapping a salute. He turned sharply and headed for the cockpit.

"Buckle your goddamned seat belt, Fallon," the Supervisor ordered, taking the chair on the other side of the aisle.

Fallon was too stunned by what he'd just been told to question the command. He automatically drew the two halves of the seat belt around him. He felt numb. Once again he sent out a psi broadcast to Keenan but it didn't connect. There was nothing there — not even a ripple — but until he stood over her, saw her for himself, he would not believe what he'd been told. There had to be a mistake. If Keenan had left his world, he would have known the moment it happened.

"Not true," he said, and the jet began to back away from the terminal. "It's not true." The pain, he thought. What had caused the pain?

"Why the fuck did you leave the Island?"

He looked over at the Supervisor. "I was trying to protect her," he said. "I was coming back to ask you to sever the Extension."

"Well, you got what you wanted. It's been severed," the Supervisor snarled.

"She's not dead. She can't be. I would know it." Again the memory of that horrible pain lashed out at him.

The plane had been cleared for takeoff, was rolling down the runway and picking up speed.

"There will be a full-scale investigation," the Supervisor said. "Nothing is to be touched until I get there. Not one shred of evidence is to be gathered until my team and I are on the ground." His glower was filled with venom. "If I find out you had anything to do with the assault on that station, I'll see you fry for it, Fallon."

Those words cut Fallon to the quick and did more than just wound his fierce pride. Not only was his loyalty being called into question, but his devotion to his duty as well.

"I had nothing to do with what happened," he said.

"We'll see," the Supervisor said then turned his face away to stare out the window as the plane took to the air.

It was the longest plane ride of his life, and when the jet touched down on the Island's runway, the first thing Fallon saw was the pier. His heart did a painful little squeeze in his chest and he had trouble drawing his next breath. He looked down at his hands and saw they were shaking. His mouth was filled with the bitter, irony taste of ashes and he had trouble swallowing.

"Why did you leave the Island?"

He looked at the Supervisor. The man was glaring at him with narrowed eyes.

"It's in me," Fallon tried to explain. "Something the creature left behind. I was afraid it would get loose and hurt her."

"You don't have to worry about that now," the Supervisor said, unsnapping his seat belt as the plane lurched to a stop.

Fallon flinched as though he'd been slapped, the words like steel barbs dragging down his flesh.

He was the last to leave the plane, left to make his way down the steps as best he could with the crutches one of the Supervisor's men had shoved at him. There was no one to help him and twice he almost fell, pitching forward as he hopped on his left leg from one step to the next, the crutches held tightly in his grip sliding lengthwise down the stair railing. No one looked his way as he stood wavering on the tarmac, trying to get the crutches under his arms. Everyone was heading for the terminal and everywhere he looked there were men and women dressed in the brown uniforms of security.

Hurrying as fast as he could into the terminal, he stopped just inside the door. There was controlled chaos as waves of white-coated technicians with gloves and face masks bent over bodies with cameras, taking shots from every conceivable angle. Three men and a woman were at the reception desk, studying something on the computer screens. The Supervisor was standing stock still, scanning the death surrounding him.

"Sir, can we begin processing the victims here in the terminal?"

The Supervisor swept his gaze over his fallen operatives, his face filled with anger and pain. "Yeah. Go ahead. Just be very respectful of our dead."

"We will, sir."

"Nine people came in on that last plane and nine people left," Fallon heard someone reporting to the Supervisor.

"Find out where the hell that plane went when it left here!" the Supervisor bellowed.

"Sir, they found the crew from the plane," another man informed him.

"Where?" the Supervisor demanded.

"Thrown in a storage room next to the refueling tanks. Dr. P. says they were dead long before the attack."

"Find Dr. Papadopoulos. Tell her to meet me in Agent Fallon's room ASAP."

"Yes sir!"

Fallon had no vested interest in the dead who lay scattered about the reception area and down each of the four corridors although he was sorry they'd been murdered. His only concern was getting to the room he had shared with Keenan. He had to make sure the woman they'd found wasn't her. As he started that way, the Supervisor and two of his lieutenants fell into step beside and behind him.

"These people didn't stand a chance," the Supervisor said, his voice heavy. "They had no reason to expect an attack. They thought they were safe here. *We* thought they were safe here."

"Like 9-11, sir," one of the men behind Fallon remarked.

"Yes, exactly like that," the Supervisor agreed.

"We'll find them, sir," the other man said.

"The plane made an emergency landing at Salvador International," Fallon said. He was fast losing breath and his armpits were screaming with pain.

"How the hell did you know that?" the Supervisor snapped.

"The security man told me when I informed him I'd be catching a flight back to the Exchange with the supply jet. He said the passenger plane would be late arriving because of a hydraulic problem."

"So they boarded the plane, took out the pilot and passengers and used the onboard information to fly here," the Supervisor surmised. He ground his teeth. "Then dumped the bodies like so much garbage."

"What about the security cameras on the flight line?" Fallon asked. They were about forty feet from the door to his room.

"We don't have any here," the Supervisor said, plowing a hand through his salt-and-pepper hair. "We didn't think we needed them."

"I don't mean here," Fallon said. "At Salvador."

The Supervisor paused with his fingers threaded through his hair. His attention was riveted on Fallon. "Good catch." He turned to one of his assistants. "Check into it. I want every second of film from the time our plane landed until it took off."

"Yes sir!" The man hurried away.

Reaching out a restraining hand, the Supervisor brought Fallon to a stop. "I don't think you had anything to do with this but..."

"I didn't," Fallon said, shrugging off the other man's hand. "You fucking well know I didn't."

"Right now all anyone has done in there is take pictures. Nothing has been touched," he said, cocking his chin toward the room toward which they were headed. "Your DNA and fingerprints are going to be everywhere, but I don't want you to touch anything. Are we clear?" When Fallon didn't reply, the Supervisor grabbed his arm in a punishing grip and repeated the question.

"Yes," Fallon snapped. "We're clear. I don't know who's in that room but it isn't Keenan. I would have felt it!"

"I hope you're right," the Supervisor said.

Dr. Papadopoulos opened the door for them when the Supervisor knocked, but she only opened it halfway, using her body to block their entrance. Her dark brown eyes flicked toward Fallon and she frowned. "I'm not sure he should see this."

"Move," Fallon said — more growl than actual speech.

She held his stare for a second or two then released a long breath and stepped back. "Suit yourself, Fallon. Don't say I didn't warn you."

Fallon wasn't prepared for what greeted him when the door swung fully open. It was like being bowled over by a steam locomotive. He staggered beneath the assault and the two men behind him — the Supervisor and his assistant — reached out to steady him.

"*Oh my God,*" Fallon whispered, eyes wide, mouth falling open.

The room looked as though a tornado had spun through it. Furniture was overturned, glass broken, drapes torn from the traverse rods. Scrawled in large crimson letters across the pale blue wall, to either side of the doorway, with a thick arrow pointing into the bedroom were the words *Just for you, Fallon! Enjoy!*

Bile surged up Fallon's throat and he had to swallow convulsively to keep it down. Instinctively he knew the message had been written — not in paint — but with the blood of whoever lay beyond the doorway.

"Sick," the Supervisor's assistant commented.

Dr. Papadopoulos had not taken her eyes from Fallon. "Are you all right, Misha?"

Despite being Matty's on-again, off-again love interest, the medical examiner had never called Fallon by that nickname, and for her to do so at that moment seemed totally out of character. He stared at her as though seeing her for the first time, searching her eyes.

"It's her, Misha," Dr. Papadopoulos said softly. "Do you really want to go in there?"

A cold wash of bitter agony flowed through Fallon and all he could manage to do was nod. Every ounce of moisture in his mouth had dried up and his knees felt weak. He could hear the blood pounding ruthlessly in his ears as he swung his crutches toward the bedroom door.

"Stay close to him," he heard her say.

Though he had killed many times over the years — often savagely — and was no stranger to brutal slayings, nothing he'd ever seen could have prepared Fallon for what was inside that room.

Lying on her belly in the center of the bed with her right cheek on the blood-soaked pillow was the naked, spread-eagled body of the woman he loved. Her eyes were open and glazed over with death. Her wrists and ankles were shackled to the bed frame and there were vicious bruises and discolorations over her back, buttocks and upper thighs.

Shot in the back of the head, there was a large black hole at the base of her brain with the radiating exit wound having blown away the top of her head. Congealed brain matter was sprayed across the bright tropical print of the padded headboard. Surrounding the grayish glob was a dark rust-colored halo of sprayed blood that arched beyond the top of the headboard.

"No," Fallon said. He shook his head. "It's not her. It can't be her." He moved a few steps closer to the bed until he could see her face clearly.

"Keenan?" he whispered. His face creased with hideous grief. "Baby?" He dropped one of the crutches and reached out to her but Dr. Papadopoulos took hold of his hand.

"You can't touch her, Misha," she said.

He looked away from the carnage on the bed and into the sympathetic eyes of the medical examiner. "That's not her," he said. "That's not my Keenan."

She held on to his hand. "I'm sorry, Misha, but it is. Don't you recognize the tattoo?"

He shifted his gaze to the dead woman's back, and the moment he saw the dark blue Celtic knot butterfly at the small of her back, an eerie keening sound came from somewhere deep within him.

"*No!*" he denied, and had not the Supervisor and his assistant made a frantic grab for him, he would have dropped to the floor like a rock, his knees finally buckling beneath him.

"Was she raped?" the Supervisor asked gently.

Hearing the question voiced that was screaming in his head, Fallon groaned. The men holding him eased him down until he was on all fours, head hanging, the brutal pain having returned full force. Fallon shuddered hard then convulsed as hot bile spewed out of him.

"I knew he shouldn't see this," the medical examiner said.

"Get him a towel, Cobb," the Supervisor ordered. He hunkered down beside Fallon and put a cool hand to his operative's forehead. He repeated his question to the medical examiner.

"Yes, it looks as though she might have been violated, but I won't know until I examine her. I…"

"*You're not going to cut her!*" Fallon shouted. His eyes were wild as he struggled to get to his feet. "*You're not!*"

"Fallon…" the Supervisor began, keeping him down.

"*She's not going to cut Keenan open!*" Fallon bellowed.

"There's no need for me to do that, Misha," Dr. Papadopoulos assured him. "We know the cause of death."

"You're not going to cut her," Fallon said, his voice breaking.

"No," the medical examiner said. "We're not."

Cobb, the Supervisor's assistant, returned with a cold, wet cloth and a towel. He tossed the towel over the vomitous and handed the cloth to his boss, who began to wipe Fallon's face with it.

Fallon was shivering violently and the Supervisor looked up at Dr. Papadopoulos. "I need something for him."

"Of course," she said, and walked out of the room.

"Why didn't I know?" Fallon whispered hoarsely. Tears were streaming down his face. "Why didn't I feel it?"

"I don't know, son," the Supervisor said. He glanced up as the medical examiner returned with a vac-syringe in hand.

"I should have felt it," Fallon said.

He barely noticed the burning sting as the needle went into the side of his neck—all he did was blink against the pain. As the pairilis took almost instant effect, he mumbled a few words, his eyes rolled back in his head and collapsed into the Supervisor's arms.

Chapter Twenty-Eight

ଥ

The next two days passed in a blur for Fallon. He was kept sedated for fear he'd re-injure his leg or—worse yet—try to harm himself in a more lethal way. He was also watched closely for that reason, and even though the Supervisor had at first denied his request, he had been allowed to sit beside Keenan's casket on the flight back to the Exchange. During all those hours of flight, he sat with one hand on the flag-draped coffin and the other shielding his face, numb to everything that went on around him.

When they landed in Iowa during a light rain, he hobbled beside the casket as it was rolled into the terminal. He refused to allow Keenan to make her last journey without him at her side. He rode in the hearse with her to the mortuary in Grinnell and had he not been forcibly removed from the premises, would have stayed with her while her body was prepared for burial. As it was, he managed to escape his escort and wound up in a downtown bar with a bottle of tequila and a shot glass never far from his fist. When the men sent to babysit him discovered his whereabouts, he threatened to kill them if they didn't leave him alone. It was decided he meant what he said so the two agents took a booth behind him to wait him out.

At closing time, the bartender came over to speak quietly to the two men everyone in there knew worked at the Exchange. "I've got to close up, guys," he told them. "Can you get him out of here without too much damage being done?"

Fallon was so drunk by then the agents didn't think they'd have too much trouble with him and they were partially right. He merely grinned nastily at them when they informed him it was time to leave.

"Fuck off," he said. "I'm not going anywhere."

"Agent Fallon, one way or the other, you *are* going to leave with us even if we have to carry you out," the senior of the two agents insisted. "Don't make this any harder than it has to be, okay?"

"Fuck. Off," was Fallon's stony reply then he threw his empty bottle at one of them.

"You want to rush him?" the younger of the two asked.

"Leave him to me."

The agents turned to see the Supervisor. How long their boss had been in the bar, they didn't know. Their main concern, their entire focus had been on Fallon all evening.

"Are you sure, sir?"

"I'll bring him home. Go on. Call it a night," the Supervisor ordered. He slid into the booth across from Fallon.

"You can fuck off too," Fallon growled, and twisted his head around. "Barkeep! I need another bottle."

"You need to sober up," the Supervisor said.

"Fuck I do," Fallon said with a snort.

"Did you forget what's happening tomorrow?"

Fallon's forehead crinkled with pain. "No. I want to but I can't."

"Then are you planning on showing up drunk for her funeral?"

More pain flashed over the Reaper's face and he slumped in the booth, putting up a hand to scour his unshaved face. His hand shook. "No," he repeated, the word so soft it was barely audible.

"Then you need to go home and sleep it off, Misha."

"I need her," he said, his voice cracking with emotion. He gave the Supervisor a pitiful look. "Why am I still alive?"

The Supervisor reached across the table to lay a hand on Fallon's arm. "I don't know. Maybe it's different with your kind."

"I should be dead. The bond..." He shook his head. "I should be dead. I wish to God I was."

"Let's go, son. We'll talk about this at home."

Fallon nodded and scooted out of the booth. His crutches were propped against the end of the table and he reached for them, so inebriated, he almost missed and staggered against the booth.

"I'm fucking wasted," he said.

"Yes, you are," the Supervisor agreed, and stepped over to slip an arm around Fallon's waist. "Lean on me."

"Sure thing, Dad," Fallon mumbled. "Just don't tell Mom."

The Supervisor smiled as he took Fallon's left crutch and helped his operative from the bar. He nodded at the bartender who was holding the door open for them. "Does he owe you anything?"

"No," the barkeep replied.

Outside in the cool Iowa night with a mist of rain still falling, Fallon turned his face up to the sky. "You think it will rain tomorrow?" he asked.

"I believe it's supposed to." The Supervisor half walked, half carried Fallon to the car where a uniformed driver got out to open the rear door for them.

"You know what they say about why it rains when a good person is buried?"

"No," the Supervisor said as they reached the car. "What is it they say?"

Fallon looked across the top of the car at the dark street. He had one hand on the top of the door, the other on the roof. "They say the angels are weeping," he said softly.

Gingerly maneuvering Fallon into the car, the Supervisor watched his operative lie his head back on the seat. He straightened and stepped back so his driver could shut the door.

"Take your time getting us home, Wend," the Supervisor asked.

The driver nodded and the Supervisor went around to the other side of the car to climb into the backseat with Fallon.

As the car turned off Fourth onto West Street and headed north toward Highway 6, Fallon rolled his head toward his boss.

"I should have been there," he said.

"If you'd been there, you would have died with her, Misha."

"I wish I had."

The Supervisor looked at him. "Then there would have been no one to go after her killers." He gave his operative a steady look. "You are going after her killers, aren't you?"

Fallon swiveled his head to the side to stare out the window. "That last day, I told her I was going to have the Extension disconnected and she told me..." He had to clear his throat before he could continue. "She told me she loved me and asked me if that mattered."

Fallon put a crooked knuckle against the glass, tracing the spirals of water falling slowly down the window. "You know what the last thing I said to her was?"

"What?" It was asked gently, fatherly.

He tapped against the glass. "I told her I had to get away from her before she got me killed."

The Supervisor frowned. "Why would you say something like that?"

"It's in me," Fallon said. "That evil the creature left behind. It's inside me and it's getting darker and meaner with every breath I take. I was afraid I would hurt her." He laughed bitterly. "Isn't that a fucking riot? I was afraid *I* would hurt her!" His voice broke. "I was afraid I would hurt her."

In the rearview mirror, the Supervisor's eyes met the driver's and the driver shook his head. No one blamed Fallon for the deaths on the Island, but everyone knew he was responsible for the carnage that had taken place there—whether at the hands of an old enemy or a new one. The message had been loud and clear.

Fallon had heard it too.

"We'll find them," the Supervisor said. "Whoever they are, wherever they are, we will find them and they will pay for what they did."

"Yeah," was all Fallon said, the word slurred. His head was against the window—the flickering streetlights overhead giving his face a deathly pale tint.

By the time the Supervisor's driver turned onto the road that led to the Exchange, Mikhail Fallon had passed out from too much booze and unbearable grief.

* * * * *

It wasn't the same suit he'd worn to Keenan's aunt's funeral but it might as well have been. The two suits were identical in cut and material. Bleary-eyed and nauseous with the headache from hell, he was fumbling with his tie, the knot refusing to look the way he wanted it to. He stripped it from around his neck and dropped it to the floor to lie beside the four others he'd mauled. Finally deciding he was neither capable of making his fingers work properly nor wanting the restriction around his neck to begin with, he gave up, crushing the tie in his fist and pitching it across the room.

"Goddamned fucking tie!" he snarled. "Who the fuck needs you anyway?"

He stared into the mirror and almost smiled. He'd nicked himself time and again while shaving—sometimes on purpose just to watch the cut close almost instantly and sometimes just to feel the slight tinge of pain the blade brought. It was the only thing he felt within the numb cocoon in which he'd been wrapped.

Leaning closer to the mirror over the vanity, he looked at his bloodshot eyes, surprised his hellion hadn't eliminated them. Not that he gave a rat's ass. He felt as though he had sand particles beneath his eyelids and his mouth tasted brutally of iron. What was a thread or two of broken whatevers in his fucking eyeballs?

"You should be dead, Fallon," he told his reflection. He cocked his head to one side. "*Why* aren't you dead?"

He felt dead, he thought as he turned from the mirror and limped over to the bed to pick up his suit coat. As he bent over, he realized he hadn't put on either a belt or his shoes. It seemed like too much, too hard a thing to do, so he plopped down on the mattress and just stared at his stocking feet, wiggling the toes on his left foot then wincing when he wiggled the toes on his right.

"It's not right," he mumbled. "Just not right. I should not be here."

Sometime during the early morning—he'd been woken by loud thunder and some deadly serious shrieks of lightning. He'd wedged his eyes open, blinked, and wondered how the hell he'd come to be in his room at the Exchange wearing only a pair of boxer shorts. The last thing he remembered was sitting at Mike's Bar in Grinnell, and he was pretty fucking sure he'd been wearing more than a pair of boxers that smelled suspiciously rank. Not that Mike had a dress code but even so...

He lifted his head and stared at the dragon head's cane he had decided to use instead of the godawful crutches. The thing had been in the back of his closet for years and he'd had to rummage for it before taking his shower that morning. There was only one thing wrong with the cane—he had to be careful with it for in its tip was a razor-sharp blade. It was an assassin's tool and he'd only used it once. He hadn't been helpless then as he was now.

"Helpless and hopeless and useless," he said aloud.

Sighing deeply, he got to his feet and made his way to the closet to retrieve a pair of black loafers. There was no way he could tie a pair of dress shoes on his swollen right foot. The loafers would have to do. Keenan would understand.

Just the thought of her name was enough to make him want to throw himself on the bed and bawl like a baby. He was barely holding it together as it was and he was afraid the funeral was going to pitch him right over the edge. Thankfully she had left instructions in the living will on file at the Exchange that she wanted no wake, no rosary said. Organs harvested if possible, and if not, a simple graveside service and quick burial in a plain oaken casket. She wanted no pomp and circumstance, no gaudy show of grief, no casket open for viewing, no frills.

"Celebrate my life," they told him she'd said. "Don't mourn my death."

"Ain't gonna happen, *lhiannan*," he said. "I'll mourn you 'til the day I die."

Moaning as he bent over to pick up his shoes, he had to grab the closet door to keep from pitching headfirst into it. He pivoted and unearthly pain ripped through his knee. He sucked in his breath and nearly heaved up the two containers of Sustenance he'd forced himself to drink. The tenerse was slowly curing the hangover, but it hadn't done anything to alleviate the bitching headache.

Straightening took some effort, but he finally got both legs to lock and grunted his way over to the bed to sit down again.

He needed help. God, how he needed help, but there was no one to ask.

"I need you so much, baby," he said, and tears welled in his eyes — tears he viciously wiped away.

Forcing his feet into the shoes, twisting his right ankle savagely and reveling in the shooting pain that flared up his thigh, he stood, plucked the belt from where it hung over the footboard of his bed and thrust it through the loops of his suit pants, cursing the entire time, fumbling with the buckle.

"Fucking fingers!" he shouted. "Why don't you work?"

He held his hands up and stared at them. They were trembling like an old drunk's.

"Shit," he spat, and snatched his coat from the bed and swung it around his shoulders, staggering a little as he almost lost his balance. With his jaw tight, he limped over and retrieved the cane and — leaning heavily upon it — left the only sanctuary he'd ever known.

* * * * *

She was there already seated in the front row with her black dress, tidy little fashionable hat with a black veil. Now and again she lifted a black-gloved hand to push a lace handkerchief beneath the veil. She nodded politely to those who came to speak to her, touched the hands of those who offered and smiled graciously as though she had every right to be the center of attention at her daughter's funeral.

Goddamn bitch, Fallon thought as he stared at the back of Lily McCullough's head.

She turned—no doubt feeling his hatred—and gave him a withering look. Her green eyes were as frigid as the tundra of Siberia. She made it clear she hated him, but he already knew that. He hated her even more.

At least Lily hadn't gotten her way concerning where Keenan would be buried. Among the dozens of forms Keenan had filled out upon coming to work with the Exchange had been one designating the disposal of her remains should she die while on duty. She had been given a choice of cremation, body donated to science, cryogenic preservation or place of burial. She had checked Iowa and her wishes had been fulfilled. Why she'd chosen Iowa instead of her native Georgia would go to the grave with her.

"Would you like to sit with us?" the Supervisor asked.

"No," Fallon replied, shaking his head. "I'll stand."

"You'd be more comfortable sitting, Misha," the Supervisor tried again. "I'll sit between you and her mother."

"I'd rather stand."

And so he had.

After that, everything passed in a blur—all leading up to the moment he found himself facedown on the Terrazzo floor with security agents bending over him—cuffing him—and the startling words he heard coming out of his own mouth.

"She's alive! *She's alive!*"

* * * * *

The Supervisor's assistant gave Fallon a pitying look as he handed the Reaper a glass of Irish whiskey. As quietly as he'd entered the Supervisor's office, the little man left, closing the door very gently behind him.

Fallon slugged back the whiskey as though it were water then set the glass on the edge of the Supervisor's desk. He used the back of his hand to wipe his lips. The man was sitting with his fingers steepled, studying his operative with a stony look that said he thought serious intervention might be in order.

"She's alive," Fallon repeated.

"What makes you think so?" the Supervisor asked softly.

"Because I know she's not dead."

The answer brought a fierce scowl to the Supervisor's face. "Not good enough. You're asking me to exhume a body we just buried because you didn't feel Keenan McCullough die, though you do admit to feeling a sharp pain. I need a better reason than that."

Fallon was battling with himself, striving to remain calm even as he wanted to scream, to shout and to punch the man across the desk in his face to get him to understand. He had already been brought to his knees with his hands shackled behind him and a doctor threatening to shoot him full of tenerse if he didn't calm down. He didn't need any more of that if he wanted to be taken seriously. Even though every instinct shrieked at him to get in a car, go to the cemetery and dig the casket up with his bare hands, he forced himself to sit like a civilized man and explain himself rationally.

"Matty Groves is missing," he told the Supervisor.

"Tell me something I don't know."

"And I'll be willing to bet if you call down to the forensics, you'll find out Dr. P. has left the building. Permanently."

The Supervisor blinked. "And she would do this why exactly?"

"Because it is her signature on the death certificate identifying the body on the Island as being Keenan's when it isn't." Fallon sat forward eagerly and had to remind himself to go slowly, not to sound like a raving lunatic. "No one other than the mortician handled that body. Dr. P. wouldn't let anyone near it down on the Island. What better way to hide the corpse's real identity. She is also Groves' lover."

The Supervisor ignored the last comment. "What is the real identity, Misha?"

Fallon shook his head in exasperation. "How the hell would I know? Some woman with the right body build, hair and eye color as Keenan."

"And who just happens to be McCullough's identical twin?"

"No, not her twin, but a woman with Keenan's face," Fallon stated. "A face built from Keenan's DNA. A face constructed by a man who is a talented plastic surgeon and biogenetics engineer."

"Do you know how farfetched that sounds, Fallon?" the Supervisor challenged.

"Groves bragged about it!" Fallon said. "He told Keenan and me that he was working up a facial replica. He called it a living mask. He hinted he had used Keenan's blood and tissue for the model." He put his clenched hand on the Supervisor's desk. "You can't tell me you don't already have cybots or clones or whatever the fuck you call them working here. I know goddamned well you do!"

The Supervisor narrowed his eyes. "You know nothing of the sort."

"Call Dr. P.," Fallon insisted. "See if she's here."

The Supervisor said nothing for a moment then swiveled his chair slightly, his fingertips still pressed together. "She left for her vacation this morning."

"Convenient, huh? You've seen the last of her. She won't be back," Fallon said, eyes bright. "She's on her way to meet Groves."

"And where *is* Groves?"

A tight smile that did not reach his eyes tugged at Fallon's face. "I don't know right offhand but..." He held up a hand when his boss would have interrupted. "But the place was christened St. Brisa by Keenan's mother although Keenan says it is under another name on maps of the region."

"Which is where?"

"Along the Brazilian coast," Fallon replied. "Somewhere below Salvador International is my guess."

"Why do you think that's where Groves is?"

"That's where Keenan is too," Fallon declared. "And where her mother is headed. It is an island with mountains on which there are mounted cannons. Keenan called it a modern-day pirate stronghold. She said it had as much security as the Island. I'm also guessing that island would be rich in iron ore and that would aid in helping block efforts to locate Matty and Roland."

"Your mother believes they are wearing some kind of suppression collar," the Supervisor said.

"They probably are, but the iron ore in those mountains would be an additional benefit to keep anyone with psi powers from locking in on their target."

Lacing his fingers together, the Supervisor stared at Fallon a long time then took a deep breath, released it slowly. He leaned forward to depress the button on the intercom.

"Yes sir?" Jonas Cobb immediately asked.

"Get a forensic team out to the cemetery and have them exhume the casket we buried this morning. Tell them Agent Fallon and I are on our way out there and they are not—I repeat—they are not to unseal the casket until we arrive."

"Yes sir!"

"Is Agent McCullough's mother still here?"

"No sir. She left for the airfield in Newton as soon as the dinner was over."

"Call the airfield and tell them I want to see a copy of the flight plan filed by her pilot."

"Right away, sir!"

"And call research. Tell them I want the name and location of any land owned by Lilith McCullough among the islands off the coast of South America, specifically Brazil."

The Supervisor released the intercom button then pushed his chair back. "All right, Fallon. Let's see if what you're surmising has any basis in fact or if I'm going to be forced to put your ass in the mental ward!"

* * * * *

"Open it," the Supervisor said.

It didn't take long for the forensics team to break the seal on the casket. A slight pop and a low hiss sounded then the upper lid was lifted and laid back.

Fallon swallowed hard then stepped closer. He had not been allowed to get that good a look at the body on the bed, but the resemblance to Keenan had been strong enough that he had accepted—if not believed—that the body was hers. The devastation caused by what Dr. P. had reported was a 9 mm hollow-point bullet to the back of the victim's head had done so much damage that it was that destruction that caught the eye and imprinted itself on the brain.

"What are we looking for, sir?" one of the forensic men asked. He was shivering, his hair plastered to his cheeks, lips trembling.

"Ask Agent Fallon."

Fallon had to compel himself to limp even closer and lean over the casket. He didn't have his cane and his leg was screaming in protest, but he drew his hands out of his pockets and reached out to tilt the corpse's face to one side. Rigor mortis and the embalming fluid made it difficult to do, but he forced the head toward the back of the casket and—fingers shaking—pushed aside the long brown hair that covered the dead woman's ears.

For one unnerving moment he thought he'd been wrong. He couldn't bear to look at the face. He willed his eyes not to wander. It took the pads of his fingers to find the evidence he'd been seeking and as soon as he touched the fine line of slightly puckered flesh, his shoulders slumped with relief.

"Sutures," he said, and moved back. "They will be all around the perimeter of her face, hidden by her hair, and skillfully concealed under her jawline and chin."

The Supervisor came to stand where Fallon had been and bent over to inspect the same line of sutures. His forehead was creased as he ran his fingers along the pathway of delicate sutures.

"Merciful Alel," he said. He looked over at Fallon. "Who is this woman and how the hell did we not notice the bruising and swelling?"

"We didn't see it because we were seeing what they wanted us to see—the mutilation caused by the bullet." He shifted his position to ease the discomfort in his leg. "If we had noticed, I'm sure Dr. P. would have explained the discoloration and the swelling as part of the wound."

"The mortician would have assumed the vic had recently had a face-lift," one of the forensic men spoke up, "and in a way she did." He was staring into the coffin.

"Get DNA and fingerprint samples," the Supervisor said. "Maybe we can at least identify her and give her a burial with her name."

"She came onto the Island with the attack team," Fallon suggested. "She isn't one of ours. I doubt she knew what they had in store for her."

"But why rape her?" the forensics man asked. "This woman was gangbanged prior to death."

"That was for Fallon's benefit," the Supervisor said. He glanced at his operative. "Just one more thing to heap hurt on him."

Fallon nodded. He was in agony, but this time it was purely physical. He knew—he *knew*—Keenan was alive but in no danger he could detect. Now all he had to do was find and rescue her from the insane clutches of her deranged mother and Matty Groves.

Chapter Twenty-Nine

ɛꙅ

"From all accounts, it was a very lovely ceremony, Kiki. The Exchange did an excellent job in saying goodbye."

If Keenan could have gotten to him, she would have broken Matty Groves' neck then and there. As it was, she glared up at him as he leaned on the teakwood railing two floors up and looked down at her. He'd dropped the newspaper down to her.

No one knew where she was, and if Fallon and the Supervisor bought into the obit she'd just finished reading, they had no idea she was still alive. Fallon must be in hell at that very moment.

Wadding the newspaper page into a tight ball, she pitched it savagely across the room.

"Go fuck yourself, Groves!" she shouted.

Furious, she spun on her heel and stomped off with a hiss of rage. With every step she took, she cursed Matty Groves, Mizhak Roland and her mother to the deepest, slimiest pits beneath Hell.

"I wanted you. I betrayed my best friend just so I could have you," Matty had told her. "I called your mother months ago and set into motion this whole scenario. She knew about the faith healing thing, where you were going to be, what we needed to do to get Fallon out of your life. She arranged the lab for me here. We left nothing to chance. Accept it, Keenan. You're mine now, and you'll never see him again."

"Fallon nearly died because of you!" she'd flung at him.

"No," Matty said, shaking his head. "I had no part in that. If I had known they were planning on killing him, I would have stopped them."

"Calm down, Keenan," she warned herself, feeling her blood pressure soaring sky-high.

Never allowed beyond the confines of the luxurious plantation home where guards were positioned at every exit and the windows were protected by lacy iron grillwork, and the phones and all other communication devices kept under lock and key, she was nothing more than a glorified captive.

"I hate you!" she said to her mother's portrait as she passed by it with an urge to take a fire poker and smash to ribbons the lovely, smiling image. "I hate all of you!"

She snagged her fingers under the thin iron choker that had been welded around her neck, she cursed again. With no way to transmit her thoughts to Coim, the Supervisor or—the thought of him literally made her ache—Fallon, she was stymied at every turn.

Stomping up the steps to her second-floor suite, she went into the room and slammed the door as hard as she could. From above her on the third floor, she heard Matty laughing and dug her fingernails into her palms.

"Yeah, Groves, keep right on laughing," she said. "You'll be laughing when I stick a blade through your lying ribs!"

Flinging herself facedown on the plush white satin coverlet, she beat her fists uselessly against the smooth surface—kicking her legs like the spoiled brat her mother accused her of being. The frustration was almost more than she could mentally bear and she flipped over to her back, flinging an arm over her eyes.

"Fallon, you have to find me. You have to, lineman! I don't know how much more of this I can take."

She'd cried every day since she'd woken to this genteel incarceration. When she'd discovered there had been no survivors on the Island, she had gone into a rage, trying her best to maul Royce Cookson—the man responsible for the deaths—but he and two of his men had easily subdued her. The same narcotic they'd pumped into her on the Island when they'd caught her had been administered again.

Thinking back to the two men who had come walking toward her as she left the pier, she realized she should have known from the expressions on their faces that they were up to no good. There had been steely determination glowing back at her and tight lips that normally would have sent up a red flag. If she hadn't been agonizing over Fallon, hurt by what he'd said, devastated over his leaving, she would have noticed the resolve in the men's behavior and taken off running. As it was, she'd walked right into their hands, passing by them only a split second before she felt something sharp puncture her neck as one of the men pivoted around. She'd barely had time to put a hand to the wound before her world began to shut down.

Thankfully, she had not been a witness to the deaths of the people on the Island. At least she did not have that to invade her nightmares each night. Imagination was bad enough and the grief was nearly overwhelming since she knew it was because of her that so many good, innocent people had died.

And what of the woman who was buried in Iowa? Who was she? How had she come to take Keenan's place? That Matty had altered the woman's appearance, Keenan had absolutely no doubt. And it had to have been done in a way that would make Fallon believe her dead. He wouldn't even be looking for her, Matty had said. Fallon had bought the entire thing.

The pieces of the puzzle fell into place so easily it made her want to puke.

"Fallon, please! Please come find me!" she pleaded, tugging uselessly at the collar that very effectively blocked any transmission she ever hoped to send to the man she loved.

If it was the last thing she did, she would make the four people who had brought this sorry state of events into play pay dearly for what they had wrought.

Matty went out to the deck and stood staring at the beautiful tropical day.

"Sure beats the hell out of Iowa," he said aloud, but oddly enough, he missed the rolling hillsides of the Midwestern state, the country life.

Leaning his elbows on the railing, he looked down at the sand and realized he even missed the black soil where corn and soybeans and hay grew in abundance.

"You gave up a lot for her, Matthew," he said softly. "More than you realized."

He squeezed his eyes shut, missing more than the rolling hills or the fertile soil or the red-tail hawks soaring through the ever-present wind. Misha had been his friend—his only friend. His conscience hurt like a sore tooth at which he kept poking his tongue. Thoughts of Fallon kept him awake at night.

Then there was Keenan, the woman for whom he'd sold his very soul now hated the very sight of him.

"She'll come around," Phyllis Papadopoulos—who was there working as his assistant—had said but Matty knew that would never happen.

The money to do the research he'd secretly planned and knew the Exchange would never sanction, the opportunities that could open up for him, the possibility of a Nobel prize—none of that mattered. Without the woman he loved so desperately applauding his triumphs, the friend he respected encouraging him, any successes he might achieve would turn to ashes in his mouth.

And there were the deaths on the Island that plagued him every waking hour. Though he'd had no hand in those deaths, they weighed heavily on his soul.

Guilt was eating away at Matty Groves.

* * * * *

"All right, we know St. Brisa is actually Santa Brigitte and we know where it is," the Supervisor said. "Just how the hell do you think we will be able to infiltrate it? By all accounts of your Brazilian counterparts, that island is invincible."

"It isn't invincible," Fallon said. He was rubbing his right thigh rhythmically. "It has mountains."

"So what? You haven't been cleared to return to work just yet and even when you are, you can't parachute into the mountains without her security picking up on your whereabouts and shooting you down. Or did you conveniently forget they also have artillery guns along with the cannons?" the Supervisor demanded. "The fucking woman is paranoid with her security!"

"All I need is those mountains," Fallon said with a merciless grin. "The mountains and one big gray shuttle bus."

"Shuttle bus?" the Supervisor questioned as though his operative had finally gone round the bend. "What the hell are you talking about?"

"A big, hairy, gray shuttle bus," Fallon amended.

"*An Fear Liath Mor,*" the Supervisor said with a sharp intake of air.

"It..." Fallon shook his head. "*He* should be back any day now. I intend to already be in the Ozarks waiting for him."

"He can travel only among mountain regions," the Supervisor said. "From one range to another in the blink of an eye." He slapped his forehead with the base of his palm. "Why didn't I think of that?"

"And he can take me with him," Fallon said. "Once I'm in the mountains on Santa Brigitte. I can make my way down to the plantation house we were told about, find Keenan, take her back up to Coim then have him get her the hell out of there while I go back and take out Groves, Roland and the dragon queen."

The Supervisor had already signed warrants for all three, had made it clear to Fallon that those warrants could be executed with extreme prejudice.

"They are responsible for the deaths of my people. They will pay with their own lives," the Supervisor had declared.

"You may need a fourth warrant," Fallon had suggested. "Someone planned that attack. I'm ninety-nine and nine-tenths percent sure it wasn't Roland or Groves. Whoever it was, I want even more than I want Roland."

"I'll have one drawn up and leave the name blank for now. That can always be filled in when we discover who he is."

It was decided the Supervisor would go down to the Ozarks with Fallon, taking along a team of his own men as well as a field medic should one be necessary. It was a precaution Fallon hoped would not be needed but he saw the wisdom in it.

So it was that two days after a woman named Danika Marie Allen—a former Marine MP turned soldier of fortune—was laid to rest beneath a stone that carried her own name instead of Keenan McCullough's, two unmarked black mini vans left the Exchange installation and took I-80 west, bearing south toward the Ozark Mountains just as the sun began to set on another rainy Iowa day.

* * * * *

An Fear Liath Mor stretched his massive shaggy arms wide and drew in a huge chest full of crisp, sweet, Scottish air. He had arrived on the slopes of Ben Macdhui in time to scare away a group of climbers who had run away bellowing, leaving behind their camping gear filled with tins and packages of food.

"Life is good," the creature said with a hearty laugh as he squatted down to tear open a box of chocolate chip cookies.

Cramming the sweets into his mouth, he chomped enthusiastically, watching the scampering of small creatures through the undergrowth and lifting his face to watch a bird pass by overhead.

He wondered how the hound and his mate were doing and concentrated on locating the young Reaper. His scruffy brow wrinkled as the hound's essence came forth in a location *An Fear Liath Mor* had not expected.

"What do you there, hound?" he sent in a gruff tone.

"Coim, you're back!"

The big gray man dropped the box of cookies and focused his attention on the words that had been sent and the emotion filling them.

"What has happened?"

Images instead of words came at the creature, bombarding him from all directions as the tale unfolded like a quick newsreel. He rose slowly to his feet, a murderous look of rage shifting over the furry features.

"The Martiya creature crippled you?"

More images of Fallon being treated, healing, and then a glimpse of the dead woman who had been foisted off as Keenan was sent to *An Fear Liath Mor* and the air around him shuddered.

"Where is your mate now?" he thundered.

From that great distance, a mental picture of the island taken from a satellite pass settled in his mind. He grunted.

"Can you locate it?"

"Aye." The word was a bark of sound.

"Can you come get me here and take me there?"

Standing on the same stretch of ground where he and Keenan had met Coim a few months earlier, Fallon stopped limping as he waited for the creature's reply.

"Coim?" he asked. "Can you come get me and take me to the island?"

When there was no answer, Fallon looked at the Supervisor with worry flashing over his handsome face. "He took Keenan. Surely he can take me."

"But *where* did he take Keenan?" the Supervisor asked. "Do you know?"

Fallon shook his head. Keenan would not tell him where she'd gone or what she'd seen there.

"Maybe it was to another dimension he took her. Maybe he can only travel from mountain region to mountain region on his own."

"Maybe," Fallon agreed, chewing on his thumbnail. He tried calling the creature again.

"You are an infuriating little pup."

Both Fallon and the Supervisor jumped at the gruff voice.

"It takes a moment or two to journey here from the highlands," Coim explained. "Now do I take you both or just one of you?"

"Vainshtyr," the Supervisor said, bowing his head respectfully and granting the title of Master to the creature. "It is my great honor to be in your presence."

"Yeah, yeah, yeah," Coim said, winking at Fallon. "That and a dollar might get you a cup of coffee, Shadowlord." He waved his huge paw of a hand in dismissal then locked eyes with Fallon. "You are sure your mate is in no danger?"

"I don't believe she is, but I want her back."

"And you will *get* her back, hound," *An Fear Liath Mor* stated.

"The Supervisor will stay here," Fallon said. "His men are down the trail a ways in case they are needed. Did you learn anything about Martiya?"

"That I did!" Coim said with a snort. "Evil thing. Primordially evil." He fanned his hand at a rock ledge to indicate the men were to sit then settled himself on the ground with enough force to make it shake.

"How do we get rid of it?"

"You destroy the one to which she is bound and you destroy her," Coim replied. "For a better understanding of her, Shadowlord, you may not be surprised to learn she is of the NightWind family of demons."

"Ah," the Supervisor said. "That makes sense."

"What is a NightWind?" Fallon asked.

"It is an incubus brought forth through the female line of witches or sorceresses who sign a blood pact with it," the Supervisor explained. "In exchange for their immortal souls—which they barter to the demon—they are given boons of wealth, beauty and power far beyond anything they could achieve on their own. The NightWind will be at the service of that family for as long as the line survives."

"While a true NightWind is bound only to the female line of a family and is primarily male in orientation, a Spirit of the Night is a succubus and is always female in orientation," Coim continued. "It is a much more dangerous creature—as are all females of any species."

"It left something behind inside me when it attacked," Fallon said. "Something evil."

Coim nodded his big shaggy head. "Aye, she would have. It is a genetic marker so she might find you wherever you go, keep track of you. One day she will return to finish what she started."

"That's what I was afraid of," Fallon said.

"He was also worried that what Martiya left inside him would erupt to hurt Keenan," the Supervisor put in.

"No, that would not happen," Coim stated in a sure voice. "The evil is for Martiya. It brings nothing with it."

Fallon breathed a long sigh of relief. "Thank God for that."

Coim smacked his big, rubbery lips together. "I have the taste of iron in my mouth when I seek your mate, hound. She wears a collar made of it."

"As do the others we're trying to find, I'm sure," the Supervisor said.

"True." *An Fear Liath Mor* pushed up from the ground. "But that is good news."

"How so?" the Supervisor asked, both he and Fallon getting to their feet.

"This Rom who controls Martiya can neither summon nor control her while he wears a circle of iron about his neck. The iron blocks his powers. Hobbled in such a way, he is as human as the next man. He will be no problem to you nor will the mother of the hound's mate or the medicine man."

"I can use my hell hound abilities to walk right past any guards without notice, but I can't sneak Keenan back past without them seeing her," Fallon said. "I..."

"In your condition, you can *limp* past them," Coim scoffed, dragging his shaggy gaze down Fallon's injured leg. "Best you let me finish healing you, pup."

"I was hoping you would," Fallon said, relieved. It would be great not to feel pain every waking moment of his life.

Towering over the Reaper, Coim laid his huge paws on the young man's body, curled the long talons over Fallon's shoulders, let his head fall back, closed his crimson eyes and let power flow from his body into Fallon's. Around them both, a faint yellow aura shimmered for a few moments then faded. When the light was completely gone, Coim removed his paws.

"There. All better, little pup," the creature said with a lopsided grin.

Fallon had felt the energy drilling through his leg. It hadn't been an unpleasant sensation, rather a strange one, but he knew even before he lifted his foot and stomped it to the ground, his leg was mended — better than it had ever been.

"Thank you, *Vainshtyr*," Fallon said.

Coim shrugged carelessly. "It was nothing, a mere parlor trick I learned at my mother's hairy knee." He rubbed his large paws together. "Now let us go and fetch that comely wench of yours! I will provide a distraction for you so you may bring your mate home."

One moment Fallon was nodding his eager agreement, the next his shoulder was clamped in a viselike grip and he was flying through the air like a missile by the scruff of his neck. It was a giddy awareness that made him squeeze his eyes tightly closed to keep from passing out as land passed by at a blur of speed.

"Merrily, merrily, merrily, merrily," he heard Coim singing off key, "life is butter dreams."

"But a dream," Fallon mumbled, swallowing convulsively to keep the vertigo from making him spew.

Coim chuckled and then banked so steeply Fallon thought he would go cartwheeling out of the creature's grip, but then his feet touched steady, rocky land and he wedged open one unenthusiastic eye to see where he was.

"Ocean!" Coim said, breathing in deeply. "Clean mountain air and pungent ocean! What more can a man want, eh, pup?"

"The world to stop revolving around him," Fallon whispered, putting his hands to his spinning head.

"Piss-poor traveler," Coim growled, letting go of his reluctant passenger. "Won't take you with me next time I go to your homeworld."

Fallon blinked and turned his head toward the creature. "My homeworld?"

"Where Reapers were hatched, pup," Coim said with a grin then sniffed the air. He sniffed again. "Human trash headed this way. Two, maybe three miles down the slope. Males, unwashed, carrying guns that have been recently oiled." He narrowed his gaze. "Want me to get rid of them?"

"Yes," Fallon said.

"An easy thing to do," Coim said, and clenched his massive paws.

It was a strange vibration that was being given off by *An Fear Liath Mor*. More a rippling of air than anything else, but it made Fallon acutely uncomfortable. He knew from experience the psychological fear the creature could instill in the unwary travelers he wished to keep at bay. In his mind's eye he saw the objects of Coim's efforts stopping, going wide-eyed and then hightailing back down the mountain—not knowing or understanding why they were reacting as they were.

"All gone," Coim said. "I will wait here." He plopped down on a boulder, crossed his hairy legs at the knees, arms across his chest and wrinkled his nose. "Well? What are you waiting for, hound? The fair damsel will not be rescued with you gawking at my handsome puss. Be off with you!"

Fallon started down a barely visible trail but turned and looked back at the creature. "Do you have a mate on your homeworld, Coim?" he asked.

Coim grinned hugely. "I have two as is my right as *An Fear Liath Mor*. I impregnated both whilst I was visiting. They will birth the cubs in seven months. Adai will have four cubs and Feei will have two." He swung his foot. "She is not the breeder Adai is, but always gives me males. I have thirty-eight males by her and fifty-two females and twenty-four males by Adai."

Fallon's mouth dropped open. "You have..." He wasn't sure if he calculated correctly or not. "One hundred and fourteen children?!"

"One hundred forty-seven to be precise," Coim said then sighed. "I was quite the hound myself in my younger days." His bushy brows lowered. "Go, pup! I've things to see to. You are not my only ward, you know!"

Shaking his head at the revelation he'd just been handed, Fallon started down the trail. As eager as he was to see Keenan, he was even more excited to tell her about Coim's brood of...

"Cubs," he said softly. "*An Fear Liath Mor* is more bear-like than gorilla-like."

He had to hold the laughter in check just thinking of the pseudo-scientists who had classified the Sasquatch and the Yeti as ape-like cryptids. He knew his mother would be very interested in what he had learned.

Chapter Thirty

ဢ

Keenan opened her eyes and smiled. "What took you so long, lineman?" she asked.

"I stopped for a couple of furburgers, an order of bearded oysters and a cherry pop," he said dryly.

"Well, just as long as you didn't dip your wick in some whore's honey pot, I guess that's okay," she said, snuggling up to him. She put a hand to his cheek, not in the least surprised he was lying beside her in bed.

He fused his gaze with hers. "I thought you were dead, *myneeast caillagh*," he whispered, voice breaking, then turned his lips into her palm.

"I know," she said, her own voice husky with apology.

His lips met hers briefly then broke away. He laid his forehead on hers and closed his eyes to keep the tears at bay.

"How many?" she asked softly.

He didn't need to ask what she meant. "Forty-nine including the one they left behind to make us think it was you."

"Oh God." Her voice trembled. "I was hoping he'd lied."

"Who is *he*?" he asked, putting emphasis on the last word.

"His name is Royce Cookson. He's based in Atlanta," she told him. "I have his contact info. I've known about him for years. He even helped me on a case once. He is head of security for my mother's companies."

"We'll see to him later," Fallon said, his eyes grim. "How 'bout getting that shapely ass of yours out of bed and taking a little stroll with me up into the mountains?" he asked. He caressed her cheek one last time then moved his fingers to the thin iron collar that circled her neck. "Let's get this off."

Fallon put his hands to the iron and with his Reaper strength snapped it as easily as if the choker had been balsa wood.

"Coim up there?"

"Yeppers, and he did a bang-up job healing my leg for me. He says he's going to provide a distraction, so hop to, missy," he ordered, rolling away from her and getting to his feet.

The house was silent, but Keenan knew the alarms were activated, the guards in place. She had no idea how Fallon planned on getting them to safety, but she trusted her man.

"Where's Matty?" Fallon inquired as he stepped to the window and pushed aside one of the vertical wooden slats.

"Screwing my mother if I know Matty," Keenan said as she peeled the nightgown over her head and tossed it aside.

Fallon chuckled lightly. "You just can't keep your boyfriends away from your mama, can you, *lhiannan*?"

"Better her than me," she replied. Naked, she padded over to the dresser and opened a drawer silently to take out a T-shirt and pair of jeans.

Distracted by her nudity, Fallon had to shake himself to return his gaze to the outside. He had counted eleven guards patrolling the grounds, five at the entrances and at least two more lurking about. He'd slipped into the house behind a maid who had gone out to empty the garbage and up the stairs, finding his lady's room right off the bat. With his hell hound powers, the maid had never known he was there.

"You were the only survivor from the Island," he said, giving her a hard look. "That's not acceptable."

She lowered her head. "I know."

"Where is her room?"

She couldn't quite look at him. "One floor up and down the hall to your right," she said as she pulled on the jeans—minus any underwear.

"Stay here and be ready to rock and roll as soon as Coim does his thing."

She could have protested—most likely should have when he pulled the Glock from under his shirt—but she didn't. She knew what had to be done.

He paused at the door—giving her a last chance to bid him stop.

She didn't. Instead, she went to the closet for her sneakers. When she looked up, he was gone.

Fallon blended into the shadows, keeping to the far side of the stair steps as he moved up so there would be little or no squeaking. He heard movement downstairs at the back of the house, but that didn't concern him. As he climbed, he reached into his left pocket and pulled out one of the three sound suppressors he was carrying and screwed it onto the barrel. He had requisitioned three because with each use, a suppressor lost some of its silencing ability. He needed to make as little sound as possible while he did his thing.

Upon gaining the landing, he put his back to the wall and pressed against it as he slid silently along the corridor toward Lily's room. At the door, he listened for a long time before trying the handle and easing the portal open inch by inch. He heard a light snore and smiled.

Creeping as quietly as a shadow across the floor of the luxurious suite and into the master bedroom, he kept his attention riveted on the bed where two naked bodies lay outside the covers. From the moonlight filtering in through the wooden blinds, he could tell which was Keenan's mother and which the bastard he had once thought was his friend.

He moved silently to the bed to stand over Lily McCullough. She was lying on her side with her hands tucked innocently beneath her cheek, but there was nothing innocent about this woman. She was evil personified.

He didn't bat an eye when he put the silencer to Lily's temple and pulled the trigger slowly. There was a slight pfftt sound. She jerked as though in the throes of a dream and then a black mushroom of inky stain blossomed on the silk-covered pillowcase beneath her head. He leveled the gun at Matty but

Groves didn't move. The man continued to snore—completely unaware he lay beside a dead woman.

Keeping his gaze on Groves and the gun steady on the sleeping man, Fallon skirted the bed to Matty's side and quietly unscrewed the silencer, sliding it into his right pocket. From the left, he retrieved the second silencer—careful not to let the aluminum bodies clink against one another—then screwed it onto the Glock 19.

He eased the 9 mm down until the 1.25 inch diameter barrel was pressed firmly between Matty Groves' eyes. He dug the silencer into the man's flesh and twisted just a little. Groves stirred, coming awake with a start. His eyes snapped wide open and in the striated light from the blinds Fallon saw terror sparking in Matty's gaze.

"Fallon, please don't," Matty said. He was beginning to quiver like a leaf in a breeze.

"Forty-nine people, Matty," Fallon said softly. "Forty-eight of them you most likely knew or at least have seen in passing. Forty-eight innocent men and women who trusted you."

Matty whimpered. "I had nothing to do with what happened on the Island, Misha," he said barely above a whisper. "I swear I didn't."

"I wish I could shoot you forty-eight times, Matty, but I just don't have the time."

"Misha, please don't..."

Fallon shot him only once, but it was the justice Groves deserved and the only mercy an old friend could bestow on a man who hadn't earned it. He eased the gun away from the staring eyes of the murdered man and tilted his head slightly as he observed the black ink stain growing under Matty's head just as it had Lily's.

Keenan was waiting in her room when Fallon came back for her. She saw what she needed to in his eyes but said not a word. His hands were empty but she knew the gun he had used to exact retribution would be under his shirt at the small of his back again.

"Where is Roland?" he asked.

"Somewhere in one of the huts where the workers live," she said. "I don't know where. I've seen him only once since I was brought here."

"Who would know?"

She thought about it for a moment. "Lee Tolbert," she said. "Mama's plantation manager. He's probably in his cottage at this time of night."

"Call him," Fallon ordered. "Pretend you're your mother and tell him to have Roland come to the house."

"If he asks why?"

"Tell him it's none of his fucking business," he said. "Just as Lily would have."

Keenan flinched at the past tense he'd used but went over to the house phone and picked it up. "This line is strictly in-house," she told him. "The outside lines are off limits to me."

"How'd I know that?" he quipped as he watched her punch in a number.

"Leland, get that gypsy bastard who came with Groves up and tell him I want to talk to him," Keenan said nastily. She listened for a moment then shouted into the receiver. "I don't want to hear any excuses from you, Leland!"

Fallon sensed something was wrong when Keenan glanced at him.

"How long has the bastard been gone?" she asked then hissed into the receiver. "No, just forget it!" She slammed the phone down. "Lee says Roland went up into the mountains earlier tonight."

"Why?"

"He and one of the workers went hunting for wild boar."

"Shit," Fallon snarled. "I don't want to have to traipse all over that fucking mountain looking for his slimy ass."

"What is Coim going to do?" she asked, rubbing her hands up and down her arms. "This waiting is starting to get to me."

"He didn't tell me what he had planned, but I figured we'd know when it started." He went to her and took her into his arms. "I've wanted to do this since I saw you lying there sleeping."

She pressed herself to him. "I knew you'd come. I knew you'd find a way to get to me."

He cupped her head against his shoulder. "Always, babe. Always." He kissed the top of her head.

"What about Martiya?" she asked. "Did Coim find out anything we can use?"

Fallon started to explain when he heard, *"Run now, hound! Run very quickly!"*

He grabbed Keenan's hand as the first thunderous boom sounded to shake the foundations of the plantation house.

* * * * *

Coim had given off wave after wave of pure terror and those men assigned the twenty-four-hour-a-day watch of the harbor to which the cannons were pointed had run away like frightened toddlers. With a huge grin on his craggy face, *An Fear Liath Mor* had plucked the heavy cannons from their bases as though they'd weighed no more than a feather and turned them toward the plantation house, lowering the barrels so the shots would fire into the pool, the fancy garden, the paved driveway in front of the building and just to the east of it. He had taken his time dancing around like a Comanche doing a war dance, humming to himself as he adjusted the aim, adjusted it again then staring down each long barrel.

"Gonna make a big bang!" he decided then stood stock still, blending his mind with every animal on the island, warning them away from the plantation. "Slink, my wee brothers and sisters! Slink away without giving warning of your flight!"

From his vantage point, he had watched the exodus of creatures and hooted with laughter, rubbing his paws together, then fired the first shot.

Now he was having a good time as he juggled cannonballs like oranges then rolled them down the barrels, singing to himself. Just before he set off the next three cannons, he howled to the bright moon and sang even louder, "There's a bathroom on the right!"

Hurrying down the staircase with Keenan in tow, Fallon had to grab the railing to keep them both from falling as another loud explosion ripped the night and the house shook again. Servants were running out the front door.

"Hurry, *lhiannan!*" he said, pulling her after him.

"If he blows us up…" he heard Keenan mumble.

Out the door and into the chaos of the night where shrieking, terrified workers were running pell-mell away from the house and toward the beach, he propelled his lady. Men with carbines were scurrying about as well, shouting in their native language, but none seemed willing to head up the mountain.

Running full out with Keenan's hand in his, Fallon saw Roland out of the corner of his eye and snapped his head that way. The gypsy skidded to a stop then raised the weapon he carried, but a mental blast from Keenan's personal arsenal set the trees around the Rom blazing and he lifted an arm to block the fiery blast, stumbling away.

Fallon knew Roland would follow. The man had no choice but to try to stop Fallon, but getting Keenan to Coim took precedent at that moment. She was keeping up with him, but he knew she'd tire quickly the higher they went up the treacherous, twisting mountain path. With his canine strength, he could literally run rings around any human—psi powers or not.

"Don't worry about him!" Fallon yelled at her over the bombardment. He tightened his hand around hers. She was craning her neck, looking back, sending wave after wave of jettisoning fire where she thought the Rom might be. He knew that too would soon exhaust her strength and she needed it to keep moving. "Just run!"

Keenan resolutely turned her attention away from the man scampering behind them. At one point she had caught his hair on fire and despite the iron collar circling his neck knew she'd pissed him off royally. He'd try to hurt her now, his expression had told her.

Dodging bushes, slapping them aside with his forearm, Fallon led his lady through the forest at the end of the property line and up the rocky incline. He was barely breathing hard but he could hear Keenan's labored breath already. Without another thought, he skidded to a stop, jerked her toward him, dipped his knees and hefted her onto his shoulder. He could run faster carrying her than dragging her behind him.

"Fallon, put me down!" she yelped as the bony part of his shoulder dug into her belly.

He didn't bother to answer. Behind them was sheer bedlam as cannonball after cannonball ploughed into the plantation house and pool. He spared a few moments of concern over the human occupants of the island, but Coim sent a reassuring mental transmission that all had fled the structure.

"Except the two to whom it no longer matters," Coim sent gleefully.

Higher up the mountain Fallon carried his protesting burden, who was slapping at his ass with her hands one minute and grabbing at his belt the next. At some point he'd felt her dislodge the Glock and it was long gone. Her "Oh no!" had made him grit his teeth as the gun fell, but he didn't have time to turn around and go back for it.

"Here, hound!"

The bellow was music to Fallon's ears and he raced toward the creature. Above Coim's head smoke from the cannon plumed.

"I'm a sawed-off Ed McMahon," Fallon heard the creature singing and winced.

"What?" Keenan asked. "What did he say?"

"He gets the lyrics wrong," Fallon told her. "He's trying to sing "Demolition Man", I think."

The closer they got to the dancing creature—now out of cannonballs—they could see he was having the time of his life. Keenan twisted around to see him and he waved at her.

"Hey, Mate of the hound!" *An Fear Liath Mor* said then started singing again. "The only boy who could ever teach me was the son of a pizza man."

"Oh my God," Keenan said, sputtering.

Fallon scrambled up the embankment and stopped so suddenly he almost dropped Keenan. Leaning forward, he slid her from his shoulder. "Coim!" he said. "Come…"

He heard the report of the rifle a second before he saw the surprise widen Keenan's eyes. His head whipped around and saw Roland—rifle up and ready to fire again. A weak blast of fire shot past him to land close to the gypsy but it was enough to make Roland dive into the undergrowth. Snapping back to face Keenan, Fallon saw the bright red bloom over her heart and he bellowed in pain. Her knees began to give way.

"Give her to me!" Coim hissed as he sprang forward and in a heartbeat caught Keenan up, disappearing with her.

With a roar of fury, Fallon spun around. He had no weapon and Roland was once more on his feet pointing the rifle at him, but that didn't matter. Fallon launched himself at the gypsy— changing in midair—and when he landed on Mizhak Roland, it was with brutal animal savagery, a black blur of beastliness.

"Marti…!" was as far as Roland got before the glistening fangs closed on his neck, ripped away the windpipe.

* * * * *

Coim slapped Fallon again, splitting his lip. "Snap out of it!" the creature barked.

Fallon staggered beneath the blow but instinctively knew *An Fear Liath Mor* had pulled his punch, making it little more than a love tap, yet it hurt like hell. He went to his knees from the momentum and shook his head like the hound he had been only a few moments before.

"You know what must be done," Coim shouted. "We do it now or you lose your mate!"

Keenan was lying on the ground and she was white as chalk. The front of her T-shirt was saturated with her blood. She was still as death. She was dead and he knew it.

He could not lose her a second time and scrambled on his knees to her. "Take it," he said, lifting her into his arms.

Coim pushed the Supervisor forward. "Your hands are smaller than mine, Shadowlord. You do it!"

The Supervisor needed no second order to act. He dug into his pocket, pulled out his multi-bladed knife and flicked it open. "Bare his back, *Vainshtyr.*"

Coim leaned over and ripped Fallon's shirt from hem to neck.

As the Reaper gently turned Keenan to her belly, he felt the cold metal of the blade on his flesh.

"Ready?" the Supervisor asked.

"Do it."

He paid little attention to the cut. It wasn't until the Supervisor thrust a hand into the wound and pulled a fledgling from his back that there was any true pain. The agony was intense as the Revenant worms bunched beneath his skin and the hellion deliberately hurt him in retaliation for extracting one of her young.

"Give me the knife," he said. "No one hurts her but me."

Shoving Keenan's blood-soaked T-shirt up her back, he took the knife from the Supervisor and made the cut—just deep and long enough—for the Supervisor to drop the wriggling, writhing fledgling into the slit Fallon spread apart with his slippery fingers.

For just a moment the creature looked as though it would balk then it raised its green pointy head, flicked out a scarlet red tongue and dove down into the wound. Within seconds, the cut closed and as Fallon eased Keenan up and into his embrace again, she took a shuddering gasp and her eyes popped open.

"Get him out of here, Coim," Fallon ordered. "I'll handle it from here."

"No, I want to..." the Supervisor said, obviously wanting to stay to see Keenan's first Transition, but *An Fear Liath Mor* snatched him up and they were gone.

"Fallon?" Keenan questioned. Death was fading from her eyes and in its place was a fevered heat that began to spark red in the hazel depths.

"I'm here, baby," he said as she bucked in his arms, her mouth open in surprise. "I'm right here."

* * * * *

She didn't seem all that happy with her tail. She kept chasing it until she became dizzy then flopped down, her little head still going in circles.

She snorted.

"I think it's beautiful," he told her.

She snorted again then lifted a back leg to scratch at the underside of her snout.

He was sitting against a rock with his knees drawn up and his wrists resting on them as she pushed up from the ground and began sniffing. Laughing softly, he laid his head back as she investigated the new abilities.

She barked and the bark echoed across the Ozarks. She barked again then threw her head back and howled.

That seemed to please her and she tried it again.

Fallon's eyes crinkled with mirth. He remembered all too well how he'd reacted to his own Transition the first time, and it hadn't been anything to laugh about.

Sniffing, sniffing, more sniffing. A bit of grass and another. More sniffing then she swung her head toward Fallon.

"What?" he asked.

She squatted.

Fallon laughed so hard tears came to his eyes. "You are something, my bitch," he said, and slapped his hand on his leg.

She tossed her head. "*I don't come when you say heel, lineman!*" she sent him, and grinned.

"Don't you want to know what it feels like to have your ears scratched?" he countered.

She moved away from her piss, scratched dirt in a lazy attempt to cover the smell then trotted over to him. He had stretched out one leg so she insinuated herself between his legs and lay down, putting her head on his lowered thigh. As soon as he put his fingers behind her floppy ear and began scratching, she kicked her back leg as she'd seen other dogs do.

"Cute," he chastised her. "Real cute."

She grunted. *"How long will I be like this?"*

"A couple of hours," he replied. "Maybe longer."

"I want to run."

"Then run."

She lifted her head. He was smoothing his palm down her neck.

"I want to run with you."

He smiled. "I thought you'd never ask."

If anyone saw the black hound and his tan bitch streaking along the paths that night, it would have raised no alarms. When the two stopped and tried to out bay one another that would have caused no unease either. Had anyone been watching—and there was one big gray someone—that person would have seen two scampering, prancing hounds playfully snapping at one another, tumbling over and over, tussling and bumping against the other.

When the puppy-like play became something more mature, the gray one turned away. The mock battle between the hounds had become love.

"Love is a plate of veal," *An Fear Liath Mor* sang as it strolled away.

Epilogue

ꝶꝶ

He placed the band upon her finger. "*Le mo ghrása mise, agus liomsa mo ghrá.*" The words of his vow were inscribed on the rose-gold band — I am my beloved's and my beloved is mine.

She looked down at the band then turned to his mother who had Fallon's band on her index finger. Svetlana smiled tearfully as she handed the band to the priest who blessed it then gave it to Keenan.

Taking Fallon's left hand in hers, Keenan slipped the identical rose-gold band onto his ring finger. "*Le mo ghrása mise, agus liomsa mo ghrá,*" she repeated.

There were only five people at the ceremony in the Supervisor's office — the bride and groom, the groom's mother, the Supervisor who was acting as best man, and the same thin little priest who less than a week earlier had officiated at the bride's funeral.

"I now pronounce you man and wife."

Neither Fallon nor his lady had wanted an elaborate ceremony. They had wanted to join their lives together, not throw a big party. Though champagne chilled in a bucket and Svetlana had insisted on baking a traditional Irish wedding cake, a delicious confection of rich fruit cake covered in white icing, there would be no fancy gown with veil, no tuxedo, no attendants in organdy and lace. The bride wore a simple pale green silk dress and the groom a black silk shirt and black leather pants.

"You may kiss the bride, Agent Fallon," the priest said.

Fallon drew her into his arms and kissed her gently as his heart raced and his blood pounded fiercely in his veins. A jet was waiting to take them to their honeymoon destination and he was more than anxious to begin their first journey as man and wife.

When the kiss was complete and the priest introduced them for the first time as Mr. and Mrs. Mikhail Fallon, they each turned to their lone attendant and either embraced or shook hands.

"Congratulations, Misha," the Supervisor said. "Well done. Very well done."

"Be happy, Keenan," Svetlana whispered. "Make him happy."

"I will," Keenan replied. "I promise you I will."

A toast, a piece of cake shared, the marriage license signed and then they were running down the hall—surprised to see people from the Exchange lined up in the terminal. To a round of thunderous applause, they hurried through the jet way and into the plane.

"Congratulations Agents Fallon," the steward said. "We're ready to leave when you are."

"Then let's get this baby in the air!" Fallon said, leaning over to kiss his bride again.

As the jet streaked through the wintry Iowa sky, Keenan sat with her head on her husband's shoulder, their fingers entwined.

"Did you see how the Supervisor signed the marriage license?" she asked.

Fallon laughed. "Yeah. John Doe."

"Who is he, lineman?" she asked. "Have you any idea?"

"Just a Shadowlord Coim told me." He kissed her forehead. "I've a feeling his story would make an interesting one."

"*I'll tell it to you one day, hound,*" came an amused voice from far away.

Fallon glanced behind them. "I need to go to the bathroom," he said, staring into her eyes.

"Okay," she said, releasing her hold on him.

He arched a brow. "I might need help."

Keenan frowned "Why would you...?"

He wagged his brows then laid her hand over the bulge between his thighs.

"Conceited prick," she said, shaking her head.

"Stiff prick," he said.

She followed him to the restroom and wedged in behind him, sliding her hand up his back as he locked the door. When he turned to face her, she trailed her palm over his arm and onto his chest.

"You going to make this a habit from now on?" she asked.

"What do you think?"

He grinned, put his hands on her waist and lifted her to the sink, pushed the hem of her skirt up to her hips. One thick dark brow rose when he noticed she wasn't wearing any underwear.

"I think you're horny," she laughed as he lowered his hand to rub her exposed flesh.

"I'm a horny, stiff, conceited prick," he corrected, and turned his hand palm up so he could insert his index and middle fingers into her wet warmth, hooking his thumb along the crease of her legs as he nuzzled her neck.

Keenan looped her arms around his waist and pulled him as close as she could get him. "Have I told you I love you?"

He shrugged. "I seem to recall something along those lines." He took her mouth in a deep, passion-filled kiss. His tongue laved hers then withdrew to flick across her bottom lip, poke delicately at the corners. He drew back to stare into her eyes while his free hand went to the zipper of his pants to free his cock.

"Do you know I love your conceited prick?" she asked in a husky whisper.

"Do you know he loves you?" he countered. He used his thumb to tease her clit.

Keenan writhed beneath his touch.

Fallon eased his fingers from her and positioned his cock at the folds of her damp channel. He rubbed it against her then slowly pressed into her, snaking his arms around her to bring her hips closer to his. Her legs locked around him. He surged upward with his hips to complete the penetration, withdrew a bit then thrust harder.

Her vaginal walls gripped him tightly. He surged into her again with more force. He brought a hand between them to mold his palm over her breast. He kneaded the soft globe, a husky growling left his throat.

Their lips fused, their tongues mated. They came at the same blissful moment, the rhythmic pulsing of their bodies taking them higher than the jet ever could.

Also by Charlotte Boyett-Compo

ଝ

eBooks:

Dancing on the Wind

Ellora's Cavemen: Dreams of the Oasis IV (*anthology*)

Ellora's Cavemen: Legendary Tails I (*anthology*)

Ellora's Cavemen: Seasons of Seduction II (*anthology*)

Ghost Wind

HardWind

In the Arms of the Wind

Journey of the Wind

Kiss of the Wind

Passion's Mistral

Shades of the Wind

WesternWind 1: WyndRiver Sinner

WesternWind 2: Reaper's Revenge

WesternWind 3: Prime Reaper

WesternWind 4: Tears of the Reaper

WesternWind 5: Her Reaper's Arms

WesternWind 6: My Reaper's Daughter

WesternWind 7: Embrace the Wind

WesternWind 8: BlackMoon Reaper

WesternWind: Reaper's Justice

WindVerse 1: Pleasure's Foehn

WindVerse 2: Secrets of the Wind

WindVerse 3: Ardor's Leveche

Print Books:

Want more? Find Charlotte's addition titles at Cerridwen Press (www.cerridwenpress.com):

eBooks:

BlackWind: Sean and Bronwyn

BlackWind: Viraiden and Bronwyn

Desert Wind

In the Wind's Eye

Prince of the Wind

Shadowlord

Taken By the Wind

Print Books:

BlackWind: Sean and Bronwyn

BlackWind: Viraiden and Bronwyn

In the Wind's Eye

About the Author

ဢ

Charlee is the author of over forty books. Married thirty-nine years to her high school sweetheart Tom, she is the mother of two grown sons Pete and Mike, and the proud grandmother of Preston Alexander and Victoria Ashley. She is the willing house slave to five demanding felines who are holding her hostage in her home and only allowing her to leave in order to purchase food, clumping kitty litter and toys for them.

A native of Sarasota, Florida, she grew up in Colquitt and Albany, Georgia and now lives in the Midwest — that makes her an official Sunshine Cracker! She writes erotic-style romances exclusively for Ellora's Cave but is also published in the speculative fiction genres of dark romance, mystery/thriller, SF/futuristic and horror. If you are a fan of her WindWorld and WindVerse series at Ellora's Cave...and especially her signature shape-shifting Reapers...you might want to check out her non-erotic novels over at Cerridwen Press.

Question: Why does the word "wind" — in one fashion or another — show up in the titles of all Charlee's novels?

Answer: Charlee was born on June 20th and that makes her a Gemini, an air sign, and she has a real affinity for the wind.

Charlotte Boyett-Compo welcomes comments from readers. You can find her website and email address on her author bio page at www.ellorascave.com.

Tell Us What You Think

We appreciate hearing reader opinions about our books. You can email us at Comments@EllorasCave.com.

Why an electronic book?

We live in the Information Age — an exciting time in the history of human civilization, in which technology rules supreme and continues to progress in leaps and bounds every minute of every day. For a multitude of reasons, more and more avid literary fans are opting to purchase e-books instead of paper books. The question from those not yet initiated into the world of electronic reading is simply: *Why?*

1. *Price.* An electronic title at Ellora's Cave Publishing and Cerridwen Press runs anywhere from 40% to 75% less than the cover price of the exact same title in paperback format. Why? Basic mathematics and cost. It is less expensive to publish an e-book (no paper and printing, no warehousing and shipping) than it is to publish a paperback, so the savings are passed along to the consumer.

2. *Space.* Running out of room in your house for your books? That is one worry you will never have with electronic books. For a low one-time cost, you can purchase a handheld device specifically designed for e-reading. Many e-readers have large, convenient screens for viewing. Better yet, hundreds of titles can be stored within your new library — on a single microchip. There are a variety of e-readers from different manufacturers. You can also read e-books on your PC or laptop computer. (Please note that Ellora's Cave does not endorse any specific brands.

You can check our websites at www.ellorascave.com or www.cerridwenpress.com for information we make available to new consumers.)

3. *Mobility.* Because your new e-library consists of only a microchip within a small, easily transportable e-reader, your entire cache of books can be taken with you wherever you go.

4. *Personal Viewing Preferences.* Are the words you are currently reading too small? Too large? Too... ANNOYING? Paperback books cannot be modified according to personal preferences, but e-books can.

5. *Instant Gratification.* Is it the middle of the night and all the bookstores near you are closed? Are you tired of waiting days, sometimes weeks, for bookstores to ship the novels you bought? Ellora's Cave Publishing sells instantaneous downloads twenty-four hours a day, seven days a week, every day of the year. Our webstore is never closed. Our e-book delivery system is 100% automated, meaning your order is filled as soon as you pay for it.

Those are a few of the top reasons why electronic books are replacing paperbacks for many avid readers.

As always, Ellora's Cave and Cerridwen Press welcome your questions and comments. We invite you to email us at Comments@ellorascave.com or write to us directly at Ellora's Cave Publishing Inc., 1056 Home Avenue, Akron, OH 44310-3502.

Discover for yourself why readers can't get enough of the multiple award-winning publisher

Ellora's Cave.

Whether you prefer e-books or paperbacks,

be sure to visit EC on the web at
www.ellorascave.com

for an erotic reading experience that will leave you breathless.

CPSIA information can be obtained at www.ICGtesting.com
Printed in the USA
LVOW041016010312

271142LV00001B/22/P